Federica

by

Hugh Chare

Publication Data

Federica © Hugh B. Chare 2015

Book and Cover design by Hugh B. Chare
Cover image based upon: Automobile Calendar for 1906, by Edward Penfield, Published 1905, by Moffat Yard & Co., New York.
ISBN: 978-0-9830013-8-6

 Kilihune Books

The James Martin series
African Encounter
Across the Zambezi
Just off the Great North Road
Well, there you go!
Back to Africa
The Sagitta Mishap
Flight 5 to Johannesburg

Marieke Englebrecht mysteries
Death in the Mopane
Revenge after twenty years

Other books
The journal of Jan Englebrecht
British Spy in the Bushveld
Federica

Preface

Car manufacturing in the early 1900s was widely distributed among many builders, large and small, of which the greater majority failed over time, with few names from the early 1900s remaining today. England lagged behind Germany and France, probably as a result of government antipathy towards the new-fangled cars and the threat they posed to horse transport, no matter how insanitary large numbers of horses were in towns and cities. The laws of 1889 reflected that antipathy with the Red Flag law that required a 'locomotive' to be preceded by a man on foot bearing a red flag. That essentially limited speeds to four miles an hour or less, and it was only the laws of 1896 and 1904 that redressed the situation and brought greater freedom to the car builders and users.

Women as engineers in the early 1900s were rare and probably regarded with suspicion by the men of the time and women who ran factories, if any in fact did, would have been regarded with even greater suspicion for pursuing a career that was one of the bastions of male supremacy, even though a great many of the factory workers were women. A woman who undertook to both design and build cars in the early 1900s would have been rare indeed, but there were women who contributed greatly to the car industry. Among them were Mary Anderson, Charlotte Bridgwood and her daughter Florence Lawrence and Helen Blair Bartlett, who were instrumental in the design and manufacture of car accessories and parts and in the arena of car racing were also Camille du Gast, Dorothy Levitt and Countess d'Albrizzi.

Our apologies also go to the Ryknield Engine Company for taking their stand at the 1904 Motor Show at the Crystal Palace.

Contents

A happy homecoming?

"Come along, Nastia, we need to leave if we are to catch the train," Federica urged.

"I'm coming, I'm coming," Anastasia replied. "Are you sure the boat will arrive tomorrow?"

"I checked again, and yes, it is due in at ten tomorrow morning," Federica confirmed.

"I wonder why it's two days late?" Anastasia asked.

"Probably the weather, or the boat is just a poor sailor, or they stopped in mid-ocean for some other reason," Federica suggested.

"Is not the Walmer Castle a new boat?" Anastasia protested. "Perhaps it was the weather. What reason would they have to stop in mid-ocean? Are you sure that George is on the boat?"

"Quite sure," Federica assured her. "He sent a telegram, if you recall, the day before he sailed from Cape Town, and having received no further telegrams telling us that he was delayed or that the sailing date was delayed, I presume that he will arrive tomorrow."

"Will you be pleased to see him?" Anastasia asked.

"Do you have to ask?" Federica laughed wryly. "He has been gone altogether too long, and I have awaited these past months with great trepidation."

"I wonder what he was doing on his Field Intelligence mission?" Anastasia mused.

"I doubt he will ever tell us," Federica said. "We may be assured that he was off somewhere in the South African veldt chasing after the Boers. Come, we may continue this conversation in the carriage or the train; we must go, if we are to arrive in Southampton before this evening, as we do not have time tomorrow to make the journey and be assured of being there in time. Sophia, how is Mr Wheelwright today?"

"He is fading fast," Sophia replied. "I pray that George is in time to see his father before he dies."

"We will be back by three or four tomorrow, Mama," Anastasia assured her. "I have said goodbye to Papa and told him that we are coming back with George."

"Well, off you go then," Sophia told her. "You two take care and let us know when George arrives."

A little while later, when the two young ladies were on the train on their way to Maidenhead, Anastasia returned to the conversation that they had been having.

"What do you think George was doing?" she asked.

"He was vague in his letters," Federica replied. "He must have been away from towns because there was a gap of many months in his correspondence."

"Whatever he was doing, it must have been really heroic," Anastasia pronounced as only a younger sister could do, confident in the knowledge that her brother was made of stern stuff and capable of great derring-do. "After all, they made him a Major and gave him the Distinguished Service Order."

"I am sure he deserved it," Federica agreed. "I confess that I was most worried that he may be wounded or even killed in whatever enterprise he was engaged upon."

"Not George," Anastasia assured her. "Will you two marry?"

"It is my wish," Federica replied. "I also believe from the tenor of his letters that George wishes it too."

"George Jacobus Wheelwright, only son of George and Anna Wheelwright, to marry Federica Giovanna Beretta, youngest daughter of Giuseppe and Vita Beretta of Florence, Italy, it sounds well, should I leave out the reference to George's mother, she has, after all, been dead these many years?" Anastasia asked.

"I do not think it is of great import," Federica thought "Although your Mama has been mother to George for some time now, she understands and sympathises with George and the loss of his mother, perhaps, George Jacobus Wheelwright only son of George Wheelwright and the late Anna Wheelwright, née Englebrecht might sound well, that should confound and alarm the people here, with Beretta and Englebrecht both unsuitably foreign."

"You're right," Anastasia agreed, laughing. "Here we are already at Maidenhead. We need to change platforms to catch the train to Reading."

"What hotel did you book for us in Southampton?" Federica asked.

"The Dolphin," Anastasia told her. "It has a good reputation, it has been there for many years, and the service is said to be excellent. It is also close to the docks. Do you think we should have driven down in the car rather than taken the train?"

"I thought about it, but if the weather turns at all inclement, then either the drive to Southampton would be unpleasant or the drive home would be," Federica commented. "I also thought that perhaps we should introduce George to the idea of cars after he has seen your Papa."

After the short train ride to Reading, there was another change, this time to the Southern Railway and the train to Southampton with yet another change at Basingstoke. From the station at Southampton, it was a short carriage ride to the Dolphin Hotel, where they were welcomed by the manager and escorted to their room, with a porter following with their luggage.

"Not much of a view," Anastasia commented after the manager and the porter had left. "A pity that the hotel is on High Street, so that the view is of other buildings also on High Street. I rather fancied a view of the docks and the Southampton Water."

"We cannot always have all that we want," Federica reminded her.

"That is true, Fede," Anastasia agreed. "I wanted to see the boats arrive and depart."

"We will go down to the docks in good time tomorrow to see boats come in," Federica assured her. "I can hardly wait for the Walmer Castle to dock, it will be so good to see George again."

"Do you know that Jane Austen used to attend balls here?" Anastasia commented.

"No, I did not know that," Federica admitted.

"Yes, she was supposed to have celebrated her eighteenth birthday here at the hotel, and while she was living in Southampton in the early eighteen hundreds, she is said to have attended several Assembly Balls here," Anastasia elaborated.

"It is good to know that this hotel has been good enough for the *haut monde* of the day, so we may expect reasonable service. Perhaps we should dress for dinner," Federica suggested.

"What did you bring?" Anastasia asked.

"The cerise dress," Federica replied.

"I like that dress," Anastasia approved. "It looks well on you and it shows to advantage your raven hair." She looked at Federica, who had been her governess for some years and who was likely to become her sister-in-law and approved. Federica was of medium height, very athletic, with well-defined musculature. She was dark with a skin colour like cinnamon and hair black like the plumage of a raven, but worn short, close-cropped, like a boy. Anastasia thought about herself and could not help but make comparisons. She was of the same height as Federica and of similar build, but not yet filled out to womanhood, having still very boyish slim hips and small breasts, not that Federica had large breasts, hers were also small. Whereas Federica was dark, she was fair, but she also wore her hair short, copying the one she adored. Her eyes were a brilliant blue, quite unlike those of Federica, which were a deep, rich brown. She envied Federica her colouring, particularly because it meant that she did not have to be as prudent with exposure to the sun as she did.

"What will you wear?" Federica asked in turn, interrupting Anastasia's thoughts.

"I brought the cerulean, the one with the silver fleck," Anastasia replied. "We should dress and attend the dining room. Will you take wine with dinner?"

"Of course," Federica assured her. "Even the English hotels are known to offer moderate wines, and I see no reason not to partake."

They dressed and went down for dinner, which could have consisted of up to eight courses had they chosen to partake of it all. They instead settled for a light dinner of lamb served with vegetables of the season, followed by a small dessert, then coffee and cheese. Anastasia looked around the dining room and was disappointed.

"There are only old men here," she complained.

"That is not altogether surprising," Federica suggested. "Many young men are off in South Africa and have yet to return, even though hostilities are over, and many more simply could not afford to stay here."

"I suppose you must be right," Anastasia sighed. "Look at the elderly man in the corner there with the exquisite creature in black, she must be eighteen or nineteen, and he must be forty if he is a day."

"It is his niece, of a certainty," Federica cynically suggested."

"Niece, my foot," Anastasia snorted. "No uncle of mine would treat me in such a way."

"I think perhaps we should retire before you march over and demand explanations," Federica laughed. "We would not wish to be asked to leave before we have stayed. I for one could enjoy a bath, I am weary from the travel and would like to be fresh in the morning to greet the day and the boat."

"It is early yet, but perhaps you are right," Anastasia agreed. "We will leave the ageing satyr to his nymph and wish them well. Perhaps we could have the hotel serve cocoa in our room later?"

"An excellent proposition," Federica agreed. "I will attend to it before we go up."

The following morning, the two were up early and breakfasted before eight. The ageing satyr and nymph from the night before were also there, but now joined by an elderly lady, who clearly was the mother of the satyr. From snippets of conversation, it became clear that Federica's cynicism from the night before had been misplaced. The nymph was, in fact, the niece of the satyr and 'Grandmama' was issuing instructions to all, it seemed they were also waiting for the Walmer Castle to dock and had come to meet an officer who was among the passengers and who was the father of the nymph and brother to the satyr. Federica enquired of the hotel the projected arrival time of the Walmer Castle and was told that it had been sighted off the coast of the Isle of White and was expected to dock a little after ten. She and Anastasia paid their account and heard from the manager the latest forecast of weather and the expected shipping arrivals that day into the docks of Southampton. The manager was clearly preparing for an influx of business caused by the repatriation of so many soldiers from South Africa, most of whom would be passing through Southampton.

The docks were only a short trap ride from the hotel, and they were on the quay by ten, joining others who were also waiting, including the satyr, the nymph and the dowager. Finally, someone saw the boat and all waiting, strained to see if they could spot anyone on the decks that they might recognise. For Federica and Anastasia, it seemed an eternity until the boat finally docked at 10:40 in the morning, which Federica wryly commented to Anastasia was probably some Government official's idea of shortly after ten. Waiting while the troops filed down the gangplanks and disappeared into the Customs' shed was frustrating, and it was Anastasia who first saw George as he came from the building, small bag in hand, rifle slung over his shoulder and with a porter in tow who was wheeling a handcart with his travel trunk. George was a little under six feet in height, and the recent war in South Africa had provided him with a deep tan, but had also given him a drawn and hungry look, that of a man who has seen much and has had to endure much.

"George," she shouted as she threw he arms around his neck. "You're home!"

"I'm home," he agreed as he kissed her and looked beyond her to see who else had come.

"What is this?" Anastasia teased. "You are not delighted to see me? Who else did you expect?"

"I was just wondering," he blushed.

"Don't worry, she's here," Anastasia reassured him, then stood aside so that he could see Federica. He reached out to her, and she rushed into his arms.

"*George, il mio tesoro, ho voglia di te*," Federica whispered in his ear, then kissed him and nibbled on his ear, whispering more words and suggestions, some of which caused him to almost blush even more.

"Mama could not come," Anastasia announced. "Papa is not well, and she stayed at home to nurse him."

"What's wrong?" George asked, not letting go of Federica, but holding her close and trying to guess by feel what, if anything, she had on underneath her light travelling coat.

"He has not been well these past few months," Anastasia told him. "I think we may lose him soon."

"I guessed from his letters that something might be amiss, but what? You are not upset by the possibility of his loss?" George asked.

"I was," Anastasia admitted. "I have made my peace and accept that when his time comes, it will be a relief for him and a release from the pain and suffering he has now. It is distressing to see him thus, and I know that Mama also waits for the day when he suffers no more."

"Why, what is wrong?" George asked.

"He has an aggressive form of cancer," Federica told him. "He has seen Doctor Ferguson and several specialists in London, but they cannot treat it and can only offer opiates to dull the pain."

"I see," said George. "There is no surgery, nothing that can be done?"

"Nothing," Anastasia confirmed. "We had thought at first that there was some surgery that could be done to remove the diseased parts, but the new Röngten Ray apparatus showed the extent of the problem upon the films that were developed and we were disappointed to see that there was nothing that could be done, except alleviate the pain and suffering."

"Has it been difficult?" he asked.

"Difficult enough," Anastasia said. "We are now really just waiting for the end. Come, we need to go so that you may get back to Hedsor and see him. A minute, I must just send a telegraph to Mama to let her know we have found you and are on our way. Where did I see that telegraph office?"

"I believe it was that way," Federica pointed. They all went that way, and Federica had been right, the telegraph office was there. Anastasia quickly wrote out her message and handed it to the clerk, who asked if there would be a reply. Anastasia told him no, then she paid, and they left to find the train.

"Are we in time to catch the train?" George asked.

"Lots, I have planned everything with my Bradshaw," Anastasia assured him. "Come, we have a compartment reserved." George dutifully followed, and the porter brought up the rear. They found the right compartment on the train and watched as the porter stowed the smaller baggage and then took the trunk to the baggage van at the rear of the train. George paid the man, who smiled broadly and nodded approvingly towards Federica. George smiled back conspiratorially and then went back to join his sister and the said delectable Federica. He stowed his rifle on the luggage rack and took his seat opposite the two women.

"We have to go to Reading, then change trains for Maidenhead," Anastasia explained. "They have no trains that go directly from here to Bourne End. So we must change trains twice, at Reading and at Maidenhead. I have arranged for our carriage to meet us at Bourne End for the rest of the journey home."

"You seem to have everything arranged," George commented. "How did you get here this morning?"

"Fede and I came by train yesterday and stayed in an hotel last night, so that we were in plenty of time to see you dock this morning," Anastasia explained.

"Ah, I see," George said. "I pity poor Federica being cooped up with you, but what of things at home?"

"What do you mean, poor Federica?" Anastasia said, trying to appear incensed. "She and I fare well together. As for things at home, I, with the invaluable help and guidance of Fede, have taken over running the estate of late because of Papa's illness and merely organising this trip is but child's play."

"The estate then is in good order?" George asked. "Would not your Mama run the estate?"

"Mama is happy to let me run things. I consult with Fede, then discuss my decisions with Mama and betimes Papa, but she and Papa have shown great confidence in me," Anastasia assured him. "As to the estate, our revenues exceed our expenditures by quite some amount, and we have made some changes to the staff to reduce unnecessary expenses. We have changed some crop types and the size of our various herds of cows and flocks of sheep. We have set up some reserves for maintenance of the house, which I fear will become necessary soon and some funds for improving the plumbing system and for the new electric light when it becomes available in our part of the country. We have other enterprises that do well, such as ploughing engines that we hire out, we have a foundry that supplies parts to carriage and wagon makers for the railways, we have a coach builder, we have a biscuit factory and we have a garment factory that manufactures clothing for the general population and some special items. We have also taken some of the excess funds and added to our investments in London, investments which Papa looked over and approved. It has been very enlightening. We are quite wealthy, Papa has set us up well, and I intend to ensure that we do not lose his fortune by squandering it on loose living and excesses."

"I did not know you were such a manager," George said. "Does Federica have a place in your plans?"

"Of course," she replied. "She is my partner in this venture, but I am willing to share her with you, brother, that is if you have the sense to ask her."

"Ask her what, pray?" George teased.

"Why to marry you, stupid," she said. "I've read your letters, I've seen you together, and I see you now, you cannot take your eyes from her, you have probably only heard half of what I have said to you, and your mind is elsewhere, probably anticipating the delights of the bedroom tonight."

"Nastia," George said, trying to appear shocked. "What do you know about such things, and when did you become so worldly wise?"

"I have been well tutored," she responded. "I only hope that when I find the one of my dreams that you will treat them with the same consideration I have shown dearest Fede in passing your letters to and fro."

"When do we get home?" George asked, anxious to change the subject completely.

"We should be in Bourne End by three this afternoon," Federica added. "Then it will only be an hour to the house, so we should arrive a little before tea."

"They are expecting us then?" George asked.

"Of course," Anastasia replied. "You recall that I sent a telegram that you had arrived, it should have been delivered already, so they know that we are on our way. I wish they would extend the new telephone service to the country; it would make things so much more convenient." George had been watching Federica during this exchange and saw in her face the love and affection that she had for his sister and the pride that she must have for her pupil.

"Well, Federica?" he asked. "Will you marry me?"

"Yes, yes, yes," she replied.

"What, that's all?" Anastasia demanded. "No down on your knees, no ring, no pomp, no ceremony?"

"I have a ring," George assured her. "My cousin Koos gave me a stone and I had it cut and set in Cape Town before I left."

"Good," she replied. "Now let me go and order some champagne from the restaurant car to celebrate."

"*Mia stella*," George said to Federica, after Anastasia had left on her quest to get champagne. "Will you truly marry me?"

"Of course *stupido*," she replied. "If you had not asked me, I was going to seduce you into asking me."

"How were you going to do that?" he asked. He watched as she stood in front of him and opened her light travelling coat. He had been right; she had precious little on underneath. He felt the growl come up from his stomach as he looked at her, and she smiled at him with hints of what was to come. They heard Anastasia coming back down the corridor, and Federica made herself decent again by closing her coat, but only because she anticipated that Anastasia would not return alone.

"Champagne," Anastasia announced, and a steward followed her into the compartment with a bottle and glasses. George thanked the man and tipped him a small amount, and then set about opening the bottle. He managed to do so without the champagne going everywhere, and then filled the glasses.

"What do we drink to first?" Anastasia asked. "Your nuptials?"

"I think so," George agreed. "Federica, my love, it is so good to see you again. I have missed you so, let us not be parted again."

"*Carissimo*," she replied. "*Te amo*, let the wedding be soon."

"I agree," Anastasia added. "Perhaps we can arrange it before Papa leaves us, and then he will be happy that he may have another in his line when you two have children."

"Nastia," George protested. "We're not even married yet, and you're already talking about children. How do you know Papa will be happy?"

"I heard he and Mama talking last week. Mama told him how it is between you two, and he was happy, surprisingly so, I would have thought that he would disapprove," she replied. "I then also talked to him and told him that I thought you two were a good match."

"Well, thank you," George laughed. "It's gratifying to know that my little sister approves."

"Well, I do," she said defiantly. "After that, he talked to Federica, and now we are here. I do think it's bold and possibly reckless of Fede to come out with hardly any clothes on, though. What would you think if I did likewise?"

"What do you mean?" George asked, choking on his champagne.

"I know what she has, or rather doesn't have on under that coat," she replied. "We do talk, you know, and we shared the room last night at the hotel and helped each other dress this morning."

"Heaven forbid, what do you talk about?" George asked.

"Everything," she told him. "Fede confides in me and I in her. We have no secrets from each other. She has been most forthcoming to me about everything."

"Everything?" George asked.

"Everything," she replied, grinning mischievously. "I know all about you, my handsome, debonair and brave big brother, but I find it hard to reconcile my stern army officer brother with the hopeless romantic that you really are, and your penchant for experimentation in the bedroom."

"Anastasia," Federica gently chided. "Have pity on me and my love, he has come many miles and travelled many days to see us, whereas we may discuss such things as women, it may embarrass him to think we have so freely shared such matters."

"I'm sorry," Anastasia replied. "I'm so thrilled that I can soon call you sister."

"As I am you," Federica assured her. "We've not even asked him about his trip. How was your trip, *Carissimo?*"

"Not that exciting," George told them. "The boat was full of others of the army, plus a civilian surgeon and some nursing sisters."

"Did you know any of them?" Federica asked.

"One or two," he replied. "There were two Liverpool regiments on the boat with a few extras like myself, I think a total of 47 officers and 1,087 men, so it was crowded. At least I had a first-class cabin, which I shared with the surgeon, unlike most of the men who had to just try to find comfortable places to sleep. I knew a couple of the Liverpool officers in passing, but not that well to engage in long conversations. It seemed like an endless voyage, steaming days on end made only bearable because you would be at the end. So, how has Anastasia been behaving herself? Has she done well in her lessons? Can she read and write yet?"

"I am here, you know," the said Anastasia protested.

"We know *Carissima*," Federica assured her. "She has done well in all her lessons; she does not need me any further."

"We'll have to continue this later, we're at Reading and need to change trains," Anastasia interrupted. She tapped her foot impatiently as she waited for George to take down his rifle and small travel bag and follow her and Federica from the train. She got a porter to retrieve their baggage, including George's steamer trunk, and they made their way to the Great Western Railway platform to catch the train to Maidenhead. They did not have long to wait. She had done her planning well, and the next train was departing in only a few minutes. This train was destined for London, stopping only at Maidenhead before speeding its way with no further stops to its final destination at London's Paddington station. The train was as well equipped as their first train, and had comfortable first-class seating, but it seemed only minutes before they were alighting at Maidenhead to catch the much smaller local train to Bourne End. The local train did not boast restaurant cars or other amenities, but it was not a long journey to Bourne End, so any inconvenience was short-lived. At Bourne End, their carriage was waiting, and the driver came to collect the baggage. George was certain that he knew the man, but could not place him immediately. He was middle-aged and seemed to handle the horses well and treated his sister and Federica with great respect, not he thought because he, George, was there, but because he seemed to genuinely respect them. He asked Anastasia about the driver. "This is Henry," she introduced him. "I had to dismiss the last driver; he was unkind to the horses. Henry is the husband of Mrs Partridge, Eleanor, our housekeeper, whom you know. Henry was dissatisfied with his last position, so I offered him the post with us, and he has joined our household."

"I'm pleased to meet you," George said to Henry. "I trust you will be happy with us."

"I believe I will be, Sir," Henry assured him.

"Which way will we go home?" George asked.

"I thought along Hedsor Road, then up Hedsor Hill and thence to the house," Henry explained.

"Very good, thank you, Henry," George acknowledged.

"Will I take charge of your rifle, Sir?" Henry asked.

"Certainly," George agreed. "It has been ever in my company these past two years, but I imagine that English roads are safe enough."

"They are indeed, Sir," Henry assured him. "No, Brother Boer waiting behind a rock here, Sir."

Once they had loaded the baggage and settled themselves for the journey home, George asked about the rest of the household, "How large a domestic staff do we have?"

"Five, plus the labourers employed on the farm," Anastasia replied. "Henry, who acts as coachman, gardener and handyman, Eleanor the housekeeper, Jane the cook and Beatrice the maid and William Forester the farm manager, who sees to the farm labour."

"I recall Eleanor and Jane, but is Beatrice new?" he asked.

"She is the niece of Eleanor," Federica said. "She is sixteen, a pretty young girl with blonde curls and blue eyes who hides herself away behind a severe uniform; she works to better herself and I teach her in her spare hours English, French, mathematics and physics."

"And Mr Forester?" he asked.

"He is quite a good farm manager," Anastasia explained. "I think he thought at first that he could fob us off with quick, meaningless reports, but after we had walked around the farm a few times and reviewed things properly, he now sees things in a different light and we get on famously."

"Where is he from?" George asked.

"He comes from a farming family with a long history in Sambourne in Warwickshire," Federica explained. "We checked his references quite thoroughly, and he is sound, unlike others that we interviewed who had stretched the truth at times and whose references fell apart when we contacted the referees. As Nastia said, he thought at first that we were just two helpless women, but after we examined the stock, audited the accounts and reviewed the general management of the estate, he now holds a different view."

"William lives in the farm manager's cottage with his wife and two daughters," Anastasia added. "Lovely little girls, ages eight and ten, they also are schooled by Federica."

"Do I have a place in all this?" George asked, a little wistfully.

"Well, what are your plans with the army?" Anastasia asked.

"That's a very good question," George admitted. "I have a mind to resign my commission, I have seen too much of war, of killing and of destruction."

"Was it bad down there?" Federica asked.

"It became total war against a people," George told her. "We interned women and children, burned farms and crops, ran off and sold stock and destroyed people's lives."

"Oh, how awful," Anastasia said. "How much truth was there to the stories that Emily Hobhouse reported?"

"Too much, I'm afraid," George admitted. "But then I suppose that is what happens when politicians get us into wars, then expect the army to win victory, no matter at what cost."

"Well, at least for the moment, you do not have to think of it," Federica said. "How long is your leave?"

"Three months," George replied. "Perchance I will extend it to indefinite if Anastasia will employ me."

"Look, we are here already," Anastasia announced. The carriage pulled up to the house, and George alit and then helped his sister and Federica down. Henry promised to have the baggage to their rooms immediately and to stow George's rifle in the household gun cabinet, and then opened the main door for them. Sophia was there at the door to meet them.

"George," she greeted him. "It is good to see you. Your father will be delighted that you are here."

"It is good to be here, Sophia. I'm so sorry that you have such distress in your life. How is he?" George asked.

"Not well," she admitted. "It pains me to see him suffer so, and we pray for a quick end that he may not suffer more."

"Do the opiates help with the pain?" George asked.

"They do," she replied. "But when he takes them, he is distressed because he is not aware of what is happening, so it is a balance. At the moment, he lives with the pain because he knows you have arrived. He will tire quickly, so you should see him forthwith."

George went upstairs to see his father and was shocked. Instead of the vibrant man he had seen just before leaving for South Africa, he was now presented with a husk of a man, clearly in pain and wasting away.

"George, my boy," his father greeted him. "So good to see you. You are safe and unharmed from the war?"

"I am fine, thank you, Father," George replied. "I am sorry that you have been visited by such unpleasantness. Is there anything I can do that will make you more comfortable?"

"Only tell me that you will see to Sophia and your sister, and tell me, is it true that you wish to marry Federica?"

"Yes, Father," George replied. "I will be sure to look to the affairs of Sophia and Anastasia and, yes, I do wish to marry Federica."

"Good, good," his father whispered. "You will do well with Federica, such a capable woman and beautiful too, but I don't need to tell you that. I have watched her of late from this window as she swims by moonlight in the lake. You are lucky to have partaken of that beauty, son, I almost envy you, if it had not been for Sophia, I might have pursued her myself, but that is by the by."

"Is there anything special you wish me to do for Sophia and Anastasia?" George asked.

"If she has a mind to remarry, be kind to Sophia, but check out any potential suitors carefully," his father cautioned. "It would be sad for me to think that Sophia were to live out her days and be lonely, but it would be equally sad to think that someone was taking advantage of her. With Anastasia, watch for the fortune hunters. I have made her equal beneficiary to you in my will, with the proviso that Sophia is assured an income for the rest of her natural days. Because you and Nastia will share the estate when she reaches the age of twenty-five, you will have to come to some amicable arrangement between you, but I think you love her enough to do that?"

"I believe I can do that," George assured him.

"Will you stay in the army?"

"I doubt it," George replied. "I have seen too much bloodletting and destruction. I may either resign my commission or go onto the reserve list. I am still considering my possibilities."

"If you resign, then run for parliament, my boy," his father urged him. "If not parliament, then look at the motor car and invest early and with good companies, mark my words, the motor car will mean great changes in the years to come. Ask Anastasia and Federica to show you what they have been doing."

"Yes, Sir," George agreed. "You are tired, shall I ring for something?"

"Thank you, son," his father agreed. "I am tired and the pain is endless, there are days when I pray for the end, but I cannot let Sophia see that, but I may tell you because you must have seen men in war that were badly hurt and looking for surcease."

"I have indeed, Father," George agreed. "I have seen a lot, but it is never easier; it is always distressing. Ah, here is Sophia. I will leave you now and visit again in the morning."

Changes

George left his father's room and went to his own room to change from his uniform into more comfortable clothes. He searched around the house and found Federica and Anastasia in the library. He was shocked to see them both dressed in what looked like pyjamas, as he had seen in India, made up of loose trousers and blouses and judging by the occasional hint of movement of their breasts, little else.

"Is this the latest style?" he asked.

"No," Federica replied. "It is more comfortable than the crinolines, taffetas, laces, high collars, pinched waists with whalebone corsets and other articles of torture that the fashionable world would encase us in; these are Chinese and very comfortable. However, do not be concerned, we are the height of conformity when we go abroad to the village or to town."

"What does the rest of the household think?" George asked.

"Well, Mama is too distracted by Papa to care," Anastasia replied. "Eleanor is shocked but hides it well, Jane and Beatrice are not sure what to think. Beatrice, I think, would like to be brave enough to follow, but her aunt would have the vapours if she did."

"Do you like it?" Federica asked.

"Very much so," George agreed. "There's just so much less to take off. What is there, trousers, shirt, I presume no hose, no corsets, nothing else?"

"George!" Anastasia giggled. "You are quite right, we have liberated ourselves from the shackles of propriety and have rebelled, but only within the house."

"So, do I have to dress for dinner?" he asked.

"Only enough not to shock Eleanor and Beatrice," Federica laughed. "So, don't present yourself for dinner like some naked African, even though that might be interesting. We have asked them to just lay out dinner on the sideboard, and we will serve ourselves."

"Good," George thought. "The idea of sitting through a formal dinner and trying to make polite conversation that will be analysed by the staff does not appeal."

"How is Papa?" Anastasia asked.

"Failing, I'm afraid," George replied. "I would not be at all surprised if your Mama does not summon the doctor later. If she does, then perhaps we should make ourselves less notorious in the village by presenting a front of conformity to fashion."

"Of course," Federica agreed. "Do you think the end will be soon?"

"I have seen many men in dire straits," George replied. "And, yes, I think the end will be soon. I'm sorry, Nastia, to bring such news, but as you said, it will end his suffering."

"I will go to Mama," Anastasia announced. "We will be comfort for one another."

When she had gone, George sat by Federica on the couch and held her hands,

"Federica, my love, how soon is it before dinner?" he asked.

"About two hours," she replied. "I think you are right about your Papa, we probably should wash and dress to receive visitors in case Sophia calls the doctor. Can you wait a little while longer?"

"Federica, my love, I have waited years in South Africa just to see your face, I can steel myself to wait a little longer to see the rest of you," he replied. "However, after the foretaste of things to come that I saw in the train, it will be difficult."

"I know my love," she agreed. "It will be difficult for me also. I have longed for you night after night, wondering if you would come back to me."

"What have you been discussing with Anastasia?" he asked.

"I shared with her my hopes, dreams and fears," she replied. "I also got carried away one day and described you as a lover, that led to inevitable questions and I realised just how ignorant she was of matters of sex between and a man and a woman, so I talked to Sophia then took it upon myself to counsel her and make her properly aware of all that was involved."

"Oh, I see," he said a little uncomfortably. "How did she take it all?"

"I think part wonder, part horror, part delight and part disgust," she said. "I believe I convinced her that with the right person, it would be wonderful."

"No wonder she was grinning and slyly suggesting things," he commented. "I wonder she hasn't asked for a demonstration."

"I told her to check the bull and the cows and the ram and the ewes," she laughed. "I think she went out one day to specifically do that and came back full of more questions."

"I suppose it's the peculiarity of our society that polite company does not discuss sex, even though they obviously engage in it, or they would die out," he laughed.

"I did point out to her that whereas men and women do engage in sex in the position of the bull and the cow, it is not the only way and it is, in England at least, more common to be face-to-face," she added.

"What did she make of that?" he asked.

"Oh, it led to more questions and more questions so that in the end I showed her the copy of Burton's translation of the ancient Indian text," she replied. "That raised her eyebrows more than a little. However, I see in her no desire to rush out and try these things, so rest easy that you will not have unpleasant issues to deal with any time soon."

"Thank God for that," he said. "In India, girls less than her age were already sexually active or married, and it is difficult to imagine her with a man."

"I have also been teaching her the defence techniques I learned in Hong Kong," she explained. "So that, if she is ever assaulted or has to fend off unwanted advances, she has the knowledge to do so, and to inflict great pain upon her attackers."

"So, Papa told me to get you to show me what you and Nastia have been doing?" he asked.

"Tomorrow, my love," she promised. "You may be surprised." Whatever else she might have said was interrupted by Anastasia, who came bursting into the room.

"Come quickly," she ordered. "Things do not go well with Papa." They followed her upstairs and were in time to see and hear Papa draw his last breaths, then descend into peace. Sophia took his hand and sat by the bed, weeping with Anastasia by her side. George went to her and took her hand, and she looked up and him and said, "He has peace at last, no more pain, no more suffering, seeing you was all he needed before he left us."

"I will fetch the doctor," he said. He wanted the doctor for two reasons: the death certificate and to prescribe whatever Sophia might need for sleep. He left the room and went to the kitchen where he found Eleanor and the others, "I am afraid Mr Wheelwright has just died peaceably," he said. "Henry, I wonder if you would mind riding over to Doctor Ferguson's house and asking him if he would attend?"

"Of course, Sir," Henry agreed. "I'm sorry, Sir."

"Thank you, Henry," George replied. "I believe these last few weeks have been a sore trial for my father, and now he is at peace, and Mrs Wheelwright and my sister no longer have to endure witnessing his pain and suffering. Mrs Partridge, I wonder if you would be so kind as to assist Mrs Wheelwright in whatever she needs in the next few days?"

"Of course, Mr George," Eleanor agreed. "I will go to her right away. Jane has the dinner prepared, but it can hold until you are ready."

George, Federica and Anastasia changed into more conventional attire, and Dr. Ferguson duly arrived about forty minutes later and, after a quick discussion with George, duly signed the death certificate, which he handed to George.

"It has been some time since I saw you last," he said. "I'm sorry about your father, but cancer is an insidious condition and one we know little about yet. Perhaps in years to come we will learn more and how to combat it."

"I hope so," George agreed. "I gather that it was a relatively recent onset, and it progressed rapidly."

"It did indeed," Dr. Ferguson agreed. "I had him visit specialists in Harley Street, but there was little they could do, beyond the palliative."

"It certainly appeared to cause him great distress," George said.

"I cannot speak from my own experience, obviously," Doctor Ferguson said. "In my discussions with other patients, I am given to understand that the condition is indeed most painful."

"Have you something for Mrs Wheelwright?" George asked.

"I will see her now and give her a light sedative if she needs it," the doctor said. "I think for her, the difficulty is going to be feeling guilty over the relief that it is over."

"That I can understand," George said. "It's like the guilt one feels when the man next to you is hit, but you are not, a relief, yes, but then a guilt over the relief."

"So, you do understand," the doctor nodded approvingly. "You will be a great help to Mrs Wheelwright and your sister in the next weeks."

"Thank you, Doctor, for coming out. May I offer you a sherry, a brandy?" George asked.

"Thank you, but no," Doctor Ferguson demurred. "I have another patient to attend, a temperance adherent, so perhaps another time. I will just see Mrs Wheelwright, then I will leave you."

Dinner was eaten late and in quiet. Each of the household had his or her own thoughts. Sophia retired early, leaving Anastasia with George and Federica.

"I am so glad you saw Papa before he died," Anastasia said to George. "It had been weighing heavily upon his mind that you would not be back in time."

"What about you, Nastia, how are you?" he asked.

"I am saddened by his death," she agreed. "But, I am so relieved that Mama does not have to watch him writhe in pain any longer. I did my crying a week ago when I realised that he was not going to recover from this and that the end was soon."

"I will contact the undertakers in the morning," George said. "I'll also talk to the local rector and then get on to our solicitors in London, is there anything else?"

"I don't think so," Anastasia said. "If you don't mind, I will retire now. I'll stop and see Mama and check on her, so will see you in the morning."

"Good night, Nastia," George said, then kissed her and gave her a hug. Federica also kissed her good night and watched her as she left the room.

"She hides her distress well," she remarked to George. "Even though she has known that this was coming, and soon, it is still hard when it is finally reality. I will go to her now and then join you."

"*Non vedo l'ora*," he whispered.

"Ah, you do remember some of the Italian I taught you," she said. "That is most gratifying."

George picked up dishes and carried them to the kitchen, to the horror of Eleanor.

"Mr George," she blurted out. "We'll do that, don't trouble yourself."

"I think it's the Army," he laughed. "I have been looking after myself for so long in South Africa, it's become second nature."

"You did not have anyone there to see to your needs?" she asked.

"I was with one other for the past few months, and we relied upon one another," George explained. "I had to fend for myself or go hungry and cold."

"Well, we'll take care of these dinner things," Eleanor repeated. "Do you wish for tea in your room tomorrow morning?"

"Don't worry, Mrs Partridge," he assured her, thinking that she might be shocked if she found Federica in his bed with him, but then perhaps he was misjudging her and she would not be that surprised. "I'm tired from the journey and the events of the day, I'll probably sleep late. When I'm up, I'll come down and bother you again."

"Oh, Mr George, it is no bother," she assured him. "I am so sorry that Mr Wheelwright died, but happy for him that he was able to see you fit and well before he departed."

"Thank you, Mrs Partridge," George said. "Mrs Wheelwright has retired for the night, and Federica has gone to see to Anastasia. I will see the undertaker and the rector in the morning, and then will talk to our solicitors in London, would you please assure the household that I do not anticipate any changes."

"Very good, Sir," she replied, obviously indicating that he was now the head of the household.

"Well, good night, Mrs Partridge," he said, then left and went to his room.

Federica looked in on Anastasia and was pleased that she was already asleep. She could now focus her attention on George and his homecoming. She entered his room and saw that he had drawn a bath and was already soaking away the aches and pains of the day's travel.

"Anastasia is abed and asleep," she said. "Is there room for me?"

"My love, there will always be room for you," he promised.

"I need help with these stupid clothes," she complained. "Can you undo me?"

"Of course," he said. He stood up in the bath and motioned her to him, then started undoing buttons. He watched as she took off the dress and laid it on a chair, then she came back over to him and turned around so that he could undo the corset, which she divested with a sigh and then threw it into the farthest corner of the room. She quickly took off the rest of her undergarments, turned to face him, then stretched her arms up towards the ceiling, showing off her breasts, flat stomach and well-muscled legs. As he had done in the train, George growled from deep in his being and feasted on the vision of her as she stretched again, she was still lithe, limber, well-formed and utterly desirable. She made a final pirouette and then climbed into the bath with him. She looked him over carefully and examined him thoroughly.

"These three scars are new," she said. "Where did you get them?"

"This one from a fight near Bloemfontein," he explained. "This one from an encounter in the Cape Colony and this from an encounter in Namaqualand."

"You sustained no other injuries that might affect your abilities?" she asked.

"No, my love," he assured her. "I am still intact, still capable and bursting with desire for you."

"Well, you are back to me finally," she sighed. "I missed you, missed your kisses, I missed the touch of you, I missed the scent of you in the morning, the feel of you in the bed beside me, the arrogance of your manhood and the way we put it to good use."

"I missed you, my love," he told her, not sure that he could ever match her descriptive terms for their separation.

"Show me how much you missed me," she challenged.

"Come closer," he told her. "Sit in my lap and put your legs around me, and I'll see if I can remember what to do." Later, when they had mopped up the water from the floor that had splashed all about, they retired to the bed and repeated the procedure, this time with less splashing but now with bed squeaks. They managed the process one more time before both fell asleep in each other's arms, sated, satisfied and blissfully happy.

They were awakened in the morning by Anastasia, who came in and threw open the curtains.

"It's time you two were up," she announced. "The whole house is wondering what is keeping you from breakfast, as if they didn't know."

"Nastia, have a heart," Federica pleaded.

"Don't think I don't know what you two did half the night, I wonder the whole house did not hear," she said sternly, or at least trying to appear stern, but failing as she grinned at them. "I certainly heard, we need a quieter bed for you."

"How are you this morning?" Federica asked.

"I am done with crying," she replied. "Papa is at rest, and even Mama is more at ease this morning now that we no longer have to witness the pain and suffering. Well, come on, up you get."

"With you standing there?" George asked.

"I won't look," she promised. "I need to supervise here and make sure you don't just go back to bed and start your amorous adventures again. There is much to be done."

"Yes, Sister," George promised. He slid out of the bed and put some trousers on then reached for a shirt. Anastasia caught a glimpse of him in a mirror and turned and looked him up and down. "Well, it looks as if you have been looking after yourself, but you are a little thin and lacking weight that would be advantageous to you," she said.

"I try," he admitted. "Life in the field in the army does require a certain level of physical fitness, but I admit to having had less to eat than I would have liked lately."

"So, I see," she said. "You have a pleasing physique, not unlike some of the famous statues in the museums in London. But, look at those scars, you've been wounded again. Does it hurt?"

"Not anymore," he promised.

"Turn around," she ordered. "All those scars, did you know about these, Fede?"

"These three are new," Federica replied, pointing to the fresh scars. "The others are all familiar to me and were presumably obtained in India, I suppose in the service of Queen and Country, unless, of course, it was a series of jealous lovers?"

"No, no, I promise, no jealous lovers," George laughed. "What about Federica, Nastia, surely she warrants some review?"

"I envy her physique," Anastasia said. "Look at her, lithe, small, high breasts, a narrow waist, that is naturally slim without the aid of corsets or other devices of torture, hips not too broad and legs that would grace a ballerina."

"You flatter me," Federica smiled. The two of them had been through this ritual many times and knew each other almost as intimately as lovers. George had not seen this side of Federica or Anastasia before and realised just how close they were, very much like sisters, but sisters who were devoted to one another, not at each other's throats through petty jealousies.

"I'll see you downstairs in five minutes," Anastasia said. "Then you can explain to Mama what you were doing last night."

"I rather think she has other things on her mind," George said. "If you will lead the way, I will go with you and Federica can go and find clothes suitable for mourning, which I note you have already procured."

"I acquired them some time ago," she admitted. "It was a way for me to begin to prepare for what was to come."

After breakfast, George saddled a horse and went to the church of St. Nicholas, where he found the rector.

"Good morning, Rector," he began.

"Good morning, Sir, how may I be of assistance?" the rector asked.

"My name is George Wheelwright," George replied. "My father, also George, died last night, and I have come to arrange for funeral services."

Of course," the rector said. "I thought you were in South Africa."

"I returned only yesterday," George explained. "In time to see my father one last brief time, and then he died last evening. He was attended by Doctor Ferguson."

"May I offer my condolences?" the rector said. "Is there anything I may help with?"

"The name of a good undertaker," George suggested.

"As it happens, I have burial services to conduct this morning and am awaiting the arrival of Mr Stanley from Cookham," the rector commented. "He is a most sympathetic man and most reasonable."

"Do you mind if I wait with you?" George asked.

"Not at all," the rector said. "Do you know when you would like to do the internment?"

"I thought perhaps we could agree a time and a date, then I will place notices in the paper," George replied. The two talked for a while, and arrangements were agreed upon. Mr Stanley duly arrived and was introduced, and he promised to call upon the Wheelwrights after the service. While they were thus occupied, Doctor Ferguson arrived and obviously knew Mr Stanley and was on good terms with him. That made George feel more comfortable; he now had two references, the rector and the doctor, normally both men of standing in any community. Leaving the church and the rector to the funeral service, George went to Bourne End and the post office and sent a telegram to their solicitors in London.

Back at the house, George was in time for lunch and over lunch, he told the others of his morning. Then lunch was interrupted by the arrival of a telegram, which was the reply from the solicitors, one of whom would be travelling down the next day. He provided the train arrival time at Bourne End and requested transport to the house. The telegram boy was waiting for a reply, so George quickly wrote out a form and confirmed that the carriage would be at the station. After lunch, Mr Stanley arrived, and George then went through the details with him of the funeral arrangements, coffin, headstone, etc. Finally, he had time to relax over coffee after Stanley had left and Federica and Anastasia joined him, no longer dressed in the attire of Edwardian mourning women, but in more comfortable black pyjamas, so that mourning conventions were still at least partially observed.

"How is your Mama today?" he asked Anastasia.

"She is more composed today," she replied. "I think she is relieved to be free of the burden of witnessing the pain and is now thinking of tomorrow. The funeral will create its own difficulties, but I believe we can manage."

"And you?" George asked.

"I am sorry he has gone," she replied. "But, also relieved that we no longer have to witness the suffering. It has been difficult, and I pray that I never have such an ordeal. What about you, George?"

"I remember when my mother died when I was only twelve," he replied. "I killed the snake that bit her and made her die, and that made it better for me. With Papa, I cannot kill the snake because we cannot see it, but perhaps one day someone will. I will grieve for him in my own way, but more I will grieve for you and Sophia, for your loss."

"I will go to Mama and spend some time with her," Anastasia stated. "I will talk to her and have her talk to me about the good times she remembers and the happiness she and Papa shared."

When she had gone, Federica turned to George and asked him how he was faring. She was concerned that he had just returned from his service in South Africa to be thrown directly into the throes of a death and the associated events that had to follow with the funeral service and the burial.

"I am fine, Fede," he assured her. "My father was a wonderful man, as I'm sure you discovered. I have seen death before, and think for him it brought a release from the pain. He is at peace, so I am at peace. Enough of that, will you join me in the garden?"

The garden included a walled kitchen garden and another similarly walled ornamental garden. They saw Henry busy in the kitchen garden, said good afternoon, then went to the ornamental garden, which included a gazebo and the small lake in which Federica took her late-night swims.

"*Carissimo*, how are you today?" she asked.

"I will be happier when the funeral, the reading of the will is done, and we may then look to our future. When would you like to be married?" he asked.

"Now, today, soon," she replied. "I think we should respect Sophia and ask her when she thinks it would be convenable."

"It's starting to rain, should we go in?" he asked.

"No, just enjoy the rain, we have not had much rain this month, it has been unseasonably dry," she said. "The walls will shelter us from the wind, which is what would make it cold, so hold your face up to the sky and let the rain wash away the ills of war and the loss of your father."

"Papa said that I should get you to show me what you have been doing. What have you been doing?" he asked, spluttering a little as the rain beat upon his face.

"For that, we must go in," she thought. "I will show you by and by, for now just enjoy the rain." George did just that, occasionally stealing a glance at Federica. She was standing with her arms spread out to her sides, back arched and face towards the sky, letting the rain beat down upon her. George looked again and this time noted how the wet pyjamas clung to her body and revealed the curves and the secret places that would normally be concealed. It was a delightful sight. Finally, she brought her arms down to her sides, bent forward and placed her head against her shins, then straightened up and announced that it was now time to go in, dry and change into fresh clothes. George agreed; he was finally getting a little chilled in the rain. Once inside, they went to George's room and she ran a bath.

"Come," she told him. "The warm water will take away the chill."

"Let me help you out of those wet clothes," he offered.

"Hurry up then," she agreed.

"You don't have much on," he said as he stripped away her shirt and trousers and discovered nothing else underneath.

"Just for you, my love," she told him. "I thought you approved."

"Oh, I do, I do," he agreed heartily. "Give me a minute and I will join you in the bath."

An hour later, they presented themselves in the drawing room and found Sophia and Anastasia both laughing about something.

"Memories?" George asked.

"Yes, memories," Sophia confirmed. "Your father was a lovely man and made me laugh a lot, our life together was happy, and I will cherish those memories always. I will probably do much laughing and crying in the weeks to come. What have you two been doing?"

"Mama," Anastasia interrupted. "I can tell you what they were doing, but it might offend our sensibilities."

"Nonsense, Nastia," her mother disagreed. "Your father and I took every opportunity we could to be together, dare I say even before we were wed. Not that I'm suggesting that you do likewise, my girl, but with a marriage date set six months away, it was difficult for us to contain our love for one another."

"As to that," George started. "At some time, when you think it appropriate, we would like to discuss our marriage with you."

"Thank you, George," Sophia acknowledged. "Let us think about two to three months from now. That way, conventions will be satisfied, the rector will not be aghast, and the village gossips will have little to talk about."

"You are not offended by our even considering marriage at this time?" George asked.

"My dear," Sophia replied. "Your father and I had a blissfully happy marriage. I celebrate his life and am thankful for the time we had together. Seeing you two marry would please me, and I believe would have pleased him as well."

"Are you going to move into George's room?" Anastasia asked Federica.

"I think that is a capital idea," Sophia interjected before Federica could reply. "You two have been separated long enough. I will instruct Mrs Partridge to move your things."

"Won't she be shocked?" George asked.

"No," Sophia assured him. "We talked about many things last evening, and on one thing we did agree, you two belong together, you make a delightful couple, and we will announce the impending nuptials soon enough. She knows you both and was surprised that it took this long for you to find each other."

"Will she spread it abroad that Fede is living in sin with George?" Anastasia asked.

"No, she regards our household as her own and is fiercely protective," Sophia assured her. "She will instruct Beatrice in what to do and what to say, and if there are rumours, why do we care, we are beholden to no one?"

"Oh, good, perhaps I will take the room that Fede has," Anastasia said. "I think I like the view better than the view from my room."

"Oh, so it had nothing to do with our welfare or happiness," George teased her. "Only your desire for a better vista from your window."

"You're lucky I had not already appropriated the room you are in, George," she retorted. "You weren't here, and I could have moved in at any time."

"I think I hear the dinner gong," Federica said. "Shall we go?"

"What were you doing of late in South Africa?" Anastasia asked George as they walked to the dining room.

"I was assigned to Field Intelligence and was essentially scouting out the Boer commandos," he replied.

"They were not in one place?" Anastasia asked.

"Not at all," he told her. "They moved around a lot, which is what made it so difficult to bring them to bay. I think in the end it was the farm burnings and the destruction of livestock that made them, at least the Transvaalers, argue for an end to the war."

"Were there some that wished to continue fighting on?" Sophia asked.

"There were," he confirmed. "They will be problems yet, but for the moment at least a peace has been negotiated and it is holding."

"Are you glad it is over?" Anastasia asked.

"I am," he confirmed. "Tracking the Boers through the bush was hard, and the risk was always there that you would be discovered, which would have been unpleasant."

"Did you spend much time on horseback?" Anastasia asked

"Altogether too long," he laughed. "I think I developed strong personal bonds with my horses."

"Horses, you had more than one then?" Federica asked.

"Oh yes," he confirmed. "I started out with a whole string, one thing we discovered in South Africa was how quickly horses lose their condition in the veldt."

"We had seen odd items in the press about remounts and the need to buy horses from all over the world," Federica said. "It seems that the need for horses was almost greater than the need for men, much of the time."

"I think that is probably true," he agreed. "Once the sieges of Ladysmith and Mafeking were over and we had marched to Pretoria, the war changed, and it was then chasing each other all over the veldt."

"Well, we're delighted that you are back with us," Sophia said. "I know your father was so pleased to see you safe and well. We have kept dinner waiting long enough, shall we eat?"

After dinner, Sophia asked Eleanor to bring coffee to the drawing room. She asked George to pour her a brandy, something that probably would have shocked the neighbours, ladies simply did not imbibe in that way, it was the gentlemen who retired to a drawing room for brandy and cigars.

"Tell me of South Africa," she asked George. "What do people do there, what do they wear, what language do they speak?"

"South Africa is much larger than England," he began. "From Cape Town to Pretoria, it is just over nine hundred miles, and there is yet more of South Africa north of Pretoria until the Limpopo River. The climate varies greatly from the Mediterranean-like weather of Cape Town to the heat and humidity of Durban on the Indian Ocean and the dry heat of the north near the Limpopo."

"Who are the people?" Anastasia asked.

"There are the Africans, of course," he started. "They divide themselves into several groups, the Xhosa, the Zulu, the Sotho and the Venda and some other lesser peoples. Then there are the two major white groups, the Boers and the English-speaking people."

"What part did the Africans play in the recent war?" Federica asked.

"Both sides used them as scouts, and both sides used them as armed combatants, more so than the leaders of both sides would have us believe."

"What did they think of the war?" Federica asked."

"I really don't know," he admitted. "I never had the opportunity to discuss it with any of them, but I cannot imagine they were supporters, the war had great effect upon them as many lost farms, stock and their livelihoods."

"What do people wear?" Sophia asked."

"The whites wear very much what you might see here," he replied. "But, with deference to the heat in the summer. The Africans wear sometimes almost nothing and other times wrap themselves up in blankets against the cold."

"It does get cold then?" Federica asked.

31

"It does indeed," he assured her. "In July and August, it can be bitterly cold in the mountains and in the open veldt at night. They do have snow there in the mountains at times."

"What language does everyone speak?" Anastasia asked.

"The best answer to that is that they speak their own language," he replied. "So, if Boer they speak Dutch, if English, English; if Zulu, Zulu."

"As I recall, you speak Dutch?" Sophia asked.

"I do indeed," he confirmed. "I learned as a child and have not forgotten."

"Was that why they wanted you in the Field Intelligence?" Anastasia asked.

"I think partly yes," he agreed, "it was of help often, but it would also have been of help to speak Xhosa or Sotho."

"What do people do there?" Sophia asked.

"Many are farmers," he replied. "They grow mealies, which is like a coarse maize, they raise cattle and sheep, there are also the diamond and gold mines which employ a great many people and which many here believe were the cause of this last war."

"What do you think?" Federica asked.

"I think in the end it was just a question of power and control," he said. "There was probably room for only one power in the country, so war was probably inevitable."

"Such a pity," Sophia said. "So many people killed, so much money spent and for what, so that some politician may stand up in Westminster and boast about the Empire and its reach."

"Well, perhaps we will be free of wars for a while," Federica said. "I am praying that will be so, otherwise I may lose George again to some foreign part."

"Well, my Dears," Sophia said. "I hate to be the one to conclude this, but I am tired and will retire. I will see you in the morning."

The reading of the will

Anastasia did not burst in and fling open the curtains of George's room, which was as well, because he and Federica were still making up for opportunities lost over the past two years. Anastasia had been right, though; they would need a bed that did not squeak as much.

"That was a beautiful way to wake up," Federica said. "If a little noisy!"

"How could I resist?" he asked. "You are so desirable, but even more so, you are here and I am here and who knows what the morrow may bring?"

"You don't think you will be recalled already?" she asked in alarm.

"No, but I did learn on the lonely nights on the veldt to appreciate life and you are to be appreciated, my love," he replied.

"Perhaps we should rise and join the others for breakfast?" she suggested.

"I suppose so," he agreed. "There is much to be said for the indolent life of the aristocracy if it would permit me to stay in bed with you for all the day."

"Perhaps," she admitted. "Think upon this, anticipation builds during the day and adds to the moment when we become one."

"Ah, true," he agreed. "I cannot look at you and not be aroused, no matter the time or place, particularly when you parade around in front of me like that, clad in nothing but earrings and a smile."

"Put away your lecherous thoughts and think about the day, we have the undertaker coming, we have your solicitors coming, there is much to do," she told him.

"You are right, my love," he admitted. "We perhaps can return to our amours later in the day."

At the breakfast table, they found Sophia reading some mail and Anastasia deep into the Financial Times. They both looked up briefly, then went back to their reading.

"So, what is so engrossing in the money pages, Nastia?" George asked.

"Ah, at it again were we?" she laughed. "Good of you to join us. I'm deciding whether we should increase our position in copper. Current prices are down, probably as a result of lower demand for brass cartridge cases now that hostilities have ceased in South Africa. As we stand today, prices per ton of copper metal are down over £20 per ton since the peak in 1900 and the same is true of most of the metals, including tin, lead, iron and steel. However, I think that the coming motor car business will use copper and brass and the electricity supply and telephone businesses both will use copper in abundance, so am considering what would be the best course of action and when. I am also considering when would be a good time to sell off the fleet of steam ploughing engines that we have, fearing that they will soon be replaced with some engine that uses the new internal combustion principles."

"Oh," was all George could say. He was rescued by Federica, who reminded him that she and Anastasia had been doing most of the managing of the family portfolio of investments for about a year, and that they had been doing rather well. She went on to detail the publications they took and the industries and businesses that they followed. All actual investment decisions had been transmitted to their solicitors and brokers ostensibly via Papa, but he had been happy to stand back and watch the two manage things.

"So, what did Papa mean when he told me to ask what you two had been up to?" George wondered.

"Eat your breakfast and I will show you," Federica promised, but as it transpired, events occurred that delayed that showing until later in the day.

"We do have some decisions to make, some more urgent than others," Anastasia said. "Perhaps later this afternoon, we could go through the books and acquaint you with our circumstances?"

"Of course," George agreed. "Sophia, how are you today?"

"I am more at peace, thank you, George," she replied. "I feel as if an enormous weight has been lifted from my shoulders, and for the first time in many months, I have been able to enjoy the birds at sunrise and the light rain that is falling."

"I am pleased to hear it," he said. "If I am able to help or provide solace in any way, please call upon me."

"Thank you, George," she said. "I was dreading the day that your father would die, but now it has come upon us, and I find I am relieved."

George was wondering what to say next when Mrs Partridge knocked on the door and announced that Mr Stanley of the undertakers had arrived. George took his leave of the ladies and went to assist Stanley with the removal of the body from the bedroom to the hearse. The funeral was set for that Friday, so Mr Stanley had time to arrange things appropriately. The burial headstone was already done, and Stanley presented George with a rubbing of the carved words for his approval. It was simple enough, George Wheelwright, 1825 - 1902, loving husband and father, RIP. Those simple words brought it home to George how much younger than his father Sophia was. It would be a shame indeed if she did not remarry; she was, after all, only forty-two, barely ten years older than himself. Stanley left, and George informed Mrs Partridge that she could now clean out the bedroom and remove and dispose of all the bedding and air out the room. Sophia had been sleeping in a spare room adjacent to that of Anastasia and had indicated that she would probably just stay there. That taken care of, George joined the ladies in the drawing room for coffee.

Mr Baker of Baker, Fielding, Higginbottom and Watts, solicitors of Chancery Lane, duly presented himself at ten, having taken the early train down from London. He was greeted by George, who showed him into the drawing room, where Sophia, Anastasia and Federica were waiting. George made the introductions and offered Mr Baker coffee, which he accepted.
"Would it be possible to assemble the household so that they may hear of bequests that may be to their benefit?" Mr Baker asked George.
"Of course," George agreed. He rang for Mrs Partridge, and when she came, he asked for more coffee and asked her if she would bring in the rest of the household. They came quickly enough, and George and Henry found chairs for all.
"Good morning," Mr Baker began. "This is the reading of the last will and testament of George Archibald Wheelwright, this Seventeenth Day in the Month of September in the Year of Our Lord Nineteen Hundred and Two, in the presence of the family members of the late George Archibald Wheelwright and in the presence of other beneficiaries. He begins with the usual form and preambles, then goes on to make specific bequests, which I will read to you. '*To Mrs Eleanor Partridge for*

her many years of devoted service to our household, the sum of £1,000 to be paid within one month of my death, to Mr Henry Partridge, recently come into our employ, the sum of £100 to be paid within one month of my death, to Miss Jane Dove, who has given us long service as our cook, the sum of £1,000 to be paid within one month of my death, to Miss Beatrice Partridge, recently come into our household, the sum of £50 to be paid within one month of my death and a further amount to cover expenses for her education should she choose to pursue it, up to and including that of university, the exact amount and conditions to be determined by my executors. Further, to Mr William Forester, our farm manager, recently come into our employ, the sum of £100 to be paid within one month of my death and a further amount to cover expenses for the education of his daughters, Catherine and Elizabeth, should they choose to pursue it, up to and including that of university, the exact amount and conditions to be determined by my executors.' That concludes bequests made to members of the household. The additional amounts that may fall due should Miss Partridge and the Misses Forester elect to pursue an education have already been funded according to actuarial figures, and the funds should be more than adequate to cover such expenses. In due course, I will return here and disburse the bequeathed funds in accordance with the wishes of Mr Wheelwright. Perhaps the members of the household could let me know how they would prefer to receive the funds, either in a banker's draft or in cash. Either is possible, but I would like at least three or four days' notice so that I may arrange for cash if that is preferred. I will be back on the fifteenth of October to fulfil the terms of the various bequests. Are there any concerns or questions? No, then the balance of the will deals with the disposal of the estate to the various family members, including Miss Beretta. If the rest of the household will excuse us?" The members of the household left, most hardly holding back tears. "I cannot believe it," George heard William say. "We have been here but a short while, and yet I am blessed with a gift and perhaps a greater gift, that of the possibility for my daughters to better themselves."

"To return to the balance of the will," Mr Baker intoned after the household had gone and the door had been firmly closed against curious ears. '*To my loving wife, Sophia, her heirs and descendants, I give the sum of £100,000, to be paid her in five annual instalments, the first being within one month of my death and the balance each on the anniversary of my death and a further £10,000 per annum payable now and on each anniversary of my death for the balance of her natural life or until she remarry, and also the use of the west wing of the house of the main house at the Hedsor Minor Estate, also known as Hedsor Grange, for the rest of her natural life, or until she remarry. To Federica Giovanna Beretta, upon her marriage to my son George Jacobus the sum of £50,000 in the hopes that she will pursue the dream that she and I shared for the development and manufacture of a motor car, to be paid in five annual instalments, one at the time of her marriage and the balance annually upon the anniversary of her marriage, should she not marry my son George Jacobus then I give unto her the sum of £20,000 to be paid within six months of my death. The balance of my estate both real and personal I give, devise and bequeath to my son George Jacobus, his heirs and descendants and my daughter Anastasia Katrina, her heirs and descendants, in equal parts, the division of which will be made upon Anastasia achieving the age of five and twenty years, providing she reach that age, if not then the balance will revert to my son George, his heirs and descendants, the division of the estate will be made by my children, George and Anastasia, trusting in their good natures to make an amicable division of the assets, but in the event they are unable to do so then the Solicitors of Baker, French, Higginbottom and Watts together with firms named by each of George and Anastasia shall negotiate and agree upon a fair and equitable division of the estate. I name as executors of this my last will and testament my son George Jacobus and the firm of Baker, French, Higginbottom and Watts.*' He goes on with the usual forms, and the will was signed and witnessed by me and Mr French of our firm approximately a year ago, on the eighteenth of October 1901."

"That seems straightforward enough, apart from the should she marry or not marry, part that affects myself and Federica," George said. "He has made provision for you, Sophia, and I pledge to ensure that you are well provided for."

"That clause regarding the potential of marriage between yourself and Miss Beretta caused us some concern, too. We tried to get Mr Wheelwright to modify the language and terms to make it less open to interpretation and possible suit, but he was adamant and the clause remained as written. He was most particular about the bequest to Miss Beretta, stating that he knew how things stood between her and you, Mr George and was saddened by the fact that he might not see you wed. The latter clause about the division of the estate was also the subject of much discussion between the members of our firm and Mr Wheelwright," Baker said. "However, he was again adamant that the conditions be so, so we trust in the good natures and sense of fairness of you, Mr George and you, Miss Anastasia."

"What constitutes the estate?" George asked.

"Well, in summary there is the real property part of the estate that constitutes this property, 587 acres in all with the house and related out buildings and certain farm related dwellings, an additional 18,233 acres in Scotland of hill country with game and fishing rights, with a tenant farmer raising sheep, 15,517 acres in Cumberland and an adjacent and adjoining 12,574 acres in Westmorland, also with a tenant raising sheep, that property also includes fishing rights along a section of a river in the County of Westmorland known for its trout and salmon, there is a further property in Lancashire of some 230 acres along the shores of Windermere, also with a tenant farmer, there is a further 1,316 acres in Derbyshire, also with a tenant farmer raising sheep and a further 900 acres of hill country, also in Derbyshire with mineral rights and an active lead mine, leased to an operating company that produces lead on which we exact a royalty, we have detailed property descriptions of each of these parcels of land that are appended to the will. There is also an extensive portfolio of holdings in various enterprises, both in factories and in shares, with an aggregate value today of some £564,320, the list of which I have here, but which I may summarise as diverse both in industry type and country. There is cash on hand of some £43,281 plus gold bars to the value of some £64,350, both these being lodged with Rothschilds Bank, and finally, there is the personal property that is upon the estate which constitutes the furniture and effects within the house, the cars, coaches, wagons, horses and other items" Mr Baker enumerated, then handed a list to each of George and Anastasia.

"Do you have two further copies?" George asked.

"I am afraid not," Mr Baker demurred. "I thought it expedient only to provide copies to the two principal heirs."

"These enterprises," George asked. "How diverse are they?"

"Well, if you consult the list you will note that they are in various categories, chiefly, mining and minerals, including oil and the new petroleum industries, transportation, which includes railways and shipping lines, textiles, merchant trading, publishing, comestibles and manufacturing, particularly in the area of household items, clothing and light machinery," Mr Baker explained.

"How has the portfolio performed?" Anastasia asked.

"It has always done well, but of late we have observed almost a resurgence of spirit as if it has been viewed with a fresh perspective," Mr Baker explained. "I confess we have been so impressed by the performance that we have taken note and made some of our own investments very much in line with those of Mr Wheelwright."

"Thank you, Mr Baker. Is there anything else that we need to be aware of at this time?" George asked.

"There is the issue of the iniquitous Death Duties," Mr Baker replied.

"Do we have an accounting for that?" George asked.

"We do indeed, Sir," Mr Baker confirmed and produced a large folio full of numbers and calculations that eventually led to the amount that the Inland Revenue would seek to collect.

"That is quick work indeed, to have such an accounting so readily to hand," George commented as he handed the portfolio to Anastasia.

"Mr Wheelwright instructed us three months ago to prepare everything as if he had just died, then to make weekly additions and alterations as conditions changed, we worked with the Chartered Accountancy firm of Leadbetter and Jones, who handle your affairs," Mr Baker explained. "Upon the actual death of Mr Wheelwright, it was a matter of only hours to amend the accounts to reflect the situation. Mr Wheelwright planned quite carefully for the death duty, and he made transfers of shares in the various enterprises he owned into the names of Mrs Sophia and into your names, Mr George and Miss Anastasia. He did this in a timely manner so that the death duty is largely avoided. There will still be some monies due and payable, but fortunately a relatively minor amount."

"Anything else?" George asked.

"No, Sir, if it would not be too forward, may we presume that we will still act for and on behalf of the family?" Mr Baker asked.

"I think there is no reason to change," George assured him. "I may or may not always be available to communicate decisions made as to our portfolio, and would ask that you treat instructions from my sister Anastasia as instructions from myself."

"If you say so, Sir," Mr Baker began. "My partners may have some difficulty, particularly because of her few years, but I will do what I can."

"What if I were to say that instructions from Miss Beretta were to be treated as mine?" George asked.

"If she were Mrs Wheelwright, there would, of course, be fewer problems, but again my partners would have difficulties taking instructions from someone not a member of the family."

"And if I were to give you a power of attorney, or I were to tell you that she has consented to marriage to me?" George asked.

"Then, of course, we would have no issues, but we may still question decisions in the normal course of prudent management," Mr Baker replied.

"That makes sense," George agreed. "I have no doubt that any decision that would be communicated by either Anastasia or Federica would be backed by sound logic and common sense, and I think mathematical analysis. I think a power of attorney that names both Federica and Anastasia would be useful."

"Very good, Sir. I will draw up a power of attorney that will suffice for us and permit us to act upon such instructions, but we will need to research whether it is permitted to grant power of attorney to a minor, my apologies Miss Wheelwright, if that is not the case, perhaps we might name Miss Beretta and Mrs Wheelwright?"

"That would be fine," George agreed. "Please let me know what the law says about granting power of attorney to a minor."

"Very good, Sir. I have some papers relating to the will and the various bequests that require your signature as the executor," Mr Baker said.

"Do you have an accounting of the immediate demands upon cash relating to the various bequests?" George asked.

"I do indeed, Sir," Mr Baker replied. He then handed over a statement that showed cash needs over the coming weeks and where that cash might come from.

"Very good," George said. "Let us proceed as you have suggested here. There is an item that I would like you to take care of. I wish to transfer to Federica half of my shares in the various companies that we hold, which transfer to be effective upon our marriage."

"We can do that under the Married Women's Property Act of 1882, if that is what you wish, Sir," Mr Baker said.

"If you will draw up those papers for me, I would be obliged," George said. "I can execute them when you come again. For the moment, let me sign these papers, and then perhaps we are done?"

"If you will attend to that, then I need not impose upon you any longer." Mr Baker assured him. "Would it be convenient to have your man drive me to the railway station?"

"Of course," George agreed. He rang for Mrs Partridge and asked her to have Henry take Mr Baker to the station.

"I will communicate with you shortly," Mr Baker said as he left. "I will return in October with the items you have requested and await your instructions as to the disbursing of funds for the various bequests that are for Mrs Wheelwright and Miss Beretta and for the payment of taxes."

When George returned to the drawing room, Anastasia pounced on him.

"Did you hear that odious man?" she asked. "My few years, hah, a minor, hah, he would probably rush out and sell the holdings they have been buying if he knew that it was Fede and me who made the decisions to buy for us."

"You must have patience, Dear," her mother told her. "Men have yet to come to terms with the fact that women are as intelligent as they, it is threatening to them and they do not like to think upon the notion."

"That is as may be, Mama," Anastasia said. "How condescending, ooh, that odious man."

"He is probably better than most, at least he had the courage to come here and face you, but he is bound by his own prejudices and education and to some extent by the law, which, I know, was written by men," George told her. "I am sure that one day we will have excellent women solicitors and barristers, probably even King's Counsellors and judges. Tell me, what is this about motor cars?"

"I promised to show you earlier, and I was hoping we would have the opportunity to show you before Baker came," Federica explained. "I was as surprised as you that your father had put such an item in his will."

"He also seems to have tumbled to the notion that you and I had an understanding long before I had expected," George commented.

"Yes," Sophia agreed. "I was also surprised by that. He was more perceptive than I thought, no wonder he approved of your relationship so quickly and easily when I told him of your love, he already knew."

"See, you weren't as discreet as you thought," Anastasia teased. "Papa saw all, but obviously approved. So when will you wed?"

"Give your poor mother the opportunity to collect herself," George pleaded.

"I know, I know," she said. "I am sorry, Mama, but Papa was obviously keen to have this happen."

"I know," her mother conceded. "Federica and I have already talked, and she has been in touch with her family, and we have agreed that December would be a good month. Even in Italy, the weather will be less clement than it is now, but perhaps a Christmas wedding, and in Florence, would be amenable, and the only difference to the current living arrangement is that the monies that Papa willed to her will be slow in coming."

"December and Christmas and Florence, oh what fun," Anastasia said. "I must look for a new dress for the occasion. Now, George, while we are on the subject of the estate, we have some items we should go over."

"We do?" he asked.

"We do," she confirmed. "The accounts that odious Mr Baker gave you are accurate enough, but if you look carefully, you will note that we have some holdings in some small firms that are merely listed as other enterprises. We need to discuss a couple of them for changes, Fede and I think we should make."

"What changes?" he asked.

"Let us begin with the traction engines we have. We have received several offers for the business, and we need to decide what to do," Federica suggested. "It is a good business, we rent out the traction engines with ploughs in the spring and with threshing machines in the autumn and throughout the year we rent others out for hauling heavy loads."

"What do we need to do, or rather what are you proposing?" he asked.

"Before we answer that, it would be useful to talk about the business. I think that in time traction engines may be replaced by either a heavy oil engine that works by internal combustion, or the system is replaced altogether by some form of car or lorry that is specially built for agricultural work," she replied.

"How long will that take?" he asked.

"Fortunately, I think not for some years to come," she replied. "We have a fleet of traction engines that is relatively new, and they will see many years of service yet. We have received several offers to buy the business. I think we should consider those offers and see whether it is better for us to sell the business now or hold the business and sell when the machines are becoming obsolete. It is simply a matter of calculating the monies we would receive from the business, either as a sale or as a going concern and see which is best."

"Oh," he said. "And you can do that?"

"Yes," she replied. "We know what our rental rates are and how many machines we typically rent out and for how long, so we just compare the incomes from each option and see which is best."

"How do you predict the future?" he asked.

"We cannot predict the future, but we can lessen the risk by creating some simple mathematics and altering the rental rates and rental numbers to give us a range of possible revenues, based upon possible events and their impact upon the country," she replied. "When you were in South Africa, how did you plan for a battle? You must have done some thinking about what might happen or not happen and what you would do if things did not go the way you expected."

"To be honest, I don't think our general staff did too much thinking about alternatives," he replied. "It seemed to be more of the 'you must take that hill no matter the consequence' type of thinking, which sometimes led us to pursue failing attacks and strategies for too long, with the attendant loss of life that in retrospect might not have been necessary."

"That is truly unfortunate," she commiserated. "We need to think a little more about the different possibilities. We have a total of twenty-five engines, three pairs of ploughing engines with the ploughs and other equipment, we have four agricultural tractors that we typically rent out with the threshing machines, and we have fifteen heavy tractors with trailers for heavy haulage. Those are rented out either on a weekly basis or to satisfy the needs of a particular job."

"Where are these machines?" he asked.

"We have a yard with a maintenance shop at Handy Cross, on the hills above High Wycombe," she replied. "The yard is well placed to serve both the Wye Valley and the Thames Valley, and the intervening hills, which are much worked with agriculture or timber cutting. When we rent out, we have to consider the travel distance and time to the job so that we may properly price the rental."

"Who runs the machines?" he asked.

"We have our own men who go with the machines," she replied.

"Do we pay them when the machines are not rented?" he asked.

"We do," she said. "It is perhaps not common to do so, but we have particular men assigned to particular machines, and they know them well. If we kept the men as casual employees only, we would lose that knowledge."

"If there is a spell when the rentals are slow, how much does that cost us?" he asked.

"It is a consideration," she agreed. "I have tried many calculations and have convinced myself that it is better to retain the men; we have not lost money with the business in the past five years, actually, we have a respectable return from it."

"If we were to sell the business, what would we sell?" he asked.

"If we were to sell the business I think the best thing would be to sell the engines and the goodwill of the business, but to keep the land where the yard is and perhaps rent the yard and the maintenance shop to the buyer, that way there is some income from the business as long as it is there," she replied.

"How much money is involved?" he asked.

"We have £15,452 invested in the engines plus another £6,876 in spare parts and equipment for the maintenance shops, that does not include the value of the land," she enumerated.

"What would be a good price for the business then?" he asked.

"We have received six offers in the past six months," Anastasia replied. "The offers range from £30,000 to £38,000."

"Why not just take the highest offer then?" he asked.

"Because we are not sure yet that the best course is to sell, moreover, there are conditions to each offer that we are still considering," Federica replied.

"Each of the offers is for the equipment and other assets," Anastasia added. "None of them included the land, which suited us. The difference between the offers is largely how they would pay; several offers are contingent upon a bank providing loans, interestingly, they are not the highest offers. The middle offer of £36,000 has the least complications."

"If we were to sell, we would want a buyer to take on the men we currently have," Federica said. "They may have other ideas, so we need to consider what our position may be, then if we choose the sell path, then we might meet with the six possible buyers and negotiate with each to arrive at the most advantageous arrangement."

"If we have received offers, why have we not already entered into negotiations?" he asked.

"Mainly because we have not yet decided that that is the best course of action," Federica replied. "And, because there are other considerations."

"That's where we need you," Anastasia said. "We had some preliminary discussions with another concern, and it was obvious that they thought we were foolish women waiting to be taken advantage of by less-than-scrupulous men. We would ask you to take the front position in any discussions, and we would provide the necessary information and analysis."

"How do we own these engines? Do we have a company?" he asked.

"They are owned by a company that we own," Anastasia explained.

"I think we should create a new company," Federica added. "Then transfer the assets of the engine business into that company, leaving the land and buildings in the original company. Then, if we choose to sell the engines, we just sell the new company to the successful bidder."

"Isn't that rather complicated?" he asked.

"Not really," Federica said. "It is a relatively simple matter that our solicitors could take care of in an hour or so."

"Who has to authorise such a company creation and transfer of assets?" he asked.

"You and Mama," Anastasia told him. "Until such time as the estate is divided between us, you hold your own shares in the various companies, including the engine company, which by the way is Handy Cross Enterprises, and have control over mine. You can effectively sign for both of us, and Mama signs for herself."

"So, you don't just need me to be the façade of the company, you actually need my approval," he laughed. "You two are devious, but I think you are quite right in this. I am confident that you have done enough investigation and analysis that whatever your decision is, it will be the right one. What do we call the new company?"

"Handy Cross Tractors," Federica suggested. "That is essentially what we might sell, and the original company can stay as it is, but with a lease agreement with the new company for the land and buildings, perhaps five years to start with, an option for another five."

"You've obviously thought about this a lot," he remarked. "Would I be wrong in assuming that you have already drawn up the relevant documents and agreements?"

"You would not be wrong," Anastasia agreed. "We have everything ready for your approval and signature, then you can instruct the solicitors to proceed with the creation of the new company and the transfer of assets, then we can examine the business carefully and determine the best course of action."

"What does this have to do with cars?" he asked.

"Nothing directly," Federica assured him. "It is one of the many issues that we have been examining in the management of the estate."

"You see, George," Sophia interposed. "Fede and Nastia have been working hard on all aspects of the estate, and you will be pleasantly surprised by it all. There are a few other similar matters that we should consider, but now we should show you what we have been doing. I think it's time we let you see what we have in the coach house."

Cars

George dutifully followed the three women as they led him through the kitchen and out into the stable yard. There, Federica opened one of the coachhouses and ushered George inside. He was greeted with the spectacle of the gleaming brass and polished coachwork of a Daimler car, and off to the side in the other coach bays, what looked like a collection of car parts, which he finally realised was a disassembled car or cars.

"So, you purchased a car?" he asked, rather stating the obvious.

"We bought four, as you can see," Anastasia told him. "We have already completely disassembled and then reassembled the Daimler, and now we have pulled apart the others and made complete sets of drawings for all the parts and drawings and sketches of the various pieces as they are fitted together."

"If this one is a Daimler, what are the others?" he asked.

"That one over there is a Lanchester and then we thought we should broaden our horizons and we bought a car from America, from Olds, that is the far one and one from Italy, to please Federica, from the Fabbrica Italiana Automobili of Turin, that is this one here," Anastasia explained.

"Who else makes cars?" he asked.

"Where to begin?" Federica laughed. "Well, there are obviously Daimler, Lanchester, Olds and the Italian, but add to them Ariel Charawacky, Arrol-Johnston, Humber, Wolseley, Riley, Sunbeam, Swift, Napier, Argyll and Albion, to name but a few.

"So many?" he wondered.

"There are more," she told him. "Some makers have already come and gone, such as Gilbert, who started last year and finished last year, so it is yet a fledgling industry, and it will be some time before the leaders and followers are sorted out. The ones I named are but the British makers, there are also the French, German, Italian and American makers."

"We picked some of the better-known cars for our researches," Anastasia told him.

"Who took them apart?" he asked.

"Why, Fede and me, who else?" she retorted. "We did have help from Henry, but it was mainly of the fetch-and-carry kind of help."

"Were not some of the pieces large and heavy?" he asked.

"Of course," Federica agreed. "We have rigged a hoist in the rafters, and we used mechanical advantage to aid us, so that we lifted little of great heft. We have most of the Lanchester together again and will next rebuild the Olds."

"Who made the drawings?" he wondered.

"I made some," Anastasia boasted. "And Fede made some. We will show you after lunch, and you will see that they are most professionally done."

"Did Papa see any of this?" he asked.

"He did indeed," Sophia replied, smiling with the recollection. "I watched him sit there for hours while the girls worked, and I never saw him happier. It has only been the last month or so when he was unable to be here. So I was in the habit of reporting to him the events of the day, and Anastasia would show him the drawings they had made."

"What would it take to build a motor car?" George asked.

"A design of a car, parts made to that design and a place to assemble the pieces," Federica told him.

"When do you think you might be ready with a design?" he continued.

"I think in another six months, I would like to have done enough work and testing that we have a model available for the Motor Show at Crystal Palace in 1904," Federica said. "We do not wish to rush into this, there are elements of the Daimler, the Lanchester, the Olds and the Italian car that are different and we need to understand why and which would be most advantageous, there is also the issue of patents held by Mr Lawson that we need to either circumvent or wait until the courts decide that the patent claims are not valid."

"What is the Motor Show at Crystal Palace, and is there any literature on the design of cars?" he asked.

"There is to be a Motor Show in late January of next year at Crystal Palace," she replied. "We will not be ready with a car for that show, but as the show is advertised as the first annual Motor Show, we should prepare for the next show to follow in 1904. As to literature, there are papers being presented at many professional institutions that discuss design and building issues and discoveries. It has been difficult for

Anastasia and me to secure invitations to those meetings, as it is assumed that we will have little or no understanding of what is to be presented. We have obtained some useful volumes, there is a very good book by a Mr Beaumont that is an excellent treatise on all things motor car and we have another from America by a Mr Homans, we also subscribe to two weekly journals, *Autocar* and *Automotor Journal*, they give us good information about current developments and inventions, and so that we do not miss something from another industry that might have application in cars we also take the weekly *Engineering*."

"You have no problems in following the arguments laid out in these books?" he asked.

"George," his sister said warningly. "Not you too. Why is it that men think that we are incapable of understanding elementary mathematics?"

"I'm sorry, Nastia," he said. "I have not seen these books and have no notion of how advanced or not their mathematics might be."

"There is nothing in them that is very advanced," Federica replied. "There are a few square functions but no Euler or Lagrange calculus, which is unfortunate, because if they were to use those methods, they might achieve better results."

"Which of the cars is the best?" he asked.

"They are all very different," Anastasia replied. "The little Olds is good for only two people, but it is cheap and it is produced in quantity in America. The others all will carry at least four people, but are more expensive, so are fit for a different set of buyers than the American."

"Who among the household drives the cars?" he asked.

"We all do," Sophia replied. "It is most diverting. Federica was the first of us to learn, then she taught myself, then Anastasia and Henry the coachman."

"Do you go abroad much in the cars?" he wanted to know, wondering how the neighbours would react to the cars.

"Indeed, we do," Sophia assured him. "We have already had several discussions with Constable Platt of Bourne End, who deems it his duty to ensure that we do not exceed the speed limits imposed by the legislation of 1896, which allows fourteen miles per hour, but which may be decreased by local authorities to twelve miles per hour, if they deem conditions to warrant, which of course they have done near the environs of the villages of Bourne End and Corse End."

"How does Constable Platt determine your speed?" he asked, intrigued.

"He pursues us with his bicycle and his watch," Anastasia laughed.

"Then it is all guesswork on his part with perhaps some calculation."

"It is most entertaining when he tries to pursue us up the hills, particularly the steep hills of Kiln Lane and Wash Hill, but then even the cars have trouble with those hills," Sophia said. "Down the hills is another matter, but he tries no matter when and where he sees us."

"And anyone may drive a car?" he asked.

"Anyone," Sophia confirmed. "I'm sure that the Government will soon enough seek to license both cars and drivers with two goals, one to raise money for the treasury and the other to in some way ensure that the people who drive the cars have some modicum of knowledge of how to do so."

"Will one of you teach me how to drive the car?" he asked.

"We'll draw lots and the loser will get the job," Federica suggested, laughing. "It can be a little frustrating until one grasps the basic concepts."

"I sense there have been some problems?" he asked.

"Not problems, perhaps some minor conflicts caused by rising levels of frustration," Sophia commented. "It was a challenge, but even Henry managed with a little tutelage."

"Did Papa ever try?" he asked.

"He did," Sophia confirmed. "Then he grew too weak and was unable to manage. We did take him for drives in the area so that he could experience for himself the thrill of it all."

"What do you do if it rains?" he asked.

"That is somewhat of an issue," Sophia admitted. "As you can see, there are rudimentary canopies, but it could be better."

"There is a lively business for ladies' and gentlemen's attire for motorists," Federica added. "It seems to be mostly clothing to keep out dust and rain. We have added such clothing to the line produced in our own factory, with quite satisfactory sales and profits."

"You may notice some of the larger and more expensive cars that have the passengers enclosed and the driver exposed," Sophia noted. "We believe that that is one of the issues that should be addressed if we design a car. Not everyone is willing to risk inclement weather just to enjoy the prospect of motoring."

"What happens if it snows?" he asked.

"That is another problem," Federica admitted. "I have seen clothing that is thick and probably proof against all weather, but one's face would surely be chilled in winter air."

"I believe it is time for lunch," Sophia interrupted. "We should not keep Eleanor and Jane waiting unnecessarily."

After lunch, George saw Anastasia go outside and into the walled garden. He followed and found her sitting on a bench, sobbing.

"It's hard, isn't it?" he asked her.

"I thought I was past the tears," she sobbed out. "Showing you the cars and remembering the fun we had taking them apart and showing Papa all that we had done brought it all back in a flood of memories."

"It sounds trite, but time will heal and you will come to remember the good things and times," he assured her.

"I know," she wailed. "It's still hard to think that I won't be showing him another drawing of a car part and explaining what it does."

"I loved a girl once," George told her. "Her name was Catherine, she was killed by a runaway wagon. I thought the bottom had dropped from my world, and it was some time before I could see certain things and not be reminded of her and descend into deep gloom and despair."

"But you overcame that?" she asked.

"Eventually," he told her. "Now my recollections are of happy times and things that I learned from her. It made me appreciate Federica all the more and how lucky I am to be blessed with you as a sister and Fede as a lover, soon-to-be wife."

"How long, George, how long will it be before this ache and sadness goes?" she asked.

"I think it is different for each of us," he replied. "My theory, and as someone familiar with mathematics, you would appreciate this, is that the mourning period is inversely proportional to the strength of the relationship when the loved one was alive. So as you and Papa were close, it seems to me that you will remember more the happy times and appreciate the relationship that you had, than regret his passing."

"Do you really think so?" she asked.

"I honestly don't know," he admitted.

"Do you not miss Papa?" she asked.

"I do, but I have been gone for some years, so have had time to consider what life would represent without Papa and, having seen him so recently in such pain, am relieved that he no longer suffers," he replied.

"Have you seen much pain and death?" she asked.

"Altogether too much," he said. "Sometimes it was my friends and other times it was men I hardly knew, sometimes it was an enemy, but it was never less distressing."

"What are you two discussing?" Federica asked. She had wondered where they had gone and had come to investigate.

"Nastia misses Papa," George told her.

"Of course you do," Federica assured Anastasia. "You will do for some time to come. Come, cry on my shoulder for a while. George, I think Sophia wants you to help her with something to do with the arrangements for Friday."

Of course, Sophia wanted nothing of the kind, but it was a convenient way to dismiss him, leaving Federica to console Anastasia. Sophia had her own concerns. She was worried about the funeral and what would be expected of her after the service. George told her not to worry, he would take care of things, or rather, he would consult with Eleanor and turn things over to her. Eleanor and Jane had already taken things in hand and had planned out what they were going to serve and how, bearing in mind that they were also going to the funeral. George was unsure just who might be at the funeral and who might then wish to call at the house to pay their respects. He had spent very little time at the Hedsor Minor house, only the occasional leave and during his last leave, he had been preoccupied with Federica, so had taken little interest in who lived close by and who might be considered friends and who would be considered mere acquaintances. Since he had been home, there had been no callers, except the doctor, but they had asked him to attend, so he had no idea who regular visitors to the house might be. He had rather imagined that there might be the odd suitor wooing Anastasia, but she had made no mention of young men, so he had no idea where things stood in that arena. Hedsor Minor was not close to the hamlet of Bourne End, but neither was it as isolated as some of the

South African settlements he had been in lately, so it was not as though it was days' rides away from anywhere. Perhaps Anastasia, in her own inimitable way, had disparaged some of her suitors, and they had left never to return. Anastasia was not one to suffer fools, and his own experience of the British upper classes had left him less than impressed with many of them, and it would be the upper classes trying to woo someone like Anastasia who would be perceived as heiress to money, something the British aristocracy seemed always in need of, often to shore up the land rich but cash poor estates and profligate lifestyles.

After dinner, Federica suggested that they return to the consideration of certain companies that they owned and that she had suggested earlier warranted attention.

"What's next then?" George asked.

"We have the Abbey Biscuit Company, which is at Burnham," she told him. "Our most serious competitors are Huntley and Palmers and Peek Freans, and there are many others that are peculiar to certain parts of the country, in particular Carrs of Carlisle, who have proven to be most inventive and fiercely competitive in that locale."

"What is it that we need to do?" he asked.

"We need to install some new equipment," she replied. "The firm of Joseph Baker has brought out a new line of machines for dough mixing and cutting, and we also should improve the ovens that we have."

"What benefit will the machines provide?" he asked.

"We will have a lower production cost," she explained. "If we properly size the dough-making and cutting machines to the ovens, we will have a better flow of biscuits through the bakery without adding any more people and thus achieve a lower cost."

"How much money is involved?" he asked.

"It is not a significant amount," she replied. "We need some new mixers for the biscuit dough and then the related cutters to properly size the biscuits, we also need a new Baker-Carr machine for sandwich biscuits, and we need to replace our wafer ovens, with the various pieces of machinery and the improvements necessary to the power in the building we need £8,350 all told as capital and a further £3,750 to cover the costs of installation."

"How many biscuits would we have to sell to recover that amount?" he asked.

"Well, ginger snaps sell for about 6d per pound," she told him. "So, you can see that it will take quite a few pounds of biscuits and a few years to pay back this investment."

"How many years?" he asked.

"Our calculations show that over a period of five years, we will have paid for the machines and will be earning a suitable profit," she replied.

"I suppose that, as with the engine business, you have examined possible ways this might go?" he asked, seeking confirmation for something he was almost certain had been done.

"Of course," she assured him. "We do that for all our businesses. We have included the possible actions that Huntley and Palmers, and Peek Freans may take in the future, because they are two of the most powerful competitors."

"I feel a little lost in all of this," he said. "This is all new to me."

"Not so new surely?" Federica said. "When you planned a campaign in the army, did you not examine the enemy and his capabilities and try to imagine what he might do? Did you also not create a list of materials you would need to wage your campaign?"

"I did, but I never had to show a profit," he said. "It was always just assumed that the action was required, so needed to be carried out with only a passing reference to cost."

"Perhaps we should leave things there for the day," Sophia suggested. "There is much to digest that we should not expect George to be able to grasp all the niceties of the estate until he has had time to review it."

"You are right, Sophia," Federica agreed. "We will continue again, George, but not tonight."

The following day, Federica announced after breakfast that she needed to go into Maidenhead to get a dress that was suitable for wearing to the funeral. She then invited all to accompany her.

"Thank you, no," Sophia declined. "I have much to do here, but do take Anastasia with you."

"Nastia?" Federica asked.

"Of course," Anastasia agreed. "And George, you will come too?"

"I will, if only to see what you two may consider appropriate attire," he replied.

"I will bring the car around," Federica said. "Bring your coats, it may get chilly later."

"Which way will we go?" George asked.

"Well, the toll across Cookham bridge is three shillings for the car, but it is five shillings if we use the Maidenhead bridge, so we will go through Cookham," Federica explained.

"Where do you buy petrol for the cars?" he asked.

"We usually buy Carless Petrol from Wilson's the ironmongers in Maidenhead," Federica explained. "We should buy some more when we are in the town."

"How does it come?" he asked.

"We buy it in two-gallon tins," Anastasia replied. "I think they use that size of tin so that it is not too difficult to pour into the tank on the car. The tins come in crates of four."

"I was thinking of buying a few crates and have a carter haul them here and storing them in the outbuilding behind the stable block," Federica added. "We will have to be careful because the Government has already started writing laws that govern the storage of petrol."

"How much is it?" he asked.

"It's about a shilling per gallon at the moment," Federica replied. "It has been as low as 7d per gallon and once as high as 1s 3d per gallon."

"Does that include the tin?" he asked.

"No, the tins are extra, or we use our own tins and have them filled by the ironmonger," Federica explained.

"What about tyres and other parts?" he asked.

"We have a small stock," Federica told him. "It is tyres that we use the most, after petrol, they only last a few thousand miles, sometimes as little as one thousand miles."

"Who makes the tyres?" he asked.

"There is a company called Dunlop and a French company called Michelin, and there are some American companies," Federica replied. "There is a debate between solid tyres and pneumatic tyres. I think that pneumatic tyres will win that debate."

"Are we going to stand here and discuss cars, or are we going to Maidenhead?" Anastasia interrupted.

"We'll go," Federica assured her. "George, instead of me bringing the car around, you can make yourself useful."

"How so?" George asked as they walked towards the coach house, where the car was stored.

"You may swing the starting handle," Federica told him. "That is one thing I am determined we must find a solution to, something to start the engine so that it is not always necessary to use the handle. I must caution you to hold the handle such that your thumbs do not wrap around the handle. If the car fails to start and it kicks back at you, it may be that you would hurt your thumbs."

"It is probably the one thing that constrains the sale of cars to more women," Anastasia commented. "It is not that difficult, but it does take some effort, and not everyone has the strength that Federica does."

George opened the doors to the coach house and then followed the others in. He stood at the front of the Daimler while Federica and Anastasia climbed aboard. Federica made some adjustments to the controls, then signalled George to swing the starting handle, which he did and was gratified to hear the engine start. He then latched the handle to the side with the leather sling that was there and joined the others in the car. Federica made more adjustments to the controls and then selected a gear and drove out of the coachhouse and off down the driveway to the road and the route to Maidenhead. George watched as she worked the gearbox of the car and adjusted her choice of gears to match the road speed and the road condition, either uphill or down. For him, it was a new and fascinating experience that he could not wait to try. He debated which of the two to ask to teach him and decided to leave it to them. He could see that there were many things to coordinate to drive the car, and he could imagine how things could become frustrating, leading to squabbles and arguments.

Twenty minutes brought them to the Cookham toll bridge. At the bridge, Federica waved to the toll collector, who came over to talk to her.

"A very good morning to you, Miss Beretta, Miss Wheelwright," he said. "Off to Maidenhead are we?"

"We are indeed, Mr Sewell," Federica replied.

"I was sorry to hear of the demise of Mr Wheelwright," Sewell said.

"It comes to all of us in time," Federica replied. "Mr Arthur Sewell, let me introduce you to Mr George Wheelwright, lately returned from the war in South Africa, you may see him from time to time in the future."

"I am pleased to meet you, Sir, my condolences on your loss, Sir," Sewell said.

"Thank you, Mr Sewell," George acknowledged. "Have you been here long?"

"No, Sir, we moved here from Wimbledon a little over a year ago. It is a most agreeable place, my wife and I are delighted to be here," Sewell replied.

"How is Christine?" Federica asked.

"She enjoys the best of health, thank you, Miss Beretta," Sewell replied.

"Christine is the daughter of Mr Sewell and his wife Ethel," Federica explained to George. "She is delightful, well, Arthur, we must be off. Here is the three shillings, we should be back in two to three hours."

"Thank you, Miss Beretta, I will be here," Sewell promised.

Federica then looked to see if all was clear to cross. The bridge was only of sufficient width to accommodate one horse and carriage or one car. There being no other traffic, she quickly crossed into Berkshire and continued on towards Maidenhead. George quite liked this mode of travel; it was in many ways more relaxing than riding upon a horse, and having Federica as a driver meant that he could enjoy the scenery as they went. Another thirty minutes brought them into the centre of Maidenhead, and Federica parked outside a fashionable dressmaker and told George that she planned to leave in an hour and to please have his errands complete by then. She and Anastasia then swept into the dressmaker's shop and got down to the business of dress shopping. George was quite relieved not to be involved in this mission and instead proceeded on his own mission to the offices of the newspaper to place notices about the funeral services for his father and the engagement notice for himself and Federica a copy of which he forwarded to the solicitors that they might be apprised of the situation and how it pertained to the conditions of the will.

At the appointed hour, George was back at the shop, but there was no evidence of Federica or Anastasia. He looked up and down the street, then spotted them coming out of a milliners. It looked as if they had both purchased new hats, as there was an errand boy trailing after them, laden down with hat boxes.

"*Caro*," Federica greeted him. "*Hai finito di fare le tue commissioni?*"

"*Penso que si*," George replied. "Or at least I think so, are *commissioni* errands?"

"How clever of you to remember," Federica said delightedly. "I'm sorry, the milliner is an Italian lady that I have come to know, and we speak Italian whenever we see each other and Anastasia and I continue in Italian outside the shop."

"Now where?" George asked as Federica supervised the loading of packages into the car.

"The ironmongers to get some petrol, then we can go home," she replied.

"Did you bankrupt us with your dress shopping?" George asked.

"No, George," Anastasia replied. "We were both quite frugal, but Fede did look at some ideas for a wedding dress for Christmas. Madame Garnier is a French émigré who has a thriving business and who has all the latest fashions from Paris and is very adept at making up quite splendid dresses."

"And you?' he asked.

"I will wear scarlet," she replied. "Quite inappropriate for a solemn occasion like a wedding, but then I feel like celebrating, and that is a bright and cheery colour. Also, it may give the Italian family something to gossip about, making me a Scarlet Woman, quite beyond the pale, don't you know. Will you wear your uniform?"

"I hadn't thought of it," he admitted. "I suppose it may depend on whether I am still in the army by then. I have given the matter much thought and have written to my CO and told him of my desire to resign my commission and return to civilian life administering our estates, even though I know you could do well without me, but it will sound well to the colonel."

"When will you hear?" Federica asked.

"Probably in a month or so," George thought. "For the time being, I am on leave, so no more army for me just now, I have new things to learn, such as driving. Which of you will teach me?"

"We discussed that at length," Federica admitted. "In the end, we decided that so as not to place unnecessary strains upon our impending marriage that Anastasia will undertake that task, that is, unless you have problems with taking instruction from your sister, your younger, very pretty sister?"

"I suppose she is passable," he laughed. "And no, I have no issues. When may we start?"

"Let us begin after the funeral," Anastasia suggested.

"Agreed," George said. "And now I suppose you wish me to swing the starting handle again?"

"Indeed, we do," Federica laughed. "You must earn your keep somehow, even though I could think of better things for you to be doing."

"You two need to be married and soon," Anastasia said, grinning from ear to ear. "I'm sure that all you think of during the day is the bedroom and what other places you may have your trysts. I see the glances and little secret smiles. Is it so magical?"

"Indeed, it is," Federica confirmed. "Let us away, we must visit the ironmongers and I wish to be back for tea."

"Now, George, when you are ready," Anastasia instructed. George dutifully stood by the front of the car, and when Anastasia signalled, he swung the starting handle and was pleased to hear the engine start. The drive to the ironmongers was short, and their business there was finished quite quickly. Mr Wilson, the proprietor, loaded the crates of tins onto a rack that was fitted to the car, a rack that George had not noticed before. Upon closer examination, he saw that it was a temporary fixture that had obviously been devised to carry the petrol tins. George helped Mr Wilson secure the crates to the rack and then paid for the petrol. He then took his station by the front of the car, awaiting the signal from Anastasia to swing the starting handle.

The drive back to the house was uneventful until the last mile, then George noticed Anastasia playing with the throttle controls a bit and asked her what was wrong.

"A minor adjustment, I think," she replied. "It will serve until we arrive at the house, but tomorrow I must disassemble the carburetion system and see what the problem is."

"You have to do your own repairs?" George asked.

"Indeed," Federica confirmed. "We must be our own mechanics. I am sure that in time, there will grow an industry that provides repair services. Nastia, we should look into such an enterprise, we should also investigate cleaning products that may be used after one has been working on the engines. Regular soap and water just does not seem quite adequate, and I fear that we may sometimes have a lingering odour of oil, grease and petrol."

"Would we link a mechanics business to the sale of new motors or keep it independent?" Anastasia asked.

"A good question, but we have arrived and must attend to other matters that are pressing," Federica said. "Let us continue this after tea and consider the alternatives and possibilities."

"Is the problem with the car serious?" George asked.

"Probably not," Federica assured him. "We often have problems with dirt in the petrol that blocks the various orifices that it must pass through. The degree of problem seems to vary with where we acquire the petrol and how long it has stood in the coach house. Perhaps we should devise some form of filter mechanism to clean the petrol between the tank and the engine."

"It does seem to me that the petrol we buy from Wilson's gives us fewer problems than the petrol we get from Bishop's on the Bath Road," Anastasia commented.

"Where do they get the petrol from?" he asked.

"Wilson's is an accredited agent for Carless, an English company from London, and Bishop's is an agent for Pratts, the Anglo-American Oil Company," Federica explained. "The actual oil is imported from America or Sumatra or Burma, and there is some that comes from the Caucasus and some from South America."

"Is there any difference?" he asked.

"Indeed, there is," Federica assured him. "It seems to me that the oil from Sumatra or Burma gives better results than the oil from America. I have also seen some papers written that expound at great length upon the calorific value of the oil and its properties. I will find some for you to review if you have an interest. As to the current issue, it has often occurred to me that there is ample opportunity for dirt to enter the tins when they are filled at the refinery or when the ironmongers refill them. Both Carless and Pratts make much of the fact that their petrol is dirt-free, yet we have issues."

George closed up the coach house after the women had gone into the main house with their packages. He looked over the cars and wondered at the changes that had occurred while he had been in South Africa and what the future would bring with the motor car. Having just fought in a long and protracted bush campaign, he could imagine a car with some armour to protect the occupants from small arms fire and armed with a Maxim or Colt machine gun. That would have been wonderful against the Boers in the open country of the Western Cape, provided, of course, that the car would have had enough petrol and spare tyres to make it independent of a large supply train. Perhaps there was a solution to that problem by matching a transport vehicle, perhaps one of the traction engines he had seen in South Africa with a trailer for supplies, to several cars and have the trailer carry extra petrol, ammunition, spare parts and extra tyres, say one traction engine plus trailer to six cars, but he was dreaming, the War Office would probably never countenance such a novel and, to them, hare-brained scheme. He had no idea that cars had already been built that served as war cars, Simms had proposed the Motor Scout in 1899, but it was essentially a motorised quadricycle with a machine gun, but no protection for the rider, then there was the later Simms car of that year, 1902, built by Vickers, that was truly an armoured car, but somewhat ungainly and the French had also produced the Charron-Girardt-Voigt car, also of that year, that had armour and a Hotchkiss machine gun. So, other people were already thinking similarly. He realised that the armoured car would have been of little use in the sieges of Ladysmith and Mafeking, but in the open veldt, they would have been of great help.

From a military perspective, the other use of the internal combustion engine would be to provide for transport of large numbers of men and supplies. The South African War had shown up the deficiencies of the transport systems. For large quantities of supplies, they had been tied to the railway lines, which were regularly mined by the Boers. Both armies had used wagons drawn by either horses or oxen. The horse-drawn wagons were quicker than those drawn by teams of oxen, but only if the horses were in good condition. Horses needed feed supplements, whereas the oxen could make do with whatever grazing could be found. In the latter part of the war, the British had started using traction engines to haul wagons and had even fielded an armoured train version as protection against raids. The traction engines required water and fuel but were well able to replace either horse or oxen. Perhaps in the future, a tractor could be devised that used the internal combustion engine that would not be so reliant upon water supplies as the traction engines were. He could imagine machines carrying loads of supplies and ammunition, and other machines towing field guns where now there were teams of horses. All this fanciful thinking assumed a military command that was not fighting the last war and that would be capable of thinking beyond the traditional, something he admitted was going to be a long shot in the odds of success. Still, he could perceive a market, so at the right time, he would raise the possibility with Federica and see what she thought. Meanwhile, perhaps he could help Federica with her dreams of designing and building cars; he was not sure what he could do, but he would support her no matter what.

Driving lessons

The funeral of George Archibald Wheelwright was conducted with due solemnity on Friday, the nineteenth of September, at nine in the morning at the Hedsor church. George, the younger, wore a dark suit in preference to his army uniform. It seemed to him more appropriate to the occasion. The ladies of the house all wore severe black dresses in deference to the conventions of the day. The service was short and internment quickly carried out. After the service, any and all who attended were invited to the house for light refreshments. In all, about thirty people chose to accept the hospitality, and of those, George knew only five, and that included the Rector, the Solicitor and the Doctor. The rest were neighbours, members of the various companies that the family owned and friends of Sophia, Anastasia or Federica. The weather had stayed good with no rain, for late September it was probably unseasonably warm, so the windows and French doors had all been thrown open, allowing people to mingle on the terraces and lawns instead of all trying to cram into the drawing room, something Sophia was quite pleased about. She bore herself well, but was glad to see the last guest depart, just before lunch, accepting the last expressions of condolence with dignity.

"I'm glad that's over," she said to George. "I have never been one to linger at funerals, and I think that half the neighbours just come to see what we have in the house."

"How are you faring?" he asked.

"Well enough," she assured him. "I think your father would have been amused by the words that the Rector said at the service. I don't think he ever saw himself as a pillar of the community."

"The neighbours all seemed to have kind words," he thought.

"Kind words indeed today, but three years ago, when he wanted to change the boundary fences, their words were less kind," she commented. "But still, I suppose it rankled that he was right yet again and the law was with him."

"If you have no objection, I may change my clothes into something less formal," he said.

"Please do," she replied. "I was myself about to do the same. This dress presents the image of a grieving widow well enough, but it is a little like doing penance in sackcloth. I may still mourn without the outer trappings that convention demands."

"Come, Anastasia," Federica said. "I think it is time for us to also change into less formal attire. Shall we see you here later?" she asked of Sophia.

"Yes, my Dear," Sophia replied. "I will be down directly, I don't even think I will even hang or fold this dress, I feel like just throwing it into a corner of my room, never to look at again."

"Will you be needing lunch, Ma'am?" Eleanor asked.

"I don't think so, Eleanor," Sophia replied. "I think I ate more than sufficient of the food you and Jane prepared and served, which, if I have not already mentioned, was delicious, thank you. I think I may take tea now on the terrace, if you would be so kind, with a light dinner later."

"Yes, Ma'am," Eleanor said. "There will be only the four for dinner?"

"I hope so," Sophia said. "I don't think I could take visitors at this time. If anyone calls, I am indisposed."

"Quite, Ma'am," Eleanor agreed most fervently. She thought that there had been too many people already traipsing through the house and was quietly and surreptitiously counting silver and other items.

"That took long enough," Anastasia said as George and Federica entered the drawing room, dressed now in much less formal attire. "Come along, it's time for your first driving lesson."

"Do I need anything?" he asked.

"Only your brains and common sense," she said. "Fede can explain the parts of the car to you, then I'll take you out and show you how to work things, then we'll change seats and start you out with your lesson."

"Of course, Professoressa," he teased.

"Well, come on then," she said.

The three of them went to the coach house and all stood around the Daimler while Federica explained the functions of the various controls, spending not a little time on the advance and retard ignition timing lever, which she explained to him would probably save him from backfires and potential hurt or even broken arms. George grasped the concepts quickly and realised that, of course, gearboxes would be necessary as the engine could not be expected to simply propel the car at varying speeds without some system of power conversion. Federica also spent some time talking about the clutch and its operation, and the idiosyncrasies of many of the clutch systems.

"The clutch is another of those items we need to improve," she said. "Along with a mechanism to start the car without the handle and something to keep the windscreen clear in inclement weather."

"Now, George," Anastasia instructed. "I have set the controls appropriately. Starter, please."

"Right," he said and then swung the starting handle and listened as the engine rumbled into life. He watched as Federica listened, then she motioned to Anastasia to move the throttle up, and they both listened to the note of the engine as the revolutions increased.

"I think the adjustments have solved the issue we had the other day," Federica said.

"It certainly sounds like it," Anastasia agreed. "Do you hear it, George? It sounds better than when we came back from Maidenhead."

"I confess to not knowing what to listen for," he said. "If you both think that it sounds better, then I am sure it is."

"Well, off you go then," Federica instructed. "George, try not to irritate Nastia with too many questions, and Nastia, be patient with my knight, he is only a man after all and wont to solving problems and taking charge of things, he may baulk at the notion of taking instruction from his younger sister."

George watched carefully as Anastasia worked the clutch, then selected the first gear. She then engaged the clutch, and the car lurched forward slightly, then settled down to a more uniform speed. "You see that, George?" she asked. "This clutch tends to grab a little, so you have to be careful not to let it out too swiftly or the wheels will spin."

"Is there anything that can be done to ease the grabbing?" he asked.

"The common solution is Neatsfoot Oil on the leather that faces the plate," she explained. "Conversely, if the clutch slips, then a light dressing of Fuller's Earth on the leather on the plate absorbs the extra oil that causes the slippage."

"I see," George said.

"Now we'll turn off here before the gate and use the farm road so that you can get the feel of the car before we venture out onto the main road," Anastasia said. George watched as she used the clutch again to change gears, both up and down, as they went downhill and uphill around the estate. "Would you like to try?" she asked.

"Yes, please," he said, a little nervously. He wanted to try, but had to admit he was more than a little concerned about making himself appear foolish in front of his sister. They stopped and changed seats, and George looked over the controls and pushed in the clutch, selected first gear and slowly let the clutch out, then the car jerked forward. "Not bad for a first try," Anastasia said. "Come to a stop and try again."

"Again?" he asked.

"Again," she confirmed. "The best way to do this is time and time again until you get the feel for the clutch and can gauge what is happening."

"Rather like riding a bicycle or a horse," he laughed. "Each time you fall off, get back on and try again."

"That's right," she confirmed. "Now again." George tried again, still with a jerk as the clutch bit repeatedly, until finally, his start was at least as smooth as that of Anastasia. "Now, as we go change gears to match the speed and the hills," she instructed.

"Fine," he agreed. "How do I tell if I am in the wrong gear?"

"In time, you will get to relate the sound of the engine with the speed and the load the engine is under as we go down or up hills, and you will know," she promised.

"This is wonderful," he said as they picked up speed and drove along the avenue of beech trees that formed the northern perimeter of the estate. "How fast are we going, and how fast will the car go?"

"We're probably travelling at about twelve miles an hour at the moment," she said. "The speed limits on the roads are supposed to be fourteen miles an hour, but local authorities have the discretion to lower the limit to twelve miles an hour and are pressing for ten miles an hour."

"Is there not some indicator that could tell us the speed at which we are travelling?" he asked.

"There are some devices available," she replied. "A man by the name of Josip Belušić invented something in the last century that he calls the velocimeter, but I have not seen many fitted to cars, but I do believe that people are working to invent new systems. Our Olds has a mechanical speedometer, but it is hard to see as it is mounted low on the dash in front of the driver."

"If there is no indication of speed, how are we to know that we have exceeded the limits set by statute?" he asked.

"That is part of the dance we do with Constable Platt," Anastasia laughed. "He stations himself somewhere on the road with his watch and times our passage over a set distance; he then calculates the speed."

"It seems to me that that would be fraught with the possibility of error," he said.

"You are absolutely right," she agreed fervently. "It seems that Constable Platt has an inexpensive watch from Switzerland that is a notoriously poor timekeeper, and I have demonstrated that to him on several occasions, such that now he is circumspect about trying to give me a summons for exceeding the speed limit."

"I pity poor Constable Platt," George laughed. "To face you and probably Federica as well must be a challenge."

"Mama is the worst," Anastasia laughed. "She is noted for furious driving, and if she is on the road, give her a wide berth."

"Do you think we could venture beyond the estate and try some new roads?" he asked.

"Of course," she agreed. "Go through the gate and turn right towards Littleworth Common."

"What do I do if I encounter other road users?" he asked.

"Slow down and grant them some courtesy," she instructed. "Horse owners have been known to complain to Constable Platt about us and other cars."

"On which side of the road should I pass them?" he asked.

"As you would on a horse," she replied. "Let them pass by in the other direction on your right."

They drove to Littleworth Common and back, and George was pleased with his progress. He admitted to Anastasia that he was not yet totally comfortable and would not relish having to drive in a town, but for the moment, he was content with country roads. At the house, George parked the car in the coach house by reversing it in, a feat of which he was quite proud.

"So, how did my knight do?" Federica asked when George and Anastasia left the coach house.

"Quite well," Anastasia admitted. "He will be fine after one or two more lessons. I confess that he grasped the idea quicker than I had expected and much quicker than Henry did."

"I knew you would be fine," Federica said proudly. "Did you have occasion to vent your frustrations upon Nastia?"

"No," George laughed. "I tried hard to control the frustrations that arose and told myself that if mere women like yourselves could manage the skills, it could not be that difficult."

"*Idiota*," Federica hissed and ran after him as he fled laughing. She pursued him into the vegetable garden and cornered him by one of the cold frames, but her attempts to strike out at him were frustrated by his gales of laughter and his dancing around. "I'll show you what skills we have," she promised. "Just stand still for a minute if you dare!"

"I would not be so foolish," he said. "I lay myself at your feet in humble apology."

"I might begin to believe that if you were not laughing so hard," she said. "You will be punished," she promised and punished he was as Anastasia crept up behind him as he danced to avoid Federica and emptied a bucket of water over his head.

"Nastia!" he exclaimed. "Have pity."

"Pity," she said. "On your knees, you hapless fool of a man, before I douse you with more water."

"Please, no more," he begged through his laughter. "I confess I offered the insult to provoke you."

"Down and beg then," Federica ordered.

"Of course, *Cara*," he agreed.

"What do you think, Nastia? Should we let him off so lightly?" Federica asked.

"His spirits have been dampened a little," Anastasia said. "Perhaps we should let him change his clothes at least before he catches his death of cold."

"Inside you and change out of those wet clothes," Federica ordered. "I will think of suitable punishment for your antediluvian ideas by and by."

Over dinner, Sophia asked about the driving lesson, and George was quick to explain that Anastasia was a splendid teacher from whom he had learned much. His attempts to gloss over his goading were foiled by both Federica and Anastasia, who told Sophia of his sins and their retribution.

"I had wondered what the laughter was all about," Sophia said. "It was good to hear, I confess there has been little laughter here of late, it is something we need more of. Do not take that as an invitation to annoy your sister or Fede, George."

"Of course not, Sophia," George agreed. "I would not dream of it."

"Toad, you utter untruths as quickly and readily as a politician," Anastasia laughed. "You live to provoke us."

"I have had little opportunity to provoke or annoy such beautiful ladies during the past two years," he explained. "I am out of practice."

"Now, it's flattery," Federica laughed. "I'm glad you think that we are beautiful; we may begin to forgive you."

"Have you heard from your commanding officer?" Sophia asked.

"Not yet," George said. "I imagine that it will be some weeks yet before I hear back."

"What do you think he will say?" she asked.

"I'm not sure," he admitted. "We have no major conflicts at this time, so I see no reason not to grant my request. There are others in the regiment who managed all my duties while I was on secondment."

"What did your duties entail?" Sophia asked.

"I was sent out into the veldt to scout the position of the various Boer commandos," he replied.

"Didn't that expose you to great risk?" Sophia asked.

"Not really," he said. "I took great pains not to be seen."

"Perhaps we will not see war for some years now," Sophia commented. "It seems that we have been ever at war, with the Ashanti campaigns, the Afghan wars, this, the second Boer war, the Sudan campaign, will we ever settle to a time of peace?"

"It is our colonial ambitions that drive many of these wars, Mama," Anastasia interposed.

"Perhaps we would do well to forego some of the Empire building and look instead to problems here in England," Sophia said. "We, as women, cannot yet vote in Parliamentary elections, even though we constitute half of the population; we have only recently won the right to keep our own household and wealth and not surrender all to our husbands."

"You are right, Sophia," George agreed. "But, the politicians in Westminster, all of whom are men, cover their fears of women by stating that you would not understand the issues."

"We saw that same stupidity with Mr Baker," Anastasia remarked. "He would have been absolutely horrified if he had learned that it had been Fede and me making the investment choices over the past months, no matter how successful we have been."

"That is the one issue that concerns me with a venture into cars," Federica added. "If people discover that the car has been designed by us and built in a factory owned by us, then will they avoid purchasing merely because of our gender?"

"Well, for the factory issue, I doubt that there are many women in our foundry, are there?" George asked.

"True enough," Federica agreed. "The foundry manager, Mr Fox, has come to accept us and perhaps even privately listens to our suggestions, but the outside world sees the foundry as run by men. It is different in our garment factory and the biscuit factory, most of the workers are women, but few of the supervisors and as yet none of the managers."

"Our garment factory is similar to the foundry," Anastasia added. "Mr Painter, the manager, now seeks us out for advice, but I am sure is careful not to let that be known to the customers, or even the employees, lest they flee in alarm."

"Indeed, they would," Sophia agreed. "Look at the situation of Ethel Charles, it matters not that she is a qualified architect, her commissions are limited to minor residences because men, and probably many women, either are afraid to give her more commercial work or the profession is actively throwing obstacles in her path."

"Perhaps if we build a new assembly factory, we should give her the design commission," George suggested.

"A capital notion," Anastasia agreed. "What of our car, what should the car and or the company be named?"

"I think the Sirius Car Company," Federica suggested.

"Why?" George asked.

"Well, not to be impolitic but Sophia has the reputation of being a scorcher on the roads, Sirius, the Dog Star, is named after the Greek for scorching, so it seems to me appropriate," Federica explained.

"I'm not such a scorcher," Sophia protested.

"Mama," Anastasia warned. "We know that to be untrue; there is no shame in wanting to test the limits of the car."

"I have often thought that I should take up car racing like Dorothy Levitt; she is a 'scorcher' par excellence," Sophia confessed. "There is an exhilaration to speed, but the limits that the government has imposed on our highways and that the local government boards want to lower are frustrating."

"So, the Sirius Car Company," Anastasia repeated. "It sounds well, do we float a new company with that name?"

"It might be a good idea," Federica agreed. "If we subscribe to the majority of the shares and allow others to purchase small amounts, then will we not have the protections of a public company?"

"We would indeed," Anastasia agreed. "I will look into the matter and draw up the prospectus, and you, George, should put it to Mr Baker to manage the registration and share offering. That way, he will not cavil at the notion."

"Do we have a badge for the car?" George asked.

"We should," Federica agreed.

"What about an enamelled emblem with a dark blue background, a single silver five-pointed star and the word Sirius also in silver underneath," Sophia suggested.

"That sounds nice," Federica agreed. "I'll sketch some examples and bring them later for you to all look over."

"What is needed to build a car?" George asked.

"As I said the other day," Federica started. "We need a design, and we have yet to finish our examination of the cars we purchased and our review of the strong and weak points of each. We need to either make or acquire parts when we have a design, and we need to assemble those parts. So, we need access to foundries, which we have, a machine shop, which we can acquire and equip, a coachbuilder, which we have in Wright Carriages, but which I think will be unsuitable, and finally, a larger building to put it all together."

"Why do you think Wright will be unsuitable?" George asked.

"Because they are hidebound in tradition," Federica explained. "It would take them months to complete the body for one car, and if we make many, we would need to add a significant number of employees. I do not think that is the best way. We need to examine other possibilities and arrive at a different solution."

"Should we divest ourselves of Wright?" Anastasia suggested.

"If we can realise a good price for the company, then I think we should," Federica agreed. "Bodies for cars need a solution that is more flexible and that takes much less time to complete each body."

"Is there still not an active market for horse-drawn carriages?" Sophia asked.

"I believe that about 40,000 new horse-drawn conveyances are built each year," Federica replied. "Given that there are at least 400 coach builders in England, with probably more if we include those that make one or two a year, that means an average of 100 per year for each. It is reasonable to assume that there are those who make only ten to twelve a year in smaller factories and that there are larger factories, like ours, that manage over 200 a year. I think as car sales increase, the demand for coaches will decline, and they will attempt to shift their focus to car bodies, which may not be successful, but that will not happen for some years to some. So, now may be a good time to sell."

"I will test the waters a little," Anastasia suggested. "There are four or five of the larger coach builders in London who have been looking to expand and who have already made approaches to us."

"You have taken apart the cars and reassembled one completely, and partly reassembled another. What have you learned?" George asked.

"Much," Federica told him. "Apart from the fact that the designs of the cars we have are very different, it seems to us that one of the greatest problems facing the car builders is that parts that should be all alike are, in fact, all slightly different, so the builders spend endless hours shaping them to fit. If you examine the parts in the coach house you will see that parts that should be alike are not exactly the same and each has been slightly altered to fit, which means we had to be careful when we disassembled the car to mark each part and matching location so that we may reassemble the car without having to address each part again. It is inefficient and costly."

"How do you measure them then?" he asked.

"We use micrometres and other measuring tools," she explained. "When I measure two or more parts that should be the same, I get different results."

"Enough different to require extra work or just enough different that you can discern the difference, but it is of no matter when it comes to assemble?" he asked.

"Enough different to be readily measurable and to be of matter when we would assemble," she explained. "When we purchased the Daimler, we asked to see the works where it was built. I was not impressed; there was much disorganisation, much clutter, and we saw many workers busy filing and polishing just to get parts to fit. All that takes time and adds cost."

"Has anyone ever looked at this before?" George asked.

"Well, what I heard in China was that in the time of the Qin dynasty, which would be about 300BC or earlier, the Chinese were producing crossbows for their army, and parts could be used in any crossbow with no special fitting, so yes it has been done before," she explained.

"Surely the situation is different?" he asked.

"I do not see why," she disagreed. "The Qin were using cast brass parts and managed without the tools we now have to make good parts. Also, in the more modern era, the armouries that make rifles and pistols for our army, including the rifle that you have and used lately in the Boer War, all use systems of manufacture that use interchangeable parts, as do the makers of sewing machines."

"Are not those parts, for the most part, small?" he asked.

"What is the difference?" she replied. "It is a matter of having the correct machine tool for the job, setting limits for the amount of difference you can tolerate and using the proper gauges, jigs and fixtures to ensure that the parts are all the same."

"So, what was your idea?" he asked.

"To make good parts from the beginning," Anastasia interrupted. "We have the foundry in Burnham, which has been producing parts for the railways, and we have already made moulds for axles, engine blocks and pistons. Mr Fox, the foundry manager, has promised actual parts by next week, so that we may conduct some trials."

"As I recall, the raw castings are quite rough and not really suitable for use in cars," George said.

"Of course," Federica agreed. "We have added space to the foundry for machines to finish the parts."

"Do we have much work to do before we may embark upon this venture?" he asked.

"We do," Federica agreed. "But, first things first, let us float the company, let us talk to architects and engineers about buildings and about the kind of equipment we may need to manufacture, then assemble the parts. Meanwhile, Nastia and I will complete our reviews and evaluations of the various concepts and complete our design. Whatever design we finally agree upon, we will still need foundry capacity, machine shop capabilities, some capability and capacity to make bodies and an assembly hall, so those activities may proceed independent of the actual design."

"I think that is enough for tonight," Sophia said. "My head is reeling from the ideas discussed, and I need a night's sleep to absorb it all. If you will excuse me?"

"I will also retire," Anastasia said. "George quite exhausted me today with his driving!"

"You will grant me another lesson tomorrow, Nastia?" he asked.

"Of course," she promised. "I did but jest. I will see you tomorrow."

"Will Nastia attend university?" Federica asked George after Anastasia had retired for the night.

"I believe she wishes to do so," he thought. "When we last talked of the subject, she said she wanted to study engineering."

"Do you know where she wishes to go?" she asked.

"I think University College London," he replied. "They at least accept women, and I understand started awarding Bachelor of Science degrees in 1881, so it is not a new thing for them. Or, perhaps she will pick St. Andrews in Scotland, they seem to be even more progressive and open to women students."

"Were the degrees from London in engineering or other scientific disciplines?" she asked.

"I don't know," he admitted. "Someone has to be first, why not Nastia?"

"Well, she would be determined enough," Federica laughed. "I would almost have pity upon some of the men in the classes she would attend."

"I'll talk to her and Sophia tomorrow," he said. "And see if she still wishes to attend."

The following morning, Federica was up and about early and dressed quickly, ready to take a run around the estate.

"Wait for me," George appealed.

"Come on then," she encouraged. "I like to be done early so that we do not delay breakfast for Sophia and Nastia."

"How far will we go?" he asked.

"It will be a short run today," she promised. "Only five miles."

"And how long should that take?" he asked.

"It depends on how well you keep up," she said. "We should be back in forty minutes or so. Are you still fit from your days in the army?"

"We'll see," he said. "Lead on, my love."

They were back in fifty minutes, with George ready to concede that he was losing condition. The good living of being back from the war in South Africa was beginning to catch up with him. He was amazed at the ease with which Federica ran the five miles; it seemed to be almost effortless for her. They quickly ran a bath and cleaned themselves of the perspiration and dust that had gathered during the run and presented themselves for breakfast, George dressed in his regular clothes and Federica clad in a tight blouse top and snugly fitting trousers.

"Did you run this morning, Dear?" Sophia asked Federica.

"I did indeed and dragged George along with me," she replied.

"How was that?" Anastasia laughed.

"Well, I tried to keep up," George said. "It was hard, she set a fast pace and was ever in the lead, but I have to say that the view from behind is most pleasing and stimulating."

"George," Sophia laughed. "Please don't let the Rector or any of the villagers hear you talk so. They would be horrified, even more so of the idea that Fede runs through the estate in scanty attire. Oh, and don't ask me why I made this association, but I have been thinking about the emblem for the Sirius Car Company, and I think just the name Sirius in silver on a dark blue background, no star, the star would detract from the simplicity of the design."

"I like that," Federica agreed. "I will modify the sketches I had drawn up, and we may look them over later.

"So, what today?" George asked.

"Today we have a meeting with the managers who run our various companies," Sophia said. "They will be here at ten, George. I will introduce you, and then you may chair the meeting. Here is the agenda, most of the time will be spent by the managers telling us how their businesses are progressing, Nastia will be present as a nascent owner, and Fede will act as secretary."

At a few minutes before ten, the managers arrived and were ushered into the dining room where the family members were waiting.

"Good morning," Sophia started. "Allow me to make the introductions. George, this is Mr Edwards, he manages Handy Cross Enterprises, the tractor business, Mr Robertson of Abbey Biscuits, Mr Wainwright from Wright Carriages, Mr Fox from the Burnham Foundry and Mr Painter, who has The Windsor Company, our garment factory in Slough. Mr George Wheelwright has recently returned from South Africa and, upon the death of my husband, his father, has taken over the majority ownership of the companies. The shareholdings of my late husband pass to Mr George and Miss Anastasia equally, and Mr George holds the voting powers for those shares of Miss Anastasia as well as his own. I retain the shares that I already had."

There were voices of condolence over the loss of Mr Wheelwright, and then Sophia called the meeting to order. George consulted his agenda and asked Federica to read the minutes of the last meeting, then asked each of the managers in turn to give an assessment of their business and the industry in which they operated. He had been given a set of questions ahead of time and noted that some were answered well, and some caused the respondents to think and admit that they had either not considered those issues or needed to do further investigation.

The meeting ran until one, and lunch was then served. After lunch, there were one or two small items to review, and approvals were given for various capital projects. Anastasia promised to have the requisite funds deposited into the bank accounts of the business concerned, and the meeting was closed at three.

"Well, what do you think?" Federica asked George after the managers had left.

"I think Fox, Wainwright and Edwards have good knowledge of their various businesses," he replied. "I was not so sure of Robertson and Painter, but I gather they are fairly new to their positions, so may have been a little reticent in voicing their opinions to us, the owners."

"I think that is a good assessment," she agreed. "What I like most about Painter is that he is open to suggestion and even seeks our counsel, now I don't know if he is being sincere or if he is attempting to ingratiate himself by asking for help, time will tell. Whereas I may not like some of the prejudices of Wainwright and Edwards when it comes to women in business, I cannot fault their knowledge of their businesses and their industries. I think Fox is the most open to new concepts, but perhaps Robertson will be too when he has been with us a little longer and is more comfortable with us."

"I would agree with Fede," Sophia added. "When we retained Painter and Robertson, we were happy with their past experience and education, but there is always the question of how well they will fit with us."

"Mama is right," Anastasia chimed in. "My feeling is that Painter will be the best manager in the long run. He has already been more open to suggestion than either Fox or Wainwright were at a similar point in their service, and I don't think he is just asking to ingratiate himself."

"So when do we meet again?" George asked.

"In a month," Federica said. "I have noted the date on your calendar and will send out notices to Fox et al, with notes reminding them of the questions that were posed but not answered and requests to address those issues in the next meeting."

"Fine," George said. "Is that it for today?"
"It is indeed," Sophia replied.

Heavy transport

The following morning, Federica again was up early and ready for a run around the estate. This time, George was better able to keep pace and enjoyed the run more than he had the previous day. When they returned to the house, breakfast was waiting, and then George asked what was the plan for the day.

"Nastia and I need to work some more on the Lanchester to complete the drawings and then finish rebuilding the car," Federica replied. "If you would like to help, we would welcome the extra hands, provided, of course, that you refrain from groping at me while I work bent over the machine."

"Fede!" Sophia laughed. "I do believe that you are incorrigible. You are just putting ideas into his head, particularly when you dress like that, showing off your figure for him to see. Those tight-fitting trousers leave little to the imagination."

"I think the ideas are there already, Mama," Anastasia remarked. "I've seen the way he looks at her and she at him. We're lucky that they're here at all and not romping around either in the bedroom or in some leafy glade in the beech woods."

"Nastia!" her mother said in pretended horror. "What do you know of such things?"

"What you told me, Mama and what Fede elaborated upon," she replied.

"Please do not talk of such things when Eleanor or any of the others are present," Sophia implored. "They have shown us great understanding and tolerance, considering some of our unconventional behaviours, but I would not wish the village to start gossiping about us, any more than they already do."

"I will be circumspect, Mama," Anastasia promised. "So, George, are you ready for another driving lesson?"

"Of course," he said enthusiastically. "Unless Fede has a mission for me?"

"No *caro mio*," she told him. "Go and enjoy yourself. When you return, I have some things that you may do for me, but I have more than enough to occupy myself for the moment."

When Anastasia and George had departed, Federica went to the coachhouse and addressed herself to the rebuilding of the Lanchester. She had the frame, engine, gearbox, and the rest of the running gear already reassembled and was working on the controls before reattaching the body. She made notes as she went and at times went to a large board where she had pinned up a chart which showed the order in which pieces went together. She spent much time at the board looking over the order and making notes, trying to determine the best order in which to do the assembly. She was already thinking of an assembly building and how it should be built, and how the work should be arranged. She recalled her visit to the Daimler works and her impressions of clutter and people falling over each other; there surely had to be a better way. It seemed to her that the car builders had focused on the engines and the rest of the mechanical components, and that the actual assembly was an afterthought. She, on the other hand, was looking at it from the point of view of how to build a car, any car, and then use the parts that they decided would be best. She already had a rough order of the way the cars went together, the Daimler had been first, and the Lanchester was following, and there really was not that much difference in how to build them. The niceties of each car might differentiate them in the market place but the practicalities and economics of building were the same.

When George and Anastasia returned later, they were still talking to each other, they were laughing, which suggested that the lesson had gone well.

"I met the famous Constable Platt this morning," he told Federica.

"Ah, and did he attempt to write out a summons for you for exceeding the speed limits?" she asked.

"No, indeed, he was the epitome of consideration," he explained. "It may have something to do with the fact that we also met, at the same time, one of the magistrates who apparently has acquired a car and who was taking Constable Platt for an excursion through the beech woods to visit some miscreant."

"Does that suggest that speeding summonses heard at the local Sessions will be treated with greater leniency?" she asked.

"I doubt it," Anastasia said. "It was old Bullard who I don't think could be reasonable if he tried. He has such an antipathetic nature."

"He certainly greeted me with courtesy," George said.

"Well, of course he would," Anastasia said. "To him, you are now lord of the manor and a 'gentleman' to boot, quite apart from the fact that you are an esteemed major in the service of His Majesty. He would bow and scrape to you, whereas he would regard me as an impudent young woman who needs a husband to keep her in line and off the roads, especially off the roads."

"I don't think he's really that bad," Federica said. "He's just a little afraid of you. I'm surprised he hasn't approached George about seeking your hand in marriage."

"Fede, how could you think such a thing?" Anastasia asked aghast.

"It is not unheard of," Federica replied. "You are of marriageable age, you will inherit part of the estate, you are passably attractive, and he needs a new wife since his died three years ago."

"Fede, passably attractive?" Anastasia asked. "Passably, I would like to think that I am beyond passably."

"I think Federica is right, passably suits," George added.

"You are taunting me, both of you admit it," Anastasia demanded.

"I confess that that was my purpose," Federica admitted. "Tell me, did Constable Platt blush when you talked to him?"

"He did indeed," George said. "She seems to have that effect on a number of men that we saw and that she said good morning to. You will break hearts yet, Nastia, passably attractive as you are."

"Toad," Anastasia laughed. "Now I know that you are both just trying to unsettle me with your teasing. But, Fede, we have left you long enough to labour on your own, what remains to be done with the Lanchester?"

"I have connected everything that needs connecting except the body," Federica explained. "So, now we need the hoist to replace the body onto the frame."

"What should I do?" George asked.

"You see the chain hoist that we have rigged to the rafters?" Federica asked.

"I do," George replied.

"Take the chain fall, that's the loop of chain that goes around the pulley and pull on it until you see that the body is raised from the stands and clear of the frame," she explained.

"This isn't very arduous," he commented as he pulled the loop of chain round and around until he saw the body rising from the stand on which it had been placed.

"That is the idea," Federica explained. "It has the mechanical advantage to make heavy lifting easy. Now swing the body this way, and when we are properly aligned, lower by reversing the chain direction."

"Tell me when I should start," he said.

"Fine, we are now aligned, so lower away," she instructed. George pulled on the chain in the opposite direction until he saw the body descend and almost touch the frame.

"Now, slowly, George, while we make some last-minute adjustments," Federica instructed. As George slowly lowered the body, she and Anastasia used some pry bars to ensure that the body was properly aligned, then George saw the hoist chain go limp as the body settled down upon the frame.

"Now, George, you can unhook the chain and remove the rigging we used to transfer the weight of the body to the single point," Federica instructed.

"Are all cars put together in this way?" George asked.

"On the whole, yes," Federica replied. "I am trying to think of an easier way, but have yet to invent something better than the cranes that assembly shops use."

"How is the body fastened to the frame?" he asked.

"Unfortunately, there are bolts that go through to the underside," Federica replied. "That entails some grovelling as we must go underneath to secure the nuts."

"There is no easier way?" he asked.

"In some assembly shops, they have pits in the floor that permit the workers access from below without having to crawl underneath," she explained. "We do not, as yet, have a pit in the coach house. Perhaps we will dig one at some time and make our own lives a little simpler."

"May I secure the nuts for you?" he asked.

"Of course," she said thankfully. "If you slide on this canvas here and pull yourself underneath, you will see the bolts protruding, place these washers and nuts on the bolts and tighten with this spanner."

"Fine, I can do that," he agreed. "There must be a better system. What if the body were held to the frame by bolts that went horizontally instead of vertically?"

"That would be a little better," she agreed. "We would still need access to the underside of the car to install the nuts and tighten things. Perhaps in our assembly building, we should include a mechanism to raise the cars above the heads of the workers so that they might easily make these final fastenings."

"Is there anything else that needs doing?" he asked.

"Some small connections and adjustments," she explained. "We are almost finished."

George watched as she bent over the car and connected cables and wires, and then secured other fasteners. He had to admit that the sight of her bent over the car with the fabric of her trousers straining over her body was most stimulating, and he was on the point of excusing himself when she straightened up and announced that all was complete.

"Now, do we start it up and see if it still runs?" he asked.

"It runs," she assured him. "I tested that before we installed the body, but you may start it up."

"Fine, let's see, this car is different to the Daimler, do I set the throttle to here and adjust the timing lever to here, then swing the handle, correct?" he asked.

"That looks just fine," she assured him and watched as he went to the front of the car and gave the handle a vigorous swing. The engine rumbled into life, and he went back to the controls to adjust the throttle and timing levers as Anastasia directed.

"Tell me, *cara mia?*" he asked. "When you enlisted the help of Henry for lifting, did you wear those adorable trousers?"

"*Madonna* no," Federica laughed. "Such a sight would have given the poor man apoplexy. No, we clad ourselves in severe grey dresses buttoned to the neck and donned aprons to save them from the oil and grease that seems to plague these cars. No, the trousers were for your benefit alone."

"Well, I cannot but admit liking them," he said. "I wonder when our society will accept them without horror?"

"I think not for some time yet," she said. "What do you think, Nastia?"

"Some time indeed," Anastasia agreed. "Look at the bathing dresses we must wear if we go swimming in the sea. We cannot all be Fede and swim in the lake with no clothes at all."

"Do you also swim without clothes?" George asked.

"I confess that I have, on occasion, followed suit and swum without clothes," Anastasia admitted. "I would not do so if you, or any other man, were present.

"I would with you," Federica said, grinning. "But, I am not for the gawping entertainment of other men, only you *amore mio*."

"Where do you plan to go?" Federica asked George.

"What do you mean?" he asked.

"Well, you started the car, do you plan to go somewhere?" she asked.

"I thought Nastia could give me another lesson," he suggested.

"I could indeed," Anastasia agreed. "Remember, though, this is a different car; it does not behave in the same way that the Daimler does, the clutch is different, the gears are different, and the controls are different, as I am sure you noticed."

"I did," he said. "The basic method is the same, just the niceties of each car that are different?"

"They are," Federica confirmed. "This clutch has the tendency to slip a little, whereas you must have noticed that the Daimler clutch tends to grab a little."

"I did experience that," he confirmed. "Nastia told me about dressing the disks with Neatsfoot Oil to counter the one problem and the Fuller's Earth to address the other."

"It is almost time for lunch," Federica commented. "Perhaps we should join Sophia for lunch and then you and Nastia can take another drive this afternoon?"

"You still don't wish to risk driving with me?" he asked.

"I would be happy to accompany you if Nastia wishes it," she replied. "But, I think she should remain as your teacher for the moment."

Lunch was partaken of, and the three motorists then returned to the coach house ready for the next lesson. George took his appointed position by the starting handle of the Lanchester, and when signalled to do so by Anastasia, he swung the handle and was gratified to hear the engine rumble into life. He then climbed aboard and took his seat at the driver's controls. Federica then pointed out the most obvious difference between the Lanchester and the Daimler.

"You will note that this is no steering wheel," she said. "Steering is effected by that tiller arm there."

"Are there other differences that I should know about?" he asked.

"There are differences in the function of the pedals," she replied. "There are other differences, such as this car has a two-cylinder engine that is arranged horizontally, and it has a gearbox with epicyclic gears, but otherwise it is similar in many respects to the Daimler. Perhaps I should drive the car to the road, and you may observe what I do."

Federica duly drove the car down the long driveway and was able to show George what each control did and how it differed from the Daimler. At the main road, she changed seats with him and sat in the back to enjoy the drive. George looked the controls over carefully and tentatively swung the tiller this way and that, and watched as the front wheels moved. Then he nodded to Anastasia, who was seated next to him as his instructor, and drove off. This excursion was a little longer than previous ones, and they ventured down the hills and across the Wye Valley and up the hills on the other side and eventually came to Handy Cross and their traction engine rental business. They were greeted by Mr Edwards, who was delighted to see them so soon after the business meeting. As George had never seen the company, he was shown around the yard and introduced to those men who were there. Mr Edwards explained that the rest were away from the yard on jobs that called for more than a single day of rental. He explained that each engine had a towed caravan that was equipped to house the driver when away from home. George talked about the traction engines he had seen in South Africa and the sterling work they had done hauling supplies for the British army. Mr Edwards was very positive about the rental business and opined that the addition of some steam lorries for heavy transport might be useful. He was particularly interested in the Foden and the Thornycroft steam lorries. He told George about some trials that the War Office had conducted the previous year in which the Thornycroft had been judged the winner, but which many said had shown the Foden to be the superior. George had had no idea that the War Office had been conducting such trials; he had, after all, been otherwise occupied in the veldt of South Africa. The notion was of interest to him, and he asked Mr Edwards where he might obtain a copy of the trials' report. Mr Edwards took them to the office and produced a copy of the report, which he gave to George, asking only to receive it back in due course.

Federica then reminded Mr Edwards about the discussion they had had the previous day about the possible addition of some lorries to their fleet of equipment and if he had any notion of to whom he might hire them out and at what rates. It was apparent to George that this was the first time Mr Edwards had really discussed this option in any depth, and he wondered if it was because he was there and now regarded as the head of the household. If that was so, he was beginning to see the problems that faced Federica and Anastasia on a daily basis. They were quite capable of running the business, but might not be furnished all the information that would be helpful in making decisions. He listened as Edwards enumerated the various industries that might be served, the typical distances a hire might entail and the tonnages.

"What are the main industries that lorries might serve in the area?" he asked.

"The furniture business," Edwards replied. "There is a steady business in hauling timber from the beech woods to the various furniture factories in the Wye Valley."

"What about the paper mills?" Federica asked.

"You're quite right, Miss Beretta," Edwards agreed. "There is significant traffic to the mills in the valley, both with the rags and wood pulp coming in and the paper going out."

"What mills are there?" George asked.

"There are quite a few," Federica replied. "We have the Hedsor mill on the cut between the Wye and the Thames, Jacksons in Bourne End,

Soho and Glory mills in Wooburn, Fords in Loudwater, and what, about ten others would you think, Mr Edwards?"

"Quite, Miss," he agreed. "If we take from High Wycombe to the Thames at Bourne End, the valley is populated with mills along the River Wye."

"Would we be competing with the railways?" Federica asked.

"Indeed, we would," Edwards agreed. "The railways have had a monopoly on the traffic for a while and are not amenable to lowering their rates."

"How many of the mills have direct access to the railway line?" George asked.

"Not many," Edwards explained. "Jacksons does not, Soho does, Glory does not, Hedsor does not, Fords does not, and for the rest, we would need to check into each one."

"How do the mills without direct access transfer materials from the railway to their sites?" George asked.

"Horse and wagon, Sir," Edwards replied.

"Their own or hired?" George asked.

"That varies, Sir," Edwards replied. "I would say that most hire transport when needed; they probably do not want the complication of running a stable."

"What about breweries?" Federica asked.

"I think breweries would probably wish to maintain their own delivery system, Miss," Edwards said. "They have regular routes to their public houses and could justify their own transport, as they do now with horse-drawn drays."

"Would you give us a proposal of how many lorries you think it may be useful to procure and how those lorries would be put to use?" George asked. "We would wish to know how much the addition of lorries would expand the business and what return we may see from any further investment."

"Just so, Sir," Edwards agreed. "I will prepare some papers and deliver them to you within the fortnight, would that be acceptable?"

"Quite," George agreed, after he had received the almost imperceptible nod from Federica.

"How are our supplies of coal?" Federica asked, recalling a comment that Edwards had made the day before.

"We have about twenty tons on hand, Miss," Edwards replied. "I think it would be to our advantage to lay in a stock before the winter months."

"I will attend to that," Federica assured him. "I will arrange for it to be delivered to the yard at the High Wycombe station, and we may collect it from there."

"Very good, Miss," Edwards said. "If I might make a request, could you see if it would be possible to get Welsh coal? We tried some from the Midlands, and it does not burn as well in the grates of the engines. The Welsh coal seems to have better-burning characteristics without too much slag."

"I will contact the colliery agents and get the appropriate specifications and forward them to you, Mr Edwards," she promised. "When last we spoke, you had alluded to problems with the boiler tubes caused by the hard water we have hereabouts. Has the shorter time between tube cleanings helped?"

"Indeed it has," he said. "It may be an inconvenience at times, but we have not had a boiler failure in a while, and we are getting better performance from the engines. Is there nothing that may be done to the water before we use it?"

"I believe there are people who are examining the problem," Federica replied. "As far as I am aware, there is not yet a viable solution in the market, but I hear that it may come soon."

"Soon would be good," Edwards said. "Because of these chalk hills, all the water here is hard, which will ever be the problem; soft water, as they get in Yorkshire, would be advantageous for us as it would increase the time between required boiler tube cleanouts."

"I will look into it further," Federica promised. "Come, George, we need to think about leaving. Twilight will soon be upon us, and the lights on the car are adequate but not the best for driving at night."

On the drive home, Anastasia and Federica berated George for the sins of men, particularly for the sins of Mr Edwards. Federica pointed out to George that although Edwards was one of their better managers when it came to dealing with them, he still was reticent about much, as they had just learnt. George was hard-pressed to defend the man, but tried to explain that it was a fault of the society in which they lived. The ladies reluctantly agreed with him and told him that they could not but be frustrated when those attitudes impinged upon every aspect of their lives. George wondered why Federica had not challenged Edwards directly about not talking to her.

"Because *caro mio*, he would only become defensive," she replied. "I believe it has been difficult enough for him in these past months since we took over directly running the estate to talk to us and not your father, but he has tried. He probably feels more comfortable talking to you, just as he was talking to your father."

"I am ever impressed by your patience," he said. "I am not sure I could have maintained my composure faced with similar circumstances."

"We have lived with it throughout our lives," she told him. "Things may change, but that change will come slowly."

"I'm sorry, *cara mia*," he said. "I will, for my part, try to be more understanding and afford you such equality as I am able."

"Talking about water," Federica said, changing the subject completely from the subject of equality for women. "If the water here furs up the boiler tubes in the traction engines, what will it do in the cooling systems of the cars?"

"When you took apart the cars we have, did you observe any build-up of the calcium deposits?" George asked.

"Not to speak of, but then I was not looking for the build-up," Federica admitted. "We should look again and see if any of the channels for the water have been obstructed."

"What happens in the winter?" he asked. "Will the water in the cooling systems of the cars freeze?"

"That is something we need to address, but it does not apply to this car. This car has an air-cooled engine. There is probably a limit to how large an engine one can air cool, but that is the system for this one," Federica commented. "I believe that many people add alcohol to their cooling water, but I imagine that the alcohol would boil off with the temperatures of the radiators, so we would have to check the system regularly. Perhaps we should investigate other chemicals, such as glycerol, that would not boil off so quickly. I suppose one could also drain the radiator water overnight if a hard freeze was anticipated and then refill the system before using the car."

"Does the lubricating oil freeze?" he asked.

"I do not believe so," she replied. "I am sure it becomes more viscous and therefore does not flow as well to lubricate until the engine warms up."

"There are papers written on the subject," Anastasia interposed. "There are different grades of lubricating oil, and there are some specifically for lower temperatures."

"You commented on the lamps earlier," he said. "As the light is now failing, should we light the lamps?"

"We should," Federica agreed. "This car has Salsbury acetylene lamps, let me show you how to turn them on and light them."

"Where does the acetylene come from?" he asked.

"There is a generator built into each lamp," she explained. "We just have to clean the lamps regularly and ensure that there is calcium carbide in the chamber and adequate water in the reservoir above."

"Do we only have lamps in the front?" he asked.

"No, we also have one at the back, it is an oil lamp that has a red light filter," Anastasia explained. "Constable Platt is ever wanting to see that the rear lamp is clean of mud and dirt and visible from behind."

"Is that not rather problematic?" he asked. "Surely, as you proceed upon the highway, there will be an accumulation of mud and dirt?"

"There is indeed," she agreed. "So, we make a point of cleaning off the lamp on a regular basis to keep it free from mud."

"Where do we buy the calcium carbide for the lamps?" he asked.

"We buy it from Wilson's the ironmongers where we get our petrol," she told him. "We also buy the lubricating oil from them."

"Is there no way to have electric lights on the car?" he asked.

"Not yet," Anastasia replied. "Lucas has offered electric lights with some form of small generator and accumulator, but they are not yet altogether reliable. I imagine that in time, Lucas and others will improve upon their designs and make them more usable in cars."

They made it back to the house without incident, possibly because of the efficacy of the Salsbury headlamps, possibly because both Anastasia and Federica knew the road well and were able to guide George along the way. Sophia wanted to know where they had been and what they had seen along the way, so Federica and Anastasia gave her a complete account while George went to change for dinner. He had the drawing room to himself for a short while until Sophia and the two others also changed, and he used the time to pore through some of the editions of *Autocar* that he found on the desk. There was much written, and he marvelled at the detailed descriptions of new cars and accessories that were featured. When dinner was served, conversation drifted back to cars.

"What issues do you think really need to be addressed to make a car that is attractive to buyers?" he asked.

"I think that the price is important," Federica said. "Until now, the car has been the almost exclusive plaything of the wealthy. That limits the number that may be sold. To grow the number of possible buyers, the price must be lower."

"How do we lower the price?" he asked.

"Well, as we discussed before, the parts must be interchangeable," she said. "Otherwise, there is much time and money spent on fitting the parts."

"As Fede said before," Anastasia added. "The cars we took apart had all been well built, but the individual parts had been filed and polished to fit. So we were at pains to record which part fitted to which when we took them apart, so that we could easily reassemble them."

"Is it possible to make interchangeable parts, and would it cost more to make such parts?" he asked.

"We believe it is possible to make interchangeable parts," Federica replied. "We have to start in the foundry or in the press shop where major parts are made, but we think that it should be possible to create the right kind of jigs and fixtures and machines that to the best of our measurement, the parts will all be the same, we believe that it would cost little or no more to make the parts better. I believe there is a false notion that higher quality automatically equates to higher cost. In our biscuit factory, we are at pains to make all the biscuits the same, and since we have done so, the costs have in fact decreased. I think in the case of fashions it may be true that higher quality equates to higher cost, only because of the fabric used, the type of stitching and the overall finish of the garments; however, none of that affects making metal parts."

"So, assembly would simply be a case of placing one part into another?" he asked.

"Yes," Federica agreed. "Why should one have to file and polish a piston to make it fit if it can be made correctly to start with?"

"That sounds reasonable," he thought. "You also said that the Daimler factory was full of clutter."

"I think that is because they set up the frame of a car and bring all the parts to it," Federica explained. "What if we put the frames on moving carts and move the cars to the places where we store engines, gearboxes and other parts, would not that be a better solution? In the biscuit factory, for those items that take an icing, we move the biscuits to the icing machine, not the icing machine to the biscuit."

"How would we do that?" he asked.

"I think we manufacture some frames that have legs, at the bottom of the legs, we affix steel wheels so that the cart may be pushed from place to place. We arrange the factory such that it is in natural sequence for assembly, and we start at one end and move the carts along until all the pieces are added," she explained.

"Would that not make for a very long building?" he asked.

"If it looks as if it would be too long, then we turn the line around at some point and reverse our direction," she thought. "We would need to determine how many steps we need to take to assemble the car and how long each step would take."

"Is anyone doing this yet?" he asked.

"We have heard rumours about Olds in America," Anastasia commented. "We know of no one here in England that yet builds in this way, but that does not mean it is not a better way, it just suggests to me that the builders of cars focused first on the design of the car and then work out how to build it."

"You said before that the makers of sewing machines use parts that are interchangeable, but how do they assemble their machines?" he asked.

"We are not sure," Anastasia admitted. "Perhaps we should arrange a visit to one of them and go and see."

"I have a chart in the coach house," Federica said. "On it, I have recorded the necessary steps for assembling a car, and there were essentially no differences between the Daimler and the Lanchester, even though they have great dissimilarities in design."

"That chart is for the assembly of the car, I suppose," he said. "What about the major pieces that go to make up the car, like the engine?"

"We would do those off to the side and bring them to the frame," Federica thought. "What we need to do is decide what are the major pieces and then how to design a building such that those pieces can be built to the side and then brought when needed."

"Perhaps you may continue this exploration into the mysterious world of manufacturing tomorrow," Sophia suggested. "There are some items for the wedding that I would like to clarify."

"Very good, Mama," Anastasia agreed. "I have decided upon dresses and colours, and Fede has also commissioned dresses."

"There is more than just dresses," Sophia commented. "If we are to travel to Italy to Florence for the wedding, how do we get there, when do we need to leave, where will we stay in Florence, and when do we return?"

"I think to get there we take the ferry to Calais and then the Rome Express from Calais and alight at Firenze," Federica suggested.

"Are there Wagons-Lits carriages on the train?" George asked.

"There are indeed," Federica assured him. "It is a well-appointed train and we should be most comfortable."

"When do we leave?" Sophia asked.

"I think the fifteenth of December would be fine," Federica replied. "It gives us ample time to arrive in Firenze but not too much time as to make us at a loss for what to do when we are there."

"Where do we stay?" Sophia asked.

"My father's house has more than enough rooms to provide accommodation for us all," Federica assured her. "George will have to stay in another part of the house until the nuptials are concluded, but I am sure he will manage."

"Poor George," Anastasia laughed. "Deprived of your close company for ten days, how will he ever survive?"

"How many of your family do you suppose will attend the wedding?" George asked, pointedly ignoring Anastasia's comments.

"My parents, probably my brother and his wife, and I suppose my three sisters and their respective spouses," she thought. "My mother will also want all her grandchildren, so there will be an onslaught of children. If they all come, there will be twelve of them."

"Uncles and Aunts?" he asked.

"Possibly six or seven all told," she thought. "Most live in and around Firenze, but three live in Pisa and may not wish to make the journey, even though it is easy on the train, we will be passing through Pisa on the Rome express, which goes from there to Firenze."

"Cousins?" Anastasia asked.

"Oh, many, too many, perhaps twenty if they all come, but my father may intercede and suggest no, that is, if he can persuade my mother," Federica laughed. "How many of us will there be?"

"Oh, so you are already wedded to George and therefore one of us," Anastasia said. "I suppose it is natural enough, you have lived here for many years now, and it is your home. So, Mama, how many of our impoverished relatives will come to the wedding?"

"I think only your Uncle Will and Aunt Esme, for the rest, the cost may be a deterrent, we should have a small party after we return where we may introduce Fede as the newest Mrs Wheelwright," Sophia replied. "Will any of your cousins from South Africa come, George?"

"I have sent a telegram to Koos and await a reply," George said. "It is possible that he may come, but he would need to organise his travel soon because of the long boat journey."

"I must refresh my Italian," Sophia said. "It has been a few years since I did the Grand Tour there, and have forgotten much. Perhaps, Fede, you might help me?"

"Of course, Sophia," Federica promised. "We should also provide George with some words and basic conversation that may be used outside the bedroom."

"Will you attend to the travel arrangements, Nastia?" Sophia suggested.

"Of course, Mama," Anastasia agreed. "I will contact the Wagons-Lits people tomorrow and book for us from London to Florence. They will then arrange the ferry from Dover to Calais, and we will board the train at the ferry terminus in Calais. It just remains for us to travel to London to catch the ferry train, but I will allow plenty of time for us to traipse across London from Paddington to Waterloo."

"Good," Sophia announced. "Now, I think time for bed for all."

Fitting

"George, there is a letter for you from the Army," Sophia said. "There is also a telegram from South Africa."

"Good, let's see what they say," he said. "Ah, Koos and Anna will come to the wedding and then come here for a short visit before returning to Oudtshoorn, and the other, the colonel accepts my resignation of my commission but he has suggested that I may be of use to the Directorate of Military Intelligence, so, as he puts it, when the next inevitable conflict arises they might have use of my services. He has been in touch with various generals in the War Office, and apparently, they want to put me on half pay to keep me around. I won't have to do anything unless we go to war again, and if we do, it's more than likely they would have me at some desk job in Whitehall. They have asked me to go up to London next week to visit with some people."

"What conflicts might arise and where?" Federica asked. She did not want George to be called up and then have to disappear off to some faraway place for years at a time.

"Well, there is still the conflict in Somalia, but the Army has enough men for that, there is always something going on in India and Afghanistan, but there are already enough men there for that, there is a war going on in Colombia, but that's not our problem, there is another in the Philippines, but again, not our problem, it looks, for the moment at least, that things are relatively quiet in the Empire," George said. "So, I don't see any particular risk at this time."

"Good," Federica said. "I'm not ready to lose you for another year or two. I am much desirous to meet you, cousin Koos, you and he spent much time together, and he kept you from harm's way."

"He did indeed. I think you will like him and his wife, Anna. What are your plans today?" George asked her.

"Well, we've finished rebuilding the Fiat, so that's all of them back together and running. Nastia and I have been reviewing the drawings and have some ideas of what we may do for our car," she said.

"Have you thought more about university, Nastia?" George asked.

"I have indeed," she replied. "I am considering submitting my application this coming year to the University College London to study mechanical engineering."

"Where will you live?" Federica asked.

"Mama and I will take a flat in London," Anastasia replied. "You two can run the estate here, and we will enjoy London."

"Are you sure that is what you want?" George asked. "Are you sure that is what Sophia wants?"

"I have thought upon it carefully, George," Sophia replied. "I have enough to occupy my time in London, and Nastia will not have to concern herself with where she lives. If, after a year, it is apparent that the arrangement is not working well, then I will return here and she will either stay where she is or we will endeavour to find her other suitable accommodations."

"Do you think they will accept you?" George asked.

"I don't see why not," Anastasia replied.

"They will probably try to place obstacles in your way," he said. "They'll say that the mathematics is too difficult, that you would not understand the concepts of mechanics and who knows what else."

"Well, I'll just have to point out to them how wrong they are and perhaps ask them how many of them have disassembled a car and rebuilt it and have it still run," she said.

"Now you understand why I took those photographs of you working on the cars," Federica added. "They can argue that they are posed, but the evidence is hard to dismiss."

"Meanwhile," Sophia interrupted. "There is the wedding to consider."

"Will you have time today to come into Maidenhead with me to attend a fitting of my new dresses?" Anastasia asked.

"Of course, Dear," Sophia replied. "Fede, we need to drag you away from your cars for a while and see how your wedding dress is progressing and how our dresses are also faring."

"Must we?" Federica said a little plaintively. "We have a month yet before the wedding."

"We must my Dear, we may have a month before the wedding, but we leave in two weeks, little enough time if there are many alterations to make to the dresses so that they fit correctly, we do not want your family to think that we have no sense of style, fashion or decorum. The weather is clement today, unlike the past two weeks that have been quite unpleasant, so we should take advantage of the sun, watery as it is." Sophia ruled. "Now change into something that will not raise the eyebrows of people in Maidenhead, and let us see what the dresses look like. The sooner we are done, the sooner you can get back to your plans."

"Shall I drive you all?" George asked.

"That is a capital notion," Sophia agreed.

"Wear your chauffeur's cap," Anastasia suggested. "Then we may all be *grandes dames* being driven around by our faithful manservant."

"I'm not so sure he is that faithful," Federica said. "He is as likely to leave us and take off to some hostelry."

"I would never abandon you, *cara mia*," George protested. "I will just get an overcoat, gloves and a hat and will draw the Fiat to the front of the house to await you."

"Make sure that there are extra rugs in the car," Sophia suggested. "I have no desire to get cold on this trip."

The drive into Maidenhead was quick enough, with only a short delay at the Cookham bridge while they waited for a steam traction engine and threshing machine to negotiate the narrow bridge, not one of their machines, but of another company. George deposited his passengers by the dress makers in Maidenhead, then went to Smith's newsagents and bookstore. He was looking for the latest texts on motor cars and hoped to pick up some volumes he had ordered two weeks earlier. Sophia, Federica and Anastasia entered the dressmaker and were greeted with great enthusiasm. It was not every day that the dress maker received orders for six dresses, all of which were high-quality productions with linings, facings and decorative additions and therefore likely to run to quite a few pounds. There were six dresses because each was getting a dress for the wedding and another for the reception that would follow. Sophia took charge and asked after the dresses for Federica; she, after all, was the reason for this expedition.

"*Bonjour,* Madame Garnier," she greeted her. "We are here for our various fittings. We are particularly concerned with the dresses for Federica."

"Ah, Mrs Wheelwright, good morning to you," Madame Garnier replied. "I have the dresses all ready for another fitting. I think you will be delighted. Please come through to the fitting rooms. Now, who will be first?"

"Fede," Sophia ordered.

"Yes, Sophia," Federica said meekly.

"Very good, Miss Beretta, I have your wedding dress here," Madame Garnier offered.

"Let me quickly change, Nastia, will you assist me?" Federica said, taking the dress.

The two disappeared behind the changing screen for a few minutes and came back for a review.

"Quite lovely," Sophia said. "The line suits you well, Dear, it sets off your narrow waist and draws attention away from your boyish hips. I like the bodice work too, it makes use of what bosom you do have and adds curves where there are usually few."

"Sophia!" Federica said.

"Madame is quite right," Madame Garnier agreed. "I recall when I measured you that you are on the small side. This style makes use of the attributes that you do have and presents an alluring picture; your husband-to-be will be entranced."

"The husband-to-be is already entranced, quite besotted actually," Anastasia commented wryly. "He does not need a dress to be entranced, I think, for him the less she wears the better," she added, grinning like the proverbial Cheshire Cat.

"Nastia," Sophia chided. "We still need Fede to look her best for the day; what they do after the day is none of our concern."

"What about the length?" Federica asked. "I do not wish to trip in the aisle of the church and make a spectacle of myself."

"Stand up here, please," Madame Garnier instructed, pointing to a small stand. "Now turn towards Mrs Wheelwright, now away. I will make some small alterations to the hem, but are you wearing the shoes that you will wear on the day?"

"Shoes, I had forgotten the shoes," Federica said in apparent horror.

"I have them, Dear, I knew you would either forget them or dare I say, leave them at home hoping we would forego our fitting," Sophia said.

She then produced the shoes and helped Federica out of the ones she had been wearing and into the new pair."

"Let me see again," Madame Garnier instructed. "Turn this way, now that, good, the hem line is perfect, there is no need for additional changes."

"Will your mother wish to acquire a wedding dress for you in Italy?" Sophia asked. "We have been treating this as if it is our wedding, but your parents may be offended by our presumption."

"It is possible," Federica agreed. "I think we should take this wedding dress, then if Mama has another notion, she may compare the two and decide for herself."

"A capital notion," Sophia agreed. "Now for the burgundy, and do not forget the shoes."

Federica duly presented herself again, this time clad in a burgundy dress that was similar in line to the wedding dress, but without the beadwork and other decoration. She also had on a pair of shoes that matched the colour of the dress.

"A perfect fit," she said, twirling around. "I like this dress. Perhaps I should wear this to the wedding."

"Fede," Sophia cautioned. "Do not even begin to contemplate such a notion. We may have our unconventionalities, but we must present a picture of some conventionality to your family, otherwise they will think of us poorly and wonder what their daughter has married into."

"I know Sophia," Federica agreed. "I was but teasing, but do you not agree that it is a beautiful dress?"

"It is," Sophia agreed.

"What will you wear under the dress?" Madame Garnier asked.

"I think what I have on at the present," Federica replied.

"Well, let us see," Sophia instructed. "We may have to purchase new undergarments for you as well as the dresses."

"That will not do," Madame Garnier said when Federica took off the dress and presented herself for inspection. "The colour is not right, it is possible that in bright light, the undergarments may be slightly visible through the fabric of the wedding dress. I know your measurements, so will provide the appropriate set. I have some very attractive items from the Galerie Rivoli in Paris, or you may wish to visit the Maison Lucile in London, which offers quite a variety. I do have some other items you may wish to examine or try, this is a *corselet gorge* from the house of Herminie Cadolle, which is most attractive and does not have the restrictions that a corset imposes."

"That sounds most appealing," Federica said. "Anything that frees one from the tyranny of the whalebone corset."

"There is also this item," Madame Garnier suggested. "It is a breast supporter from Marie Tucek, a most daring garment."

"I'm not sure that one could call it a garment," Sophia said. "There is little enough to it."

"May I try?" Federica asked.

"Of course," Madame Garnier agreed. Federica went behind the screen and reemerged wearing the Tucek supporter and her drawers.

"Well, what do you think?" she asked.

"It certainly supports," Sophia commented. "Is it comfortable?"

"Not particularly," Federica replied. "But even though it is not the most comfortable, I prefer it to corsets, I should like to take one in white for my wedding dress and one in another colour for the burgundy. Can you do something to make it more comfortable?"

"I have some ideas that may help with comfort," Madame Garnier replied. "For the burgundy dress, the colour is dense enough that it matters not what you wear underneath, so I would suggest something that will intrigue the groom and bring him to a high sense of desire."

"The groom needs nothing to intrigue him," Anastasia said. "Fede just has to look at him and crook her finger, and he runs to do her bidding. But, Madame, you are right, we should present the bride in the best possible way, so what to wear?"

"Black, I think," Sophia suggested. "If we are going to be risqué, then we might as well do it properly."

"What about the dresses for Nastia?" Federica said, wanting to get away from this subject as fast as she could.

"They are ready, but first, I will note that we should provide Miss Beretta with a set of undergarments, black in colour and with appropriate lace finishings to intrigue and present a picture of desirability. Now, Miss Wheelwright, which do you wish to try first?" Madame Garnier asked.

"I think the blue," Anastasia said.

The blue was duly tried on and approved of, as was the scarlet that Anastasia had selected for her dress for the wedding. Next was Sophia, who had selected beige for the wedding and a deep Tyrian for the reception gown. Madame Garnier had excelled, and the dresses fit perfectly, but all were left with the strict admonition to adhere to a rigid diet between then and the wedding day lest the dresses no longer fit when they arrived in Italy. The next port of call was the milliner and hats. That took some time as the conversation switched into Italian and all matters relating to the impending wedding were discussed and reviewed at length. Sophia managed to keep up with most of the conversation, which pleased her greatly as it showed her that her Italian had improved over the past weeks and that she would not be left like a wallflower at the wedding or the reception, alone and unable to join in the festivities. When finally they were done, they went looking for George and found him lolling against the car and looking at his watch.

"Are we done?" he asked.

"We are done," Sophia assured him. "We must return on Friday to collect the dresses, but no further alterations are required, and you may be assured that we will not embarrass you."

"I could never be embarrassed by you, Sophia," he assured her. "By Nastia perhaps, but by you, never."

"Your sister will not in any way embarrass you," Sophia promised. "She is agog with excitement over this wedding and the chance to spend time in Florence."

"What if she falls for some handsome Italian cousin of Fede's?" he asked.

"If that happens, it happens," Sophia said. "I will be keeping her close at hand to minimise such a contingency,"

"What are your cousins like, Fede?" George asked.

"Reprobates all," she assured him. "I would not let any of them within a mile of Nastia. She is far too romantic and would fall prey to their blandishments too quickly."

"What will we wear for the journey?" Anastasia asked.

"I think something warm," Sophia suggested. "It will, after all, be the beginning of winter, and it may be cold."

"Gabardine, gauntlets and goloshes then?" George joked.

"I cannot say for certain," Sophia said. "Fede, what will the weather be like in Florence in December?"

"It has been known to snow in Firenze in December, rain is possible, and the temperatures will be cool, almost to freezing overnight at times," Federica expounded. "We will be sheltered from the weather in the house, and when we go to the church, it will be carriage, or at least I presume it will be."

"Will there be a problem that you are marrying a man who is not of the Catholic Faith?" Sophia asked.

"I doubt it," Federica assured her. "When we moved to Hong Kong, religion rather took second place to commerce. If there are any issues, it will be with the priest or priests involved, then we may have to promise to raise any children in the Catholic Faith to keep them happy."

"Will there be children?" Sophia asked.

"We are not desirous of a family," Federica replied. "It is, of course, possible, would it be a problem for you, George, if we were to make such a commitment to the priests?"

"None at all," he promised. "If I may change the subject here, perhaps we should return home post haste, I sense a change in the weather and fear that we may be rained upon."

Rain it did, but only as they were driving the last short distance down the driveway to the house. They got slightly wet, but were thankful to have escaped the worst as the downpour increased in intensity and it rained hard and steadily for the next two hours. Anyone driving in an open-topped car in that rain would have been drenched, even with a cloth cover that some cars came with; the result would have likely been the same: drenched passengers and driver.

"You see why we need to consider some form of coachwork that fully encloses the car?" Federica pointed out to George as they were changing out of wet and damp clothes.

"I do indeed," he agreed. "I have been on a horse in the pouring rain in South Africa, and I am not sure which was more unpleasant, that or this most recent dampening."

"There are cars with enclosed compartments for the passengers," she said. "Often they leave the driver exposed to the elements."

"Is that because the cars are designed for the wealthier market and the assumption is that there will be a chauffeur?" he wondered.

"I think that is the case," she agreed. "If we are to build a car that appeals to a wider number of people, we need to provide some reasonable protection from the elements, but it is bandied about that a closed coach would cost about twenty per cent more than an open coach and would also weigh more."

"How much would that cost?" he asked.

"That is a very good question," she said. "If we were to build a body for the car that was based upon coachwork, then I think the costs would be prohibitive, after all there are cars that one may purchase today were the price is quoted as being so many pounds for the car and an additional number of pounds for the type and style of coach that will sit upon the frame."

"So, how do we build coachwork for the car that is not too costly?" he persisted.

"Perhaps we should talk to our Mr Wainwright, such an apt name for a coach builder, don't you think, about the possible ways to build car bodies," she thought. "At least he may have some ideas."

"I thought you said that he was not the most liberal in his thinking?" he asked.

"True," she agreed. "Even among the reactionary thoughts, there may be some kernel of an idea that is worth pursuing."

"So tomorrow then?" he suggested.

"Tomorrow at ten I think would be an appropriate time," she agreed.

Ten in the morning the following day, Federica, together with George and Anastasia, presented themselves at the offices of Wright Carriages in Slough, near the railway station. Mr Wainwright was there and expressed delight in seeing them again so soon after their normal meeting, but Federica was sceptical of his reception as their last meeting at the factory had not been that harmonious. Mr Wainwright did not take kindly to women telling him what he should and should not do, particularly as she was not yet a part of the Wheelwright family, so her insistence in seeing the books was not welcomed but only tolerated because Sophia happened to be with her at the time and because she acted as the secretary to the various companies. Anastasia excused herself and went off to closet herself with the bookkeeper, leaving Federica and George with Mr Wainwright.

"Good morning, Mr Wainwright," Federica said. "We have come to seek your advice."

"Really, Madame, on what subject?" he replied.

"I wish to build a car and am seeking the best and least cost way to construct the coachwork," she explained.

"You wish to build a car?" he repeated.

"I wish to build a car," she reiterated, ignoring the condescending manner in which he repeated her statement. "I understand that most cars come with coachwork that is built in traditional ways by coach builders such as ours."

"That is so," he said. "I am not sure I understand. You wish to build a car?"

"That is so," she replied, playing back his own words to him. George moved to intervene quickly because he saw her left hand clench and unclench, which was not a good sign; it meant that she was running out of patience.

"We wish to build a car," he stated. "I thought that was clear?"

"Clear, Sir, of course, Sir, you wish to build a car," Wainwright said. "Well, if you have the mechanicals sourced from somewhere, then we can provide a body. We would need some drawings to show us the size, and then in about six months we could produce a suitable coach."

"Is there a way to shorten the time?" she asked.

"Madame," Wainwright began. "There is the frame to make and cure, there are the panels to form and affix, then there is the finishing and painting, all of which takes time, it is not like baking where one mixes ingredients and then puts the item in the oven to be done in an hour. These things take time."

"If the panels were already painted and shaped?" she asked.

"We could not do that because we would not know if the panels would fit," he said dismissively. "All our work is custom-made, and as I said, these things take time."

"Let us assume for the moment that the panels would fit," she said. "Would that make a difference?"

"I suppose it would," he admitted. "It would never happen because we cannot know how the frame will be exactly, so there may be gaps between the frame and the panels, or between panels."

"And if the frame was known?" she pressed.

"Then, yes, I suppose it would be a matter of hours or days to affix the panels, but no one does that," he protested. "How would we know ahead of time what the frame would be?"

"We make a jig and fit the frame to it," she suggested.

"We would never do that," he said. "Each frame is different and made to order. Madame does not clearly grasp the intricacies of such manufacture."

"If we made but one model and they were all the same?" George asked, interposing again, knowing full well that Madame did indeed grasp the intricacies of such manufacture and was hardly impressed by the techniques used in the shops of the car makers she had seen.

"I suppose that may be made to work," Wainwright admitted. "Who would buy such a creation, a car the same as the car the next man is driving? What gentleman would stomach such a travesty?"

"Must the panels be of wood, or may they be of the steel plate?" she asked, ignoring the last.

"Steel Madame?" he asked aghast. "We build our coaches of wood, good English ash and other woods; we would never use steel, except to provide for reinforcing gussets and plates."

"Can the frame be of the laminate form that some of the furniture people are now using?" she asked.

"Madame, the furniture industry makes lightweight items that do not see the stresses and wear that a carriage does; those laminates would never be strong enough," he said, dismissing the idea.

"And yet, laminate beams have been used in churches and schools to hold up the roof," she commented. "Were they not used in the roof of one of the buildings at King Edward VI College in Southampton?"

"Perhaps, but those laminates must be of significant size, and they are in buildings where weight is not of a concern," he replied.

"Well, thank you for your time, Mr Wainwright," Federica said. "You have been a great help."

"I am sure that Madame will come to realise that such an enterprise is not something that the fair sex should undertake," he said. "It is, after all, replete with oils and greases which are quite unladylike."

"Well, we will see," Federica said. "We will bid you good day. We will collect Miss Wheelwright on our way out."

Outside, George looked at Federica and said, "That was not much help."

"On the contrary," she said. "We learned much."

"We did?" he asked. "What, other than the man, is, to use the words of Nastia, odious?"

"We know that preformed and pre-shaped panels would reduce the assembly time," she said. "We also know that laminated forms are worth considering."

"But, he dismissed that idea," he protested.

"His words did, but did you see his reaction? He has considered it himself at some point and is still doing so," she said. "We should visit some furniture factories and see what they do."

"Why do we retain such a man?" George asked.

"Because in his own way, he is very good at his job," Anastasia said. "I reviewed the books, and we are still making handsome profits. It is fortunate for us that his dealings with women in commerce and business are limited so that his condescension is not an impediment to our success."

"The books are honest and reflect the true situation?" he asked.

"They do indeed," Anastasia assured him. "Mr Wainwright is a deeply religious man, and his sense of right and wrong may be a little warped in our view, but to his honesty, there is no doubt. How close did you come to striking him, Fede?"

"She was close," George laughed. "I had to intervene twice or there may have been blood."

"Did she start clenching and unclenching her left hand?" Anastasia asked.

"She did indeed," George said. "I had not appreciated until a few weeks ago that that was a sign of impending doom, but I learned to recognise the symptoms and took action."

"It's just as well I took her gun out of her purse," Anastasia laughed.

"Her gun, what do you mean?" George asked.

"She habitually carries a gun in her purse," Anastasia explained. "I think she got the idea from something that Dorothy Levitt said."

"That is not the issue," Federica interrupted. "Another thing we learned is that if we pre-shape and preform the panels and paint them, then the frame must be exact so there are no gaps and spaces."

"Quite, *cara mia*, but you carry a gun?" George asked.

"Only when I go abroad on my own," she assured him. "The road to Handy Cross and some others we take are not well-travelled, and it is useful to have the means to protect oneself. Now, if we pre-paint the panels, then assembly and finishing time will be reduced surely?"

"I would agree with that," George said. "How would we know what colour to paint the panels?"

"Simple. They are all ultramarine to match the background of the Sirius emblem," she said.

"What if someone wants red?" he asked.

"Then we charge them more and add to the delivery time," she said. "Ultramarine is standard and any other colour is a special order with the concomitant increase in price."

"If we assume that the frame is some laminate, then what are the panels, wood or steel?" he asked.

"I think we need to investigate the costs of both and the weight; we do not want this car to become too heavy," she replied.

"What if we made panels from wood veneers and corrugated card interiors?" Anastasia asked.

"We could try," Federica agreed. "It would certainly reduce the weight and the cost and would still have the appearance of a quality product."

"How do we seal the body between the panels?" George asked.

"We can form seals from rubber," Federica suggested. "We form them to a tee shape and then affix the panels to the frame with the tee shape between the three pieces. That would seal the body and provide a cushion against the vibration of the car that might otherwise affect the coachwork."

"Would these panels made from card and wood have the necessary strength for use in a car?" he asked.

"I believe so," Federica replied. "I think Anastasia may have hit upon something there. It would be an elegant solution to the problem of weight."

"We should use the new honeycomb paper structures that are now available from Mr Heilbrun in Germany," Anastasia suggested. "If we glue wood veneers on each side, the panels will have a pleasing appearance and I believe they will be at least as strong as ordinary wood panels, but at much less weight."

"We should try some," Federica agreed. "We need an experimental shop, George, so that we may try some of our ideas and see if they are practical."

"Has anyone tried these honeycomb panels?" he asked.

"Not that I am aware of," Anastasia told him. "That does not mean it is not a good idea, merely that it has not yet been tried. It was not so many years ago that Daimler first produced a working car with a petrol engine; no one had done that before, someone has to be first."

"Could you not make the body from steel?" he asked.

"The mudguards on many cars are already made of steel," Federica said. "They typically have a curved shape that is made by beating the panels over forms. I suppose a body could be made in the same way, but what of the weight?"

"If the mudguards are formed to a curve, could the body panels also be curved?" he asked.

"Some companies use steaming methods to curve the wood," Anastasia replied. "I think if we were to use thin wood veneers, then the steaming would be minimal, and perhaps the paper honeycomb can be easily formed to a curve; we would have to see.

"How are the frame members that support the engine made?" he asked.

"Either wood or pressed steel or in some cases even tubular steel," Federica explained. "The wood frames often have gusset plates made of steel to reinforce certain parts."

"If we have a body that encloses the car, how do we see out?" he asked.

"We put in windows, and to keep the inclement weather out. We'll borrow from the railway carriage industry and have windows that open by lowering," she replied.

"Doors?" he asked.

"Ah, yes, doors," she thought. "I think we will have to look at how the coach builders and the railway carriage people manage doors. We will need to have a frame that is sturdy enough to hang the doors from and then we will need to decide whether we need one door on each side, in which case how do the passengers in the back seat get in and out, or do we have two doors on each side, in which case do we hang the doors from a central pillar or have two pillars, so many questions?"

"And the wheels?" he continued.

"The two most common solutions are the wooden artillery-style wheels or the wire wheels that developed from the cycle industry," she replied. "I was thinking of wire wheels for our Sirius."

"Do we make all these parts ourselves or purchase them already made from another?" he asked.

"That is a question that has occupied us for some time," Federica admitted. "It has probably also exercised most others in business at one point or another. I think we should make our own frames, bodies, engines, gearboxes, axles and the like, but perhaps buy wheels, lamps and other smaller items. Unless, of course, we find that it is to our advantage to buy bigger parts from someone else."

"How will we know that?" he asked.

"We will have to estimate the costs of making parts ourselves and then compare those estimates to prices we get from possible suppliers," she replied.

"If we buy parts, then do they come from England or should we also consider France, Germany and America?" he asked.

"All, I think," Federica replied. "The Americans have skills in high rates of production, and perhaps for us, that would mean lower costs."

"Perhaps we should take lunch somewhere," he suggested. "Do you have any suggestions?"

"We might go to Skindles Hotel in Maidenhead," Anastasia suggested.

"Will Sophia be wondering where we are?" he asked.

"No," Federica assured him. "I told her that we would take lunch out after our visit with Mr Wainwright. After we have dined, I also want to stop and talk to Fox at the foundry."

Sophia was not wondering where they were; she was musing over shoes and whether or not she liked the shoes she had selected for her trip to Italy. The shoes for the wedding itself were of no issue, but the shoes she had selected for travelling were giving her cause for reflection. It was not that she did not like the shoes; they were among her favourites, but she was concerned that they did not quite match the clothes she had picked out for the journey. That gave her further cause for reflection. Here she was deciding that this particular pair of shoes might not be appropriate, and yet there were many who had only one pair of shoes, perhaps even none, and could never have the luxury of the quandary in which she found herself. Her musings were interrupted by the return of Anastasia, Federica and George, so she happily turned to less philosophical issues.

"How was Mr Wainwright?" she asked.

"Oh, probably as forthcoming as ever," Anastasia replied.

"We did learn some things from him," Federica added. "The trip was not a waste of time; we have more investigation to do."

"What do you think of all this, George?" Sophia asked.

"Fascinating," he replied. "I confess I had never thought about what it might take to build anything. It has all been very interesting and I have already learned much."

"Should we go ahead and build a car?" she asked.

"Absolutely," he said. "I think between Fede and Nastia, they should be able to arrive at a design and some method of manufacture that will be good for us."

"Will there be resistance to yet another car on the market?" she asked.

"I doubt it," he replied. "I'm sure that there will be many more car companies that come and go in the next few years, as people try their skills and luck with new designs."

"Will it make a difference that Fede and Nastia will be the designers?" she asked.

"Ah, that's a different question," he admitted. "I think if it becomes known that Fede and Nastia are the designers, then there will be a great amount of scepticism about the design, and people may be reluctant to try the car. I think Fede may be right, we may need a public face that is different to the private face."

"I was forgetting," Sophia said. "Where did you luncheon?"

"We went to Skindles," he replied. "It was most pleasant, and you?"

"I dined in," she replied. "I had much to think upon and am almost decided about what to pack for our trip to Italy. It will be upon us soon enough, and I have no desire to be frantically searching for something at the last minute."

"We also stopped at the foundry and spoke to Mr Fox," George added. "Federica gave him a list of materials that she asked him to purchase, and they also discussed the castings that she wants for the engines."

"So, she has settled on a design then?" Sophia asked.

"I don't think entirely yet," he replied. "But she is far enough along in the process that she wants to try her ideas to see that they will work."

"What did our Mr Fox think of that?" she asked.

"I think that in spite of himself, he is quite excited by the idea and even seems to have forgotten that it is Federica who has designed the engine and with whom he is discussing the niceties of castings," he said.

"She can be most persuasive," Sophia commented dryly. "I have not yet met a man who would not bow to her will."

"Absolutely," he agreed. "I watched her at work with Fox, and I could tell the point at which he stopped thinking of her as a woman and just started to listen to her design philosophies."

"Will he do a good job?" Sophia asked.

"I believe so," he replied. "He was most enthusiastic when we left and was scurrying around ordering people left and right to do things. We are well served with him as a manager."

"Good," Sophia said. "Now, is everything set for Florence?"

"I believe so," he said. "If you will excuse me, I will go and see if Fede agrees with me or if she has things for me to do."

"I would like to see the biscuit factory and the garment factory," George said two days after their visit to the coach builder. "It would be interesting to see a different type of manufacturing."

"Why don't we go tomorrow?" Federica suggested. "If we leave early in the morning, we can be there at a reasonable hour."

"What do we have there?" he asked.

"We have several lines of biscuits that we mix, bake, decorate and box up for distribution to our customers," she replied.

"Who do we sell to?" he asked.

"We have made arrangements with several of the larger shops in the area and four in London," she explained. "We sell to them wholesale and they then sell on to the actual customers."

"And the garment factory?" he asked.

"We can go there this afternoon," she said. "It is close to the foundry."

"How do we sell the clothing items that we make?" he asked.

"Again, we have arrangements with various shops and we supply to them," she explained. "The garment business is a little different to the other businesses we have, fashions change and we must stay alert and not be caught with large amounts of clothing that is not easy to sell."

"Who checks on that?" he asked.

"We have some women who stay abreast of what is fashionable and what will sell no matter what the fashion trends," she replied. "They do a good job and will identify changes in fashions quickly so that we are not left behind."

"That was most interesting," George said after they returned from their visit to the biscuit factory. "I saw a number of machines from Baker Copland. Who are they?"

"Baker is one of the leading manufacturers of machines for the mixing, dispensing, cutting and finishing of dough products, be it for bread or biscuits," she explained. "They have been working closely with Carrs to develop new machines, and I would look to them for equipment in the future."

"I like the way the biscuits disappear into the oven and then come out the other end fully baked," he said.

"That is one of the reasons I think we should consider building cars by moving the basic frame along and adding to it," she said. "What were your thoughts about Windsor?"

"I had not appreciated how many women actually work in certain types of factories, at both the Windsor and Abbey Biscuits factories, most of the workers were women," he replied.

"But, did you also notice that almost none of the supervisors or managers were women?" she asked.

"I did see that," he said. "Why is that?"

"I think history and cultural biases," she said. "It is my intent that we start to promote from within the companies so that women do advance. Until now, we have retained men directly as supervisors or managers; there is the perception that women cannot do the job, something that is patently untrue. Nastia, Sophia and I have been working on a plan for some time. The next challenge is to get Mr Painter and Mr Robertson to both agree and implement our desires."

"Let's hope that they accede to your desires soon, then," George said. "I would not wish to see them replaced too quickly."

"So, you think we would dismiss them if they failed to carry out our wishes?" she asked.

"Wouldn't you?" he asked.

"You're probably right," she laughed. "Now, *caro mio,* enough of work."

Anastasia wrote to the University College London and applied to be admitted as a student of mechanical engineering. She included all the materials that they said they wanted to see and the names of appropriate referees. She was mildly surprised to actually receive a reply requesting that she go for an interview that week. So, she and Sophia travelled to London and she had her interview.

"That was quite a long interview," Sophia remarked when Anastasia finally rejoined her.

"It was indeed," Anastasia agreed. "They seemed to be at great pains to discover whether or not I had the academic preparation for the degree. I believe I finally convinced them."

"What is next?" Sophia asked.

"They actually offered me a place there and then," Anastasia replied. "The term begins next October, and I will need to be here the last week in September in order to register, pay fees, and meet my tutor and other instructors."

"When should we take up a London residence then?" Sophia asked.

"The weekend preceding Monday the 28th of September of next year would be fine," Anastasia said.

"Well, we will need to find an appropriate address then," Sophia said. "I will investigate the possibilities."

Florence

The Rome express left Calais bound for Paris, Turin, Pisa and Florence before its last leg to Rome. The Channel crossing had been choppy and the record time of just over sixty minutes for the crossing was not equalled In fact it had been close to ninety minutes and many of the passengers on the boat had succumbed to sea sickness, so it had been a relief to all when Calais was reached and solid ground was again underfoot, with no heaving and pitching of the deck, just the lingering sensation that the ground might actually be moving. The Wagons-Lits staff were as efficient in Calais as they had been in London and Dover, and the Wheelwright party was soon ensconced in the sleeper car. The sleeping arrangements were quite simple: George and Federica together and Sophia and Anastasia sharing. The Wagons-Lits staff just assumed that George and Federica were husband and wife and always addressed her by the title Mrs Wheelwright, which amused Sophia and Anastasia.

The Rome Express came with dining cars, so dinner was partaken of between Calais and Paris before retiring to bed for the overnight run to Italy. George told them of his last train ride that had been in South Africa from Beaufort to Matjiesfontein and the colonel who had talked and talked when he, George, had least felt like talking. That train had not had the comforts of the Rome Express, but at least the danger of derailment and gunfire had stopped with the cessation of hostilities. Anastasia asked him about other train rides in South Africa, and he had told her of the previous adventure he had had when travelling the other way from Matjiesfontein to Beaufort. He left out much of the detail that dealt with death, but focused instead on his riding in the goods wagon that was filled with boxes of ammunition. Anastasia was duly horrified that he, a British officer, would have to travel in anything less than style, but then painted a romantic picture of derring-do as he defended the train from all comers. Nothing could top that, so George suggested that it was time to retire and enjoy the more lavish comforts of the Wagons-Lits accommodations.

"Before we retire," Federica interrupted. "Tell me about your trip to London and your meetings with the generals."

"I did not meet with any generals, "George admitted. "I did meet with an Under Secretary of State for War and we had a most interesting discussion."

"That sounds like an impressive title," Anastasia commented. "Who does he report to?"

"William St. John Brodick, the Secretary of State for War," George replied. "He is a member of the government, and if the Conservatives lose the next election, he will be replaced by a new man."

"What did your Under Secretary want?" Federica asked.

"Essentially, would I help them in time of war with intelligence methods and instruct officers and others how to gather intelligence? They have people who are very capable of analysing intelligence but have yet to develop good systems for gathering, apart from the classic spies that have been used by governments since societies were formed," George elaborated.

"Do they want you now?" Federica asked.

"No," George said. "Apparently, whatever conflicts we are currently embroiled in do not require such meagre skills as I have."

"They cannot be so meagre if you saw the number two man," Anastasia stated.

"I agree," Sophia chimed in. "Whatever you did in South Africa must have impressed someone."

"I did little enough," George said. "I merely trailed around the veldt after the Boers and passed back intelligence as to where they were and where they might be going."

"Well," Federica announced. "I'm very glad that they never caught you and put you in some kind of prison."

"Perhaps it is those skills that your Undersecretary wants," Anastasia suggested.

"At any rate," George said. "They have no need for my services at this time, so I have dismissed them from my mind. Do you not think it is time to retire?"

The train travelled on into the night, stopping in Paris to pick up passengers and then leaving for the run down through France to Lyon before branching off to take the line that included the tunnel through the Alps at Mondane. The tunnel took miles off the route to Rome by not going through Marseille and along the Mediterranean. The disadvantage was that, through the tunnel, the train was invaded by the smoke from the steam engines that hauled it. Electric traction had not yet reached this tunnel, although it was part and parcel of the London Underground system and its use there was expanding, particularly in the deep tunnels, displacing steam traction and the associated smoke and ventilation problems. Once through the Mondane tunnel and south of the Alps, it was full steam ahead for Turin.

Past Turin and Pisa, the train finally came to Florence, and the party disembarked to a welcome from fifteen or so excited Italians. Federica made introductions that included her parents, her brother and sisters and their respective spouses, together with assorted nieces and nephews. Sophia was known to many of them from her days of the Grand Tour, but George and Anastasia were new. Anastasia's ability to speak Italian was greeted with delight, and even George's attempts were dutifully listened to, and his poor grammar was forgiven, for after all, this was the man who finally had brought Federica to book and had had the nerve to ask her to marry him and had been accepted! The family had despaired of her and had long ago given up hope that she would ever marry. Fortunately, from their point of view, she lived abroad in England, so their friends and neighbours were not constantly reminding them of her status as single and asking the inevitable question, why?

As they left the railway station, they were greeted by the sight of a line of five Fiat cars, which Federica's father proudly announced belonged to the family and would be their transportation whilst in Florence. Federica was delighted and wanted to know which one she could take. Her mother gasped at the notion and pointed out that they had chauffeurs to do the driving. Her father looked at her over her mother's head and nodded to the third one in the line and mouthed the word,

"*Domani*". That satisfied Federica for the moment, and she was content to be driven through the streets of Florence to the family residence. Their drive to the house was quite quick, and in short order, they came to an impressive structure that sat opposite the Institute of Galileo Galilei and abutted the Giardino già Gheradesca. The carriage house had been turned into a space for the cars, and Federica noted that all the trappings for horses that normally adorned stables and coach houses had been replaced with tyres, petrol tins, driving clothes and other motoring paraphernalia. Clearly, her father had embraced this new fashion with gusto.

Inside the house, they were shown to various guest rooms, and Federica had been right, George was given a room seemingly miles away from hers and in a completely different part of the rambling house. Still, after the wedding, conventions would have been satisfied, and they would be housed together. Sophia and Anastasia were offered separate rooms but elected to share a large room that overlooked the gardens. After a brief period allowed for unpacking and settling in after the journey, Federica's mother wanted to know about wedding dresses and other matters, so George and Federica's father, brother and brothers-in-law left and went to the coach house to talk about cars. Left with her mother and the other ladies of the house, Federica decided that the best way to move forward was to take the offensive, so she produced the dress that she had brought with her and asked her mother's advice on some trivial matter having to do with the finish. She hinted that she was thinking of ripping the whole lot off and starting again. Her mother immediately said no, as Federica guessed she would, and castigated her for wishing to deface such a beautiful dress. That effectively settled the issue of a wedding dress, and she was content then to sit back and let her mother manage the other items. Her mother had a List, or rather many lists, lists of guests that had been invited, lists of flowers that she wanted to be carried by the bride and the others in the party, lists of tasks that she would assign to various family members and lists of items to be served at the reception that would follow the wedding. Federica quickly scanned the lists and decided that there was nothing that she really took exception to, so there was no need to go to war with her mother over the arrangements. Finally, the men rejoined them and arrangements for weddings were put in abeyance until the morrow, and the family settled down to the serious business of the evening meal.

Federica arose early the next day, just after daybreak, and went to the coach house and found the car that her father had indicated. She looked it over and then opened the coach house doors, started the car and drove off towards the city centre. By the time she returned, the rest of the family was up and about, but her absence had not been noted, except by George and Anastasia. Breakfast was on the table, and she found a seat and helped herself to something light. She leaned over to George and whispered in his ear, "Later, we must take the car and go for a drive in the hills to the North."

"Which car?" George asked.

"The one my father indicated yesterday when we arrived," she replied. "I took it out earlier this morning, and it is a fine machine, very fast and powerful; it is the larger model of the Fiat we purchased."

"You were out already this morning?" he asked.

"Shh," she told him. "Mama does not need to know, she wants to review dresses again today, but only I think to assure herself that the one I brought from Maidenhead is quite suitable. I think she likes the dress but does not wish to admit to me too quickly that I made a good choice."

"Where did you go?" he asked.

"Only into the centre of the city," she said. "Quite a short drive, but enough to test the car. I attracted the attention of several young men along the way and received such whistles of approval."

Their conversation was interrupted by Mrs Beretta, who told Federica that meetings had been arranged that morning with seamstresses, bishops, florists, cooks and photographers. Whether or not Federica wanted the trappings of a wedding, she was going to receive them. Her mother wanted to be sure that the other significant families in Florence knew that she could arrange a spectacular party for her daughter. So it looked as if outings with George would need to be postponed, at least for a day.

George was duly dispatched with Franco, Federica's brother, whose English was excellent, on a tour of Florence while the women got down to the serious business of The Wedding. Federica imagined it as described, thus with the emphasis as it was turning out to be much more than she had anticipated or even desired. In time, though, she met with the seamstress, who admitted that the dress that Federica had brought with her was well made, very stylish and most suitable for the occasion, conveniently confirming Federica's mother's opinion and striking one item from The List. The next appointment was with the florist, who discussed the flowers that Federica's mother had suggested and pointed out those that were in season and those that were not available, one more item struck from The List. The meeting with the bishop was delicate as she skirted around the issue of her attendance or lack thereof at services in the Catholic church closest to Hedsor. She was vague about children but assured the bishop that she would bring George with her to an interview at the church when they would satisfy all his concerns. She planned to manage that interview by telling the bishop that George spoke no Italian so she would translate. She had tested the bishop and his knowledge of English and was satisfied that it went no further than Good Day.

The photographer suggested that the family come to his studio the following Wednesday for the requisite pictures to be taken. That suited Federica even when she was told that she would have to take along the wedding dress and that everyone would be dressed up as if they were attending the wedding. The last appointment of the day was over lunch and was with the cook. Mrs Beretta had a menu planned, and the cook was submitting samples of the dishes for tasting and approval. The tasting and approval process lasted until almost four in the afternoon, after which it was time for a siesta before the evening meal. Anastasia remarked to Federica that at the rate they were going, they would all need the seamstress to let out the dresses they had come with.
"Never fear, Nastia," Federica assured her. "Tomorrow we start on the regime that will ensure our figures on the day of the wedding. I have

already spoken to cook and she quite understands and will fend off Mama."

"But, the food and wine are so good it is hard to resist," Anastasia complained.

"We will just be sensible with the sizes of our portions," Federica said.

"I'll wager that George and the other men will not be so reticent," Anastasia commented.

"Why don't we take George's trousers in a little to alarm him about his gain in weight," Federica suggested.

"Oh, Fede," Anastasia giggled. "That would be unkind, but so much fun, a capital notion."

"You will have to acquire his trousers for me," Federica said. "I am watched by Mama so that I may not approach his room."

"We should wait a few days so that he may be convinced that it is the food that has added to his waistline," Anastasia suggested.

"So, it is agreed then," Federica said. "Now let me find my husband-to-be and see if I cannot spirit him away for an hour or so, or at least to see the sunset."

George was duly found and Federica spirited him away to the hills that bounded Florence to the North in the car that she had taken earlier. Once out of the city and into the hills, Federica told George of her various meetings and then asked him about his day with her brother.

"We never actually made a tour of the city," he replied. "We met instead in the coach house where your father told me about the wonders of this car and the others."

"Indeed?" she said. "What else did they talk of?"

"The offer of financial support," he told her.

"I see," she said. "How much and at what cost, remember my father is a trader at heart and nothing comes without an expectation of a return."

"He said something about a gift to his last daughter," he explained.

"That on the face of it sounds very generous, how much?" she asked.

"He said something about £100,000," he replied.

"So much," she said aghast. "What will he want for that, control of the company?"

"He did say it would be a gift," he said.

"Nothing is ever a gift," she said, dismissing the notion with a wave of her hand. "We may offer him some shares in the company, but we need to be sure that we retain the majority so that he does not become the controlling shareholder."

"Are you being unfair to your father?" he asked. "He may be wishing to bestow a gift upon you."

"He may," she agreed. "However, my past experience is that he will not be able to contain his basic instincts to look for a return, gift or not. I will talk to him and see if I may get some sense of whether or not he has stepped away from his own nature with a true gift or if he wishes to help us with our endeavour, with the caveat that his idea of help is invest and expect a return."

"Do you think we will succeed and generate a return?" he asked.

"Of course," she said, quite confidently. "It is not that complicated, we design a car, we build a factory to manufacture the car, and we sell cars. There will be difficulties, but they may be overcome."

"I admire your confidence," he said. "I wish I had your assurance."

"When you went into your various encounters with enemies in South Africa and India, did you not have confidence in your success?" she asked.

"Of course," he said. "I had been well schooled and had gained enough knowledge and experience to trust my capabilities."

"So it is with business," she said. "I have confidence that we can succeed where others may fail."

"Perhaps we should return to the house?" he suggested.

"We should indeed," she agreed. "We have much to discuss with Papa."

"Don't fight with him," he pleaded. "I don't want our marriage to start on a bad note."

"I won't fight with him," she promised. "It may sound like it to you, but remember, we Italians tend to get dramatic in our conversations. Our discussion will be a negotiation. I will start by telling him that I thank him for his gift and offer nothing in return, and then will wait to see how he responds."

"Will he?" he asked.

"Of course," she said confidently. "I know my father. He will tell me that the gift is the least he could do for his daughter, and then he will begin to allude to various things that he would like to see happen. After that, it will get entertaining."

"And you will agree on something?" he asked.

"Eventually," she assured him. "It may seem to you that we will never agree on anything, but we will agree. He probably has his most desired situation already in his mind and will just argue and argue until he gets it or something close to it, just as I will argue and argue, fending off his more outrageous proposals."

The discussion took place after dinner. It began peaceably enough, then the tone changed. Mr Beretta hinted at what he might like, not related in any way to the proposed gift, of course, but clearly a *quid pro quo*. Federica gave as good as she got, and George watched in horror and fascination as the two obviously negotiated towards an understanding that was apparently mutually acceptable. George had been convinced several times that either or both parties would storm out of the room, but then he began to see that it was as much theatre as anything and that there was sound reason behind each demand, no matter how dramatically it was delivered. With agreement reached, Federica then announced that she was retiring for the night, but not before giving George a quick look and smile. After Federica had left, Mr Beretta suggested to George that they take a cognac, then he proceeded to wax eloquently about his daughter's business acumen and how proud he was of her. Having been convinced not too many minutes earlier that he was going to disown his daughter, George was surprised at Mr Beretta. He seemed to be delighted with the final solution, and even Franco was making approving noises. Mrs Beretta just shook her head and left as well, presumably to join her daughter.

"Federica," Mr Beretta started. "Drives a hard bargain, as you English would say. In return for my gift to you as a wedding present, she has agreed that I may enjoy a small ownership in your new company, not enough to dictate but enough to interest me."

"How much?" George asked.

"Ten per cent," Mr Beretta replied. "I had hoped that she would grant me more, I would have settled for less, but in the end, I think she felt generous and agreed to ten."

"And for that, what are your expectations?" George asked.

"I expect that you will succeed and would also like the tenth production car that your factory produces," Mr Beretta explained.

"The tenth, not the first?" George asked.

"The first may have some minor issues as you prove the manufacturing systems," Mr Beretta explained. "By the tenth car, you should have most of the minor issues resolved, and I want to be able to show off the car made by my daughter before others in Firenze."

"Papi," Franco interrupted, "there are also Anastasia and George in this enterprise."

"Of course," Mr Beretta agreed. "*Una bella ragazza*, Anastasia, you will have problems with suitors, George."

"I agree," George said. "I believe there have been a few, but she has sent them on their way, so perhaps it will not be so bad, but as you say here, *sono molto stanco*, so if you will excuse me, I will retire."

"*Buona notte*," Mr Beretta said. "*A domani*."

The following day brought more items to be crossed off The List and little time for much else. Federica was beginning to question her own wisdom in agreeing to come to Florence for this spectacular. On the other hand, she was not unhappy with the agreement she had struck with her father; ten per cent of the company was little to give in return for essential financing. She had considered British banks but was reluctant to start with debts, and they had yet to publicly float the company, so she was unsure how much subscription to shares might yield. Financing from her father meant that she could begin without having to worry about satisfying investors in the short term or the costs of carrying debt from banks. She would apply some of the money he had pledged to share purchase, and the rest would be held as cash reserves for working capital. She sought out George and Anastasia and told them that she wanted to settle on a design for the car.

"Do we know enough yet?" George asked.

"We know more than enough," Federica assured him. "We have a design that is similar in many ways to the Olds car, and I think we should look to the larger market of less affluent people. I see greater possibility there than merely being another competitor in the market for larger cars."

"So, we have a car that seats four, it has a four-cylinder engine, we have a steel frame that is stamped, there is a gearbox with four gears, for springs we use semi-elliptic leaves secured to the frame, and for the body we construct a body that includes a roof and doors. Is that correct?" Anastasia asked.

"That sounds right," Federica confirmed. "When we get back to Hedsor, we will need to seek out premises for the assembly works and will need to retain a manager."

"How many cars do we need to produce and sell such that our costs do not exceed a reasonable selling price?" Anastasia asked.

"That we still must confirm," Federica admitted. "This wedding is now an obstacle; now that we have the financing from my father, I am keen to begin, and every day we spend here is a delay."

"Should we not at least appear to be enthusiastic about the wedding?" George asked.

"My Love, I would marry you at the meanest chapel in Florence," she replied. "If we could manage that tomorrow, I would gladly do it, but as that might cause some consternation in the family, I promise I will rein in my desires to get to work and at least pretend to enjoy the festivities."

"It will not be for much longer, *mia stella*," George promised.

A week later, Federica saw George tugging at the waistband of his trousers. "Is there a problem?" she asked

"I'm sure it's nothing," he replied. "My trousers seem to have shrunk a little."

"You don't think that it's possible that you have been overindulging in the hospitality?" she asked, pretending innocence.

"Perhaps," he thought. "But I have tried to be careful, I want to be able to fit into my dress suit for the wedding, perhaps I should stop taking wine with dinner and look to eating smaller portions."

"That may be advisable," she agreed. "What did you have for breakfast?"

"Oh, the usual," he said, shrugging his shoulders.

"And, what is the usual?" she pressed.

"Oh, you know, coffee and light toast," he said.

"So, it is not breakfast," she confirmed. "But, while we talk of breakfast, you would do better to eat more at breakfast and less at dinner."

"I know, I know," he said. "It's just that your mother's cook makes such divine meals, how can I resist?"

"George, you need to go to the station," Sophia said after lunch. "Your Uncle Will and Aunt Esme arrive today, as does your cousin Koos and his wife Anna."

"I wonder how they all will fare with everything around them Italian?" he said.

"Your uncle will probably be like most English people and complain loudly that no one speaks English, and then he will add some vowels to the ends of words in the hope that it makes them almost Italian, failing that, he will speak louder until they understand," she laughed.

"Sophia," Federica laughed. "Not everyone has your ability with other languages. Have pity on those who feel lost and at sea."

"What about your cousin Koos?" Sophia asked. "Does he have any Italian?"

"I have no idea," George admitted. "Koos speaks Dutch, English, the Hottentot language and at least one other African language, and I recall that he also speaks French, so it may be that he has acquired Italian along the way."

"Does he have an ear for languages?" Federica asked.

"He does," George confirmed. "He is also a great mimic, so be careful when you hear things that it is not him playing a joke upon you."

"Well, we should be going if we are to meet the trains," Federica said. "I think the train from Rome arrives at almost the same time as the train from Calais. I will drive us there and we will take Marco and another car for the luggage."

The drive to the station was quick, and Federica and George stood waiting for the trains to arrive. First to come was the Calais train, and they watched as passengers disembarked. George saw his aunt and waved, and she came over to them.

"George, so nice to see you and Federica, you look lovely as usual, do you ever not look like a portrait?" she gushed.

"Aunt Esme, if I may call you Aunt, I doubt that I look like a portrait," Federica protested. "Is Uncle Will with you?"

"He is negotiating with the porters for the retrieval of our suitcases," Esme replied. "He should have left it to the train porters; they know what to do."

"Never mind," Federica assured her. "Marco here will take care of the suitcases."

"Marco?" Esme asked.

"Marco is one of our drivers," Federica explained. "He is well versed in the art of facilitating all things."

"George, Federica," Will said, coming up to join them. "Can you tell these blighters to take care with my suitcases? I don't seem to be able to get them to understand."

"Marco?" Federica asked.

"*Si, certo Signora,*" Marco said, then he turned and launched into a tirade directed at the porters who sprang into action and cradled the suitcases as if they were babies.

"Well," Esme said. "It certainly looks as if he can manage things. Do we go to our lodgings now?"

"Not just yet, Aunt Esme," George said. "We're also expecting my cousin from South Africa on the Rome train."

"One of your mother's relatives?" Will asked. "Is he Dutch?"

"Koos, yes, he's Dutch," George confirmed.

"Did he fight in the recent war?" Will asked.

"He did indeed," George confirmed. "But he fought with me."

"You know your father was very proud of you and your decorations that were awarded you for that affair," Will said. "What did you actually do?"

"Koos and I scouted the Boer positions and their commandos," George explained.

"Must have been bally difficult for you chasing after your mother's people," Will commented.

"It had its moments," George agreed. "But, here is the Rome train."

"George," Koos hailed from the crowd disembarking the Rome train. *"Hoe gaan dit man?"*

"Baie goed, dankie," George replied, then he went on to greet Anna and then introduce Federica and his uncle and aunt. *"Anna, so lekker om jou weer te sien. Kom ek stel jou Federica, my oom Will en tante Esme bekend."*

"Federica, molto lieto," Anna said, and then she added, turning to Uncle Will and Aunt Esme. "Pleased to meet you."

"You speak Italian, I gather?" Will asked.

"Only a little," Anna replied. "Koos has a much greater facility than I."

"It is wonderful to meet you both," Federica said. "George told me a little about his recent experiences. I am grateful to you, Koos, for keeping him safe and from harm's way. Which is your baggage?"

"It's over there," Koos said, pointing to two suitcases and a trunk.

"Marco, per favore?" Federica asked.

"Certo," Marco replied and went over to the porters and indicated where the car was. He soon had all the baggage loaded and then told Federica that he would go to the house and arrange for the baggage to be placed in the appropriate rooms.

"Now, shall we go?" Federica asked. "I thought we might take a short drive through Florence so that you may see a little of the city. Unless, of course, you are too fatigued from your journeys. George, would you mind going with Marco, so that there may be more room for us in this car?"

"Of course, perhaps Koos, you would like to come with me?" he asked.

"Fine," Koos agreed. "Anna, I will see you soon."

"Aunt Esme and Uncle Will, you are fine with a short tour of Florence?" Federica asked.

"It would be wonderful to see some of Florence," Esme said. "Unless you are too tired, Anna?"

"I am fine," Anna assured her. "I think it would be delightful to see the city."

"How was your trip, Anna?" Federica asked.

"The boat ride was long, but we were comfortable and did not suffer from any ill effects from the motion of the sea," Anna replied. "The accommodations were quite acceptable, and the food was surprisingly very good. We did meet an interesting man on the voyage, he had fought with the Italian Ricchiardi and had much to say about the war."

"Which side did this Ricchiardi chap fight on?" Will asked.

"He fought for the Boers," George replied. "There was a whole Italian brigade among the several brigades made up by foreign fighters."

"Where is this chap Ricchiardi now?" Will asked.

"He accepted an offer made by the Argentinians to go and settle the area known as Chubut," George explained.

"How is it that you have heard of this chap?" Will asked.

"Because he was very good," George replied. "He had a price on his head of £3,000, but he kept coming back."

"Why?" Esme asked.

"A girl, what else?" George laughed. "He married Myra Guttman, she is a niece of General Joubert, and her sister married Frikkie Eloff, who is the nephew of *Oom* Paul."

"You seem well-informed about all this," Esme commented.

"It was well to stay informed," George said. "It may have meant the difference between life and death."

"Well. I'm glad it's all over," Federica said. "Anna, were you not afraid when Koos was away with George?"

"I was," Anna admitted. "But I had faith that they would keep safe and that Koos would come back to me and the boys."

"You have sons, how many?" Esme asked.

"We have four scamps," Anna said. "They are with my parents at the moment."

"Heaven help your parents," George laughed.

"I'm sure that Anna's parents will be fine," Federica said. "Shall we go?"

"As you suggested, Koos and I will go with Marco," George said. "That will leave more room for you. We will see you at the house."

Federica drove into the city and pointed out the sights as she went. She was a good tour guide who knew her city well and was able to answer all the questions put to her. Esme and Will were a little uneasy about riding in the car, but Federica assured them that her driving was quite good and that most other road users would give way to her. Esme had not wanted to take the front seat next to Federica, so Anna was privileged to sit in the front and get a splendid view of all that they saw. Before the group tired of the sightseeing, Federica brought them to the house and drew up by the front door. Marco was waiting with George and Koos, and he took the car to the stable yard while Federica escorted the guests into the house and introduced them to the members of the household. She then showed them to the rooms they would be using and told them that dinner would be served at eight and that dressing for dinner, such a British tradition, would not be necessary.

"How was your trip with Koos?" Federica asked George.

"We talked about his farm, his ostriches, how the boys are growing and what is happening in South Africa," he replied.

"All is well with them?" she asked.

"According to Koos, everything is well with the family, and his farm is now recovering from the depredations of the war," he replied.

"How did they afford this trip?" she asked.

"I assume that he sold some of the diamonds that he has left from those that his father collected years ago," he thought. "I know he had quite some left when I was with him. It was his guarantee of future security."

"The diamond that you gave me came from that same collection?" she asked.

"It did indeed," George agreed. "Koos gave it to me as a present when I left South Africa because I had told him that I would ask you to marry me."

"How big is their farm?" she asked.

"Big enough," he replied. "You can just about ride across it in two days."

"It must be huge!" she exclaimed.

"Not particularly," he said. "There are many farms larger, but size does not imply that much can be made from the animals or crops; much is fairly arid and not particularly fertile, worse than the hill country land we have in Scotland and the Lake District."

"I would like to go and visit one day," she announced. "Do you think that would be possible?"

"Of course," he said. "Unfortunately, it takes some weeks to get there by boat, so it may interfere with our Sirius venture."

"Let's think about it when we have a factory running and good managers in place," she suggested. "Perhaps four or five years from now, we can leave Nastia in charge and you can show me the places you went on your missions."

"Those are places that are less than attractive," he laughed. "But, there are places that I would like to show you."

"Including the town where you were born?" she asked. "And the town that your mother came from."

"Beaufort and Renoster Kop?" he replied. "Beaufort has little that would attract, unless you like sheep, and Renoster Kop even less."

"Still, I would like to see, didn't you say that the railway ran through there?"

"It does," he agreed. "If we were to take a train from Cape Town north, then we could stop in Beaufort, take an excursion to Renoster Kop and then on to Oudtshoorn to see Koos and Anna and then proceed on to Johannesburg."

"Capital," she said. "It will be an adventure to anticipate."

Christmas Day, the day of the wedding, dawned clear but cold, and the household was up early to be ready for the ceremony. Federica enlisted the help of her mother and her sisters to get ready, mainly to be politic and avoid any complaints. George went off to the church early in the company of Koos and Anna, Will and Esme and Sophia and Anastasia. The Beretta family followed, and Federica and her father went last. The family cars were busy shuttling back and forth to take the various waves of family members to the church. Federica had schooled George about the ceremony and the mass that went with it, so that he was prepared. She had no doubt that everything would proceed without issue and just wanted it to be over quickly, but, nothing happens quickly in Italy and in the Church, so it was late morning, almost lunchtime before the wedding party arrived back at the house for the reception that followed. Cook and her staff had prepared a feast for all comers and it seemed to the new Mrs Wheelwright that there was enough food to satisfy half of Florence. She had anticipated much of this, but the reality of seeing the mountains of food and wine was still a shock. Federica allowed her mother to play hostess, and she stayed as it were on display with George for all the wedding guests to see and talk to. It was not until quite late that night, before everyone had gone, that the family was left in peace.

Then the ribald comments started from Franco and the sisters, who were pushing Federica and George towards what had been designated as the bridal chamber. As the comments were all in Italian, many were lost upon George, but all were heard and appreciated by Federica, who gave as good as she got to the hilarity of the family. Finally, she and George were ushered into the bridal chamber, and the door was shut.

"Finally," she said to George. "It's been a long day, help me out of these clothes, will you?"

"Willingly, *mia stella*," he said. "I see that someone has prepared a bath."

"Yes, I asked for that," she told him. "But come, hurry up, I want you in the bath first and then again in the bed. We must keep up appearances and satisfy the household that we have consummated the marriage, even though we dispensed with that particular ritual some time ago."

"And such a pleasure it was too," he said, reminiscing.

"*Bene, mio marito*," she said when they were in the bath. "*Ho voglio di te. Ti voglio anima e cuore!*"

"*Sei la più bella donna nel mondo*," he said, exhausting his knowledge of Italian amorous compliments.

"*Ancora*," she whispered in his ear. "*Ancora. Non fermare!*"

"*E tanto buono*," he whispered back, and so it went with water splashing out of the bath onto the floor until they both shuddered with the final release and clung to each other, relaxed and happy.

"Take me to bed," she suggested. "Then we can do that again."

"For you, my love, anything," he promised. "Will we clean up the floor?"

"I think not," she said. "Let the maids clean up in the morning and report back to the household that you consummated our marriage with energy and thoroughness. That should satisfy everyone."

The next morning at breakfast, Federica and George were greeted with smiles and sly grins from the rest of the family. George missed most of the passing comments, but Federica heard enough to wonder what had gone on the night before. She discovered later in the morning when she caught two of her nephews up on a ladder, removing a string from the ceiling of the room under their bedroom. She took them by the ears and interrogated them and learned that they had attached a string to the underside of their bed and had fed it through a small hole in the floor and had attached a small bell to the end of the string. Any movement in the bed was telegraphed via the string to the bell. So it was perhaps not surprising that she and George had been greeted with sly grins and comments, their nocturnal activities had been witnessed by all. She decided to just leave the subject and let the family have their fun. George, at least, had now a solid reputation with her brother and father and all the nephews and brothers-in-law, and who was she to gainsay that. She recalled with some amusement her comment to George the night before about the maids cleaning up and reporting back to the household, which was now rather moot as the household had had a ringside seat, so to speak. She made a comment to her mother and learned that her mother had discovered what was going on and had berated all and sundry, including her own husband and had shooed them from the room and then locked the door but not before observing for a few minutes and satisfying herself that George was indeed performing his husbandly duties.

The new Mr and Mrs Wheelwright stayed only three more days in Florence before setting off back to England. Federica was now keen to get back and start work on their project. The Wedding was now behind her, and she could devote all her energies to the task at hand and finish the design of her first car and set about constructing the factory or factories that would be required for production. Uncle Will and Aunt Esme travelled back on the same train as did Koos and Anna, so it was quite a party that they made, and the dining car was noisy and cheerful with their conversation and laughter. Anastasia had not fallen for any of the Italian cousins, not for want of trying on their part, but because they tended to treat her as a girl with little business acumen or knowledge of world affairs, and that offended her. So, no matter if she found at least two of the cousins passably attractive, she could not get over the fact that they did not see her as an equal, and she was not prepared to be seen as anything but equal or superior.

Crystal Palace

England for Koos and Anna was all new and exciting, the weather might be dreary and cold, but it was nowhere near as cold as it would be for Scott, Shackleton and Wilson, who were journeying south towards the pole and who reached as far south as 82 degrees on that day. England was so different to the Cape Colony, everything was close, towns and villages and hamlets were not scattered far and wide as they were in the African veldt, there were roads aplenty and railways and canals, and the place was teeming with people. Koos commented to Anna that if he lived there he would feel hemmed in by his neighbours and would miss the wide expanses of the Karoo and the feeling of spaciousness that was part of the Cape, but for all that, he was still excited to be there and to see for himself where the British came from and wonder how such a small place could have expanded to control such a large empire.

Henry had laid on additional carriages at the Bourne End station so that all could be transported to the house at Hedsor. The trip up the hill was made in the light rain that was falling, and it was almost dark when they arrived. Eleanor had aired out the rooms in anticipation of the return of the family and the visitors. She was delighted to have them all back and wanted to hear all about the wedding and events in Italy. Sophia gave her a detailed account, and then they settled into the planning for a reception to be given for family, friends and neighbours who could not journey to Florence.

Dinner interrupted this planning, and Sophia promised to resume in the morning. Over dinner, Federica asked Koos and Anne about cars in South Africa. Koos had seen some and was keen to learn more and perhaps buy one for himself.
"What cars are there now?" Federica asked him.
"The first to arrive was a Benz," he replied. "That went to Pretoria but was destroyed by fire after only a few months."

"What happened?" she asked.

"I don't know," he admitted. "But the fire did not deter people from investigating cars and buying them."

"Are all the cars from Benz?" she asked.

"No, we have some French cars from Darracq, some Italian cars, and there are those that are looking towards America," he replied.

"What kind of car would you like?" she asked.

"One that keeps us sheltered from the weather," Anna said. "We may have sunshine for many months, but we do get rain and sometimes snow, so I would prefer some shelter."

"I have very much the same prejudices," Federica said. "I cannot abide being cold and wet, and the clothing that we manufacture and sell for the motorist is among the best, but it still does not protect one as well as I would like."

"You make clothes?" Anna asked.

"Yes, we have a factory for garments," Federica confirmed. "We added a line of clothing for the motorist about a year ago, and sales have been brisk."

"When might you have a car ready for sale?" Koos asked.

"Not for a little while yet, Federica apologised. "We have yet some work to do with the design, and we have factories to build."

"Could you not build some in the coach house?" George asked.

"Not in the coach house, but at the foundry in the building that Fox has cleared out," Federica replied. "But they would be mainly for testing purposes. Building at the foundry would not tell us what we need to know about building in large numbers."

"If you were to build some at your foundry, could I take one for road testing in the Cape?" Koos asked. "We would send back comprehensive reports of performance and reliability."

"That is a capital idea," Federica agreed. "When do you depart for South Africa?"

"We have passage booked in two weeks," Anna said.

"We cannot have a car ready so soon," Federica said. "But, perhaps in a month, we will have our first test models. Could we ship one to you in the Cape?"

"That would be really exciting," Anna said. "We would journey to Cape Town to meet the boat and then drive home, that is, of course, if you could teach Koos to drive."

"Why not you?" Federica asked.

"Oh, I couldn't," Anna protested.

"Why not?" Federica asked. "I drive, as do Nastia and Sophia; we even taught George how to drive."

"Oh, do you think I could?" Anna asked.

"Of a certainty," Federica promised. "Nastia can teach you both in the time you have remaining here. She is the best teacher we have and is most patient and understanding, she must be, for she taught George!"

"Oh, that would be *baie lekker*," Anne said. "When may we start?"

"Tomorrow," Anastasia said. "Tomorrow I will explain the controls to you, and because you will be far away from us and probably any help, I will also explain how the car works and show you basic repairs."

"What fun!" Anna said. "Will we have the first car in Oudtshoorn, Koos?"

"Probably," he laughed. "I can only imagine how the *dominee* will react; he'll probably want to exorcise the demons from it and will condemn us to a life of perdition."

"The what we must do is convince the *dominee* that he should be among the first to buy a car, that way he could better minister to his flock," Anna suggested.

"I like that idea," Koos said. "So Nastia, when do we come?"

"Tomorrow?" Anastasia reiterated.

"Tomorrow, yes," Anna confirmed.

For the next week, Anastasia spent her time instructing Anna and Koos, first on the basics of internal combustion and then on the practicalities of driving cars. Federica spent her time closeted with George preparing the final designs of their car and then sketching out the kind of factory she envisaged and working on the assembly of the engine parts that had been made. She also made arrangements for hotels near Sydenham, within easy drive of the Crystal Palace Exhibition Hall. They had another week before Anna and Koos left to return to the Cape Colony and another week beyond that before the Motor Show, so time was passing and there was much yet to do.

"Which car do we take to go to the show?" George asked her after dinner one night.

"I think the Daimler," she replied. "It is comfortable and we all four can go in one car."

"What do we need to study at the show?" he asked.

"I just want to see how designs are progressing," she thought. "I want us to pay particular attention to the coachwork styles and manufacture."

"You are looking at a closed-in car?" Anna asked.

"We are," Federica confirmed. "But the problem that most car builders face is that the coachwork is done by coachbuilders, and they take time, inordinate amounts of time. It is probably the governing factor in the length of time it takes to build a car. Engines, axles, the frame and other parts can be done quite quickly, but the coach builders have their own time, built on years of tradition, and they are unlikely to change quickly."

"We already have engine castings and the pieces to build up several complete engines," Anastasia added. "The foundry has been producing parts for Sirius, and they are quite acceptable."

"Are they all the same?" George asked, remembering what Federica had said about the necessity for interchangeable parts.

"They are," Anastasia assured him. "Mr Fox complained a little at first about the time to prepare the moulds and then the machining that we specified afterwards, but even he is quite proud of the parts he is now producing and is looking to see how he might improve other products and reduce the amount of time his people have to spend making things fit together."

"Have you built an engine yet?" Koos asked.

"We have," Federica confirmed. "It is on a stand at the foundry. Perhaps tomorrow we might all watch a test?"

"What fun," Anna said. "Have you tried it at all yet?"

"I have," Federica said. "There is a need for some adjustment to the carburetion system, but that is only a minor matter. What we need, George, is a dynamometer, perhaps one of the Heenan and Froude models. That way, we could apply the output of the engine to the device and measure what we are achieving from it."

"You should buy one, my Love," he said. "We can afford it, can we not?"

"We can indeed," she said. "We need a facility in which to install it, perhaps that building adjacent to the mould-making facility at the foundry would be suitable, what do you think, Nastia?"

"Yes, but you mentioned the coach builders before," Anna interrupted. "How are you going to deal with that?"

"We will build a new and different kind of factory," Federica replied. "We have some different ideas about how to make the coachwork, and it will be simpler, use materials that are new and novel and which will enable us to build the body of the car in a day or so, instead of the months it now takes."

"There is so much to all this," Anna wondered. "How do you keep it all in order in your mind?"

"It is not so complex," Federica assured her. "It takes only a short while to become acquainted with all the parts and what is required to put them all together. After we start production, will come the challenge of ensuring that we have enough of the various parts to produce cars with no waiting for the one part that we really need. That will take some thinking, but I am sure it may be done."

"Well, I wish you luck in your endeavours," Koos said. "When may you have time to visit us in Oudtshoorn?"

"George and I have talked, and we think that perhaps in five years we may be sufficiently well-positioned to leave everything in the capable hands of Nastia and come a calling," Federica replied.

"Come around Christmas time when it is warm, not in July when we may even get snow in the mountains," Anna said. "George can tell you how unpleasant it can be in those midwinter months."

"So, it is settled then, Christmas 1907, we will be there," Federica said. "Now, if you will excuse me, tomorrow I intend to start building the first of our cars, and I need some rest!"

Federica and George drove the next day to the foundry to start on their first car. Mr Fox had cleared space in one of the buildings adjacent to the main foundry, and there he had also stored all the materials that had arrived over the past weeks. Federica asked for two men to help, and

Fox called off two of the younger apprentices to be her helpers. Mr Fox went with them to the building, and they all stood around the stand that had the car engine. Fox had set up a stand close by with a tank on it for petrol, and he told one of the apprentices to fetch a tin of petrol and pour it into the tank. That done, Federica set the controls and then nodded to George to swing the handle and start the engine. She noted with amusement that Fox and his two apprentices stepped back away from the engine stand, almost behind a column.

"It works," Fox said, a little in wonder, coming out from his hiding place. "It works and sounds good, does it not?"

"It does indeed, Mr Fox," Federica agreed. "You have done an excellent job with the castings and the machining, the parts went together easily, and I had to do no hand finishing or filing. I am most pleased."

"I confess that I had doubts," Fox admitted. "I had been labouring under the prejudices that ladies might not be capable of understanding castings and the functioning of such a complex device, I realise now that it is not a matter of one's gender, but of one's intelligence and knowledge. How may I be of further assistance?"

"Well, it would appear for the moment that we have a workable design for the engine. We'll leave it running for a while to see if there are any issues when it heats up," she replied. "What we will need next is a plan to increase production without sacrificing the quality of the job you have done on these parts. Do you have some ideas for that?"

"I have given the matter some thought. Perhaps when you are done here, we might discuss my ideas?" he replied.

"That would be quite agreeable," she said. Mr Fox then left to attend to the normal duties of the foundry manager, and the apprentices looked to Federica for instructions.

"And you are?" she asked them.

"John, Ma'am, and this is Thomas," was the reply.

"Fine, would you set up a stand over here and then fetch those two long channels that are over there by the wall?" she asked. John and Thomas fetched and carried until all the major pieces were where Federica wanted them, and then she started marking out locations where she wanted holes drilled and cross members and brackets mounting. She gave them each jobs to do, then she asked George to move the back axle to another bench. Before she could do more, Anastasia arrived with

Koos and Anna. They were there to see the engine test, and Federica was happy to show them. Anastasia listened with a critical ear, but she could find nothing to complain about and was as pleased with their progress as Federica. Koos and Anna both looked on in amazement that someone in their family had designed and created such a thing.

"What else do you need to build a car?" Anna asked. "Are all those bits and pieces part of it?"

"They are," Federica confirmed. "Some, like this axle here and those wheels there, we purchased already made; other parts, like the frame and the springs, we will make up ourselves."

"How long before it is ready?" Koos asked.

"In another two days, we should have everything together and working, except for the coachwork," Federica replied. "We will probably add a simple structure for seats for now and perhaps a cover to keep out the elements, and then we will run some tests on the road."

"When will you have coach work?" Anna asked.

"I have a project for that," Anastasia replied. "I have a small workshop near here where I am trying different kinds of materials and designs to get a simple body for the car that will be weatherproof, not weigh too much, nor cost too much."

"That sounds like a big challenge!" Anna said.

"It is," Anastasia agreed. "But it is a challenge we have to solve so as not to be held hostage to the conventional methods of coach building that will then govern how long it takes to build a car."

"I had no idea there would be so much involved," Anna commented. "It must cost prodigious amounts to do all this."

"There are costs," Federica agreed. "But, we have sufficient financing to take us through the period of development and into the first cars we would build for sale, and that would include the construction of some special factories for the assembly of the engine and frame and for the building of the body and then for the final assembly of the whole."

"Where will you build those factories?" Koos asked.

"We have recently acquired the land next to the foundry here, there are 15 acres that we may use for construction of buildings and for storing materials and we can extend the railway siding that comes from the Great Western main line to make it easier to bring parts in and ship finished cars out," Federica replied.

"Will that be enough?" Koos asked.

"I think so," Federica replied. "It may behove us to acquire the land to the west of us, towards the Taplow end of Burnham, in case we need more. In the event that we do not, we may always either sell or develop that property."

"How big do the factories need to be?" Koos asked.

"The Clément-Talbot company of Ladbroke Grove has been talking to an architect about a new factory in London," Federica replied. "I saw the preliminary sketches and he envisages a large, spacious factory with columns spaced every 35 feet or so in one direction and 38 feet in the other direction, with a total of 120 bays in all, each 35 feet by 38 feet. I think the architect will spend more time on the façade of the building, which may well be quite grandiose, rather than the layout of the factory, which will probably be quite traditional."

"Will that be large enough for you?" Koos asked.

"I think it would be more than adequate," Federica confirmed. "The Talbot people will probably build their cars in the traditional way by bringing parts to assembly stands. I plan to do something different."

"In what way?" Anna asked.

"In our biscuit factory, the biscuits flow down a line, and we add fillings and icing at certain places in the line. Why not do the same with the car?" Federica asked.

"I suppose," Anna thought. "How would that work?"

"Well, suppose we make some little carts, put the frames on the carts and then push them down the line to the next place where we fit the engine, then push it down the line to the next place where we add the gearbox and so on?" Federica posed.

"Can you do that?" Koos asked.

"Why not?" Federica countered. "Just because it has not been done yet, does not mean that it does not make sense. If we look at other industries, people are always doing things that seem odd at the time, but that eventually make sense. In the brick-making industry in the 1880's there was a man named Henry Chare, and he installed some continuous kilns to make bricks, when everyone else used batch kilns. The product was never as good as that from the batch kilns, but with time, that would have been corrected. Unfortunately, Chare sold his brick business and went back to furniture before he solved those problems, so we will never really know, but the thinking was sound."

"What would you do, make up the engine somewhere else and bring it to your assembly line?" George asked, intrigued now by the extent of his wife's thinking and research.

"Yes," she confirmed. "I envisage several sidelines where the main parts are built up and they all deliver to the main line in the way a river builds from its tributaries."

"Clever," Koos said. "Then you don't have benches full of stuff all over your factory, and when the car is done, it just rolls out the end."

"That's what I was thinking," Federica agreed. "The last things to be fitted would be the wheels, and then the car is ready to go. The little carts we would wheel back to the start, ready to be used again."

"Does all this have to be in one long line?" Koos asked.

"Probably not," Anastasia said. "We've sketched various possibilities, and we're thinking perhaps of a U shape with the various other lines around the edges."

"Could you do the same thing with your coach factory?" Koos asked.

"I don't think so," Federica said. "The concept only works if the parts fit when they reach the right place in the line. Any fitting or filing that has to be done delays everything, so the secret is to make the parts all the same so that they fit immediately. Most of our coaches, carriages and wagons are built to order, so they require much custom hand work."

"Will this take lots of people?" Anna asked.

"That remains to be seen," Federica said. "We will need people to put together the various parts and deliver them to the assembly point. I think we will start with few people and then add when and where we see problems and delays."

"But does that mean ten to start with or a hundred?" Koos asked.

"I think to start, perhaps fifty," Federica replied. "I anticipate that with sales of cars, we will have to add people to increase production."

"How will you sell the cars?" Anna asked. "You can hardly have a shop where people walk in and just buy one."

"Why not?" Anastasia laughed. "Just like a bakery, you walk in and, if you have enough money, you drive out. But that is something we want to investigate further when we go to the Crystal Palace Motor Show later this month, just how are all the makers of cars selling their wares?"

"I almost wish we had booked passage on a later sailing," Koos said. "I would have been intrigued to see this Motor Show. But, we need to return, first to rescue Anna's parents from our boys and second to attend to the farm. We cannot really stay away any longer."

"I will send you a programme," Anastasia promised. "And I will make notes and give you my thoughts and impressions of the show and the people exhibiting."

"That would be wonderful," Anna said. "Then, when we get one of your Sirius cars and people see it, we may compare it to others with some exactitude."

"We've taken up far too much of your time," Koos apologised. "We really should let you get back to your work."

"It's fine," Federica assured them. "John and Thomas have been busy while we have been conversing, and I think now is a good time to give them their next jobs."

"We'll see you at home later, Fede," Anastasia said. "Don't be too late!"

"I won't," Federica promised. "It is still getting dark early, and I have no real desire to drive home in the dark if it is not necessary."

Two days later, Federica came home after a day at the foundry, driving their first Sirius car. The bodywork still left much to be desired, but the car ran! The family and the household staff all assembled outside to look over the car and were delighted with what they saw.

"When might we have a nice top to the car?" Sophia asked. "This one does rather look like a box perched atop the chassis."

"I have three possible solutions," Anastasia said. "We plan to try them all over the next week and see which is easiest to fit and which looks the best."

"How does it run?" George asked.

"Well enough," Federica replied. "The engine runs well, and we seem to have settled on a good combination of gears. It will be interesting to see how much the added weight of the top changes the performance."

"A pity we leave tomorrow," Koos lamented. "I would have liked to have seen the finished car."

"We will send you a photograph," Anastasia promised. "But tomorrow we will take a short break from building cars and all come to the docks to see you off on your way."

"You are taking the new boat from London?" Sophia asked.

"We are indeed," Anna confirmed. "The SS Ionic makes her maiden voyage to New Zealand tomorrow from London. She will stop in Cape Town, then go to Hobart and finally Wellington."

"The Ionic is of great interest to us because it's a refrigerated ship for transporting meat from New Zealand," Koos said. "If we could get lamb onto a boat like that, we could also ship to England without having to worry about spoilage."

"I suppose the New Zealanders have the boat to themselves," Anastasia commented. "Still, from the passengers' point of view, if it's a maiden voyage, the service should be good as they will be trying to attract passenger business. How many passengers will it take?"

"I think a little over 650," Koos said. "I'm not certain, but when I booked our passages we were offered three classes of cabin on the boat and I seem to remember numbers of passengers between six and seven hundred all told."

The morning of the following day, the 16th of January, found the whole family on the train to London to see Koos and Anna off on their voyage south to Cape Town.

"One day I would like to visit the Cape," Anastasia announced as they found their seats. "I would like to take an expedition and see the wild animals in their natural habitat. Regent's Park is nice and all, but I think the animals would act differently if they were not caged and behind bars."

"We could arrange that," Anna said. "If you decide on university, then perhaps during your summer months you could come and see us and we could show you animals."

"Are there then animals near you?" Anastasia asked.

"There are," Anna confirmed. "We would not have to take you far from the town to see all manner of antelope and other animals."

"I would like that," Anastasia said. "Perhaps by then you will also have one of our cars and we can explore together."

"We will," Anna promised.

"Take a gun with you," George commented. "And take warm clothes, it can get unpleasantly cold in the mountains in August and September."

"I suppose that would be wise," Anastasia said. "I presume that you are well equipped, Anna?"

"We are," Anna assured her. "George tells me that you shoot well, so we would be well protected. Can you ride a horse?"

"I can indeed," Anastasia assured her. "I cannot claim the level of skill that George has, but am confident that I would not in any way hold you back."

"When will you have your car finished?" Koos asked.

"I think in a week or so," Anastasia replied. "Federica gave me the hard job of working out the seats and the tops for the car. I have three designs ready to try, and when we have settled on the best, then I need to work out how to produce the tops at the same rate as we build up the rest of the car."

"Will you take your car to the Crystal Palace show?" Koos asked.

"Not this year, but definitely next year," Federica replied. "We want to be sure that it runs well and the top we put on is sufficient to protect from the elements, so we plan some trials, perhaps even one of the distance trials that are being run now."

"Would you enter a Sirius car in one of the races?" Koos asked.

"They are not really suitable for racing," Federica said. "If we were to build a racing car, then we would change the engine and keep the body to the bare minimum to give the driver some protection, but not a complete top. All the extra weight for comfort would just be dead weight to carry that would do nothing for speed."

"We might build a special sporting version for Mama," Anastasia said. "Then she could satisfy her dream of emulating Dorothy Levitt and scorching everywhere."

"I don't scorch everywhere," Sophia said, trying to sound indignant. "I only give the appearance of scorching to provoke Constable Platt."

"Well, here we are at Paddington," Federica said. "George, will you arrange for cabs to take us to the docks?"

After Koos and Anna had departed on their voyage south, the rest of the family spent time touring the various showrooms for cars that they found in London. They wanted to see how the cars were displayed and how they were sold. The tour was instructive, and Federica and Anastasia spent most of the journey home planning their own showroom. What they had not decided upon yet was where that showroom should be, adjacent to the factory or in London or another town. Slough did not attract too many people as visitors, so perhaps London would be better. That did mean either buying or leasing premises in London, preferably close to one of the underground railway stations, for easy access. Sophia said that she would look into that and perhaps buy a property herself and lease it back to the car company. She thought that she would also investigate the possibility of a flat above a showroom, so that she could achieve two aims with one purchase, a flat for herself and Anastasia while Anastasia was at university and a suitable showroom. George wryly remarked to Federica later that it was also a clever way to have the expenses for a London flat paid for by the company. The Sirius Car Company had just been floated, with a capitalisation of £50,000, with shares at par of £1 and the shares were oversubscribed. Now they had to decide how to award shares to the various subscribers and how they would maintain control of the company. It was amazing to George that so many people were willing to bet money on a company that had yet to publicly display a car and for which sales were probably six months to a year away. The prospectus that Federica and Anastasia had written was a masterpiece of literature, not quite fiction, but offering a tantalising view of potential car production and sales. In the end, Federica decided that she, George, Anastasia and Sophia would each take 15% and she allotted her father 10% as promised, and the balance was divided among subscribers until the shares were all gone, on a first-come, first-served basis. All that remained now was to actually build some cars and sell them to prove the projections included in the prospectus.

Mr Baker of the firm of solicitors duly visited the house with new share certificates in various companies that now reflected the ownership of Federica Giovanna Wheelwright. Federica was delighted, but would have been less delighted if she had heard Mr Baker expressing his misgivings about the transfer to George. George explained as carefully and politely as he could to Mr Baker his reasoning, but realised that for some people, the idea of women owning businesses and conducting their own affairs was still difficult to accept, even though the 1882 Act had addressed that legally. Legality outside the law courts was of interest but typically had yet to have a significant impact upon common practice and custom.

On January 29th, the family motored in the Daimler to Sydenham and their hotel. It was then only a short distance to the Crystal Palace centre where the Motor Show would be held. They were all excited to see what might be on display and how the various cars and services were shown; it would help them design their exhibit for the following year. The show was scheduled to run from January 30th until February 7th, and they had allowed themselves three days, assuming that would give them time enough to examine all the exhibits.

The opening of the first Automobile Show of the newly formed Society of Motor Manufacturers and Traders was greeted with great enthusiasm by thousands of people who had journeyed down from London and from the surrounding towns and villages. Judging by the number of visitors, the exhibition would be a success. Federica and family went in via the main entrance, then stood and looked at the spectacle in front of them. To either side, the great Crystal Palace stretched hundreds of feet and the open space was taken up with stands displaying cars, clothing, accessories and parts. Federica consulted the catalogue she had and led the way to her left down the aisles, starting with the stands of the publishers of various magazines and booklets, interspersed with stands for car frames and parts. Opposite those stands were those of car companies, including Edge, De Dion, Germain, Auto Carriage, Wilson and Pilcher and many more. When they came to the stand of the Straker Steam Vehicle Company, Anastasia reminded them that it would be prudent to stop and get information, as they were considering the purchase of several steam lorries.

"Good morning, Miss," a representative greeted her. "What might we interest you in today, perhaps something in your colour to match your dress?"

"We have been considering the purchase of several heavy lorries lately," she replied. "Perhaps you have some information?"

"If your father would like to call upon us, we would be happy to acquaint him with our products," the representative said archly.

"Listen, my good man," Anastasia said. "I am in the market for up to seven heavy steam lorries for my company."

"What company would that be?" the representative asked.

"To whom am I providing that information?" she asked.

"I am William Fields, the Sales Manager for the Straker Company," was the reply.

"Very well, Mr Fields, I am Anastasia Wheelwright of the Handy Cross Company. We currently run a fleet of twenty-five traction engines, none of which is a Straker, and I am thinking that perhaps Foden or Thornycroft would give us a better reception."

"As you wish, Miss," he said, turning away from her to talk to a man who had come onto the stand.

"Idiot," Anastasia said to the rest as they walked away from the stand.

"You surely expected something like that?" George asked.

"Why?" she retorted. "This is 1903, not the Middle Ages. Women do actually participate in the economy."

"Yes, they do," he agreed. "But for many men, the idea of women running companies and making decisions is threatening; they see their power and control eroding.

"Well, when we get to Thornycroft, we'll see," she said. "You would think that they would want to sell something."

"There are probably two problems with that," Sophia said. "First, I don't think many of the people here came to sell specifically, more to show their wares and raise awareness, and second, very few men expect women to have the authority to purchase anything beyond clothes and household items, certainly not heavy tractors and lorries."

"I suppose you're right," Anastasia conceded. "But when, when will it not be so?"

"I fear not for some time yet," George said.

"To change the subject a little," Federica interrupted. "Look at this car from Langdon-Davies. What do you think?"

"It has a chain drive," Anastasia commented derisively. "It is not the latest design, there are better here."

"That's very dismissive," George joked. "What is so bad about the chain drives?"

"The location of the chain impedes an intelligent design of the body," she replied. "It makes, by necessity, the body to be high from the ground. It is why so many early cars had access for the rear seats from the back of the car, like a horse carriage. If we are to have an enclosed body, we need to avoid chain drives and stay with gearboxes and drive shafts to the differential. We are here to see the latest, are we not?"

"We are indeed," Federica agreed. "Look, George, this is the stand of the Simms company. You may recall that Simms brought out a vehicle at the end of the Boer War that may have served you well if it had been available."

"I see they have mainly motors and ignition systems on display," he said. "Is any of that of interest to you?"

"It is," Federica confirmed. "Come, Nastia, we should look at their ignition systems."

After an extensive stay talking to the Simms people, they continued their walk of the halls, examining cars as they went and making notes of what they considered good and poor attributes. For George, it was a fascinating process; he was in awe of his wife and sister and their grasp of matters mechanical. He watched several times as Federica worked her magic and had representatives falling over themselves to be helpful. She had a gentler touch and was more willing to tolerate male egos and insecurities than Anastasia, who, with the zeal and passion of the young, could not understand why the men did not immediately see things from her perspective. George called a halt to the perambulations and announced that perhaps it was time to consider luncheon. The others agreed, and they repaired to the Grill Room situated behind the Photographic Court. Over lunch, Federica and Anastasia compared notes and made a list of particular car companies they wanted to see and then consulted the guide to see where they were.

"We will have to come back tomorrow," Federica said. "We will not have time today to see all that we wish."

"That's fine," George agreed. "We have the hotel for three nights, so there is no need to miss anything that you particularly wish to see."

"I would like to look at some of the clothing," Sophia said. "Where are they?"

"It looks as if they are concentrated in the group of stands numbering in the 220s, and they are all located in the Gallery," Federica replied. "Now, we need to determine how one accesses the Gallery."

"I will enquire," George promised. "Now, if I just pay the account, we can begin again."

The Gallery was located, and clothing examined by Sophia and George while Federica and Anastasia continued their tour of evaluation. They finally met at five in the afternoon to return to their hotel, all tired from the day and all in need of respite from the crowds. At the hotel, Sophia ordered tea and asked for the dinner menu.

"Aren't you a little premature, Mama?" Anastasia asked. "You have just ordered tea for us all, and yet you are examining the dinner menu."

"I wish to see what may be served so that I can decide what to eat now of these sandwiches and cakes," Sophia explained.

"Have you learned much today?" George asked Federica.

"I have indeed," she replied. "There are one or two items of our design that I think we will revisit, but generally, I would rate our car as equal to or better than most here. I have seen nothing here that makes me wish to totally reconsider our design, just small refinements that I think will improve the final design."

"What was the general response to you from the men on the stands, similar to the man from Straker, or more amenable?" George asked.

"I think generally the car people see a potential sale, whereas the heavy lorry people cannot understand why we would have any interest in their machines," Federica replied. "If I asked the car companies if Dorothy Levitt had ever tried one of their cars, they usually were happy to discuss racing and how their cars might perform. I think all men picture themselves as winners of some high-speed race."

"The Foden's man was nice," Anastasia said.

"That's because you fluttered your eyelashes at him and he succumbed to your charms," Federica said. "I told her to try a different approach than the one she had used with the Straker man," she told the others. "It worked, didn't it, Nastia?"

"You're right again, Fede," Anastasia complained. "I obviously have much to learn yet about bending men to my wishes."

"The trick is not to allow them to realise that they are being manipulated," Sophia laughed. "So they may preserve their vanity and yet still do what you wish."

"So, you manipulate me?" George asked of the three.

"Of course, *mio amore*," Federica confirmed. "How else would I be sure that you would marry me? You will, of course, be wary now in the future, thinking that you are being manipulated, but, of course, you will not know, so you may as well just surrender yourself to the inevitable and enjoy life as it comes."

"I will do that, *mia stella*," he promised.

"Well, I think I will bathe and change before dinner," Sophia said. "Nastia, are you coming?"

"Yes, Mama," she replied. "We will see you at dinner, then Fede."

At the dinner table, George brought up something that had struck him as they had wandered the halls, "With the new licensing laws, who has to license a car if it is purchased new?"

"I don't know," Federica admitted. "Nastia, do you remember?"

"No," she replied. "I know that the taxation, which is the car licence, is based upon weight, so we will need to determine what the final unladen weight of our car will be. I do not recall whether we should pay that before selling the car, or if the new buyer must do so."

"I would have thought that it would be the responsibility of the seller to ensure that the car is licensed before it leaves the showroom," Sophia suggested. "If we have cars built for testing purposes only, do we also have to license those?"

"Another good question," Anastasia agreed. "Clearly, I must read the Act again, but now paying closer attention to those points. When we were at the show today, did you notice if the cars had licences?"

"They did," George confirmed.

"As our licensing authority has an office in High Wycombe, perhaps it would be a good idea to visit with them soon and work out how we will manage this," Federica suggested. "I am supposing that we license all the new cars we sell, then when we make the actual sale then we inform the County Council of the name of the new owner. Perhaps we will need to buy blocks of licences monthly based upon our production."

"I confess that this is a subject I had not thought to investigate," Anastasia admitted. "I wonder if we would have any responsibility to ensure that a purchaser of a car has a driving licence?"

"This show is being staged by a manufacturers' association, is it not?" George prompted.

"It is," Federica agreed. "Of course, they will have already covered this. We will check with the show office tomorrow, enter our names for the show of 1904 and also ask about the licensing issue. We may also ask at the office of the Royal Automobile Club, they were very active in the work done to draft the Motor Car Act and will probably have the answers to these questions immediately to hand."

"Well done, George," Anastasia applauded. "Fede and I have been so concerned with the design and building of our car that we have missed the obvious, someone has, of a certainty, already addressed all those questions."

"So, I have my uses after all," George laughed.

"*Caro mio*, we will not be able to do this without you," Federica said.

"What else do we need to look at tomorrow?" Sophia asked.

"I think we should check with wheel and tyre suppliers," Federica suggested. "I have no desire to set up a wheel-making line at this time, but we should investigate if there is not a way to make wheels other than the artillery wheel or the wire-spoked wheels."

"I think we should take a closer look at the interiors of cars, perhaps look at seats, we could perhaps add an upholstery line to our garment factory and make seats ourselves," Anastasia suggested.

"I imagine the sewing techniques are similar to heavy outer garments," Sophia commented. "We would need to acquire the necessary sewing machines that are sufficiently robust to sew leather or other heavy fabrics. It occurs to me that it would be worth investigating who makes the seats for railway carriages, perhaps we could look at purchasing seat cushions from the same people."

"Perhaps tomorrow we should split up and each pursue a different goal?" George suggested. "If I register us for the show next year and also investigate the licensing issue, then perhaps the more technical issues can be better addressed by Fede and Nastia?"

"That is a good idea," Federica agreed. "Sophia, would you be amenable to investigating upholstery?"

"Of course, my Dear," Sophia agreed. "I presume that you and Nastia each have things you wish to check upon?"

"We do," Federica confirmed. "We have a list here of things we wish to check and will divide it between us. Let us each go our separate ways tomorrow and meet for lunch to check upon our progress."

"I have marked on this list those things that I will check tomorrow, if you will take the rest, Fede," Anastasia suggested.

"Fine," Federica agreed. "I look forward to tomorrow, George. Are you ready to retire?"

"Yes, my love," George confirmed. "Sophia, Nastia, will we see you for breakfast?"

"We will be here at eight," Sophia confirmed. "Have a good night."

The following day was one of specific tasks to be done rather than a general meandering around the show. Federica went off to look at gearboxes and axles and managed to charm representatives on those stands into giving her their undivided attention. She got specifications and prices for everything in which she had an interest and had to actually cut short her discussions with one axle company in order to keep her lunch date.

"So, how was your morning?" George asked her as she joined the others at a table in the dining room.

"Quite instructive," she replied. "I think we may have a source for axles that I like and will be looking at our costs for gearboxes to see which is most advantageous, our building or buying. What about you?"

"I have booked us space for the show next year, and we will be entered into the drawing to see which location we actually get," George replied. "As to the licensing issue the Motor Car Act says that when one registers a car with the local authority there will be a fee of twenty shillings and then added to that there is the annual tax, based on weight, that is two guineas for a car of less than one ton and four guineas for a car between one and two tons, that will paid at the Post Office. There is a facility for manufacturers with the local authorities, upon payment of an annual fee of three pounds, to have temporary licence plates for the purposes of testing and delivery; the only difference is that they have to be a different colour, so perhaps red letters instead of black. The Act appears to be silent on the subject of who licenses a new car. I rather think that the responsibility lies with the purchaser because there is a clause that refers to proceeding to the licensing office without plates, which is permissible."

"What about you, Sophia?" Federica asked.

"I have some ideas," Sophia replied. "A lot will depend upon how we decide to furnish seats in the car. If we make an appropriate frame, we can use ready-made cushions that we either make or we buy from one of the carriage builders. Many of the car companies seem to have opted for leather armchair-like seating, which is expensive. I think we can do as well with less expensive, simpler seats, similar to those of the first-class compartments of railway carriages."

"What are railway seats made of?" George asked.

"Typically, there is a frame, then spring cushions with horsehair stuffing and a covering of a heavy fabric, often patterned," Sophia explained.

"So, not so hard to make?" Federica asked.

"Not at all," Sophia assured her. "We would need to add appropriate sewing machines to our own factory, but I see nothing that we could not do."

"Perhaps it would be worthwhile looking at an upholstery business to acquire?" Anastasia suggested. "Then we would gain the knowledge to make the cushions and, in all probability, the equipment."

"I like that idea," Sophia agreed. "I will look into suitable companies. I think it would also be prudent to ask our Mr Fox who he knows in the railway carriage business and arrange a visit to one or more of them."

"I think that is a capital notion, Sophia. I will talk to him as soon as we return home. Nastia, how were your investigations?" Federica asked.

"I think our ideas for the body are different to anything I saw today," she replied. "We may well lead the industry if we are successful. One thing I did learn, quite by chance, talking to an American I met, was that some railways in America are experimenting with cladding wood with thin sheets of copper for the exterior of their carriages."

"That sounds interesting," Federica agreed.

"It does," Anastasia said. "But, I don't think we should get too diverted from our plan. Perhaps we could run some tests to see if it would give us a better result than our sandwich panels that we have settled upon."

"Is there anything else that we need to check on?" Sophia asked.

"I don't think so," Federica replied. "Perhaps this afternoon we should view those cars that are being demonstrated outside and see if it is possible for us to drive a few of them."

"A capital notion," Sophia applauded. "A pity that the course is so confined, it would be fun to see how fast we could get each of them to go."

"Mama, you're thinking of scorching again," Anastasia accused.

"Not really," Sophia said. "I just would like to have a little enjoyment."

"Then shall we return home tomorrow?" George asked.

"I have nothing else that I wish to see," Federica said. "Sophia?"

"Not I," Sophia added. "Nastia?"

"I could stay for days, but that would just be for the fun of touring the halls and checking every little thing," she replied. "But, I am satisfied that I have seen what I came to see, all else is entertainment."

"Fine, then we will return after breakfast tomorrow," Sophia said.

Interviews

The Crystal Palace Motor Show behind them, the family concentrated on getting a workable prototype car, complete with bodywork, and also set about finding people to run the factory they had planned. Federica replaced the basic frame of the car after she found cracks in the gussets and cross members; clearly, they had not designed it adequately. She also placed advertisements in the Times and various trade publications for a manager to run the assembly factory and another to run the body shop. Replies came a plenty, and then it was time to sort through the various letters they received and invite some for an interview.

"How many responses have we had to date?" Federica asked George.

"Forty-three," he replied. "That was as of Monday last."

"Are there any from women?" she asked.

"Not that I can discern," he said. "Perhaps there are one or two hiding behind initials rather than names, but I rather doubt it."

"How many of those do we ask to come for an interview?" she asked.

"I have a list of fifteen that I think we should see initially," he said. "It may be that I have missed some in my reading of their letters, but fifteen should give us a good sense of what we may find."

"We should retain the services of a secretary," she said. "I have no desire to spend hours typing letters to all and sundry."

"Where do we find a secretary?" he asked.

"I will ask Mr Fox if I can get one of the girls we have at the foundry," she said. "He seems to have a clever talent for finding bright young girls who can not only type but who can think for themselves."

"Is Fox interested in the job at the motor works?" he asked.

"No, I asked him and he declined," she said. "He loves the foundry business, and since we have been trying new casting and machining methods, he has become quite enthusiastic. I think we should change the ownership structure of the foundry and make him a part owner, so that he may benefit from his efforts in a different way than just receiving a salary."

"Should we do that for all the companies we own?" he asked.

"Not yet," she thought. "I'll talk to Nastia, perhaps Robertson from the biscuit factory, but I think we would need to look carefully at Edwards, and at Painter "

"I think Edwards is nice enough," George commented.

"Nice, yes, but not I think of the type to make his own destiny. He will run the company well enough, but would shy away from ownership and the added responsibility that he would see there," she thought.

"What about Painter?" he asked.

"Mr Painter has only been with us a few months, and although things seem to be improving nicely, he has yet to be tested in a softening of the market," she said. "Perhaps that will never happen, but we should look at him again in about six months."

"Well, we'll see them all again at the regular meeting next week," he said. "Perhaps we should look at them again with a view to offering some shares."

"We should indeed," she agreed. "Nastia and Sophia are both very good judges of our managers, and we should ask them for their views."

"Perhaps we could put an item on the agenda and ask them if any of them would have an interest in the position?" he suggested.

"I don't think that would be wise," she replied. "If they express interest and we don't offer them one of the positions, they might be disheartened, and we don't want that. Better, I think, to build up their confidence in the businesses they are currently running and see what we can do with them."

"Have you thought any further about the potential sale of either the tractor business or the coach builders?" he asked.

"Nastia and I have been over the various offers, and we are of a mind that we will not sell the tractor business at this time, but for Wright, we should seriously look at the offer of Marshalls of Croydon," she replied.

"And what of Mr Wainwright?" he asked.

"It is my understanding that they wish to add to their facilities and would want to keep Mr Wainwright in place," she explained.

"So, what's next?" he asked.

"We should meet with them and negotiate the terms of the sale," she replied. "It may be best if you take those discussions, Nastia and I will be present in the form of scribes, but will note all that they proffer and will advise."

"Good," he said. "I would not wish to try that on my own. You and Nastia have the knowledge of the business and have done all the work."

"I will send them a letter expressing our interest in pursuing their offer," she said. "Shall we say the 24th of this month to meet, and perhaps we should meet at the Reindeer Inn."

"Good idea," he agreed. "It's not far from the station and I'm sure that we can have an upper room for our meetings. While we think of that, perhaps we should also set our interviews at the inn. It would be more convenient than asking people to come here."

"I will do that," she said. "I will set the interviews, five a day, for the 25th to the 27th of this month."

"Who shall do the interviewing?" he asked.

"You, me and Nastia," she replied. "We need to be sure that whoever we retain is willing to work with me and Nastia. We also need you there so that they have the comfort of knowing that there is a man somewhere in this enterprise."

"How many of the possibles are from other car companies just trying to find out what we are about?" he wondered.

"We'll probably never know," she said. "But a good discussion of where they work now and where they have worked may reveal that, if it is a possibility."

The Marshall Carriage Company owner and entourage duly arrived at the appointed hour on the 24th and were greeted by George.

"Good morning, Mr Laird," George said. "I trust that your journey was uneventful?"

"Fine, thank you, allow me to introduce Mr Harding, my accountant and Mr Lancaster, my solicitor. I presume that I am addressing George Wheelwright, and may I be introduced to the ladies and gentlemen?" Laird responded.

"My wife, Federica and my sister, Anastasia and our solicitor, Mr Baker, and from our chartered accountants, Mr Archibald Jones of Leadbetter and Jones. Both my wife and sister have shareholdings in the company and have a keen interest in the proceedings," George explained.

"Good, let us to business," Laird suggested.

"Very good," George agreed. "May I offer you coffee or tea?"

"Coffee would be most welcome, thank you, Mr Wheelwright," Laird replied. "James, David, anything?" James Harding also asked for coffee, but David Lancaster declined. "Tell me, Mr Wheelwright, why are you selling the Wright Company?" Laird asked.

"We are embarking upon a new venture and have a need for the cash," George explained.

"There are banks that I am sure would be happy to extend you sufficient credit," Laird commented.

"That is true," George agreed. "But I have an aversion to bank debt, my father was a banker for many years and showed me the inner workings of banks and their lending practices, I would just as soon keep my dealings on a cash basis and use the banks for that purpose only."

"Fair enough," Laird laughed. "I have often thought that the only people the banks will lend to are those who don't actually need the money. So, there are no entailments on the Company and no debt?"

"There is always the matter of monies owed suppliers and employees, but beyond that, no, no debt and no entailments," George replied. "I have here the past accounts for the Wright Company, perhaps you would like to review them while I pour coffee. If you have any questions concerning the accounts, please address them to my sister; she will have the answers, and if she does not, then I am sure that Mr Jones will." That raised the eyebrows of the visitors, but after one or two test questions, the eyebrows went back down as they realised that she had their measure in every sense and had an encyclopædic knowledge of the company and the accounts. After an hour or so, Mr Laird sat back and remarked, "Well, that seems very satisfactory, let us to terms for the purchase."

"Before we proceed to that, please tell us why you have an interest in acquiring our company?" George asked.

"Fair enough," Laird agreed. "We've expanded our business to the limits of our existing premises. We have a choice of buying land and buildings and hiring more people, or acquiring a going concern with an existing place in the market and with existing competent managers. We know your Jack Wainwright and would be delighted to have him in our company."

"So, you would have no plans to reduce the number of people working at Wright?" Federica asked.

"Far from it, Mrs Wheelwright," Laird replied. "We have several large orders that are better suited to the equipment you have at Wright and would, in all probability, need to add to the number of people."

The negotiation of terms took a little while, probably because both solicitors were keen to show their respective employers how skilled they were in negotiation and their knowledge of company law, but finally, terms were reached to the satisfaction of all.

"Good," Laird said. "What's next, the transfer of money?"

"I agree," George said. "With whom do you bank?"

"We have an account with Barclays in London," Laird replied.

"Why don't we have Mr Baker meet your representative tomorrow in London at the bank, and upon receipt of a banker's draft, he will hand over the share certificates. Meanwhile, you and I can go to the factory and introduce you to Wainwright as the new owner?" George suggested.

"Good, I like that," Laird said. "Shall we say one in the afternoon then, that will give the solicitors and bankers time to execute the necessary papers, and then they can telegraph us notice of success, and we can proceed?"

"Excellent," George agreed. "Until tomorrow, then."

"Until tomorrow," Laird echoed. "Miss Wheelwright, if ever you have a falling out with your brother and are looking for employment, please call on me, I would be delighted to have you in my company."

"Thank you, Mr Laird," Anastasia said. "But, I think things between George and me are fine and are likely to remain so."

After the Laird party had gone and Mr Baker and Mr Jones had added some small suggestions to the process and then left, George turned to Federica and asked, "Well, how did I do?"

"Perfect *caro mio*," she said. "The only problem is that we have interviews set for tomorrow."

"Ah, forgive me," George said a little ruefully. "It slipped my mind. I know that you and Nastia can manage the interviews on your own, and I am curious to see how the interviewees will react to no man present."

"Let's see who is on for tomorrow at one," Federica suggested.

"I doubt that I will be gone long," George said. "I will introduce Laird to Wainwright, then leave, as Laird will be by then the owner, and I will have no further need to be there, so should be back here before two. Will you be finished by then?"

"I doubt it," she thought. "Good, it will give us the opportunity to see how he reacts to dealing with us, then dealing with you."

The first candidate on the list arrived just before nine the following morning and was shown to the room by the innkeeper.

"Good morning, Mr Williams," Federica said. "Please be seated, may we offer you tea or coffee?"

"Tea, please," Williams replied.

"Milk and sugar?" she asked.

"Both, please," Williams said.

"Allow me to introduce myself and my colleagues," Federica said. "I am Federica Wheelwright, the managing director of the Sirius Car Company. This is my sister in law, Anastasia Wheelwright, our chief designer, and this is my husband, George Wheelwright."

"Is this some kind of joke?" Williams asked. "There are no women car designers; what would a woman know of such things?"

"Thank you for your time, Mr Williams," Federica said, smiling a little. "George will see you out and compensate you for your travel expenses."

"That didn't take long," George said when he came back. "If they all are like that, this may be a difficult task."

"I expected some like that. What did he say when you took him out?" Federica asked.

"He wanted to know if it really was a joke, and when I disabused him of that notion, he wanted to come back for a chance of redemption," George replied.

"I assume that, as he is not here, you did not accede to that request?" Anastasia asked.

"No, I told him that he had had his chance and that perhaps on another occasion he might consider first what he says, before he actually says it," George explained.

"We'll see what the next one is like," Federica said.

"When is he due?" George asked.

"At eleven," she replied. "So what shall we do for an hour and a half?"

"Shall I leave the room and come back later?" Anastasia said, only half jokingly.

"As much as the prospect of a tryst in a strange inn with George is attractive," Federica began. "We must behave, the candidate may be early, what if he found us *in flagrante delicto*, that would hardly inspire confidence for the future!"

At eleven, a Mr John Forester presented himself, and the situation repeated itself. This was disheartening for George, but Federica and Anastasia told him that this was the kind of behaviour they had had to put up with their entire lives. They took an early lunch, and George excused himself after receiving the telegram that the monies for the Wright Company had been received and the share certificates duly handed over. So, it was Federica and Anastasia only who welcomed the next candidate a Mr Gerald Bishop.

"Good afternoon, Mr Bishop," Federica greeted him. "Thank you for coming today. I am Federica Wheelwright, the managing director of the Sirius Car Company, and this is Anastasia Wheelwright, our chief designer."

"Thank you for seeing me," he said. "I understand that you are looking for a factory manager to oversee production of a car?"

"We are indeed," Federica confirmed. "We have a workable design that we are testing at the moment and would like to start producing cars to sell."

"Is it possible to see this car?" he asked.

"By all means," Federica said. "It is in the stable yard of this inn, if you will come with me?"

They traipsed downstairs and out into the yard, where the car stood, resplendent in ultramarine.

"May I?" Bishop asked.

"Please do," Federica said. They watched as Bishop opened the engine compartment and quickly scanned over the works, then he crouched down and looked underneath the car, then climbed inside, finally he got out and announced, "Delightful, and you designed this, Miss?"

"I did indeed, together with Mrs Wheelwright," Anastasia confirmed.

"I resent this bare-faced lying and sham that you are trying to play upon me," he stated. "There is no woman who can possibly have done this; it displays thinking and concepts that are far too advanced for a mere slip of a girl. I wish to speak to the gentleman in charge."

"There is no gentleman in charge," George said from behind him. "My advice to you, friend, is to leave before I take the insults to my sister very personally. Here is five pounds for your travel expenses, I trust we will not meet again."

"Please," Bishop said back, backpedalling as quickly as he could, taken aback at the appearance behind him of a man who looked like trouble. "Try to understand my scepticism. Your sister must be a remarkable person indeed if that is her design."

"That is as may be," George said. "But to insult her is to insult me, and I don't take such insults lightly."

"Please forgive me, Miss Wheelwright," Bishop pleaded. "May I have a chance to redeem myself?"

"Give him the chance, George," Anastasia said. "We will see what he has to say. Let us return inside and continue this discussion."

Once inside, George left the interviewing to Federica and Anastasia. It turned out that Mr Bishop had a good understanding of engineering and something of manufacturing. But Anastasia was not going to let the comments about her design abilities rest. She put Bishop to the test, asking him about engineering concepts that left him spluttering at times, and she returned time and again to Bishop's attitudes towards women in industry and business and finally concluded that, sadly, he was just another victim of his own prejudices and fears. Although he was promising, she struck his name off her list. After he finally departed, Federica asked George something that had been nagging at her all during the interview. "Would you have hit Bishop?"

"Me, hit someone," George expostulated. "I would never do anything so crass."

"I truly have never seen you so cold," she commented. "You reminded me of my father once. I saw him in Hong Kong, deeply offended by something another trader said about my mother. That trader was never seen again."

"Yes, but that is the Italian way, *cara mia*," he commented. "We British would never be so bold; we would probably hire the Italians to do the job for us."

"Well, don't go telling my father or my brother," she said. "I don't want a blood feud on my hands."

"Perhaps the next man will be better," Anastasia said hopefully, but she was disappointed in not only the next but also in the last of the day.

"How were the interviews?" Sophia asked when they returned home.

"I think as Fede and Nastia expected," said George. "But, I confess to some disappointment in my fellow males. I had not appreciated the extent to which prejudice against women still reigns. I know that in the army we did not have women, but that is perhaps to be expected. I don't see combat as a place for women, no matter how emancipated they be, but I had expected things to be different in the business world, I should have thought more about it and would have realised that it is essentially the same class of person running the army and running our businesses and industries."

"We had one possible," Federica added. "But he blotted his copybook by saying that Nastia was only a mere slip of a girl and not capable of designing anything."

"He did compliment us on the design, though," Anastasia said. "He liked what he saw, but he could not accept that we did not have a man or two lurking in the background and doing the actual design."

"I suppose that that is good to know, that the design has its merits," Sophia said. "Perhaps tomorrow will bring better luck."

The candidates of the 26th were to a man dismissed early, with not one of them even briefly considered. Federica was beginning to despair that they would ever find anyone. The first man in on the 27th was a Mr Ian Stuart, a Scot who arrived well before the appointed hour. Federica suspected that he had actually stayed overnight at the inn.

"Mr Stuart, good morning," she greeted him and went through the ritual of introducing herself, Anastasia and George.

"Good morning," he echoed. "Did I hear aright that Miss Wheelwright is the designer behind a new car?"

"You did indeed hear correctly," Anastasia said.

"Wonderful," he said. "I canna wait to tell my daughter that she should not give up her dreams."

"You have a daughter, Mr Stuart?" Federica asked.

"I do indeed," he said quite proudly. "The lass is quite determined to study engineering and have a career in some related field, but until today, I had found little to encourage her."

"Tell us what you do today, Mr Stuart," Federica invited.

"I manage projects for Mirrlees Watson," he said. "As you may know, they are one of the best builders of machinery for the sugar industry."

"Would you like to see the car that we built?" Anastasia asked.

"I would indeed," he said. "What will I tell Kirsty? How long did the design take? How many successes and failures did you have before it worked?"

"The design took several months, " Anastasia explained. "But only because we examined the designs of four other cars before settling on our own. Does Kirsty design things now?"

"Oh, aye, she does," he confirmed. "The stable at our house is full of machines and tools of mine that she has used to create all kinds of devices. It is so much fun, but I had found little to encourage her."

"Well, here is our car," Federica said as they entered the stable yard.

"Well, isn't that nice," he said. "May I look further?"

"Please do," Federica said. They watched as he poked around the engine, peered underneath and opened the doors and sat in the seats. He was shaking his head as he emerged from the interior of the car.

"What is this bodywork made of?" he asked. "I canna place the type of material."

"It's a sandwich of different materials," Anastasia explained. "We tried to achieve strength without adding too much weight and also tried to standardise on the shapes and sizes so that we may assemble the body quickly, unlike the coach building styles used elsewhere."

"Brilliant, brilliant," he said almost to himself. "I can see an assembly shop, but you must have already thought of how you would design such a shop."

"We have a concept," Federica agreed. "If we were to come to terms on employment, we would want your views on the design and the first task would be to manage the construction of the shop."

"I built a car myself," he commented. "But I lack the wherewithal to do anything with the design."

"Come upstairs and tell us of your design," Federica invited. For the next ninety minutes, the conversation went around on his design and his thoughts and philosophies of manufacturing and engineering. Finally, George had to step in. "Mr Stuart," he interrupted. "Do you have to be somewhere tonight?"

"Not particularly," Stuart replied. "I was planning to take the night train to Glasgow later."

"Could you put that off until the night train tomorrow?" George asked.

"Oh, aye," Stuart agreed. "I would just need to telegraph my wife to let her know that I will be one day more."

"Why don't we do that?" George suggested. "I will arrange for a night here at the inn, and you could continue your discussions with Federica and Anastasia tomorrow. Would that be acceptable?"

"Oh, aye, fine, thank you, Sir," Stuart agreed.

"Fede, would you see the next candidate while I organise things with Mr Stuart?" George suggested.

"*Madonna,* look at the time," Federica said. "I got quite carried away there. Tomorrow, then, Mr Stuart, we will send a car to collect you at eight."

Of the next four candidates, there was a definite possibility for the body shop, a Mr Andrew Coates of Durham, so they asked him if he would also stay another day. Of the rest, there was one other who showed good promise, so they said that they would contact him soon, keeping him in reserve in case the other two did not work out. Sophia was delighted when they gave her the news that they believed they had found candidates for both positions and looked forward to meeting them the next day. "What do you propose to do tomorrow?" she asked.

"I thought we would send Henry to collect them at the inn, then we would meet them at the foundry and show them our test stand and the work that we have done," Federica said. "We would also show them Nastia's laboratory for experimenting with body materials, then come here for lunch, and after lunch, see if we cannot reach agreement with both to come and work for us."

"What are your views, Nastia?" Sophia asked.

"I am in agreement with Fede," she confirmed. "I thought yesterday that we would never find anyone, then today our luck turned, and we found three; it was most gratifying."

"George?" Sophia asked.

"I think Stuart turned it when he started talking about his daughter," he said. "He clearly has seen some of the same problems that Fede and Nastia face and is sensitive to them. He got quite enthusiastic about the car, and he's built his own car to boot!"

"He has?" Sophia asked. "Why is he not in business for himself then?"

"I think funds are the issue," Federica said. "We gather that he has six daughters, so costs at home are quite high. I would imagine that six girls between the ages of fifteen and five could be quite a financial burden."

"Poor man," George laughed. "To be plagued by seven women day in and day out."

"Well, you have three," Federica pointed out. "Six, actually, if you include Eleanor, Jane and Beatrice."

"I do, and it's a blessing," he said, realising that he had better say the right thing and not dig a hole for himself.

"Are you satisfied with the day?" George asked Federica later that evening after they had retired for the night.

"At the moment, yes," she confirmed. "We will see what tomorrow brings with the discussions with Stuart and Coates."

"Have you thought any more about the building that you want?" he asked.

"I have, I still think we should retain the services of Ethel Charles," she replied.

"Will you contact her or do you wish me to do so?" he asked.

"I will," she said. "I'll write to her on Sunday and see what kind of reply we receive. Now, *caro mio*, you have been neglecting me of late. I think it is time you returned to your husbandly duties!"

"I neglected you, I thought it was the other way around," he protested.

"No matter," she said. "It is time to remedy that. What do you propose?"

"Let me help you undress, and I will think of something," he suggested.

After breakfast the following day, Federica and Anastasia drove to the foundry where they met Messrs. Stuart and Coates. It seemed that they had breakfasted together and were on good terms, both excited to see what the opportunity for them might be. Federica showed them her test stand and the trial pieces she had, then Anastasia showed them her shop where she was running trials of various materials for the body. Then Federica took Stuart to look at more parts while Anastasia talked more to Mr Coates about the ideas she had for the bodywork. Coates was intrigued and asked question after question. Just before twelve, Federica came to get Anastasia and Mr Coates, and they drove to the Hedsor house for lunch.

"Welcome," George said as he greeted them at the door. "Please come in. Did you have a good morning?"

"Fascinating," Coates said. "I have worked with coach building and railway carriage building, but the concepts of Miss Wheelwright are very interesting and novel."

"I can see where my car design lacked," Stuart bemoaned, but only half-heartedly. "Your car is very advanced, and I see a potential for many sales."

"It will all depend on keeping our costs well under control," Federica said. "Much of that burden would fall upon you, Mr Coates. Many cars today have bodywork that costs as much as the rest of the car."

"That is true," Coates agreed. "But perhaps the greater problem is the time it takes to build a body for a car. That seems to me to be overly long."

"We agree," said Anastasia. "That is why we are looking at a completely different way of making the body. I want to do it in the same time as Mr Stuart would build the rest of the car, so that the final operation would be to mate one to the other, make the appropriate connections and fastenings and be done."

"Allow me to introduce Mrs Wheelwright," Federica interrupted as Sophia joined them.

"Good afternoon, gentlemen, I trust that you both had an interesting morning?" Sophia said.

"Fascinating," Coates said again.

"Yes indeed, fascinating," Stuart repeated.

"Shall we go in for lunch?" Sophia invited.

Over lunch, the conversation switched back and forth between cars and the lives of the two candidates. They learned that Stuart's wife was named Mary, they had already learned the name of the eldest daughter and learned that the other daughters were in order of age, Kathleen Mary, Susan, Elizabeth and Deirdre. They also learned that Mr Coates was not married but that he was courting Miss Mabel Lloyd, a well-known and successful actress. That he admitted was difficult as it was a long-distance relationship with her in London and he in Durham.

"So," Federica said after the luncheon, things were cleared away. "Do you have an interest in our enterprise?"

"Most assuredly," Coates said, and then Stuart chimed in with, "Aye, certainly."

"Perhaps you could take Mr Coates for a look at our other cars while I talk to Mr Stuart, Nastia? You have no objections, Mr Coates?"

"No, none at all, I understand completely," he replied.

After Coates had left with Anastasia, Federica got down to business quickly, "We are delighted that you came to see us, Mr Stuart and would like to offer you the position of General Manager of the Sirius Car Company with an annual salary of £1,200. We would like you to start as soon as possible. What period of notice would you need to give to your current employer?"

"Thank you, Madame, so much?" Stuart said. "That is considerable more than I currently receive."

"That is what we believe the position is worth," Federica said. "I have no desire to try and obtain people at less than reasonable salaries, it does not serve my purpose, I am looking for people who will dedicate themselves to the task at hand, and worries and concerns about meeting daily expenses should not be a consideration."

"In that case, Madame, I accept. I will need to give my current employer two weeks' notice. After that, I will be yours to command," Stuart said. "If I may ask, is there someone that you know who may help us find a suitable property that we may purchase? I will, of course, need to put our current house on the market for sale, but I have received several offers over the past year to purchase it, so do not anticipate any delays or problems there."

"We will provide an additional £150 as recompense for your expenses that you will incur in selling and buying properties and in moving yourself and your family to your new abode," Federica suggested. "And I will give the name of a reputable agent who will help you with your search here."

"I thank you, Madame, I have never heard of such generosity, except perhaps with some select senior civil servants," Stuart exclaimed.

"It is worth it to me to facilitate your move," Federica explained. "I would rather have you concentrate on our business than fret about the move and related expenses. Shall we say that you begin with us on Monday, the 16th of March?"

"That would be fine," Stuart agreed. "I will travel back tonight and tell my family the news, and then will give my notice on Monday morning."

"Why don't we reserve a room for you at the Reindeer for a week or so when you come in March, so that you will have a place to stay while you find a more permanent place to live?" Federica suggested.

"That would be most generous," Stuart said. "Might I ask for assistance in getting to the railway station later to catch the train to London?"

"We will arrange that, I have already booked you on the night sleeper to Glasgow, here are the reservation details, is there anything else that we need to discuss at this time?" she asked.

"There is one more thing," he replied. "My girls are all continuing their education, and three are currently at the grammar school level. Can you recommend a school that they might attend?"

"Unfortunately, our county has been dilatory when it comes to schools for girls, no matter what the recent Act may call for," Federica replied. "Your best option is the Halidon School for Girls in Slough, it has been going since the mid-1860s and has a reputation for excellence."

"I will certainly investigate the school when I return. Do you know the current headmistress?" he asked.

"No, but I would be happy to pay her a visit on your behalf," Federica promised.

"That would be most appreciated," he said. "Again, I thank you for this opportunity and will be here on the 16th."

"Splendid," she said. "Now, if you will excuse me, I should spend a little time with Mr Coates. Mr Wheelwright will settle up with you for your expenses in coming to see us these past two days."

After Stuart had left, Federica rang for Eleanor and asked for coffee. When George returned, she asked him how he thought things had gone.

"Perfect, *cara mia*," he said. "If Coates has a similar notice period, what do we need to do in the next two weeks to be ready when they arrive?"

"I think some office space," she replied. "We need space large enough for four offices, enough for Stuart, Coates, Nastia and myself, we need secretarial help for them, and we need some space to lay out drawings of buildings. Their first tasks will be to oversee the construction of their respective premises. I think if we get secretarial help for them, then I can turn over a lot of the mundane tasks that I have onto her, then when Stuart and Coates each get their premises built and staffed, then the secretary can stay with me as the secretary for our enterprises."

"Shall I find Coates?" he asked.

"By all means," she agreed.

When George returned with Anastasia and Mr Coates, Federica went through the same basic offer as with Stuart, but with a salary of £1,000.

"Thank you," Coates said, more than a little taken aback. "That is a significant increase from my current situation."

"I am looking for someone who will devote their energies to this job," Federica said. "You will have to first agree upon the layout of the factory with Miss Wheelwright, and then you will need to oversee the building of it and finally start up production. There will be much to do."

"I am looking forward to it, Madame," Coates said. "The prospect is most exciting, and I am eager to begin."

"Do you have a house to dispose of in Durham?" Federica asked.

"No, I rent at the moment and would rent here for a while until I decide where I may like to live," he replied.

"Well, to assist you in your travels, we will provide an additional £50 to help defray those expenses," she said. "Are you travelling to Durham tonight?"

"No," he replied. "Mabel is appearing at the Royal Princess on Oxford Street tonight, so I thought I would try and see the show and travel back tomorrow."

"I hope you enjoy the show," she said. "We look forward to seeing you soon. Mr Wheelwright will see you out and also recompense you for your travel expenses."

"Thank you again, I'm looking forward to the adventure," he said. "Good day, Madame."

"Well?" Federica asked George when he returned.

"I think we'll be fine," he said. "What do you think, Nastia?"

"I spent more time with Coates than Stuart, but I like them both, and Coates has ideas and enthusiasm; he is not constrained by his previous experience in the carriage business," she replied. "Are you happy, Fede?"

"I am," Federica confirmed. "Now we must look to getting some office space, but all that may wait until Monday, for the balance of the day and for tomorrow, I intend to be indolent."

"I wonder what is playing at the Royal Princess?" Anastasia said. "What fun that one day we might get to meet a famous actress. I wonder what it is about Mr Coates that attracts such a personage?"

"You might check the theatrical reviews in the paper and see what, if anything, is written about her," Federica suggested. "As to what attracts, who can tell? Perhaps they have known each other from the time before she became famous, perhaps he just makes her laugh, or perhaps he is just a steady refuge from the whirlwind of the theatre set. Now, I think I will go and relax in a bath before dinner, George?"

"*Cara mia*, the invitation is one I would never decline," he said.

"You two," Anastasia said despairingly. "I doubt that there will be much relaxing. Will you always be so lovey-dovey?"

"Of course," George replied. "Well, Nastia, we'll see you anon."

On Monday, Federica and Anastasia made an expedition into Slough looking for some offices that they might take for a while. They found three possible sites and finally settled on one that had four offices, an ante room and a large room in which they could set a table on which to lay out drawings and papers. They talked to the lessor and struck a deal for a year with an option to renew and then left with the keys. Their next stop was at the foundry to persuade Mr Fox to give up one of his secretaries.

"Good morning, Mr Fox," Federica greeted him.

"Good morning, Mrs Wheelwright, a delight to see you, how may I be of assistance?" he replied.

"We are seeking to steal away one of your intelligent young ladies," she explained.

"Are you looking for clerking skills or secretarial skills?" he asked.

"I had not thought of that," she admitted. "Let me put the need to you and you can advise me. We have retained two managers for the car assembly factory and the car body works factory. While they work at constructing their respective factories, we need some administrative help, and I had thought of one of your admirable young ladies."

"What you really need then is some skill with the typewriter, but a greater skill in organising files, project folders and works to be done," he suggested.

"Capital," she exclaimed. "You have hit upon the need excellently."

"As much as it pains me to do so, I can recommend Miss Alice White," he said. "She has typical secretarial skills but also is possessed of an agile brain and an ability to organise; she also can read and understand the drawings that would be required to construct a building."

"Where did she acquire such skills?" Federica asked.

"Her father is an inventor of sorts and, having no sons, shared all his dreams and ideas with Miss White," Fox explained. "I was lucky to have her come and work for us. I know her father, and he was looking for situations for his daughters, as his ability to support the family was not as good as he would have liked. His inventions, while fascinating, have yet to generate enough cash to make the family comfortable."

"I don't wish to leave you with a problem," Federica said. "If we were to talk to her about the opportunity, how would you replace her?"

"I have another already in mind," Fox replied. "In fact, it is the younger sister of Alice, Constance by name, whom I would have liked to hire on sooner, but had no space for; this gives me the opportunity to do so."

"Should we then talk to Miss Alice White or to Miss Constance?" Federica asked.

"Alice," he said. "I will arrange for her to be here forthwith, and you may see for yourselves her capability."

Alice White was duly interviewed and approved of. Alice expressed surprise that the design of the car fell to Anastasia and Federica, as she had supposed that all really creative work came from men, particularly men like her father. Her mother took no part in the projects that her father dreamed up and was fond of saying that it was beyond her. Alice had therefore assumed that her understanding of the sketches and drawings that her father made was an aberration. Her schooling had had no such classes, and even her mathematics classes had included only basic arithmetic with no geometry and certainly no algebra or calculus. Federica then talked to Mr Fox and arranged for Alice to be transferred to the rolls of the Sirius Car Company, as its first real employee. Federica then took Alice to the offices they had found and told her that they needed to be furnished and equipped, and to prepare a budget for that task and then with monies approved to furnish them. Federica gave Alice some petty cash for travel expenses and suggested that she check on possible suppliers in Slough and Maidenhead, and that if should suitable suppliers and furniture to acquire it and have the invoices sent to the Sirius Car Company at the new address. Then she gave Alice the keys and told her that she and Anastasia would be back later in the week to see how she had progressed. Alice was delighted with the challenge and said that when Mr Stuart and Mr Coates came to work on the 16th of March, she and the offices would be ready for them.

When Federica and Anastasia arrived home, Sophia and George both met them, eager to learn what they had achieved that morning.

"May we have lunch first?" Federica pleaded. "I have a great hunger for food and will surely fade away if it not satisfied."

"We could talk as we eat," George suggested.

"I suppose that is an option," Federica agreed. "At least then, when Nastia is talking, I can eat and vice versa."

"Good, shall we go in then?" he asked. "We waited for you."

"How sweet," she said. "Perhaps I will forgive your hasty enquiries after our morning."

"Did you find an office? Did you persuade Fox to part with one of his girls?" he asked.

"George, give your dear wife time to eat at least one morsel before she answers all your questions," Sophia chided.

"You are quite right," he said to Sophia, then to Federica, "I'm sorry, *cara mia*".

"To answer your questions," Anastasia interrupted. "The answers are yes and yes. We found quite satisfactory premises, which may in time become the showroom for Sirius, if we take the rest of the building, but for now we contented ourselves with office space for four, space for a secretary and space for a meeting room. We signed a lease for a year with an option to renew and an option to purchase. We also got good advice from our Mr Fox, who provided us with an admirable young lady who types and reads engineering drawings."

"She does?" George remarked. "That is not very common in young ladies today. How is it that she has this facility?"

"Her father is an inventor, and she assisted him," Anastasia explained. "Fox gave her employment because her father's inventions do not pay the rent. To replace Alice White, the young lady we purloined from Fox, he will retain the services of her younger sister, Constance."

"There you have it, dear," Federica said. "Thank you, Nastia, that was most helpful. Now, please eat before you faint away. What did you do today, *caro mio?*"

"I sent off our enquiry to Ethel Charles," George said. "It left with the postman this morning when he came with the first post. Then I took the Fiat for a drive into High Wycombe to the county offices there and had a discussion with them about special licence plates for us when we need them as a manufacturer. They were most helpful, I will return in January of next year and pay the requisite of £3 and then have some plates made up, I think with red letters and numbers upon a white background."

It was Thursday before they heard back from Ethel Charles, and then it was a disappointment. She apparently had some commission that she had already taken on and regretted that she had not the time to devote to their project.

"What do we do now?" George asked Federica.

"We have to find a new architect and engineer, but who?" she replied.

"Who has the project for the Talbot factory?" he asked.

"The architect is William Walker, but I understand that his real purpose is to address the façade and the immediate entrance. I also understand that the factory itself will be a single storey with a saw tooth roof line set with many windows to give the most natural light," she replied.

"Should we approach this Walker?" he asked.

"I don't think we need anything so grandiose," she said. "The factory itself, without the façade, intrigues me. We need to find a competent engineer who can specify the building and supervise the construction."

"Who is supervising the Talbot factory?" he asked.

"I believe it is Charles Garrard, but he is an employee of the Clément Talbot people; he is an interesting man, having been involved with the business of motorised cycles, but he is not our man, he is Talbot's man," she replied. "I think it would be prudent to contact the editors of *The Engineer* publication and get some assistance in creating a list of possible candidates."

"Will you do that or shall I?" he asked.

"Let you do it," she suggested. "You are more likely to elicit intelligent responses. Why don't you go up to London to their offices and see what you may learn?"

"I will do that tomorrow," he agreed. "How is our car performing?"

"Well," she replied. "I have noted no issues, and Nastia has not made any comments about things she wishes to change. We replaced the body on the first car, and it looks much better now. We have a second car almost done, and I am thinking that the third one we build should go to Koos and Anna for really rigorous testing."

"When will it be ready?" he asked.

"I think at the end of March," she said. "We have the parts, but we have been so busy of late that Nastia and I have been slow in our assembly. When Stuart and Coates join us, I will tell them that they will need to build up a workforce."

"What kinds of skills do we need?" he asked.

"That largely depends upon how we assemble the cars," she said. "We need experienced machinists to make the parts, then for the assembly, the skills will be different. I am thinking that I would like to see more women in the factory."

"Are there skilled women machinists?" he asked.

"I doubt that there are many, if any," she lamented. "But for the final assembly, it seems to me that we can teach women to do the job equally as well as men."

"What about the weight and size of the parts?" he asked.

"What was the famous quote, 'Give me a place to stand, a lever long enough, a fulcrum strong enough and I will move the world'?" she replied. "If we design the assembly process well enough, there will be no need for brute strength, more a need for fine fitting and assembly, tasks for which I think women are as well suited as any man, which is why we have women in our garment factory."

"How may I help?" he asked.

"I think your best help now is to find us an engineer who will do the calculations for the building design and then produce a construction plan that Stuart and Coates can execute," she replied. "But, enough of cars, come for a run around the estate with me, I have been lax of late and feel the need for some exercise."

"It's wet out and muddy underfoot," he said.

"No matter," she said. "If we get wet, we can always bathe afterwards, and clothes and shoes can be cleaned. *Andiamo caro mio.*"

Construction

On the Friday that followed the acquisition of the office space, Federica, accompanied by George and Anastasia, stopped to see how Alice was faring. They were all pleasantly surprised to see the four offices already furnished, a table set in the large room and Alice seated at a desk with a typewriter and filing cabinets.

"Good morning, Alice," Federica said. "How delightful this all looks."

"Thank you, Mrs Wheelwright, may I bring you tea or coffee?" Alice replied.

"Tea, thank you, Alice, you know Anastasia of course, and this is my husband, Mr George Wheelwright," Federica replied. "How did you manage to have all this done so quickly?"

"Good morning, Miss Wheelwright, Mr Wheelwright. To answer your question, Madame, I visited the various possible suppliers and hinted to the one that the other had promised such and such and asked what they might do," Alice replied.

"Have you decided who shall be in which office?" Anastasia asked.

"No, I thought I should defer to you," Alice said.

"If you had a suggestion, what would it be?" Federica asked.

"Well, those two offices have ready access to the large room, so I would place Mr Stuart and Mr Coates in those offices and perhaps yourself there and Miss Wheelwright there," Alice suggested.

"Nastia?" Federica asked.

"I think that is a capital notion," Anastasia replied.

"So be it," Federica said.

"I have an accounting for you of all that I have spent," Alice said. "If you would review it, I would be much happier."

"Nastia?" Federica asked.

"Let me see Alice," Anastasia requested. She then glanced down the list of items and noted that apart from the furniture, there was also the typewriter and various and sundry office supplies, including the very tea cups that she was now handing around. Finally, she nodded to Federica and then said to Alice, "Thank you, Alice, would you file that under office supplies?"

"Yes, Miss," Alice said. "I had done so provisionally, pending your approval of the expenditures and my filing system. I also have a list of all my petty cash expenditures. We have received only one invoice to date of all the purchases I made, but I expect others soon."

"We should list you as a signatory on the company's bank account," Federica said. "Then, for items such as this, you can create a cheque when the invoice is presented and pay the account. Are you familiar with bookkeeping entries?"

"No, Madame," Alice said.

"Do we need a bookkeeper, Nastia?" Federica asked.

"We should have one," Anastasia replied. "During the construction process, there will be many bills to be paid and we need to account for everything, but I think we rather need an accountant, not just a bookkeeper."

"We will engage such a person then," Federica said. "Where will we put him or her?"

"If you will permit Madame," Alice said. "I have talked to the landlord and he would be delighted to let us have the space adjoining, which would give us offices for an accountant and a place to store the many files that I anticipate being generated in the coming months."

"George, Nastia?" Federica asked.

"Excellent notion," George agreed.

"How did I miss something so obvious?" Anastasia wondered.

"Because, dear sister, you were concentrating on what you should have been, which was and is the car design. Shall I see the landlord then, Alice?" Federica asked.

"Yes, Madame," Alice said.

"Shall we discompose the admirable Mr Fox again and steal away his accountant, or should we look elsewhere?" Federica asked.

"I think there is one in the employ of Mr Painter," Anastasia suggested. "Mr Painter was telling me only the other day that a Mr Douglas Wilson is an aspiring accountant who is probably not used to his full capability, positioned as he is as second to Mr Roberts, the works accountant."

"Let us talk to Mr Painter then and see what may be arranged," Federica said. "Alice, could you get a desk for an accountant and whatever other equipment or supplies they may need?"

"Of course, Madame," Alice agreed. "Do we have any company paper or stationery with the appropriate letterhead?"

"Not yet, please add that to your list of things to do," Federica said. "Use this address as the company address. I wonder when it will be possible to get telephone service here? We should talk to the National Telephone Company and badger them into extending their lines as far as here."

"Alice, do we have any biscuits?" George asked.

"Indeed, Sir," she replied. "Excuse me for not setting them out sooner."

"These are not ours," George said, turning them over and looking at them carefully.

"I'm sorry, Sir?" Alice asked, a little perplexed.

"We own the Abbey Biscuit Company," Federica explained. "We should have Mr Robertson send you a supply."

"I'm sorry, Madame," Alice said. "I had no idea you also owned Abbey Biscuits."

"It is our fault," George said. "We did not tell you, nor do I think we have told anyone of the other companies that are associated. We have the Abbey Biscuit Company, the Handy Cross Tractor Company, not that you are likely to be using their services unless you have fields to plough, harvests to thresh or really large loads to move, the Windsor Company, manufacturer of ladies' garments and motoring wear and the Burnham Foundry."

"Perhaps we should extend to all employees within the companies that we have the benefits extended to those individual companies," Federica suggested. "Is there any reason why Alice should not be able to purchase items from Windsor at the same rate as employees of Windsor?"

"The only issue may be that I don't see many employees wishing to buy castings or hire traction engines," George laughed.

"True, but let us talk to Mr Robertson and Mr Painter and work out how we may extend those benefits to all our employees," Federica said.

"Is there anything else that Alice should do to prepare for the arrival of Messrs. Stuart and Coates?" Anastasia asked.

"I don't think so," Federica said. "Except, Alice, have you ever taken a ride in a motor car?"

"No, Madame," Alice replied.

"Well, we should take you with us and go and see Mr Painter," Federica announced. "Let us go, we can luncheon afterwards, perhaps in the company of Mr Painter and Mr Wilson. We have two cars with us today, Alice, both are Sirius cars, one is brand new, we only finished building it a few days ago, so this is in part a test of that car to see if it performs properly. Nastia, please take Alice with you, and George may come with me."

It was only a short drive to the Windsor garment factory, and Mr Painter happened to be walking between buildings and saw them arrive.
"Good morning," he said. "Are these your new cars?"
"They are indeed," Federica confirmed. "These are the first cars that we have built, I hesitate to say production models because it would be like saying a new garment is in production when you have just laid it out on a cutting table and have yet to run it through the sewing line."
"May I see?" he asked.
"Of course," she agreed. "Tell me, Mr Painter, would it be an idea for us to have a delivery vehicle of sorts, emblazoned with our name and the company image, with which to deliver boxes of clothes to the various local shops?"
"I think that would be wonderful advertising," he said. "How large a vehicle would it be?"
"Nastia?" Federica asked. "If we built a special body with no rear windows, how large a space would we have, and how many clothes boxes could it accommodate?"
"I will think about it," Anastasia promised. "I will have some ideas for you, Mr Painter, in two or three weeks."
"Mr Painter," Federica started. "Miss Wheelwright tells me that you have an aspiring accountant by the name of Douglas Wilson. We are in need of an accountant for the Sirius Car Company. Would you recommend him, and would it discommode you greatly if we were to take him?"
"As to the latter, no, it would not be a great disruption, my accountant, Roberts, can manage for the moment, and I would get a bookkeeper to help him. Would I recommend him? Yes, he started with us as a bookkeeper but has continued his learning and has qualified recently as

a Chartered Accountant. That gives me two with the same qualification, and I need only one. I would recommend him to you, he is dedicated and desirous to learn, and I believe would serve you well," Painter said.

"Might we meet him?" Federica asked.

"Of course, please come this way," Painter replied. "I have not met this young lady before. Is she also part of the Sirius Company?"

"She is indeed," Federica confirmed. "Mr Painter, Miss Alice White, recently in the employ of Mr Fox at the foundry and now our sole employee. Alice has accepted the position as our secretary, clerk, tea maker, filer, purchasing agent and whatever else we may find to impose upon her."

"Congratulations, Miss White," Painter laughed. "Make sure they do not overload you with tasks. Watch out for special projects and the ever-alarming, 'have you ever thought about', questions. But, here we are, let me find Wilson."

Mr Wilson was brought to the office of Mr Painter and introduced to all. He was a young man, in his late twenties, and they learned that he was married to Agnes with one small daughter, Agatha. He told them of his recent qualification and the examinations he had had to take to get that qualification. His experience to date had all been with the Windsor Company, but he was willing to try something new.

"Would you join us for luncheon?" Federica asked Painter and Wilson. "We may continue this discussion there."

"Where do we go?" Anastasia asked.

"There is the Crown," George suggested. "We can take both cars and have room for all."

"Good," Federica agreed. "Shall we go?"

At the Crown, the landlord was delighted to see a party of six and was most solicitous. He knew Federica and George and knew that they had considerable means, so were customers to be cultivated.

"Mr Wilson," Federica began. "We have recently formed the Sirius car Company and are looking for an accountant to join the company. As we are at this moment, Miss White is the sole employee, but she will be joined on the 16th by two managers who will take care of the assembly of the body work for the cars and the assembly of the finished car. There will be much work during the next few months as we construct suitable buildings in which to do this work, and then there will be the parts to make or purchase and the people to retain. What think you of this prospect?"

"It sounds most attractive," he said, glancing at both George and Mr Painter.

"Let me help you a little," Painter said. "The person you need to address your replies to is Mrs Wheelwright."

"I'm so sorry, Madame," Wilson said, clearly embarrassed. "It is rare to find such enterprises that are headed by the ladies of the house."

"Is it an impossibility?" Federica asked.

"I confess to having not ever considered such a possibility," he replied.

"What does your wife do?" Anastasia asked.

"She maintains our household and cares for our child, and she gives piano lessons to paying pupils," Wilson replied.

"Does she manage the expenses involved in that, or do you handle all the money?" George asked.

"She manages the money for the household very well," he said proudly.

"And she cares for your child," prompted George.

"And she gives piano lessons and collects money for that?" Anastasia added.

"Yes, she does," Wilson agreed.

"Is she then capable of managing an enterprise?" Federica asked.

"Well, they are different," Wilson hedged.

"Different, in what way?" Anastasia asked.

"Well, the amounts of money are greater, and there are multiple accounts that are usually set up to cater to different demands," Wilson said.

"Does your wife know what she spends on food, clothing and other items?" George asked. "Does she know how many hours she has spent teaching pupils and what to charge for that?"

"Of course," Wilson admitted.

"So, apart from the difference in the size of the numbers, there is no difference between running your household and running an enterprise on, what would we call it, Nastia, a cash basis?" George asked.

"I suppose not," Wilson said. " I confess I had not thought of it in those terms, but why not, a really large household as one might find in the estates of the aristocracy, is usually run by the housekeeper, who is most often a woman with much experience."

"One final thought," Federica added. "The late queen, did she run a large enterprise?"

"Yes, but she was educated and raised for the job, and she had advisors and people to do her bidding," he replied.

"So, with the right education and with appropriate advice and people, a woman could run this enterprise, it is so much smaller than the British Empire," Federica said, pressing her point home.

"Yes," he said. "I confess that my own education and learning to date have included strictures that women are not mentally equipped to handle complex issues, but I can see that I was sadly led astray. How may I be of help?"

"We need an accountant to track the business of the Company, and we will need advice as to changes in tax laws and how we may comply," she replied.

"I would be delighted to accept that challenge, Madame," he said. "Where are the premises of the Sirius car Company?"

"We have offices that we occupy now and have land upon which we will construct the two factories that we need," she replied. "Would it be convenient for you, Mr Painter, if we took a quick drive to both?"

"That would be most interesting," Painter replied. "If I may be back at Windsor by three, I have a meeting then with my manufacturing staff."

"Good, then let us eat and then repair to the offices," Federica said.

After lunch, they drove to the Burnham Foundry and parked, then walked beyond the foundry to the land beyond.

"This is where the two factories will be," Federica said. "One for the car bodies and one for the mechanical parts manufacture and the final assembly. You can see that we have ready access to the main road, and we plan to extend the railway siding that leads to the foundry."

"Is there room for expansion if required?" Painter asked.

"There is," Federica confirmed. "We have purchased more land to the west and will see how things progress."

"Is there a building design yet?" Wilson asked.

"We have a building concept, and that should be reduced to drawings by a competent engineer," Federica replied. "We will involve our new managers in the design process, and their first task will be to manage the construction of their respective factories."

"Are the offices far from here?" Painter asked.

"No, they are on the far western edge of Slough, almost into Burnham, so a short drive," Federica replied. "As there is little to see here apart from dead grass, perhaps we should inspect the offices?"

At the offices, Alice led the way and opened up the building. She stood aside as the others entered, then asked if tea or coffee was desired. The consensus was for coffee, so she disappeared and returned a few minutes later with cups and saucers and then in a few more minutes with coffee, milk and sugar. Federica took orders and poured the coffee, which Alice then passed around.

"There are biscuits," Federica added. "But through our own lack of thought, we neglected to tell Alice that there is a sister company that makes biscuits, so they are not our own. I will rectify that with a short conversation with Mr Robertson at Abbey and collect some for our use here."

"You own Abbey Biscuits?" Wilson asked.

"We do," George confirmed. "Our other companies are the Burnham Foundry and the Handy Cross Tractor Company. We owned, until recently, the Wright Carriage Company, but that was sold, and the proceeds will be used for Sirius."

"We are going to add some space here for the accounts office and for document storage," Federica explained. "Until such time as the factories are built, those offices will be occupied by the two new managers and Miss Wheelwright and myself will take those two."

"And Mr Wheelwright?" Wilson asked.

"For those times that I need to be here, I will share the office of Mrs Wheelwright," George replied.

"Would it be possible to get telephone service at Windsor?" Painter asked.

"We were just talking about that very subject earlier," Federica said. "We will be contacting the National Telephone Company to see what may be done to install telephones here and at Windsor, Abbey and Burnham. Handy Cross, being more remote, may be a little more of a challenge, but if High Wycombe is well served, then it should not be a great issue."

"Why don't I run Mr Painter back to Windsor while you discuss things with Mr Wilson?" George suggested to Federica.

"Good," she agreed. "*Ciao, ci vediamo presto.*"

Mr Wilson was sent to London to meet with the firm of Leadbetter and Jones to discuss how best to set up the accounting for the period of construction and the financing of the project. Federica and George were trying to keep their own finances discreet from those of the company, which they thought just made good sense. George obtained the names of several engineering firms that had good reputations and arranged for them to meet with him at their offices. The first to arrive was a Mr Freeman. Freeman came in and started at the sight of Federica and Anastasia sitting with George in the large room.

"Good morning, Mr Freeman," George said. "George Wheelwright, this is my wife Federica and sister Anastasia. They are major shareholders in the Sirius Car Company, and we would like to discuss with you works to design and build two factories."

"Good morning," Freeman said. "Do you have some basic sizes and needs that you can share with me?"

"I do," Anastasia said. She unrolled some drawings and started to explain her ideas. "As you can see," she said. "This is the property, it is adjacent to another we own and is served by this railway siding and by a short side road to the A4. There are a total of 45 acres; the ground slopes generally in this direction at about six inches in every hundred feet, there is a twelve-inch water main here and large drains here. The soil conditions are detailed in this report that we had done when we made some expansion to our foundry on the adjacent property. We are thinking of two buildings along these lines." With that, she unrolled another drawing that showed a basic building layout with columns and other features marked.

"You have been well coached, Miss Wheelwright," Freeman remarked, smiling. "I congratulate you, Sir."

"Until the latter part of last year, I was on active duty in South Africa," George said. "I am no expert on land or buildings, congratulations, if any congratulations are due, should go to my wife and to my sister."

"Really?" Freeman said. "I find it difficult to accept that you, Miss, have done this work without the assistance of an engineering concern. I think you are using me to check their proposals."

"Why would you think that we are not capable of creating this simple design?" Federica asked.

"Well, look at it," he said. "It's obvious that the spans have been well thought out and calculated. I have never heard of a woman talking about soil reports and such. No, whatever scheme it is you have going here, I want no part of it, good day."

On that note, Freeman left, leaving George Federica and Anastasia all looking at each other and wondering how difficult this was going to be.

"Perhaps we should do the coaching, George," Federica suggested.

"We may have to resort to that," he admitted. "We'll see what the next firm brings."

The next engineer was a Mr Pitt. Alice showed him in and introduced those in the room. "Good morning, Mr Pitt," George greeted him. "Thank you for coming to see us."

"Thank you for seeing me, I understand that you have a factory that you wish to build?"

"We do indeed," George confirmed. "If you will allow, my sister will explain the basics."

Anastasia went through the same explanation that she had done for Mr Freeman and Pitt, then asked a barrage of questions, all of which she answered. Pitt looked at her carefully as if seeing her for the first time.

"Where did you get your schooling?" he asked.

"I was tutored by Mrs Wheelwright," Anastasia replied.

"And, excuse my curiosity, Madame, yours?" he asked.

"Mainly Hong Kong," she replied. "Before that, Florence."

"Ah, so you are familiar with the works of de Vinci?" he asked.

"Very," she replied. "My father was an admirer and insisted that we all take note."

"Well, I have to say that the project is intriguing," Pitt said. "My only concern is what my partners will make of working with you ladies. They will have difficulty communicating because they will not accept that you can obviously understand the engineering and the calculations. That much is clear from the preliminary sketches you have here. You have engaged no other firm to assist in preparing these documents?"

"No one," George assured him. "What is about the idea of my wife and sister doing such work that is so hard to believe?"

"I think it is the accepted wisdom, if that is the right word, of the day that women do not have the capacity to understand such things," Pitt replied. "I am beginning to wonder how much validity there is to that premise."

"If Nastia will permit," George said. "Draw a structure and ask her if she will calculate the loads."

"If you wish, Miss Wheelwright?" Pitt asked.

"Go ahead," she said. "It rather smacks of a prize exhibit at a fair, but let us see how I fare."

"Very well," Pitt said. He drew a truss on paper that George placed in front of him and indicated some loads. Anastasia looked at it and said, "This is an indeterminate structure; the loads cannot be calculated using equilibrium methods."

"Very good," he said. "What if I do this?"

"Then we have a determinate structure and the loads would be," she paused, did some calculations and then wrote down numbers.

"Excellent," he said. "Well, I am convinced. Now I need to see what my partners will say."

"We have been rude," George said. "You have been here for some time now, and we have not even offered you tea or coffee."

"Tea would be much appreciated," Pitt said. George left the room and came back in with Alice, who handed around tea and placed biscuits on the table and gave George a folder.

"Ah, Abbey biscuits, my favourite," Pitt said.

"That is good to hear," George laughed. "Abbey is our company, in fact, you may be interested to hear that my sister just finished overseeing the installation of new dough and icing machines."

"Really, one day I would like to see what a biscuit factory looks like from the inside. I have only seen façades in the past. What of the Sirius Car Company?" Pitt asked. "Do you have a car that I may see?"

"Of course, please come this way," Federica said. "Bring your tea, it is only a few steps to the stable yard."

Outside, Pitt looked at the cars, he looked under the bonnets, under the cars and inside. Finally, he looked at Federica and Anastasia and said, "Let me guess you designed these yourselves?"

"We did indeed, and built them," Anastasia replied.

"Is the Sirius Car Company traded on the stock exchange?" he asked.

"It is," Federica confirmed. "But it is a closely held company and most of the shares are held by us, Anastasia's mother and my father."

"I will look to see if there are shares to be had," Pitt said. "I will get you a quotation for the design of the building and for costs to construct. I will ensure that my partners will listen to me."

"Thank you, Mr Pitt," Federica said. "You will find all the information you need here in this folder."

"Very good," Pitt said. "Tell me, Miss Wheelwright, what are your ambitions?"

"I would like to go to university and study engineering," she replied.

"You'll terrify the professors," he laughed. "They will not know how to deal with you. I wish you luck and will follow your adventures, as they surely will be. Look at this car, it is a delight. When might I purchase one?"

"That will depend upon how quickly we build the factories for the bodies and the rest of the car," George said. "But I would be happy to take an advance order, the price yet to be announced and delivery yet to be determined, but we will exhibit at next year's Motor Show at the Crystal Palace and will have cars for sale then."

"I'll hold you to that," Pitt said. "Well, Ladies, Sir, this has been a very instructive day, I should leave and catch my train back to London."

The next two engineers fell into the same category as Mr Freeman, one being as dismissive, the other a little less so. The last was another Mr Pitt, and with him they also elicited a promise of a quotation for the engineering and for the construction costs. When the last had gone, George asked Federica, "Did things go as you thought?"

"They did," she confirmed. "I was a little taken aback by Fox and Paxton, being called a liar is not something I am used to, and having them walk out was a surprise. Davies was a little more polite but just as unbelieving as Fox and Paxton. Pitt and Watson both took a little while to get used to the notion that not all good ideas and knowledge lie with men, but once they had accepted the idea, both seemed enthusiastic."

"Which do you think will give us the better price, and which do you think would be better to work with?" he asked.

"I think Pitt," she replied. "Watson was keen at the end, but I think a little out of his depth; this would be a big project for him. He might quote us a lower price, but unless Pitt is outrageous, I think we will have better success with him."

"We should end the day then, Alice, would you clear up and lock up?" George suggested.

The next day, Alice wrote to Stuart and Coates and obtained their travel plans so that they could be met at the railway station and transported to the Reindeer Inn. She also received driving lessons from Anastasia, and by the time Stuart and Coates arrived, she was quite capable of driving the Sirius cars, so met each at the station from their trains. On Monday morning, the 16th of March, Federica, Anastasia and George all went to the offices to meet with Stuart and Coates. Federica introduced them to Douglas Wilson and showed them each their offices. Then she called for a meeting in the large room and had Anastasia lay out the drawings of the property and the sketches of the buildings.

"These building sketches are preliminary," she said. "Pending work to be done by an engineering firm, and pending your thoughts on the flow of work through the factories. We will have presentations this afternoon by the two engineering concerns that have quoted on the project, and I would like all your opinions afterwards. Alice will assist you with correspondence and filing and such and Douglas will keep a tally of our costs and expenses during the construction process and afterwards. Our desire is to exhibit cars at the Motor Show at Crystal Palace next February 12th to February 24th, in fact, the first ballot for space is being held today, so we await their response. We will need cars for the stand and cars for the outside exhibit, and then cars to fulfil orders that we anticipate will come pouring in." This last pronouncement got the laugh that she intended and generally lightened the mood of the meeting.

Mr Watson was the first presenter that afternoon. He was introduced to Stuart, Coates and Wilson and seemed more comfortable with more men around. Federica and Anastasia had to prompt Stuart and Coates a little to get questions from them, but eventually, they relaxed and put their own questions to Watson. When Pitt arrived and went through his proposals, the questions came from all parties without prompting from either Federica or Anastasia. After Pitt had departed, Federica then asked for comments on both proposals and for votes on which proposal to accept. The comments and voting both favoured Pitt, even Douglas Wilson, who one might have expected to opt for the slightly lower bid, voted for Pitt. His comment was that a first cost is often the least cost, and he anticipated that Watson would add changes to the project and that those changes would carry additional costs, which would take his bid over that of Pitt.

"Very good," Federica said. "I will communicate our decision to both, perhaps Alice, we could quickly draft up a letter?"

"Yes, Madame," Alice replied.

"I have other meetings in the morning," Federica said. "I will be back tomorrow afternoon and can sign the letters then, perhaps by then we will also have the results of the space ballot for the 1904 motor show. Meanwhile, Mr Stuart and Mr Coates, would you please start listing the machines and equipment you will need to make the various parts of the car? Here is a list of those parts that we plan to purchase, at least to start with, and here is a list of the machines that we used to make our test cars, most of which are at the foundry. We should introduce you to Mr Fox of the foundry, he will be a great help to you and will also be supplying some parts."

"Is there anything else we need to decide today?" George asked. "No, then perhaps we should adjourn for the day and meet up again on the morrow."

At the regular meeting of the various business managers, Federica reported, as the managing director of the Sirius Car Company, that they had retained the services of the two managers and were about to engage an engineering firm for the construction of the factories. George then told them of the sale of Wright carriages to Mr Laird, but assured them that there were no plans to divest any of the other businesses. He then took the rest of the meeting, and Fox, Painter, Robertson and Edwards reviewed their respective businesses. George then raised the issue of offering employee discounts for the goods and services of the company, which led to some discussion and then consensus. It was decided that each would inform his staff of the opportunity and what was available, and then collect orders and pass them to his colleague for fulfilling. Federica was asked if there would be an employee discount for Sirius Cars, and she said that she had thought it over and that employees could buy the cars at work's cost. That led to the obvious question: what was that going to be? Her short answer was that they would know in about six months, but that she would keep them informed.

At the offices, Alice had news: they had received a notification from the Society of Motor Manufacturers and Traders, and they had been allocated Stand No. 221 in the Concert Room. Anastasia consulted the diagram sent and found Stand 221, which was adjacent to the tea room and generally in the centre of the building. "That is good, don't you think?" she asked.

"I think so," Federica concurred. "All those going to take tea will have to pass by and will see our cars."

"So, now all we have to do is produce some cars," George added. "Have you thought any further about the idea of a van to deliver goods, Nastia?"

"I have," she said. "I think we could use the same engine, gearbox and axles, but change the body to essentially a simple box with doors at the back. I think the frame should be a little longer, but not too much, and we may have to use slightly larger springs."

"Shall we look to build delivery vans as well and exhibit them at the show as well?" Federica asked.

"I think we should," Anastasia said. "We should display one that has emblazoned on it Abbey Biscuits and the picture that we use for the biscuit tins. That way we can also advertise our biscuits!"

"Capital," George said. "How long before we see work at the factory?"

"It will depend somewhat upon the weather," Mr Stuart said. "If we have no more snow or frosts, then we only have rain to contend with."

"Have we made the appropriate notices to the council?" George asked.

"We have given them notice that we intend to build the factory, and they were happy to assist when we told them that we might employ as many as two hundred people," Federica said.

"That many?" George asked.

"I have no idea," she admitted. "Mr Stuart and Mr Coates are going to have to tell us how many people they need. But, the number will not be insignificant, so the council will be happy."

"What do we need to do now?" he asked.

"We need to review the lists that Mr Stuart and Mr Coates have started, and then we need to put in place contracts to acquire the parts and materials that we need and when we need them," she said. "We have much work to do while the factories are being built."

It was not until the 15th of April that work actually started on the site. Federica organised an official groundbreaking ceremony and invited all the council members and Mr William Grenfell, the local Member of Parliament, he was, after all, a near neighbour, living at Taplow Court. They all attended, eager to show that they supported industry with an eye to how many votes there might be in it for them. They would have been horrified if they had learned that Federica was keen to get women working in the factories as well as men; women did not mean votes, so were less of an incentive to attend. Mr Pitt was present with his various foremen, and they set to work immediately thereafter. Federica watched as earth was moved and the site flattened, trenches were dug, and foundations were constructed. She watched the workers pour concrete in what was one of the first uses of reinforced concrete in the country. Mr Pitt had been researching building methods from around the world and saw no reason not to see this new technique in their buildings. Fairly soon thereafter, columns went up and then support beams and roof trusses, and then the roof and walls were closed in. Pitt had suggested that they use the reinforced concrete for the floor of the factory, and Federica was delighted to concur. Messrs. Stuart and Coates were kept busy checking on the works of the engineering firm and ensuring that all was done according to the specifications. It was also good for them to see the buildings from the very beginning; they knew how they were built and could begin to imagine production lines and layouts. Stuart had carts constructed that met Federica's requirements so that the cars could be moved readily from place to place, where different parts would be added.

While the construction was proceeding, Federica and Anastasia built a few more cars and shipped one of them to Cape Town to Koos and Anna for testing. They also built a delivery van, one designed to take stacks of biscuit tins or boxes of clothing. During this time, they made some minor improvements to the process for making the body panels and, in doing so, reduced the amount of time it took to make and the costs. Messrs. Stuart and Coates each got a car to use, and Federica also assigned one of the delivery vans to the Sirius Car Company. The first two cars built they pulled apart and rebuilt using new parts. Now all that remained was to finish the buildings and then start the production line. Federica worked with Messrs. Stuart and Coates to employ people to do the work. They found a few who had worked in small factories where machines had been built, and even found two who had built cars. This gave them the nucleus of a workforce that would be able to build upon later. To the great disappointment of Federica, they did not retain any women among this first group. She was then at pains to point out to both managers that she would view very favourably women in the workforce. In her view, they would be just as capable, and Anastasia had already designed tools that would allow even the smallest woman to properly tighten nuts and bolts. Mr Coates was dispatched to review the manufacturing processes of Mulliners of Nottingham, and he came back with his report. They were still using methods and techniques from the coach-building industry, so although he learned some things, there were no dramatic revelations.

George talked to Federica and suggested that while she was busy with the project, he might take a trip to Scotland, the Lakes and Derbyshire to visit with their various tenants. Federica thought that an excellent idea and together they planned his journey and where he would stay. He would be gone for almost a month, but he promised faithfully to write regularly. Mr Pitt had now accepted both Federica and Anastasia and would discuss the project with them as easily as he did with Messrs. Stuart and Coates. Federica placed orders for machine tools of the latest designs that each came with their own electric motors, obviating the need for the complex pulley system that was often found in factories, as the machines took their power from a central drive unit feeding an overhead shaft. Federica felt that that imposed constraints on the layout of the machine shops that she did not want, so spent the extra money to have self-contained machines. She also bought machines that were larger and more precise than those that conventional wisdom said would be appropriate. She wanted to have some assurance that the parts they made would be usable without any further finishing or filing to fit. As June came, the weather turned warm, and building proceeded apace. Now they had building shells and the foundations for the power house equipment were in, and machinery was expected shortly. Federica was happy with progress and pleasantly surprised that Mr Pitt was staying within the budget they had agreed to.

Then, on the 13th of June, everything changed. It started to rain, and it rained and it rained for two solid days.
"What happened to the weather?" George asked her on the morning of Monday, the 15th of June, as they both stood in the factory and looked out at the rain still coming down.
"The meteorologists say the eruption of Mount Pelée in Martinique has put so much ash and dust in the air that it has changed the normal weather pattern," she replied.
"Do they know how long this will go on?" he asked.

"I don't think so," she said. "The annoying thing is that it is not raining everywhere; elsewhere in the country, it is quite dry."

"How much time will we lose?" he asked.

"We will probably lose a week in all, but if we get more bad storms later in the year, we may lose a little more time," she replied. "The amount of rain we have had has filled the ditches and drains, and look how it has turned the road into mud. If we try and bring too much equipment in now, we will make it so much worse."

"Will we have enough time to build cars for the Motor Show?" he asked.

"If we have to, we'll build them at the foundry," she said. "We don't need that many for the show itself, what it may mean is slow deliveries against orders we may receive at the show. Here is Mr Pitt, let's see what he has to say."

"Good morning, Madame," Pitt said. "Terrible rain, isn't it?"

"It is indeed Mr Pitt," she agreed. "What are your plans today?"

"I think it would be inadvisable to try and do too much today," he said. "We could work inside, but that would mean bringing heavy machines and equipment up the road, which I am afraid will not take it and will then turn into a quagmire."

"I agree," she said. "It is unfortunate, but this weather is unusual, isn't it?"

"It certainly is," he agreed. "I have never seen rain like this in June."

"Are you satisfied with the progress to date?" she asked.

"Very," he said. "We have completed far more than I had expected, and I am delighted with the new reinforced concrete. If we lose no more than a week to this inclement weather, I would still expect to have everything complete according to your timetable."

"That would be wonderful," she said. "We were just discussing what other plans we might make in case we would need to build cars for the motor show next year"

"There is some empty warehouse space on the Bath Road," he said. "If you need to, you could at least store parts there for a while."

"We may need to," she thought. "We have adjusted the deliveries of parts from our suppliers, but we may have to take delivery or lose our place in their manufacturing timetable."

Work resumed a week later, and then it seemed to go in peculiar spurts of obvious progress and then less obvious. Federica was concerned about the periods when progress was less obvious and asked Pitt about it. He took her on a tour and pointed out what was happening. It was all the small finishing tasks that needed to be done, but which did not change the overall appearance of the factory. Satisfied, she was content to let Pitt do his job. Sophia and Anastasia found premises in London that would be quite suitable as a car showroom room and there were living quarters above that were quite elegant. Sophia signed a lease for three years with an option to renew for another three, then set about making the necessary changes to the showroom itself that would best display their cars. In late September, Federica sat down with Anastasia and they reviewed all the projects that Anastasia had been working on and made sure that everything was transferred to Mr Coates. He had become quite enthusiastic over the past months and had developed clever ways to quickly produce the panels, paint them and attach them to the frame of the body. The last weekend of September, Sophia and Anastasia moved to London, taking clothes and the like. Furniture for their rooms had already been acquired and delivered, so the place was quite livable.

During the second week of October, during another rainstorm, as it happened, Mr Pitt talked to Federica and said that they would be ready for her inspection on the following Monday. So, paper in hand, Federica then toured the factory on the following Monday, together with Messrs. Stuart and Coates and took note of all the things that they felt were not quite right. Mr Pitt and his foremen also made notes as they went and at the end of the day agreed a timetable to correct all the minor issues that had been noted. After Mr Pitt had left, she turned to George about her next question.

"Do we have a grand opening?" she asked him.

"Yes, we should, and it might be politic to invite the local council and Mr Grenfell again," he suggested.

"I shall arrange it," she said. "Or, should I be honest and say that I will ask Alice to arrange it. We could set up chairs in the assembly area and have speeches and such, and then serve refreshments."

"Should we do it now or when our first cars are complete?" he asked.

"I think we can display the cars we have already built and invite the trade press as well as the council members," she thought. "Perhaps we should have a couple of frames partially complete so that the trade can take photographs."

"Do we explain the manufacturing line?" he asked.

"I think not," she said. "If we gain a cost advantage because of the process, I do not wish to lose that too quickly to competitors."

"So, we should store away the carts that we will use to move the cars along the line?" he asked.

"Yes," she agreed. "We can explain that we cleared away the cars that are under construction to make room for the festivities."

"Do we give people a tour of the body works?" he asked.

"I don't think so," she said. "That is all so novel, it may lead to more questions and discussion than I wish to have at this time. I will invite Papi and Franco, so if Mr Pitt can correct all the small items, we could have the opening in two weeks."

"What do we include in the factory tour for the council members?" he asked.

"I think we bring them to the assembly area, have the grand opening and then take them on a tour," she replied. "We will start with the power house where we are generating our own electricity, and then we will move to where parts and materials arrive and how they are moved to the various places for the assembly. Then the engine shop, and then perhaps we do need to see some car bodies in various stages of construction, so we should move two or three into the general assembly area."

"Will you organise that or would you like me to?" he asked.

"I think we should let Stuart and Coates do the tours," she replied. "I will give them some basic instructions and then ask them for a tour route and what they plan to say. I will also give them some guidance as to how to respond to questions, both about the car itself and about the number of people we may eventually employ. That will be of greatest interest to the politicians, as to them it means votes."

"Should we invite potential buyers?" he asked.

"I think that would be an excellent idea," she said. "We should ask local doctors, solicitors and other professionals and perhaps local business owners. We should, of course, invite our own business managers and perhaps a few relatives and friends, and I think we should invite Mr Wainwright and Mr Laird."

"If we invite business people and we are asked how much the car will cost if they wish to buy one, what do we say?" he asked.

"Prices of cars vary so greatly," she said. "One may acquire a voiturette for as little as £168 or pay £1,000 for an imported car from Italy. I saw a report on imported cars that said that for the month of January, there were 540 cars imported, and the average price per car was £309. There is also the complication that some cars are actually only the chassis with the engine and related parts, and the body must be acquired separately. I think that given the cost of parts that we purchase, parts that we make ourselves and the labour to put everything together, we should set a price of £250. That is then not out of the reach of all but the very rich, and perhaps will increase the number of sales."

"At that price, will the company show a profit?" he asked.

"Yes, providing we sell more than fifty a year," she replied. "Nastia and I have done calculations and have tried different costs for the pieces we buy and the time it takes to put it all together. That is where we must make our profit. If we make less than fifty cars a year, we will not make any profit, but beyond that, we will be successful."

"I suppose that is because we have to consider the cost of the factories themselves," he commented.

"It is indeed," she confirmed. "We are allowed to charge some money against each car and spread the cost of the factory over many years."

"Do you think we will sell that many a year?" he asked.

"I do indeed," she said. "I know that Nastia and I are biased because the design is ours and we built the first few cars, but I do believe that it is a pretty-looking car and quite serviceable."

"That I would agree with," he said. "Our premises in London are quite ready to accept cars for sale, we just need to retain a manager and people to do the selling and deliver cars."

"Will you attend to the task of finding and retaining a suitable person for the job?" she asked.

"Of course, *cara mia*," he said. "When do you think he, or she, should start?"

"She, do you actually think we could have a woman in the job, or are you merely humouring me?" she asked.

"I confess to jesting with you," he said. "Although I can see no reason why a woman could not do the job, I think there would be resistance from buyers who would cavil at the idea."

"Sadly, you are probably right," she agreed. "I will leave it to you then, but I think we should retain a sales manager soon and then have him spend a week or so here when we get the production line running, so that he is intimately familiar with the car."

"We must not forget to ensure that Sophia and Nastia are also at the grand opening," he said. "We would never be able to look them in the eye again if we forgot. I will telephone now while I think of it."

"Good," she said. "I will telegraph Papi and Franco now as well."

"Oh, I almost forgot," George added. "I saw a brief note in one of the scientific journals the other day that a French scientist, by the name of Édouard Bénédictus, happened upon a notion to hold glass together if it breaks. Apparently, he had some cellulose nitrate solution in a flask, which had dried; he dropped the flask and it broke, but the pieces all stayed together. Perhaps we should coat the glass for our windscreen and the other windows in like manner?"

"An excellent notion," she agreed. "I will instruct Mr Coates to run some trials and see how we can do this, and if we are successful, then the first coated windows can go in our own cars."

Saturday, the 7th of November, the grand opening was held. All the items that Federica and the others had noted had been addressed, and Mr Pitt was quite proud of the new factories. Representatives from *Autocar* and *Automotor Journal* were invited, as were members of the local press. Federica expected the local press to focus on the jobs that would be created, while the trade press would dissect the car and provide details of design and construction. As the focus was typically on the chassis and running gear and not the body work, Federica was not overly concerned about giving too much away. The engine was a fairly standard four-cylinder engine, with a single block, cylinders of a bore and stroke that were well within the norms of the day, and a gearbox and axle set-up that used third-party components that had already been reported on and essentially approved by the trade. Mr Grenfell made a nice speech and then cut the ribbon, declaring the factory open. George and Federica then escorted him on a tour of the factory while Messrs. Stuart and Coates toured groups of councillors and business people. Anastasia got the unenviable task of seeing to the reporters, something for which she threatened dire revenge against Federica and George. Signor Beretta and Franco, who had arrived a few days earlier, tagged along with Anastasia, posing as reporters from the Italian press.

That evening at home, Federica asked for impressions of the day.

"I think things went well," George replied.

"I did also, but one day you will both pay for leaving me with the men from *Autocar* and the *Journal*," Anastasia said. "I had difficulty getting them to take seriously what I had to say. I rather think they finally decided that I was just the tour guide assigned to them while George, the brains behind the design, was swanning around with our MP."

"It was really the only thing that could be done, Nastia," Sophia said, defending the decision of Federica. "She could not really not escort Mr Grenfell, could she?"

"How are classes, Nastia?" George asked.

"Well enough," she replied. "Much of what we do now is basic, but it has not hurt to refresh myself."

"And the other students?" Federica asked.

"A mix," was the answer. "There is one other girl, Annabel by name, who is very clever of the men; they are, for the most part, accepting of us, but there are four or five who let us know that we are not cut out for engineering. The professors are, for the most part, fair, but two seemed to have it as their life's work to see if we can keep up with the men; so far, they have been sadly disappointed as we have routinely done better than the men."

"Have you had any other issues?" George asked.

"What, with unwanted advances?" Anastasia laughed. "Only one, and he took a day from classes to recover from his fall, or so it was put about. He has since stayed well away from me."

"Who is this man?" Signor Beretta asked. "Do we need to deal with him?"

"No, Papi," Federica assured him. "Nastia can see to herself very well."

"I like your factory," Signor Beretta said. "When do I get my car?"

"Soon, Papi," Federica temporised. "You will get the tenth."

"When, tomorrow, next week, should we return to Firenze and then come back to collect it?" he asked.

"Or, we could ship it to you," she suggested.

"No, I will stay until it is ready," he announced.

"You are very welcome in our house," George said. "Franco, will you also stay?"

"No, I must return and ensure that there are adequate funds coming in to pay for Papi's holiday," Franco replied.

"When do we see the articles in the magazines?" Signor Beretta asked.

"Not until Saturday," Federica replied. "The magazines are published weekly and are in the shops on Saturday."

Federica and George were quite happy with the press reports in the local papers that dealt with their opening. The newspapers made much of the visit by Mr Grenfell and his remarks. For the motor journals, the wait until Saturday seemed interminable, but eventually the day came and George collected the two magazines from the newsagents.

"What do they say?" Federica asked.

"In the *Automotor Journal,* there is a detailed description of the car," he said. "And they have photographs, some of which are theirs and some are those that we provided. There is also commentary, which you may not like."

"Why, what do they say?" she asked.

"I quote," he said. '*This is a simple-looking car that is clearly designed for the general market. The chassis and works are fairly well set up and the body is innovative and creative in that it completely encloses both driver and passengers, the interior reminds one rather of the interior of a railway carriage, there is no leather upholstery, just wooden seats with cushions that look as if they came from a railway carriage. The railway carriage analogy goes further with the windows that are built to drop down to afford the driver and passenger either protection or ventilation. The charm of the car may be that it is obviously designed to be low-priced. The one aspect that will need to stand the test of time is the design itself. It is rumoured that the designers are two women, and it is not clear whether they grasp the arduous nature of the use of motor cars. It would be interesting to see how the cars would fare in a 1,000-mile endurance test.'*

"What does the *Autocar* say?" she asked.

'They also run through the standard physical description of the car, and then they also have comments," he said. "Their comments are, *the low suggested price of this car makes one wonder if either the builders have little knowledge of manufacturing costs, or they have underdesigned the car for the sake of cheapness, that will mean that it will be unable to withstand the rigours of daily use. We learned from the factory manager that the designers are two women. This, to us, offers explanations as to the apparent issues with the design and its low price; they simply do not have the knowledge and experience to more appropriately set the price of their car. If the car were to be entered into one of the 1,000-mile duration tests, it would be interesting to see if it were capable of handling the test. Our recommendation is not to buy until such time as this car is proven, even though the concept of a fully enclosed body is a particularly attractive feature, obviously designed to attract the widest market.'*

"*Idioti. Da non credere! Sono senza parole!*" was all Federica could say.

"Why have you no words?" her father asked as he came into the room.

"The motor journals have not been kind to Fede," George explained. "They thought the car was fine until they discovered that she and Nastia had designed it, then they questioned the design and its ability to withstand the rigours of daily use."

"So, what do we do?" Signor Beretta asked.

"Nothing yet," George replied. "But, I think an entry into the next long-distance duration trial would be useful."

"When I get my car, I will drive it back to Italy," Signor Beretta said. "I will keep notes of my journey and send them to the journals and see if they will publish them, that should settle the issue."

"*Si,* Papi," Federica agreed. "But, what if it breaks down?"

"Will it?" he asked.

"Of course not," she stated quite categorically. "The reports we have been getting from George's cousin Koos in South Africa have been most encouraging. One cannot say that service in South Africa is easy and lacking in situations to test the car."

"Why not have your cousin Koos send in reports to the journals, even if they don't publish them as editorial comment, they could appear as letters, which people will read," Signor Beretta suggested.

"An excellent proposition," George agreed. "I will telegraph Koos and ask him to do so. By the way, you recall when we talked about coating the windows, well, Koos says that that is the greatest problem he is having. There are just too many stones that fly up on the South African roads."

"We should coat some windows and send them to Koos for trial," she suggested. "That will give us a real test of the process."

First production

The production line was started on Monday morning. Both Ian Stuart and Federica supervised the loading of a completed frame onto one of the movable carts. Stuart had staged the various parts that would be needed in the appropriate places and had positioned people to do the specific tasks of affixing those parts. He and Federica followed the car down the line and noted things that were not right or that could be made easier. Several times, Federica stopped the work altogether to review some issue that arose, until finally the work stopped because of a purchased piece that did not fit properly. "We need to institute some better form of control to be sure that the parts that we purchase are correct," she commented to Stuart. "We cannot have delays and problems caused by parts that are not correct."

"Yes, Madame," Stuart agreed. He had been thinking that it would be just as easy to take a file and make the parts fit, but acquiesced to her suggestion.

"I do not wish to see the line stopped because there is a part that will not fit, and I do not wish to see little work benches cropping up where we make those parts fit," she instructed. "We should be able to do this right the first time without having to do extra work."

"Yes, Madame," Stuart said. "I will have the supplier of the part come here, and we will see why it does not fit."

"Good," she said. "Do we have the measurements of this part?"

"We do, Madame," he said.

"Well, for today, we will not add anything further to the car until we have corrected this situation," she instructed. "I think it would be wise to get the drawings and specifications of all the parts and check to see if they are correct; the men can do that for the balance of the day."

"Yes, Madame," Stuart said. "I will attend to it forthwith."

Next, Federica went to see how Mr Coates was progressing. She noted that the first of the bodies they had mounted on a movable cart was being moved from one workplace to the next and was satisfied that the system seemed to be working. Coates was smiling broadly when he came to talk to her. "It works," he announced.

"Pray, what works?" she asked.

"I spent time with Ian and we constructed some frames that match the frames of the car, we put wheels on the frames and upon the frames we built up the body," he explained.

"And the fabrication of the pieces that make up the body?" she asked.

"We are using the side shops and have developed some presses for the glueing process, and over here we have set aside an area for painting. It would reduce the time if we could acquire some low-temperature ovens to dry the parts," he said.

"Give me a proposal and we will see what may be done," she said. "When do we match the body to the chassis?"

"As soon as this body is finished, we will take it across the road to the main factory to make the final assembly," he said.

"Well, Mr Stuart has a few small problems at the moment that delay the readiness of the first chassis. Please coordinate with him and only move the completed body when he is ready for it," she instructed.

"Of course, Madame," he said.

"Do not make too many bodies ahead of our chassis production," she cautioned. "We don't want too many bodies sitting and waiting; the longer they sit, the greater the possibility there is for damage."

"Yes, Madame. I have a small experiment set up over here," he said. "I coated some glass with a cellulose nitrate, and it is now dry. I was about to break it to see what would happen."

"Excellent," she said. "Please do." Stuart walked to a workbench and picked up a hammer, then he collected the glass sample and went outside. He set the glass up on a frame that he had obvious built for the test, then swung the hammer and hit the glass. The glass broke, but it did not fly apart into pieces; but stayed together as though all the broken pieces were somehow glued together.

"That is splendid," Federica said. "Do you think we could incorporate this process into our cars?"

"Of a certainty, Madame, he agreed. "I will attend to it forthwith. Meanwhile, if you agree, I will continue experiments with glass and the coatings to see if we cannot improve upon the idea."

"Of course," she agreed. "Do you need anything for that?"

"No, we can get glass easily enough, but I would like some form of containment for the area where we apply the cellulose nitrate," he said.

"Draw up what you need and let me know," she said. "Thank you, Mr Coates, oh, and please get your people to clean the floor around where they have been working, too much debris, and we could create a fire hazard, which would not be good."

"I will do that, Mrs Wheelwright," he promised.

At home, Federica related to George the events of the day and the issues and problems they had encountered.

"How long do you think it will take to build a car once you have those problems resolved?" he asked.

"I see the final assembly taking less than a week, and I think as we learn, we may even be able to finish a car in one day," she thought.

"As little as that?" he asked.

"Perhaps even less," she said. "We have all the parts necessary; we just need to learn the best way to put them together quickly."

"If we can produce that many cars, we need to look to how we will sell them," he said. "Our reviews in *Automotor* and the *Journal* did not help."

"Perhaps we can persuade Papi to be a dealer for us in Italy," she said.

"I'll send a telegraph to Koos asking him if he would be able to sell any in South Africa," he added. "Meanwhile, I have interviews in London tomorrow for the sales manager post. I will travel up on the early train and conduct the interviews at the Savoy."

"I talked to Mr Robertson late today, and he tells me that he would like four more of the vans we built," she said. "Apparently, he likes being able to deliver our biscuits with our own vans. He also told me that he has been approached by others asking where they may obtain similar vans."

"Should I see him and then contact these others?" he asked.

"Please do," she said. "It is possible that we may need to emblazon the names of those companies on the side of the vans."

"If we do that, are you going to change the way the body panels are painted?" he asked.

"No, I thought we would finish the vans, then contract with a local sign writer to apply the company emblem and name," she replied. "I will talk to Ian Stuart tomorrow, and the next four motors on the line can be our vans, and after that, we will see what transpires."

"Perhaps there is a ready market for delivery vans?" he suggested. "I did send some photographs of our Abbey Biscuits van to Koos, perhaps he may help us."

"You may be right," she agreed. "I confess I had thought of them as only a novelty, but they may yet save the day. What did Papi do today?"

"He went for a drive into High Wycombe, then he took it upon himself to teach Jane how to make *Cognilio alle olive e timo.*"

"Where did he get the rabbits?" she asked.

"From the estate," he said. "He took one of the small rifles and went out after rabbits. At least as he used a rifle, we won't be spitting out shotgun pellets."

"How has Jane taken to this?" she asked.

"Oh, he has charmed the household, and he has all the staff at his beck and call, and he's cooking enough for an army, so they'll get to eat it as well," he replied.

"Do we have any wine?" she asked.

"Of course, *cara mia*, what would you like?" he asked.

"Something white and cool," she said.

"We have an excellent Chablis," he suggested. "I will get a bottle and you may try it, and I will peek into the kitchen and let your father know that you are home."

When George returned, he had Federica's father in tow. Things in the kitchen had reached a point where he could take a break from culinary pursuits.

"*Ciao* Fede, when do I get my car?" he asked.

"*Presto* Papi," she promised. "You have no concern for me or my welfare, just your car?"

"No, no, I have the news from George, and he tells me that you have encountered a few delays," Signor Beretta explained.

"A few," she admitted. "But better to resolve them now than continue forward and encounter the same delay again and again, don't you think?"

"*Certo*," he agreed. "This Chablis is very good. Where did you get it?"

"There is a small shop in Maidenhead run by a French couple, and they seem to have contacts with many of the vintners in France," George explained. "Certainly their clientele comes from far and wide."

"Papi, would you consider distributing our car in Italy?" Federica asked.

"I think that could be arranged," he said. "I have driven the ones you have built and am quite satisfied with the performance. What terms would you give me?"

"*Madonna*," she said in mock exasperation. "Always the trader!"

"*Certo, sempre*," he agreed. "So, what terms?"

"£225 cif Livorno," she offered. "Payment upon sale of the car or 30 days, whichever is sooner."

"30 days," he protested. "That's hardly enough time to get the car to the showroom, 150 days would be better, cars to be crated and time to start upon receipt of customs documents at Livorno."

"60 days then, and yes to the crating and time to start upon notice of the vessel docking in Livorno, I don't want you playing games with your friends in Customs," she offered.

"I could come as low as 120 days, but then life will become difficult," he countered. "And what friends do I have in Customs? I suppose I can always facilitate release from Customs if I approach the right person."

"Final offer, £225 cif Livorno, crated, 90 days to pay from the date of notice of docking in Livorno," she said.

"Done," he agreed.

"No quibble on the price, Papi?" she asked.

"I think those margins are slim enough," he said. "And I have to protect my investment, small shareholder that I am, since you limited me to 10%."

"Have you purchased any more shares on the market?" she asked.

"Me, no," he protested. "Perhaps your Mama now has a small interest, but I am still at 10%."

"I see," she said. "Well, it was to be expected. How many cars will be in your initial order?"

"I was thinking of 20 of the cars and one of the delivery vans," he said.

"That would be wonderful," she said. "When do you want them?"

"Shall we say the 15th of January?" he suggested.

"Perhaps the 22nd of January," she countered. "I will let the factory know tomorrow that we have a firm order, and that will give them an incentive to resolve the problems we have. Do we include the car I promised you in the 20, or do I still owe you a car?"

"I still would like the tenth car off the line," he said. "And will hold you to the other 20, plus the one delivery van and will accept the 22nd of January as a delivery date on the docks in Livorno."

"Very well," she agreed.

"*Bene*," he said. "Now I need to check on the kitchen."

"Is there enough time to make that many cars by January?" George asked after Federica's father had left.

"We need to resolve some of the small problems, but yes, I think it is adequate time," she replied. "We have enough parts already, and it is now a question of building the bodies and assembling the cars. I think that as we learn what to do on the assembly line, we could produce several per week."

"We only have about seven weeks to make the cars and get them to the docks and shipped," he said.

"We need to allow two weeks for shipping time, so that only gives us five weeks," she said. "That means at five a week, or at least one a day, *Madonna*, we have work to do!"

"With all the expenses of the construction and the cars we are building now, how are we doing with the finances?" he asked.

"We are fine," she said. "I went through all the costs with Douglas last week, and we are still well within our cash reserves. I see no need at this time for an additional infusion of cash."

"Hopefully, we can get some sales soon and start showing income," he said. "I would be distressed if we were to go under before we really got started."

"That will not happen," she promised. "I still have some of the first £10,000 that your father left me in his will, and there is the £10,000 that will come in December."

"Goodness, we will have been married a year already this Christmas," he said. "What would you like to do?"

"I think if we have shipped all the cars for this order to the docks, then I would like to take a week and go somewhere quiet," she said.

"I will arrange it," he promised. "Ah, here is your father with our meal!" Signor Beretta came in bearing a platter on which were arranged the rabbit pieces, and following him came Eleanor, Jane and Beatrice, each bearing a dish. "*Ecco,*" Signor Beretta exclaimed. "*Cognilio alle olive e timo,* thank you, Jane, Mistress Eleanor and Beatrice for your invaluable assistance. I trust that you will also enjoy this dish."

"I am sure we will, Sir," Eleanor said. "Will that be all, Ma'am?"

"Thank you, Eleanor," Federica said.

Later that evening, when they had retired for the night, George returned to the question of what to do and where to go for their anniversary.

"I really don't mind," Federica said. "All I want is to spend time with you without the interruptions of the business. I know I have neglected you of late and am desirous of atoning for that omission."

"You have been preoccupied," he said.

"That is little excuse," she said. "Come help me undress, and I will see if I cannot atone a little here and now."

"I will draw a bath and then will see what penance I will exact," he said.

"Penance?" she laughed. "You were gone in South Africa for years, and what penance did I exact for that?"

"None that was not pleasurable," he admitted. "*Mia stella, ho voglia di te!* Here, let me help you out of those clothes."

"When, I wonder, will it be convenable for women to wear clothes other than these restrictive long gowns and undergarments?" she said.

"What is this?" he asked.

"You remember the breast supporter by Marie Tucek that I had for our wedding?" she replied.

"I do," he said.

"Well, this is our own improvement on that; we are testing several for Windsor, and if they are successful, we will start to sell them," she explained. "Do you like it?"

"Oh, very much," he said approvingly. "How does it fasten?"

"There is a hook and eye fastener at the back," she said.

"Ah, I see," he said and undid the garment. The rest of the disrobing took only moments, and then followed the bath and the inevitable conclusion.

Federica was at the factory early the next day to meet with Ian Stuart and Andrew Coates.

"We have an order," she told them. "An order for 20 cars and a delivery van. The order needs to be completed by the 5th of January, it is an export order, so we need to crate the cars and deliver them to the docks for shipping. We also have another order for a single car that we may take from the line at any time. I suggest we build the cars first, then the delivery van, and we will add an additional four delivery vans for Abbey Biscuits."

"How will we do all that in such a little time?" Stuart asked.

"Did you resolve the issue that stopped the line yesterday?" she asked.

"We did," he said. "We found all the parts that had been shipped to us had the same discrepancy, so we modified them, and they will now fit, and we have called in the supplier to see how he may correct the issue."

"So, today we will continue from where we stopped yesterday and see what else we uncover," she said. "Mr Coates, will you be able to supply the requisite number of bodies?"

"Indeed, Madame," he confirmed. "I see no particular problem. I can have the first body to Ian as soon as he is ready."

"Good," she said. "Then let us to it."

Out on the factory floor, Ian Stuart and his foremen set the men to work again and watched nervously as the chassis proceeded from station to station, acquiring parts as it went. By lunchtime, it had passed the station where it acquired wheels, so now was detached from the frame and was ready for the body, so a man was dispatched to the body works to let Andrew Coates know. He returned with three other men, and they were pushing the cart with a body attached. The body was detached from the cart and hoisted up onto the monorail, and then the chassis was wheeled underneath. Lowering the body and making the necessary connections took about an hour, and then they were ready for the final moment. The car was wheeled to the last bay and fuel and water added, then Federica climbed aboard and made the necessary adjustments and signalled Ian Stuart to swing the starting handle. The car started on the first swing, and she drove it off the bay and into the yard to the cheers and applause of all the workmen.

"Splendid," she said when she came back to Ian Stuart. "Now we should clean and polish it and perhaps cover it from the elements until such time as we crate it for shipping."

"Yes, Madame," Stuart said. "Should we take it for a trial run?"

"Yes," she agreed. "Run it for a good hour and send someone along to observe and make note of anything that needs correction, then do the cleaning and polishing. Now let us start the other cars on the line and see how long it takes to build one."

"Perhaps we should extend the monorail from the factory to the body works and then use that to move the bodies over as we need them?" he suggested.

"An excellent suggestion, Mr Stuart," she agreed. "Please work with Mr Coates and see to it, and perhaps when you do that, investigate how much it would cost to enclose the passageway between the factories that we may make the transfer without regard to inclement weather."

"Yes, Madame," he said and then left to get the next cars started on their assembly journey.

At home, Federica told George and her father that the first car was off the line and that things had gone well. There had been no further issues of parts and pieces not fitting properly, so now she was focused on the next step, selling cars. To that end, she asked George about his day.

"I have found a sales manager," he confirmed. "He will be at the offices tomorrow to settle terms of employment and to view the factory."

"Good," she said. "Then, if he is available, he can spend the next few weeks at the factory working with the men to build the cars; he will then have an intimate knowledge of the car."

"*Alora, Fede, tutto va bene?*" her father asked.

"*Molto bene*," she happily replied. "Unless there are unforeseen issues, you should have your car by the end of next week or the very beginning of the following week. If you plan to drive it back to Firenze, will you have problems with snow in the Alps?"

"I will not take that route," he said. "I think I would drive down through France from Paris to Lyon, then follow the Saône to the sea and then along the coast through Nice and Genoa to Pisa and then inland to Firenze."

"We will provide you with extra tyres and perhaps a second spare wheel, in fact I think we will put together a small kit that we will include with each car that has a jack, pliers, spanners of sizes to suit the nuts we use, screw drivers, an oil can, a grease injector, a tyre pump, a sparking plug, some valves and a few other small items, that should provide enough for most quick repairs, we will provide a box for the tools that we will affix to the rear of the car," she said. "When will you get Marco to join you?"

"I will telegraph him tomorrow to take the next train to Paris, and from there he can make his way to London, and we will collect him there," her father replied.

"I will make sure that at least when you leave here, you have food and wine," she promised. "Will we need to modify our car design to put the steering wheel on the left?"

"I will check when I return to Italy," he replied. "I have seen cars with the drivers on both sides, but I do think that we are slowly moving to a convention that all drive on the right; therefore, the steering wheel will be on the left. Does that present a problem?"

"No," she said. "Nastia and I discussed the possibility some time ago, and we already have the design done and know which parts will be different. The challenge for us will be to ensure that we build the right number of each on the assembly line."

"Leave the car as it is for now," he said. "But, perhaps the next order will need to specify that the steering wheel will be on the left."

"I will do that," she said. "Now, if you will excuse me, I need to divest myself of these clothes and find something less restrictive."

The planning, trial runs and focus on having the parts all be the same paid off because the next cars sailed happily down the assembly line to the delight of all. The new sales manager, Mr Arthur Dent, duly arrived and was indoctrinated and spent hours on the assembly line helping to add parts and learning all about the car. He knew how to drive, so was often dispatched as the test driver to ensure that each car would run as desired. Each test drive exposed some minor issues, and they were quickly resolved. Marco arrived in London from the Channel Ferry and was collected by Signor Beretta, who then instructed him on the niceties of the Sirius car. Federica thought that it would be advantageous to have him also spend some time on the assembly line and to do some of the test driving, so that when they came to drive back to Italy, he would be very familiar with the car. Federica observed with some alarm that Alice seemed to have taken to Marco, and she was concerned where that might lead. She was relieved when Alice finally came to her and talked about Marco and her feelings for him. Apparently, things had not yet gone to the stage of intimate relationships, but Marco had invited her to Italy, and she was considering going, at least for a visit. Acting as the intermediary, she then interviewed Marco to try and get a sense of his intentions and feelings and was quite surprised to hear that they were genuinely of affection and that he was seriously thinking of asking her to marry him. That relieved Federica but presented her with another problem, that of replacing Alice if she accepted his proposal.

Federica's father came to her and told her that he had been to see the editor of the *Automotor Journal.* For a moment, she had horrifying visions of her father exacting dire retribution upon the poor man for the article that had appeared in the *Journal* about their car. But it turned out that he had talked the editor into publishing a series of reports about his drive from England to Florence, a distance of a little over 1,190 miles. He omitted to disclose the make of car he was going to use, but focused instead on the information that he could relay on the state of the French roads and how easy or difficult it was going to be to make the journey. He also promised photographs, so had had to acquire a camera, which he duly had done from a shop in London and was now the proud owner of a Kodak No. 3-A Folding Pocket Camera. He got film for the camera and tried some practice shots around the estate and of the cars.

On the 27th of November, Federica came back from the factory to the house to collect her father. "Your car is ready," she told him. "We have just driven it off the line."

"*Bene, bene*," he said. "Let us go and see the car."

"George, will you come too?" she asked.

"Of course, *cara mia*," he said. At the factory, Ian Stuart met them and took them to the bay where the cars were now being stored inside. He indicated the car in question, and Federica told her father, "Car number 16, the tenth off the assembly line, the previous being hand-built by us in the annexe to the foundry."

"*Fantastico!*" he said. "*Che pensi Marco?*"

"*Molto buono, Signor*," he replied. "*La macchina va molto bene.*"

"*Eccellente!*" Signor Beretta said. "Tomorrow I will arrange for passage across the Channel for us and the car. I will telegraph Vita also and let her know that we are finally on our way home. I should take some photographs of the car now so that I may begin my reporting to the *Journal*. Should we take it for a test drive?"

"*Certo*," she said. "If there are any issues at all, we need to correct them before you leave." Marco and her father left with the car and were gone a little over an hour. When they returned, she was gratified to learn that they had discovered nothing that needed attention.

"Now, how is the rest of my order progressing?" Signor Beretta asked.

"We have nine of the cars finished and parked there," she said, pointing to the parade of cars lined up in the bay. At the rate we are proceeding, we will have the rest done by the 14th of December. Then we will crate them up and deliver them to the docks. We have booked space on a freighter from Tilbury that will arrive in Livorno on the 16th of January, then the clock begins, and I will be looking for payment!"

"What will the delivery van have emblazoned upon it?" he asked.

"Nothing," she said. "We thought here to have a sign writer apply names and images according to the wishes of the customer."

"I can have that done in Firenze, good," he said. "I have an idea for a customer for the delivery van, and if he likes the proposition, he could probably use six or seven more."

"Would you want those with the steering wheel on the left or the right?" she asked.

"I think the left, but I will check," he said. "Can you change the design to put the steering wheel on the left?"

"We can indeed," she confirmed.

Signor Beretta did not leave until the 5th of December, it was chilly and overcast, and both Signor Beretta and Marco were wrapped up against the winter cold as they drove off in the early morning before it was yet light. Federica and George had suggested that they drive to Dover to see them off, but were assured that that was not necessary and that the focus should be finishing building the cars on order. Federica was happy with her production line; things were going well, and it looked as if they could easily complete a car a day, probably in even less time as they learned and improved. Ian Stuart had some ideas that he wanted to discuss, one in particular that had to do with painting parts. He felt that instead of repainting the parts that came from suppliers, they should buy them already painted the right colour.

"Do you think that our suppliers will cavil at the idea?" she asked.

"They may," he said. "Because, like us, they would probably prefer to have everything the same colour and ours would then be a special order."

"I presume then if we asked them to do that, we could expect higher costs?" she asked.

"Indeed," he replied. "But, would it be more or less than it costs us to do the repainting?"

"Would you investigate?" she asked.

"Of course, Madame," he said. "It may also be advantageous for us to investigate some new machine tools. There are some new lathes out that would significantly reduce the time it takes for us to turn the pistons."

"Then we should acquire one or more as we need them," she said. "Please get me the details and the costs. Have you any thoughts about how we may start the car without using the handle?"

"I saw a notice the other day of a patent issued in America to a Clyde Coleman that purports to address that. I will obtain a copy and see if it indeed does work," he promised.

"What about the cleaning of the windscreen?" she asked.

"Ah, yes," he said. "There was another patent granted in America to a Mary Anderson for a window cleaning device. I have a copy of that one and am awaiting the time to conduct some trials to see if it works as advertised."

"If it does, do we buy the patent from Miss Anderson or do we license it?" she asked.

"I think first we see if it works and how easily we may apply it to the design of our car," he replied.

"Finally, electric lights that we may dispense ourselves of the need for acetylene generators?" she asked.

"There is the Electric Vehicle Company of Connecticut in America that has electric lights on its cars," he replied. "But, the trade journals do not rate the system highly as the light from the lamps is dim and the filaments in the lamps either burn out quickly or break from shocks received from poor roads. I do not see this as something we can use at this time."

"Thank you, Mr Stuart," she said. "We need to keep looking at the latest developments to ensure that we are not left standing."

"I could use some help in that area," he said. "I have concentrated on the production line and see items that we may improve upon and thus reduce the time it takes not only to assemble the car, but also to make the various parts."

"Of course," she said. "And that is, and should be, your concern. Would it help if we retained someone to do the investigating and the testing?"

"It would indeed, Madame," he said.

"Do you know that Alice's father is an inventor of sorts?" she asked.

"I do and have met him," he replied. "He has an inquisitive nature and is wont to disassemble everything to see how it works. He would be ideal for the post, shall I contact him?"

"Please do," she agreed. "Give him a place that he may experiment and work, but give him specific tasks; we do not want him to investigate for the sake of investigating, perhaps start with the three issues we have just reviewed."

"An excellent proposition, Madame," he agreed. "I will attend to it."

At home, Federica confided in George all her misgivings and concerns about the design of their car. She felt that the brakes were inadequate, that the rear axle and differential combination was adequate but not good, that the ignition system was reliable enough, but could be simpler and a whole host of other items.

"Are there better systems on other cars?" he asked.

"Not yet," she said. "But I know that there must be people working on ideas to improve all these things. I miss Nastia, she had the ideas and was able to put them into practice."

"Can you find engineers that we can employ investigating all those things?" he asked.

"We could, but they all cost money," she said. "And, we really do need to see some income from car sales to balance the books."

"In time, *cara mia*," he said. "In time. We have the Motor Show in February, and our display should attract attention."

"Yes, but what of the reviews by *Autocar* and the *Automotor Journal?*" she asked.

"When your father sends in his reports of his trip through France, we should get good advertising," he assured her.

"Only if the articles make proper reference to our car and the focus is not solely on road conditions in France," she commented.

"Do not be overly concerned," he told her. "When I was in South Africa, they had had the debacle of the siege of Ladysmith and the efforts to relieve the town, and if one had believed the press, then we would never have eventually won through."

"I suppose you are right," she admitted. "But, it does concern me that the car works well and that we are able to sell adequate numbers. Our assembly procedure is novel and ensures that we have low costs, but if the various parts and components are not adequate, then that is of little comfort."

"How is it with Stuart and Coates, are they up to the job?" he asked.

"Yes," she replied. "Both are now fully seized of the idea of making things right the first time and reducing the time it takes to assemble the car. I think Ian Stuart took a little longer than Andrew Coates, but he is now proposing improvements to reduce the time it takes. It would be a poor thing if we were to lose either one."

"And Douglas, our erstwhile accountant?" he asked.

"Douglas has already proven his worth and has instituted clever systems to follow particular cars through the manufacturing process and collect the costs associated, that information has already given us some ideas for improvements," she replied. "He has also created a system for the stock of parts that we have, and when we need to order more."

"To change the subject completely," he said. "I was thinking further about our anniversary. I propose that we take a week away over the Christmas period. You will have the order for your father complete by then, and although we should continue with building cars, there will not be the urgency of an order to fulfil."

"That is so," she agreed. "What do you have in mind?"

"We take a week to go to Windermere in the Lakes," he suggested.

"Windermere, what would we do there?" she asked.

"Very little," he said. "We can walk if the weather is nice, perhaps take a boat on the lake, but for the most part, we can just spend time together."

"That actually sounds very appealing," she said. "How do we get there, where do we stay?"

"We take the train from Euston to Windermere and stay at the Hydro Hotel," he suggested.

"Do you know what Sophia and Nastia plan to do for Christmas?" she asked.

"No, but do you wish to invite them as well?" he asked.

"I think we might," she said. "They will not in any way impose upon our time together, in fact, I think Sophia would ensure that we had time alone for each other."

"I will telephone Sophia tomorrow and propose that they join us," he said. "I will also make the necessary arrangements for the train and the hotel."

"What clothes do I take?" she wondered.

"Enough to satisfy convention when we are in public, but otherwise the less the better," he said.

"*Sei un uomo molto arrapato!*" she laughed.

"You have that effect upon me, *cara mia*," he said.

Federica made a special trip on Saturday, the 12th of December, to the newsagent to pick up a copy of the *Automotor Journal*. She scanned the pages quickly and found the first of the promised reports from her father, under the byline of *Motoring Marco;* apparently, he had chosen not to use his name, but send the articles in under the name of Marco. A quick examination satisfied her that the editors had treated them if not well, at least fairly, and she hastened back to share the news with George.

"They have published Papi's first items," she said as soon as she came in the front door.

"What does he say?" he asked.

"He starts out with a description of the car, as he calls it, The Sirius Model 1, with a 12hp engine of four cylinders, each with a bore of 3" and a stroke of 31/2", and there is a very nice photograph of him and Marco. You remember that we took it as they posed in front of the car? He goes on to talk about the fact that the driver and his passenger are enclosed and protected from the elements, then he provides some technical details about the carburettor, and the ignition, the clutch, gearbox, rear axle and the brakes. He describes their journey into the centre of London, getting slightly lost in London, then finding their way out to Canterbury, then Dover, the last part of their journey being in the failing light at sunset. That was the first day. They took the next day, crossing the Channel, he comments that in the future, there may have to be boats capable of allowing cars to be driven on and off, obviating the need for a crane to hoist them on and off. There is a photograph of the car being hoisted aloft to load it onto the boat at Dover."

"Were there any problems or issues that day?" George asked.

"It seems not," she replied. "He comments on the fact that they could pick up some speed on the old Roman road that runs to Canterbury, but he cautions against zealous local police forces."

"So where did they go after they had crossed the Channel?" he asked.

"They went as far as Amiens," she said. "He comments that the French roads are no better or worse than the English roads, but he now begins to talk in kilometres instead of miles. I see the editor has added the mileage in parentheses. He says that they had to repair one puncture that they experienced just outside Amiens."

"Where next?" he asked.

"That's all for this issue," she replied. "His reports for subsequent days may have reached the office too late for publication in this week's issue."

"I think that's wonderful," he said. "Two days of solid motoring and no mechanical or electrical issues."

"Let's hope that it lasts all the way to Firenze," she said.

On the 15th of December, one day later than they had planned, all the cars were ready for shipment to Federica's father. Ian Stuart had the firm of Pickfords come in and crate all the cars to be ready for shipping. On the 17th of December, they received a telegraph from Signor Beretta to say that he and Marco had arrived in Florence, safe and sound and that he had sent off his last report and photographs to the *Automotor Journal*. Unfortunately, he included no details of his trip, so they had no idea whether or not he had experienced any problems. The crating of the cars continued, and on the 22nd of December, they were loaded onto railway wagons that had been shunted onto the siding that served their factories. Pickfords would take care of the transfer to the docks at Tilbury and ensure that the crates were loaded onto the boat. Federica telegraphed her father in Florence with the news that the cars were now on their way to the docks at Tilbury. She then met with Messrs. Stuart and Coates and went through the work schedules for the next week or so. They had one van yet to finish for Abbey Biscuits, and there were the cars to be built for the Motor Show. They also had an order from Cape Town from Koos, who had sold four of the delivery vans to the *Cape Argus*. He had sent them the information regarding the signage that would be required on the vans and promised payment as soon as the vans were received and delivered to the *Argus*. She told them to finish up the van for Abbey, then to build these next four and then to continue production of the cars at the rate of five a week until the show, which would give them twenty-five to sell. Arthur Dent she dispatched back to London with instructions to ready the showroom for cars that they would deliver early in 1904, before the Motor Show. He was confident that he would actually sell a few before the show, which was good to hear, but which all the others took with a pinch of salt, salesmen were wont to overestimate numbers. Finally, she instructed

Douglas and Alice to negotiate with the landlord at their offices and obtain the space required for a car showroom. That done, she said goodbye to the office and the factories and went home to tackle the task of packing for the week away. George had offered to do this, but she knew that her idea of what might be needed and his differed more than a little, so she declined his offer and packed after dinner that night.

The following morning, Henry drove them to the station early to take the train to Paddington Station in London. From Paddington to Euston was a short cab ride, and there they met Sophia and Anastasia. "*Ciao*," Federica greeted them.

"*Ciao*," Sophia replied. "Are you certain you want us along on your trip? We do not wish to impose ourselves."

"No, it is fine," Federica assured her. "Nastia, *como vai?*"

"*Bene gracie*," she replied.

"How is university, Nastia?" George asked.

"Good, actually," she replied. "I think the professors have now accepted that I can do the work with some facility, and my fellow students seem to have all accepted me now."

"I have missed you," Federica said. "I have so many ideas and questions, and I need your brain."

"Perhaps, if George will let you go for a short time, we can talk about them at Windermere," Anastasia suggested.

"I will, reluctantly, agree to some time," he said. "How could I deny you?"

"Easily," she said wryly. "If you had lecherous thoughts about Fede, we wouldn't see you, the pair of you."

"That is true," he admitted. "But, in my defence, how could I not be attracted to Fede? She is the light of my life."

"Do we know where our compartment is?" the light of his life asked.

"Let me check the reservation board," he said. He was gone for a few minutes and returned with a porter who took charge of the bags and showed them to their compartment. Shortly thereafter, luggage stowed, they settled down for the trip. At 10:15 precisely, the London & North-Western train pulled out of the station and sped on its way north.

Not long after they had left, George handed around the latest copy of the *Automotor Journal*. "There is another from Fede's father in this issue," he said.

"How far did they get this week?" Sophia asked.

"His report goes as far as Nice," George replied. "Let's see, from Amiens where we left them last week, to Paris, thence to Troyes, Dijon, Lyon, Montélimar, Marseille and finally Nice."

"Were there any breakdowns?" Anastasia asked.

"None that he reports," George replied. "Four more punctures to repair in various stages of their journey, some fuel blockage problems caused by dirty petrol and complaints about the rain and the necessity to stop and clean the windscreen on occasion to remove the mud."

"Well, at least on the Mediterranean the weather would have been a little more clement" Sophia commented.

"It looks as if things went well," George said.

"So far," Federica agreed. "I imagine his next stop would have been Genova, then he must have stopped somewhere before the final drive to Firenze. I may write to Mama and get her to give me all the details."

"Does the *Journal* make any comment about the reliability?" Sophia asked.

"None that I can see," George said. "But, there are a couple of days of the trip yet to be published, so perhaps after it is complete, they may say something that counters their previous comments."

"We'll see," Federica said. "*Vedere per credere!*"

"So, how much farther to Windermere?" Anastasia asked.

"Quite a long way yet," George said. "We have only just passed Rugby."

"Does this train go all the way to Windermere?" Federica asked.

"The train, no, but this carriage, yes," George explained. "We get shunted off at Carnforth and then the Furness Railway picks us up and takes us the rest of the way."

When they reached Carnforth, while the carriage shunting was taking place, they took advantage of the dining room there and had a late lunch. Over lunch, the conversation was all about the recent news of the first powered flight of an aircraft by the Wright brothers in America.

"Have you ever thought about trying to build an aircraft?" George asked Federica.

"I have toyed with the idea," she replied. "Flying through the air sounds so exciting, I have tried to imagine what might be needed."

"Perhaps that will be our next venture," Anastasia commented.

"Perhaps," Federica agreed. "But, for the moment, we have a fledgling car company to make successful."

"I'm sorry to interrupt," Sophia said. "But, we need to leave, the train is now ready to leave for Windermere."

They arrived into Windermere late in the afternoon and took a cab to the Hydro Hotel, an impressive edifice overlooking the lake that was built around mineral springs and "healing" baths. Unfortunately, the sun had set by the time they reached the hotel, so were unable to appreciate the views.

Over dinner that evening, Federica apologised to George, then raised the subject of the Motor Show scheduled for late in the upcoming February. She had some ideas about the layout of the stand that they had and wanted views from Sophia and Anastasia. George sat back as the three talked over her ideas and then made modifications until they were all happy with the final layout. It was going to be a stand with two of the cars and one of the delivery vans. They also decided that they would take two cars for the outdoor demonstration drives. Finally, Federica announced that she was finished with car matters and turned to George and asked him what he wanted to do the next day.

"Tomorrow the weather is forecast to be at least dry, if a little chilly," he said. "I propose that we hire a launch for the day and tour the lake."

"I would enjoy that," Federica said. "Shall we take Sophia and Nastia with us?"

"Of course," he said.

"Tomorrow is Christmas Eve," Anastasia said. "It is almost a year since you were married."

"Already?" Federica marvelled. "So much has transpired this year."

"Nastia, do any of your fellow students hold any attraction for you?" George asked.

"There is one," she admitted. "His name is William McIntosh."

"Is he tall, short, thin, fat, where is he from?" George pressed.

"He is about your height and build," she replied. "And, he comes from Kimberley in South Africa."

"Oh, and if you take up the offer of Koos and Anna to visit South Africa next summer, would that also include a visit with the said Mr McIntosh?" he asked.

"Probably not," she said. "I understand that he will be with his aunt and uncle in Inverness when not at university."

"Sophia, have you met this William?" Federica asked.

"I have," she replied. "He is one of four or five students who are often at our rooms in London. I think they come as much for the food as to study with Nastia."

"Well, I wish you well, Nastia," Federica said. "I will see you all on the morrow, I am for bed, good night all."

"Shall we see you for breakfast?" George asked of Sophia and Anastasia.

"We will be up, perhaps not with the lark, but we will be up," Sophia replied.

In their room away from everyone else, Federica unburdened herself to George about her worries and concerns with the car business. "Have we been too hasty?" she asked. "We have invested considerably and have yet to sell many cars."

"Do you believe in your design?" he asked.

"I do, but I was quite taken aback by the comments in *Autocar* and the *Journal*," she said. "I did not really expect such criticism, not based upon actually experience but merely upon conventional wisdom, if it is indeed wisdom and not simple bias."

"I think we may face that for some time," he said. "Men are afraid to admit that women may be their equals in intelligence; our whole body of law since Roman times has been structured to keep it that way."

"Why?" she asked.

"I have no good answer for you," he replied. "How is it in Italy?"

"Publicly, probably worse than here," she said. "But behind the doors, women wield surprising power. Perhaps that is the case here, but why was it only late last century that the law was changed so that a woman could keep her own property? Why cannot women vote in elections?"

"We have to hope that as time passes, those issues are addressed and put behind us," he said. "To return to our car, are you satisfied with the way they are now produced on your assembly line?"

"Yes, for the moment," she said. "But we can all see things that may be improved, so we will make some changes throughout the year."

"Perhaps we'll get some better reviews when your father's last report is in and he discloses that he drove for some twelve hundred miles and had no breakdowns with the car along the way," he suggested.

"*Speriamo*," she agreed. "Now, enough of cars and fears, it is time to think of other things!"

"I have hired the steam launch Kittiwake for the day," George said as they gathered for breakfast the following day. "We need to be at the Bowness Pier at ten to meet the boat."

"Will we go up the lake or down the lake?" Anastasia asked. "Can we go up the lake towards Waterhead? I have a fancy to view the property we have on the shore."

"We can certainly do that," he agreed. "Fede, Sophia, any requests?"

"No," Federica said. "I just wish to spend the day relaxing and enjoying the views from the lake."

"I agree with Fede," Sophia said. "When will we return?"

"Unless inclement weather forces us to abandon our trip, just before sunset, which is just before four this afternoon," he said.

"*Bene, andiamo*," Federica said. It was a short trap ride to the pier, and there they boarded the boat and pushed off for their trip.

"I wonder how long it will be before these steam launches are replaced with petrol boats?" Anastasia mused.

"Well, if they are, I doubt that they will be as quiet," Federica said. "The very nature of the petrol engines is one of explosions, so I am sure they will be noisier, which may detract from the ride."

"Look at the tops over there," Sophia said. "Snow!"

"Well, it's probably cold enough up there," George said. "It's chilly enough here!"

"Over there," Anastasia said, pointing. "That's the property, isn't it?"

"It is indeed," George agreed. "I was here earlier in the year and met with the tenant, a Mr Postlethwaite."

"As I recall, he is a very nice man," Sophia added. "Your father and I had several meetings with him and the other tenants that are hereabouts."

"What did you get Fede for Christmas, George?" Anastasia asked.

"A little something," he replied. "But really, what I did was entice her away from the daily worries of our car business and give her the chance to do nothing."

"For that I am grateful," Federica said. "I had not realised until just now how much I needed the time away, just to spend looking at the hills with their snow caps and the trees around the lake, it is so peaceful."

"Shall we try the picnic lunch?" Sophia asked. "I see there is soup as well as sandwiches, one of the benefits of a steam launch, there is always hot water!"

"You never thought of a steam car?" George asked Federica.

"We investigated them, but concluded that they will be replaced by petrol engines completely in a few years," she replied. "One simply cannot go far enough in the car without having to consider more water and fuel. Companies like Weston and White will be with us for a while, but I would not invest in them."

"But steam seems to still be popular in agriculture," he commented. "How long before that also changes?"

"The first oil engine tractors have already been produced," she replied. "It will probably take longer than the car to replace steam, but it will happen. In perhaps five years' time, we should again consider selling Handy Cross Tractors."

"And electric cars?" he asked.

"There are at least a couple of companies, such as Electromobile and the City and Suburban Electric Carriage Company," she said. "But, they all have the same problem, the cars will go about forty miles on a charge, then what? Battery life is just not good enough yet, and they are heavy."

"How far does our car go on a tank of petrol?" he asked.

"About one hundred miles," she replied. "It all depends on the capacity of the petrol tank. We could put in a larger tank, but it would have to go in a different place, and then we would have to work out a way to pump the petrol up to the carburettor and not rely on gravity feed."

"George," Sophia interrupted. "You promised Fede a week away from work, and yet you are taking her back to it."

"*Cara mia*, can you forgive me?" he asked of Federica. "Enough of cars and such, tomorrow is Christmas Day, we should enjoy the occasion."

Christmas day was one of exchanging gifts and doing little else. Federica did remark on the situation of the hotel staff who had to work on the day, something she felt mildly guilty about. Anastasia made a note of the various shops and enterprises that made deliveries to the hotel and commented at dinner that night that there she was convinced that there was actually quite a large market for inexpensive small delivery vans. She had seen a baker, green grocer, dairy, florist, vintner and fishmonger, all of whom had made deliveries to the hotel. Sophia chided her gently for thinking of their company again, but only gently. She had herself noticed the same thing and had wanted to talk about it, but had been reticent because the holiday was supposed to be time away from the business of cars.

Crystal Palace revisited

"Good morning, Alice," Federica greeted her went she went to the office on the 4th of January, refreshed from her break away from the company and ready to take on the world again.

"Good morning, Madame," Alice replied. "How was the trip away?"

"Most relaxing," Federica said. "A little chilly at times, but I enjoyed the time I was able to spend with Mr Wheelwright and the rest of the family. How was your Christmas?"

"Very nice, thank you, Madame. We got the news late last year that my father is going to be retained to check on inventions and try them to see if they actually work, which quite made the day," Alice replied.

"I am pleased that we have been able to do something that is mutually beneficial," Federica said. "Have you seen Mr Stuart or Mr Coates?"

"They were both here early and are both in their respective factories," Alice said. "They are both keen to have models available for the Motor Show next month. Mr Wilson is in his office, working on the accounts for last year."

"Thank you, Alice," Federica said. "I think I will see what Douglas has to say first, then I will take a tour of the factories."

"There are two other things, Madame," Alice said. "The telephone people will be here today to install our telephone, and they will be at the two factories tomorrow to do the same, and workmen will be here soon to start putting in large windows for the car showroom next door. They should be done with all the changes by the middle of February."

"Good," Federica said. "When they come, would you be so kind as to ask the telephone people when they will also install the telephones at Abbey Biscuits, Windsor Garments and the Burnham Foundry?"

"Of course, Madame," Alice said. "Are you also going to request service for Handy Cross Tractors?"

"If they have service out that way, it would be most convenient," Federica said. "Would you see if the installation people have a notion of when that may happen?"

"Certainly, Madame," Alice said. "Will there be anything else?"

"I don't think so, Alice, thank you, except perhaps tea, would you mind bringing tea to Mr Wilson's office?"

"Not at all, Madame," Alice said.

Federica went to Douglas Wilson's office and found him delving through papers. "Good morning, Douglas," she greeted him. "I trust you had a good Christmas."

"Indeed, I did, Mrs Wheelwright," he replied. "And yourself?"

"It was most pleasant," she said. "I am most refreshed and eager to see what 1904 may bring us."

"It will be interesting," he said. "I am currently preparing the accounts for 1903. I should have them complete in a week or so. Much of the work is around the construction phase of the business, with only a small amount of actual car production."

"Very good, Douglas, thank you, ah, here is Alice with some tea," she said. "Tell me, how soon can you give me some idea of the actual costs per car?"

"I should be able to do that when I have completed the accounts for the year," he said. "As I said, there will be a section for the building of the factories, then we will have expenses associated with acquiring parts and materials, then as we build cars, some of those costs will be assigned to the cars."

"When you have the accounts complete, would you forward a copy to our accountants in London, so that they may aggregate them into the accounts for all our enterprises?" she asked.

"Of course, Mrs Wheelwright," he promised. "I have already been in touch with them and have agreed upon certain treatments of costs that will serve us best when we deal with the Board of Inland Revenue."

"Thank you, Douglas," she said. "That will be most helpful. I should visit the factories and see what is afoot. Tell me, do you possess a driving licence?"

"I was planning on getting one this week," he said.

"Good," she said. "We will probably have to inveigle you into the team that goes to the Motor Show, perhaps you could do some demonstration driving for us?"

"That would be most interesting," he said. "I look forward to that."

"Please mention to Alice that she should also obtain a driving licence," she said. "Perhaps you could go together to the licensing office in one of the company cars, draw from petty cash for the licence fees."

"I will attend to that today," Douglas promised.

"Alice said that we had come to terms with the landlord regarding the extra space to use as a showroom," she commented.

"We have indeed," he said. "We have the most advantageous terms, and Alice is currently working with a builder to put in windows and doors and some flooring that will stand up to the cars being placed upon it."

"Good," she said. "Alice told me that the work should be done by the middle of February."

"That is what she also told me," he replied. "That may be optimistic, but she seems to be able to achieve the impossible."

"Now we just need to be sure that we have cars to display," she said.

Federica left the office and drove to the car factory. There she found Ian Stuart deeply engrossed in some drawings. He was looking at some new ideas for the final mating of the body to the chassis. He and Andrew Coates had come up with the idea, and he was now seeing how to put it into practice. Federica said hello and had a short discussion with him to determine how many completed cars they had, then left to obtain a driving licence for herself and also to register all their cars, their personal cars and those of the Sirius Car Company and obtain numbers for them, she also was going to pay the fee and obtain the numbers that they as a manufacturer could use on temporary plates. That activity took her the best part of the day, but it was finally done, and they could now bravely drive past Constable Platt without fear of being hauled over and cited for failing to have registered the cars or for driving without a licence. The licensing office had been busy, as many who had cars or drove cars as a chauffeur were seeking to comply with the new law.

George had also obtained his driving licence as he told Federica later that evening when she returned from her marathon licensing session, but he had gone directly there and had been one of the first in line. He had then spent the balance of the day checking on the biscuit factory and the garment factory. As Federica was occupying her time almost wholly with Sirius Cars, he felt that he should stay involved with the other businesses. She gave him a report of her day and then began planning for the Motor Show outing.

"We should book the hotel soon," she said. "Or there will be no rooms close to Crystal Palace."

"How many rooms do we need?" he asked.

"One, two, three, four, five, six," she counted. "One for us, another for Sophia and Nastia, and one each for Ian Stuart, Andrew Coates and Douglas Wilson and finally one for Alice. Arthur Dent has already indicated that he will travel down by train on a daily basis."

"You are taking them all?" he asked.

"I am," she confirmed. "We need someone on the stand in the show, and we need at least one driver for the outside display. Would you prefer to drive or be on the inside stand?"

"I think it may be politic if I stay with the stand," he said. "Whereas we may get some sales from the driving demonstrations, I think it more likely that we will see results from the exhibition itself."

"Thank you," she said. "I was thinking that I would use Douglas and Alice for the driving and then have the rest of us take turns upon the stand, so that we will not have to be there all day long."

"Will some potential buyers demur in the face of Alice driving them?" he asked.

"It is possible," she agreed. "But I think it may be more likely that people will be attracted to the car just because Alice is driving, it shows that the car may be readily driven by a man or a woman."

"What do you hear from your father?" he asked.

"The boat is on the water between Gibraltar and Civitavecchia," she said. "After Civitavecchia, it will go to Livorno, and then Papi will have his cars, he wrote to say that he has a building ready for them and that he already has interested parties. My supposition is that he went to his wealthy friends and talked them into buying cars from him."

"The forecast is for snow tonight," he said. "If you take a car to the office tomorrow, have a care, I would not like to hear that you have gone off the road."

"I will be careful," she promised. "I just need to decide what to wear as it has been so cold lately, and the car is cold."

"Is there no way to heat the car?" he asked.

"There is a patent held by a Canadian, one Thomas Ahearn, which has among its claims the ability to electrically heat a car, whether or not that applies to cars as we know them or what the Canadians call street cars, or trams, I am not sure. We do not have enough electricity in our design to consider any form of heating. I have seen people with small paraffin stoves in their cars, but that seems to me a recipe for disaster," she explained.

"So, something yet to invent?" he asked.

"Indeed," she agreed. "If we were to consider heating the car, we should first look at insulation to avoid losing too much heat, but would that make it unbearable in the summer?"

"So much to consider," he said. "It would seem that you and Nastia will be busy for years to come."

"If we can sell enough cars to avoid bankruptcy," she said. "We will see how sales are this year after our introduction at the Motor Show."

It did indeed snow that night, and Federica's drive to her office was slow. The snow was not so much the issue as the odd patches of ice that she encountered. After one or two slides across road intersections, she learned how fast to approach another road so that should could, in fact, stop. Alice had tea ready when she arrived, and Ian Stuart was there.

"Mr Stuart, good morning," Federica said.

"Good morning, Madame," he replied. "You will be pleased to hear that we have finished the delivery vans for Abbey and the Cape Argus. Douglas is currently organising shipping for those from Southampton. We have three cars done and have now got the process reliable enough to build as many as six a week quite easily, perhaps seven."

"That is good," she said. "Did the telephone company complete their installation yesterday?"

"They did," he replied. "We now have telephone service between here and the two factories as well as to anyone else who had a telephone."

"Alice, have you already modified the stationery?" Federica asked.

"Yes, Madame," Alice said. "I only included this office number, should I also add the numbers of the factories?"

"I think just the office number for now," Federica replied. "I would not like to think that Mr Stuart and Mr Coates are being bombarded with calls they do not want. Now, to the Motor Show, Alice, please make hotel bookings in Sydenham for six rooms. There will be myself and Mr Wheelwright, Mrs Wheelwright and Miss Wheelwright, then Mr Stuart, Mr Coates, Mr Wilson and yourself. I had thought of asking two of the gentlemen to share a room, but that may not be convenient, so a room apiece, I think. We will need the rooms for the nights of the 11th of February until the 25th of February."

"Yes, Madame, you wish me to come to the Motor Show?" Alice asked.

"I was rather hoping that I could persuade you to share the driving of the cars in the outside exhibit," Federica said. "We have the stand that we must have people on and the cars outside, so we will need quite a party."

"What do I wear for such duties?" Alice asked.

"You and I will go shopping and find appropriate attire," Federica said. "Mr Stuart, do you have a suit that might be appropriate for the occasion?"

"I regret that what I have is what you see, Madame," he apologised.

"No matter," Federica said. "I think I will send you three gentlemen on a similar shopping expedition; the Company will fund suitings that are appropriate for the duty."

"Thank you, Madame," he said. "What will we be required to do?"

"We will need you on the stand to explain the features of the car and the delivery van with the view to stimulating interest so that people will buy our cars and keep us in business," she explained. "Perhaps we should meet at some time and discuss what there is to say and how to best answer the questions that may be put to us. It would also be prudent if you and Mr Coates toured the other stands to see what may be learned from the other exhibitors."

"Very good, Madame," he said. "If you will excuse me, I need to return to the factory."

"One more thing quickly before you go, Mr Stuart," she said. "Who will you leave in charge when you are gone to the Motor Show?"

"I thought that Thomas Harding would be very capable," he replied.

"Thank you," she said. "Please convey my thanks to all your staff for their hard work and dedication in getting our orders filled and the cars ready for the show."

"George, did you see this item in the paper today about the Russians and the Japanese?" Federica asked, over breakfast, a week or so later.

"No, what happened?" he asked.

"They are at war," she said.

"Really?" he said. "Well, I suppose it's not all that surprising; they have had disagreements about Manchuria and Korea and mistrust one another."

"It says here that the Japanese fleet attacked the Russian fleet in Port Arthur," she read. "It seems that the Japanese did some damage to some Russian boats but were unable to completely disable the Russians as they stayed protected by the shore batteries of Port Arthur."

"I hope we have the sense to stay out of it," he said. "We really do not need another war so soon after the last one in South Africa."

"Will it all be naval engagements?" she asked.

"No, there will be land battles as well," he thought. "The Russians have troops in Manchuria, and the Japanese have been building up their army, so I expect them to engage ground troops soon."

"Will the Army ask you to go back?" she asked.

"I don't see any reason why they would," he replied. "I have not been to Manchuria and can offer no real advice on how to proceed with any intelligence gathering. I also see no reason for us to get involved. But, our politicians may see things differently."

"Well, I hope not," she said fervently. "I have no desire to see you go off to China never to be seen again!"

"I see no danger of that," he said.

"We are almost ready for the Motor Show," Federica told George that evening, after they had had dinner and were in the sitting room in front of a fire. "The only decision we need to make is how to get the cars to the show, do we drive them or rely upon the railways for transport?"

"I think it would be good to drive them," he replied. "But we will then need to find somewhere we may wash them upon arrival, we would not want muddy cars on the stand."

"I agree," she said. "I will have Alice look into possible places."

"I heard from Nastia today," he said. "She tells me that her classes will keep her in London on the Friday, so we may only rely upon her for the weekend."

"That is a shame," she said. "But, no matter, her schooling is important and we should not pull her away from her classes."

"What will you wear?" he asked.

"I have yet to decide," she said. "I am taking Alice with me to shop and find something appropriate."

"You could always wear nothing or next to nothing," he joked. "That would draw the crowds."

"And probably a constable or two," she commented wryly. "Perhaps not, the world is not quite ready for exposed skin, the most we may see are bare shoulders."

"I wonder why?" he said. "Why do we cover up so completely? In South Africa, the black population often wore little to nothing."

"Perhaps because it was warmer, so there was less need to cover up so completely," she suggested. "When you were in India, what did they wear?"

"It depended whether they were Hindu or Mussulman," he said. "If one saw a Hindu woman, she probably had on a tight bodice top that covered the breasts but left the midriff exposed. Then she would have a wrap-around skirt and perhaps the whole covered by a sari, or a sort of soft fabric cloth that was draped around. What did they wear in Hong Kong?"

"That depended very much on social status and wealth," she replied. "Most people, men and women, wore trousers and tops, similar to the ones I wear. If one had money, then clothes of expensive silks were worn, and one's attire could become quite extravagant."

"So, still covered up?" he asked.

"Yes, still covered up," she confirmed. "Even in Hong Kong, where it was warm."

"So, I suppose you will have to cover up, but now there is no need," he suggested.

"That is true," she agreed. "It is warm enough in here with the fire. Help me with the buttons on this dress, will you?"

Undressing led to the inevitable conclusion, which was consummated on the rug before the fire. "Do you wonder what Eleanor would say if she were to come into the room now?" Federica giggled.

"She'd probably just say excuse me and then leave hurriedly to pass on the gossip to the rest of the staff," he said.

"Would you get me a glass of wine?" she asked.

"Of course," he said, and got up from the floor to get them both glasses. "Are you happy?" he asked.

"Absolutely," she said quite categorically. "I have you, we are blessed with more than enough to make life very comfortable, we have the car company, which is challenging, what more could we want?"

"Do you have any desire to start a family?" he asked.

"Perhaps in a year to so," she said. "Do you feel the need to have an heir?"

"Not really, but a child would be nice," he said. "If we had a child, we would have to make changes to our lives, but I don't want to impose upon you and cause you to give up what you are clearly enjoying."

"Perhaps then, in a year or so when the company is running tolerably well," she suggested. "If we are to do this, then I should not leave it too long, I understand that risks in childbearing increase with age."

"We will look to this in the future, then," he said. "Meanwhile, we need to practice more so that we may know what to do."

"Oh, confident are you that you can so quickly satisfy me again?" she laughed. "Are you sure that your body can match the desires of your mind?"

"You are all the stimulation I need," he said. "Come, let me show you."

Eleanor did not burst in upon them, which was as well, for they had returned to the works of Burton for ideas on how to make love in new and different ways, the positions of which would have probably shocked Eleanor. George was dispatched later to collect a dressing gown so that Federica would not shock the staff if any of them happened upon her as she went upstairs to their bedroom. Federica had been feeling a little guilty about neglecting George and was happy that they had found the occasion and time for lovemaking. It served to bring them closer together and reinforced her views that they had a love match that would stand anything. As she had told George, she was deliriously happy, her life was good and complete, and he was the one who made it so. How many husbands would so support their wives in whatever venture she embarked upon. She was fortunate in George that he was secure enough in himself not to be threatened in any way by her successes. He could in no way be described as a shrinking violet; his wartime service had proven that he was a man of action and capable of great bravery, perhaps that was what made him so willing to support her. He had no need to prove himself to anyone; he had already done that.

The weekend before the Motor Show, Federica decided to hold a party for all the managers of the Sirius Car Company and the other managers of their various enterprises. She asked them to bring their wives, and in the case of Andrew Coates, she suggested that he bring Mabel Lloyd. She threw open their home and laid on food and drinks that would feed a regiment. Sophia and Anastasia came down from London for the weekend on Friday night and were met by George at the station and transported to the house. On Saturday evening, John Edwards from Handy Cross tractors came with his wife, Elizabeth, in a trap drawn by a nice-looking bay, arriving at the same time as William Forester and his wife, also Elizabeth, who had made the short trip from the estate farm in the farm trap. Henry took care of the horses and was back in time to direct motor traffic as Ian Stuart arrived in company with his wife, Mary, and with Winston Fox and his wife, Victoria, followed quickly by Stephen Painter and his wife, Jane, they came in the Abbey Biscuits delivery van, followed by Henry Robertson and his wife, Esmerelda. Last to arrive were Douglas Wilson and his wife, Agnes, together with Alice White and Andrew Coates, with Mabel Lloyd. For all the spouses, it was the first time that they had been to Hedsor Grange, and they were more than a little intimidated by the surroundings and the very fact that they were in the house of Mr Wheelwright, one of the local dignitaries. Federica did her best to make everyone feel less ill at ease and was helped by Mabel Lloyd. All of them had heard of Mabel Lloyd and knew of her acting roles, and she had the gift of quickly making people relax and talk to her. Federica envied that a little at first, but was soon happy to let her take on that role. George hovered and picked up snippets of conversation. He was amused to hear Agnes Wilson chiding her husband for not telling her what a beauty Mrs Wheelwright was. For a moment, George wondered which of the two Mrs Wheelwrights they were discussing, but then saw that it was Federica in their field of view. He had to agree with Agnes that Federica was a beauty, but then he admitted to himself that he was biased. He also heard Mary Stuart talking to Victoria Fox and Jane Painter about schools and the merits and demerits of the Halidon School for girls. It seemed that that had been a good suggestion as the reviews from the two ladies were both positive. He also heard plans being made for lunch appointments, which he was happy about because it meant that the management was becoming more of a team. He realised that it would never have the same esprit de corps as that of his old regiment, but social interaction as well as business interaction was important. He worked his way around the room and joined Federica.

"They are nice," she said. "But, so stiff!"

"They're intimidated," he said. "They are all afraid that if they say the wrong thing, then someone will be dismissed."

"I suppose you are right," she admitted. "Was this a mistake?"

"I don't think so," he assured her. "It will take time. In the army messes I was in, any poor new subaltern was very much aware of the possibility of committing some kind of grievous social gaffe, until they became more comfortable with the others. This was good because when we go to the Motor Show, Coates and Stuart will be more relaxed, as will Douglas and Alice, more importantly, so will their wives."

"Andrew Coates asked me if I had any objection to his inviting Mabel for the weekend while we are at the Motor Show," she said. "What do you think?"

"I have no issues," he replied. "I am not sure what the hotel may make of things, but they may assume that Lloyd is just her stage name."

"I was thinking that if she comes, we could get her to pose on the stand with the cars and use the pictures as publicity," she suggested.

"A capital notion," he agreed. "Have you asked her?"

"Not, yet, but I will do before the evening is done," she said.

They were interrupted by John Edwards, who apologised for intruding and for bringing up business issues at the gathering, but who asked if he could attend the Motor Show to see what the trends were in heavy lorries and also if her could get a Sirius van emblazoned with the Handy Cross Tractor emblem and name.

"Of course, Mr Edwards," Federica replied. "I am sorry that I did not think of both those items sooner. Are you and your wife enjoying the evening?"

"We are, Mrs Wheelwright," he said. "It seems we have family in common with Andrew Coates, so Elizabeth and he are deep in family matters."

"We understand from Andrew that Mabel has no performance tonight" Federica commented.

"Indeed," he replied. "She told us that she is preparing for the Spring season and took this weekend off. I believe her next engagement starts this coming week and runs through until after Easter."

Before everyone left for the night, Federica handed out badges for the men and brooches for the women with the Sirius emblem set in them. She asked the men who were going to the show to please wear the badges so that potential customers would know that they were part of the Sirius Car Company. She also handed out copies of the *Automotor Journal* and the items from her father that described his journey across France and into Italy, and the lack of breakdowns or other mishaps. That was worth pointing out to people, she told them and was in the way of an endurance trial. She also told them that of the twenty cars shipped to Italy, twelve had already been sold and that the balance was probably spoken for, which was really good news because it meant some revenue would be forthcoming.

"Your father must have worked quickly," George commented. "The boat only docked yesterday!"

"I think he had them sold while the boat was on the water," she said. "He probably used the one he drove back in to demonstrate the car, then coerced his friends into committing to purchases. At any rate, he has told us that twelve are sold, so we may expect money from him soon. Let me quickly see Ian and tell him to add another van to the production line that we can assign to Handy Cross Tractors, and also get Douglas to make the asset transfer on the books."

Later that month, they received word that Koos had received delivery of the Cape Argus vans in Cape Town. Koos also told them that he was going to deliver them personally to the Argus, after which they presumed he would be paid.

"How will he transfer the funds?" George asked Federica as they read through the messages that Koos had sent.

"I will get Douglas to work with our bankers and set up a transfer of funds," she said. "We had to do the same with Papi, so it will be a good exercise for Douglas"

"I wonder if Koos will be able to sell any cars in the Cape," George mused. "It seems to me that they would be most useful there."

"Perhaps we should suggest that he take on dealers in the different towns so that he might extend his reach?" she suggested.

"That may be an idea," he agreed. "Perhaps a dealer in Port Elizabeth and another in East London, for the interior, I cannot think of a large enough town that would warrant the work needed to set up a dealer, unless we include Johannesburg and Pretoria."

"Should we be doing that here?" she asked.

"Let's see what the Motor Show brings and then look at the question again afterwards," he suggested.

"That is sensible," she agreed. "We will see if anyone approaches us and then make a decision."

On the morning of the 11th of February, a convoy of cars assembled at the factory, and they were all given a last-minute check before setting off for Sydenham. Alice had made arrangements with the hotel to use their coach house and yard to clean the cars and van the next day before taking them to the Crystal Palace for display. They briefly discussed the route to take and agreed that the best way was to follow the Bath Road into the centre of London, then cross the river and then go south to Sydenham. By three in the afternoon, they were there, with, thankfully, no mishaps along the way. The hotel was pleased to see them all and promised water, hot or cold, on the morrow for car washing. Federica suggested to Ian Stuart that they take an additional bucket with some cloths to make last-minute cosmetic touches to the cars as they positioned them on the stand. He suggested that, because it looked like rain that they take quite a lot of cloths to dry off the cars before moving them inside the building. He was sure that the show marshals would want that so that the floor was not damaged. Federica then asked them all to meet for dinner, where they would discuss and agree upon the tasks for each for the next few days. She wanted to go into the show with a plan of action, something the others could understand. Arriving with no assignment of duties meant milling around aimlessly until decisions were made; better to do it ahead of time.

"Move the back a little to the left," Federica said as they positioned the first car on their stand. George and Arthur Dent used the long lever they had procured and gently lifted the back end of the van and nudged it to the left. "That's fine," Federica said. "Now let me see what it looks like. Good, the two cars on that side of the stand and the van on that, with the chairs between, it works. What do you think, George?"
George handed the lever to Arthur Dent and walked away from the stand, then turned and looked with a critical eye. "I think it looks most inviting," he said. "Both from here and from the other side."
"What do you think of some of the other stands?" she asked.
"There are some that draw one's attention," he said. "And there are others that may have information of value, but which hold no initial attraction. I think ours falls into the former category."
"Good, I'm very pleased that you thought to bring some old clothes," she said. "I confess I had not thought that we may have to do the stevedoring work ourselves. Where did you get those dreadful clothes?"
"They are what I wore in South Africa," he said.
"No wonder you blended in with the Boers," she said. "You look as scruffy as we were led to believe that they were. Tomorrow, before the show opens, we will get the flowers that I ordered and place them there and there, then we'll change them each day so that they do not look stale and wilted. Alice, do we have the brochures for the cars and the van?"
"Yes, Mrs Wheelwright," Alice confirmed. "I have a thousand of each, the packets are under the stand at that end. I will set out a few of each

tomorrow morning, and then if you or Mr Coates or Mr Stuart could replace them when they go?"

"We can do that," Federica promised. "Now, is there anything else? No, good, then let us return to the hotel."

"How do we get there, *cara mia?*" George asked.

"Ah, good point," she conceded. "We don't want to muddy up the cars we will use for the outside demonstrations. We need to call a cab, are there any to be had?"

"I will check," Douglas volunteered. He disappeared and was gone for a short while. When he returned, it was with the news that he had found a cab large enough to accommodate them all, and that the driver would also bring them to the exhibition hall the next day. Arthur excused himself and said that he would take the train back into town, but that he would be back out again the following day, bright and early.

At the hotel, Federica asked the others if they had seen anything of particular interest at the show on the stands that were being set up.

"I saw two delivery vans similar to ours," Ian Stuart said. "One was on the stand of the American company Cadillac. The one thing that struck me was that whereas the van part was enclosed, the driver is left exposed to the elements. The other was on the stand of Langdon-Davies, and again it encloses the van but leaves the driver exposed."

"I think that is a problem most car companies have," Federica said. "There are cars that have bodies, but most of those have bodies for the passengers only and not the driver, who I think most assume is a paid chauffeur. I am hoping that our innovation will attract attention and buyers."

"I saw many cars with very elegant upholstery," Andrew Coates added. "Should we make some changes to our design and add leather seats?"

"That would raise the cost," Douglas commented. "I suppose we could make that an option, but then we would be complicating your lives as you try and build either to specific orders from buyers, or build to stock a showroom somewhere, in which case, what option car to build?"

"I think we stay with the simple seats for the moment," Federica said. "Let's see how many sales we get and if that is an issue raised by our buyers."

"When your father drove the car to Florence, did he complain about the seats?" Ian asked.

"No, he made no mention, neither good nor bad," Federica replied. "I think he was concentrating more on the mechanics of the car and if it would survive the journey without breakdown."

"I was struck by the number of smaller voiturettes," Douglas said. "I counted thirty, all of which were less than £200."

"Perhaps there is a realisation that there may be a larger market with less expensive machines," Federica said.

"I did see some heavy steam lorries," George said. "Mr Edwards will have something to look at when he comes up on Saturday."

"I suppose we should keep the fleet up to date," Federica said. "We cannot afford to be left wondering why we have lost business."

"The grand opening is tomorrow. Is there anything else we should do?" George asked.

"I don't think so," Federica said. "We have the stand set up, we have brochures for people to take, and the cars outside have petrol. We have a number of days ahead of us, I think we should divide up the days into four-hour periods and take some time to rest. We may call upon you, Alice and Douglas to relieve one of us on the stand. When we do that, then the one relieved can take a spell at the driving demonstrations."

"Very good," said George. "To the present, the dinner the hotel served last night was very good. Shall we eat here again? Why don't we all eat together, and then if there is anything else that we need to discuss, we will have the opportunity?"

"Did we make the others uncomfortable?" Federica asked George later when they were in their room.

"Well, after last night and tonight, they can see that we are not in any way overbearing," he replied. "So, I think they are becoming more at ease with us. I don't know if they were on their best behaviour, but I saw no excessive imbibing. Are you excited about the show tomorrow or apprehensive?"

"A little of both, I think," she replied. "To be at the show with our own car is exciting, but what if no people stop by our stand?"

"I think they will stop," he assured her. "If only because our car is one of the few, if not the only one, with a full body that protects the driver and passengers from the rain. I saw cars from Thorneycroft, Daimler, Napier, Maudeslay, Winton, James and Brown and Elswick, all with various styles of body that offer protection to the passengers and in some cases limited protection for the driver, but typically only from the front, not the sides."

"I looked at many of those," she said. "Most were in the higher price range and I assume are designed with a chauffeur in mind."

"That makes sense," he agreed. "I think we have a unique machine that should attract attention."

"It should," she said. "But enough of cars for the day."

"So, now what?" he asked.

"I know that look," she laughed. "At least this room has a bath that looks as if it is large enough for two if we squeeze in. Will you help me with these buttons?"

The 1904 Motor Show opened with due pomp and circumstance, and there was an immediate flood of visitors. There was plenty to look at, and there was a stream of people who went by the Sirius stand. Arthur Dent had arrived early, eager to prove his worth and was greeting people in the aisles and directing them to the stand. Federica was gratified that many stopped to look, and some even asked questions. The reports in *Autocar* and the *Automotor Journal* had obviously been read by many, but almost as many had not, and were just curious. George had been right, the big attraction was the unique bodywork. There were journalists aplenty, those of the two major car publications, but also others, such as the *Engineer, Tatler,* the *Strand Magazine* and *Punch,* as well as the major newspapers of the day. Federica gave a number of interviews, and they all came back to the same theme: had she actually designed the car without the help of men? Finally, tired of answering all the questions, she let George take some of the interviews, and he just skirted around the issue of who had designed the car with practised ease. His time as a British agent had served him well in the art of dissembling. He managed to drag them back from the issue of who had designed the car to the design itself. It was, after all, very novel in having bodywork that provided protection from the elements. To a man, the journalists were intrigued by the materials used to build the body, and George gave little away, except to say that it was an innovative use of existing materials.

By lunchtime, Federica was ready for a break away from the stand and was happy to be relieved by Ian Stuart and Andrew Coates. She and George made their way to the dining room and ordered lunch. "How do you think it is going?" she asked him.

"Well enough," he said. "There was a lot of interest this morning."

"I felt that too," she said. "I did get a serious enquiry from one of the large shops in London for five of the delivery vans."

"When do they want them?" he asked.

"In March," she said. "I see no problem with completing five by then, we just need to agree on the price and the name and emblem they wish to have emblazoned on the sides."

"No buyers of cars?" he asked.

"Not yet," she admitted. "But, I rather think that people will look at everything in the show, then compare, then decide. As long as they know where to find us after the show, we may yet see some sales."

"Our brochure shows the London address as well as the Slough one, doesn't it?" he asked.

"It does indeed," she confirmed. "Alice did a splendid job of that and the stationery."

"Arthur said that he had received a number of enquiries as to where our showroom is in London," he added. "I didn't see him distribute the brochures, but I trust that he did so."

"He did," she confirmed. "In fact, he has been distributing so many, I fear we may run out."

"I wonder how Alice and Douglas have fared?" he said.

"We should see them as soon as we finish lunch, to give them a break," she said.

Alice and Douglas had been busy with driving demonstrations. Both had had a stream of people eager to take a drive in the enclosed cab of the car. Some had commented that they preferred the openness of most cars, with the wind in their hair. That Alice said to Federica was before it started to rain lightly, then the opinions changed, and the attraction of the enclosed body was then obvious.

"We had a number of people who were surprised how easily the car started," Douglas said. "Several watched Alice start the car and remarked upon the ease with which she could do so."

"Any takers for buying a car?" George asked.

"Possibly," Douglas replied. "I think that three I talked to could be real purchasers."

"We will do the driving for a while," Federica said. "You and Alice should rest for a while and take some lunch."

"Thank you, Madame," Alice said. "The morning has been interesting, but I confess I would be happy for a break."

"So, which car do you want?" George asked Federica after Alice and Douglas had left.

"I think this one," she replied. "I see no great lines of people; perhaps they are all taking lunch somewhere."

"Perhaps," he agreed. "I think tomorrow we should persuade Sophia and Nastia to do the driving in the morning, the novelty of two ladies driving our cars may attract some attention."

That evening at the hotel, Federica asked for views of the show and was pleasantly surprised to hear from the others that the response to their car had been very positive. Before Arthur Dent had left to return to town, he had told her that he had fifteen appointments booked for the week after the show. That brought up the obvious question of did they have cars to send to London to exhibit in the showroom. Ian Stuart assured her that they did and promised to have some there as soon as the show was over; in fact, he suggested that the cars on the stand be driven to London and left there at the showroom. Sophia and Anastasia joined the group and were regaled with tales of the day. Anastasia told them that most of her class would be at the show the next day, along with their professors. It was a college excursion, partly to see the show and partly to see what she had had a hand in designing. Andrew Coates then announced that Mabel Lloyd would also be there the next day and that she was bringing a photographer with her. She was keen to get some publicity pictures for herself and quite happy that the Sirius Car Company should also benefit. That was good news; it meant that the car would feature in publications other than the usual car journals.

When Mabel arrived the next day, she was followed by a large crowd of admirers, including many of the students who had ostensibly come to see Anastasia and her car. Glamorous actresses held more attraction than mere iron and steel, especially for young men. Federica was happy to cede the stand to Mabel and watched from a short distance the process of creating just the right pose for the photographs. She was delighted to see that in nearly all the photographs, the Sirius badge was quite evident and that in some cases, Mabel was actually pointing it out. The really good thing about the visit was that it brought crowds of onlookers who were curious about what was happening. The stand close to the Sirius stand was also happy, with that many people milling about, they could not help but attract attention.

"Well, *cara mia*, how do you feel about things today?" George asked.

"Today is a good day," she stated. "I am wondering how much Mabel would charge for the use of one of her photographs in an advertisement. I did not get the opportunity to approach her before when she was at Hedsor."

"We can ask," he suggested. "She may, for the sake of Andrew, be kind to us and offer a reasonable price."

"Do you know in which publications these pictures may appear?" she asked.

"I imagine *Vanity Fair*, *Tatler* and *Country Life* at least," he replied. "I asked Andrew which magazines follow Miss Lloyd, and he named those three and some others."

"Well, perhaps with the publicity we will get some potential buyers," she commented. "If nothing else, she has brought many people to our stand."

"I wonder how Sophia and Nastia are faring?" he said more to himself than to Federica. "I think I will take a walk outside and see."

Sophia and Anastasia were actually both faring very well. They were busy, but not overly busy, and each had had a steady stream of visitors all anxious to take a ride in the novelty of a car with full bodywork. Among the visitors were two of Anastasia's professors, who had both asked many questions about the design and construction of the car and where the ideas had come from for the bodywork. George met one of them as he was alighting from the car and introduced himself.

"Delighted to meet you, Sir," the professor said. "Herbert Walker, I teach mechanical engineering. Tell me, where did Miss Wheelwright get such a comprehensive education?"

"We had a governess," George explained. "She had been schooled in Florence and in Hong Kong."

"I would be delighted if I might meet her," Herbert Walker said.

"By all means," George agreed. "Please come with me." Inside the hall, he sought out Federica and led the professor to her. "Fede, this is one of Nastia's professors, Professor Herbert Walker, Professor Walker, my wife Federica."

"Truly delighted to meet you, Mrs Wheelwright," Walker said. "I have been impressed by the depth of knowledge that Miss Wheelwright has of many subjects."

"I tried to give her the best education I could," Federica replied. "Tell me, how does she fare at university?"

"I confess we are all a little at a loss of how best to provide her with the education she expects," he replied. "Many of the faculty have deep-seated prejudices and have had difficulty coming to grips with the fact that her work is her own and not cribbed from someone else. In fact, I rather think it is the other way around, many of her fellow students turn to her for help. My greatest concern is what she will do when she leaves university. Sadly, our society is ill-prepared to accept women in the fields of engineering."

"We have talked about that," Federica said. "At least for the moment, she may come back to our Sirius Car Company, where she is assured of employment."

"That is good to know," he said. "Would it be possible to arrange for my students to visit your car factory at some time?"

"By all means," she replied. "Obviously, at the moment it would be a little difficult to give you the best tour, because we are all here, but when the show is finished, we may make arrangements."

"I am most grateful," he said.

"Here is my card," she said. "Please call the week after the show, and we will agree upon a day and time. If you would please excuse us, it seems we are wanted on the stand."

"Mr and Mrs Wheelwright, you remember Mabel, of course," Andrew Coates said after they had returned to the stand.

"I am delighted to see you again, Mabel," Federica said. "I am also delighted that you have graced our poor stand with your presence."

"The pleasure is mine," Mabel said. "When Andrew told me that he was now engaged in building motor cars, I could hardly wait to see what the car would be like, and then when we came to your delightful home recently, I experienced the benefits of the enclosed cab first hand when it rained lightly."

"And what do you think?" Federica asked.

"I think it's just delightful," Mabel gushed. "So compact and unlike all the others, I see it offers me protection against the rain and snow. I plan to purchase one as soon as I return to London."

"That is good news," Federica said. "We have a discount that we offer to all our staff, perhaps we could extend that same courtesy to you?"

"Really?" Mabel exclaimed. "How lovely, to be considered one of the company, and not the theatre company to which I am contracted."

"Good, that is settled then," Federica said. "Forgive me for asking, but do you currently drive a car?"

"No, sadly," Mabel said. "Andrew must teach me how."

"Allow me to offer a service," Federica said. "We will provide lessons through our London showroom."

"Oh, what a good idea," Mabel agreed. "I would be distressed to think that we might fall out because of my inability to quickly grasp the skill of driving. Has that been a problem?"

"It has been noted that there can be a degree of frustration," Federica said wryly. "Our advice to novice drivers is to have someone other than one's spouse do the teaching. My husband was taught by his sister and not by me, to preserve harmony between us."

"A most sensible suggestion," Mabel agreed. "Please excuse me, I see the photographer for *Country Life* trying to attract my attention. I agreed to an interview and some photographs, now I have news to tell them, that I will be soon driving a new car. I also have interviews later with *Hearth and Home*, the *Illustrated London News* and of all publications, *County Gentleman*."

"We should ensure that we have a car set aside for Mabel in London," Federica said to George after Mabel had gone. "We should also let Mr Dent know that he has some driving lessons to give."
"I doubt that he will cavil at that," George said. "To be seen about town in the company of a famous personage will probably delight him."
"Perhaps we should offer driving lessons to all potential buyers, what do you think?" she asked.
"I think that is a good idea," he agreed. "The question is then, do we charge for the lessons or build it into the price, and if it is in the price, does one receive a discount if no lessons are needed?"
"I think we build it into the price and gloss over the issue with buyers that already are skilled," she said. "We can ask if they already know how to drive and if they do, point out the various features of the car and where it may differ from models they are familiar with, and if they do not, offer them."
"Who will do the teaching?" he asked.
"I was thinking that we should take two of the people from the factory who currently do the test driving and make them part of the sales department and make them available for lessons when needed," she said.
"And in London?" he asked.
"We tell Arthur to retain the services of someone to give the lessons, and when he is not teaching, then he can deliver cars, collect cars and do other jobs as needed," she thought. "Ah, here is Arthur now, we can tell him the good news."
"Good morning, Mrs Wheelwright, Mr Wheelwright," Arthur said.
"Good morning, Mr Dent," Federica replied. We were just talking to Mabel Lloyd, and she wishes to buy one of our cars. Would you please earmark one of the cars we have scheduled for delivery to London for

her, and we committed that you would teach Miss Lloyd how to drive, I trust that is acceptable to you?"

"It is indeed, Madame," he said. "That might be a wonderful way to promote sales of our cars, to be seen about town with Mabel Lloyd."

"Good," Federica said. "We also thought that for future sales to people who are unable to drive that we should retain a driver instructor at the London showroom."

"A most excellent suggestion, Madame," Dent agreed. "I will attend to it as soon as the show is over. I was also wondering if we are to provide a repair service for cars we have already sold?"

"That is something we have been discussing," Federica said. "I think we should and need to plan how we would manage such a service. Perhaps this next week, when there is a quiet time, we might meet with Douglas Wilson and Mr Stuart and discuss the matter. We would need to understand how we would charge for services, for parts and for a mechanic to fit the parts."

"Very good, Madame," Dent agreed. "I will mention it to Douglas and Ian, and perhaps they may mull over what may be practical."

For the next few days, the routine was simple enough. They would leave the hotel, go to the Motor Show, spend time on the stand or with the cars outside and then return to the hotel in the evening. By Tuesday the 23rd, everyone was looking forward to the end. It had been a tiring week, not too trying, but definitely tiring. It was difficult to remain polite and welcoming all the time. It was difficult to listen to essentially the same questions and comments day after day. It was difficult to stand all day and not get back ache. It was difficult to drive around the same outdoor circuit time after time and not get bored. Federica would have liked to leave early, but the show required that all exhibitors be there for the duration.

"One more day," George said to her when they were at the hotel on Tuesday night. "Then we can remove the cars from the stand on Thursday and go home."

"I will be glad to be home," she said. "I have laundry that needs doing, I am looking forward to a long, relaxing soak in a decent-sized bath and to some different meals, hotel food is fine, but we have exhausted their menu."

"It has been long," he agreed. "We will come next year?"

"What do you think?" she asked in turn. "Has the show been worth it?"

"I imagine we will not know that before we have to commit for next year," he said. "My sense is that it has been worth it, but the final test will be whether or not we see increased sales. I think it may be politic to tell the others to take Friday off and return to work Monday next," he added.

"Definitely," she agreed. "I plan to do that as well, do nothing on Friday or Saturday, just sit with my feet up!"

"Arthur Dent has asked that we leave all the cars at the London showroom," he said. "So if we do that, we can take the train to Burnham and have Henry collect us at the station, but one of us will have to drive the van back to Slough."

"We'll let the others decide tomorrow," she said.

"I asked him to check with the customer and confirm the order for the five vans you had mentioned earlier in the show," he said.

"Excellent," she said. "Is there anything else we should do?"

"I told Arthur not to bother to come tomorrow," George said. "I said that he would be better employed preparing the showroom for the extra cars we would be delivering. He mentioned that he was sorry that we had not been able to find time to discuss the repair business, but suggested that he make a trip to Slough in the near future to meet with everyone."

"I had not forgotten about that," she said. "We should have Douglas look at the cost of parts and also at the costs of removing broken parts and then replacing them. It will not be like the assembly of a new car, there will be the necessity to determine what is wrong, then removal of parts if required and then replacement. All of that will take time, and that means having people skilled to do that, and they need to be paid, and we will need premises in which to do the work."

"I will talk to Ian and Douglas next week and see when we may be able to have a discussion about the business prospects," he said. "Leave it to me."

Thursday saw them removing the cars from the stand and cleaning up the little that was left of their display. All the brochures had gone, and they had collected quite a few from other companies along with the cards of many people and businesses. Federica suggested that the cards and brochures be wrapped up and put in the back of the van. She was surprised to hear that both Ian Stuart and Andrew Coates wanted to take the van back to Slough. She had thought that that would be a duty that would be hard to assign. By lunchtime, they set off in convoy for London and their showroom. Federica and George were together, and the others had a vehicle each. In London, they handed the cars over to Arthur Dent, said hello briefly to Sophia, said goodbye to Ian and Andrew as they drove off in the van, then took a cab to Paddington and the train home. Alice and Douglas left the train at Slough, returned finally into the arms of their loved ones, and Federica and George stayed on for the next station, where Henry was waiting with a car to drive them home.

"Well, I'm glad that is over," Federica said when they arrived home. "Was it worth it?"

"Only time will tell," George said. "We certainly had a lot of interest and people apparently keen to look at the car and even drive one."

"It seemed to me that we had much genuine interest in the van," she thought. "Did you get that impression?"

"I did," he agreed. "I looked at the other vans that were at the show, but they none of them had enclosed space for the driver, only the cargo."

"I think that is a point we may sell," she said. "But, I have had enough of cars for the week, it is time for a bath and a change of clothes and something to eat."

"I will see Eleanor and arrange dinner for seven," he suggested.

"Excellent," she said. "I will await you in the bath."

Aftermath of Crystal Palace

"Good morning, Mrs Wheelwright," Alice said when Federica arrived at the offices of the Sirius Car Company on Monday morning.

"Good morning, Alice," Federica replied. "You're in early this morning."

"I wanted to check that we had missed nothing of consequence while we were away at the show," Alice explained. "There is nothing that requires immediate attention. The alterations next door for the showroom are complete."

"Good," Federica said. "We should talk to Mr Stuart and move some cars here to display, and I suppose we need to also think about a sales manager. Did you enjoy the show?"

"I did indeed," Alice said. "Although I confess to be have been less enthusiastic at the end. It was a long time to be polite and sociable."

"It was indeed," Federica agreed. "I think if we exhibit next year, I will gather a larger group and have no more than three or four days each."

"I think that would be perfect," Alice said. "Then we could still be fresh but also gain in the experience in dealing with the public over a day or two. I noted that I was better able to deal with questions and the like after a day or two, but that my enthusiasm waned after four days. Did we engender much interest in the cars?"

"That remains to be seen," Federica replied. "It will be interesting to see if our enquiries increase in the next month or so. I did get the feeling that our delivery vans may sell. Many people seemed quite taken with the notion of their own delivery van, adorned with their name. I received what I believe was a credible order for five vans from Carrier and Bulstrode of London while we were at the show, and others asked for more information."

"That may explain these letters we have received," Alice said. "They are from two of the better-known chocolate makers, and both seem to want vans painted in their colours. They both ask for quotations and delivery dates and want to know if the carrying space may be modified to fit their box sizes."

"I will reply to them today," Federica said. "As I recall, our stand was visited by a whole host of chocolatiers and biscuit makers, including our major competitors."

"Perhaps the notion of Abbey Biscuits delivering by motor van caused them to think that perhaps they should follow suit," Alice suggested. "I wonder if they know that you own Abbey as well as Sirius?"

"We will let them live in blissful ignorance if they do not," Federica laughed. "And, if they do, then apparently it is not important to them."

"I'm sorry, Mrs Wheelwright," Alice said. "I have been remiss in asking whether you would prefer tea or coffee."

"I think coffee, thank you," Federica replied. "Bring some to my office, for yourself as well, and we will review the mail and dream up some witty replies. Have you seen either Mr Stuart or Mr Coates yet this morning?"

"No," Alice said. "I imagine they both went straight to the factory to see if it is still there. I did see Mr Wilson, he was here just before you arrived, but left to visit the factory to get figures for his accounts."

"Has the latest issue of the *Automotor Journal* arrived yet?" Federica asked.

"It has," Alice confirmed. "It is in that pile of periodicals on the left of your desk."

"Let's see if they say anything about us," Federica said. "Ah, yes, here we are. Just a short note as part of the first article on the show. They say that we exhibited, but nothing further yet. Wait, there is more later on. There is a longer item that recapitulates the articles that Papi sent to them, and the editor notes that it looks as if the car survived its test of a thousand-mile trip very well. Listen to the last paragraph. *It would appear that our misgivings about this car may have been somewhat unwarranted; certainly, the reports by Motoring Marco indicate a trouble-free journey of well over a thousand miles through France and Italy to Florence. We will be interested to see if others report similar results. If they do, then this car perhaps has merits that we were unwilling to ascribe to it before, and perhaps the earlier reports that it was designed by two women were unsound, or perhaps they had help from other quarters.*"

"That sounds a little tentative and rather insulting," Alice said. "Did your father send in his reports under an assumed name, or did Marco send them in?"

"I think that Papi was forestalling future comment by not revealing our relationship," Federica replied. "Otherwise, there are critics who would say that he failed to disclose any shortcomings in the car because he has an interest. As to the comments about us getting help for the design, I have come to expect nothing less. It would seem that the industry press is the victim of its own prejudices and fears, and the idea that design is not the sole province of men is unthinkable."

"Still, it just sounds really insulting," Alice said. "Now, if you will excuse me, I will get the coffee."

"How many enquiries is that that we have for delivery vans?" Federica asked when Alice returned with the coffee.

"Fifteen," Alice replied. "The two that we noted before for the chocolate makers, seven for drapers and milliners, three for grocers and two for fish mongers and one for a veterinary surgeon, and that does not include the five you mentioned."

"I wonder if we should not find some way to insulate the van walls, so that grocers and fishmongers can protect their product?" Federica mused.

"Would that not also benefit chocolatiers?" Alice asked.

"I'm sure it would," Federica agreed. "I will ask Anastasia if she has any ideas, and then put it to Mr Coates."

"There are several enquiries here from people wishing to sell our cars," Alice said. "I have them in this separate pile."

"Where are they situated?" Federica asked.

"They are scattered throughout the country," Alice replied. "There is one from Glasgow, one from Edinburgh, one from Durham, then as we come down the country, Manchester, Nottingham, Birmingham and Bristol."

"I wonder if that would be worthwhile?" Federica asked, more of herself than of Alice. "Let's send the same form of reply to each, asking what terms they propose. Do they propose to buy cars at some form of discount, then sell them to purchasers, or do they wish us to place cars with them on consignment and only pay when the car is sold, and if they do, what kind of commission do they think they deserve? Draft up a reply, would you, Alice, that asks those kinds of questions and let's see how they react."

"Very good, Madame," Alice agreed. "Do we have a form of agreement with Signor Beretta in Italy and Mr Englebrecht in South Africa?"

"Not yet," Federica said. "So far, our dealings with Papi and Koos have been for particular orders and on faith, but we should probably look at some form of distributor agreement that covers how they buy from us and, more importantly, how they pay us. Oh, that reminds me, would you please send a copy of the show catalogue to Mr Englebrecht. Anastasia had promised him one when he was here in January, the notes she said she was going to make and send, she will have to attend to herself?"

Federica left Alice to the correspondence and sat back and thought about the next steps. Everything for success now hinged on making sales of cars. They had proven to themselves that they could build cars, and in fairly short order, the cars had demonstrated reliability in South Africa and on the trip to Florence, so now it was time to sell. Federica thought about advertising and in which papers or magazines it might be prudent to buy space. She had noted a Vauxhall advertisement for their 5hp model, which sold for £150, less than the Sirius car, but which was a two-seater and had no enclosed cab for the driver. That advertisement turned up in quite a few publications, which she thought reasonable as the car was priced to appeal to a fairly wide market. She thought that she might try the *Illustrated London News*, *Tatler* and *Country Life* to start with. Given the level of interest shown in the delivery vans, she also thought about which publications might be best to promote the van to the various trades that would find it useful. She set herself a task to research the various trades and what publications they had. She also thought about the position of sales manager for their showroom and whether or not there was someone at the factory who might be suitable, or if she should look outside, as they had done with Arthur Dent. All those things could wait, she decided; it was time to visit the factories and see how things fared. Before she could depart, the telephone rang, and it was Arthur Dent.

"Mrs Wheelwright, I have good news," he said. "I have sold all the cars you delivered from the Show."

"That is good news," she agreed. "How did you manage to sell so many so quickly?"

"A newspaper reporter had the story from the Show that Mabel Lloyd was buying one of our cars, and the fashionable set came a calling," he laughed.

"Well, that is wonderful," Federica said. "Did Mabel collect her car?"

"She did not collect it, but I have it set aside," Arthur confirmed. "She is coming later today for driving lessons?"

"Is there anything we can do to help?" Federica asked.

"Send more cars," Arthur said. "Based upon the crush that was here on Friday and Saturday, I am in need of another twenty cars to meet orders placed with me and would like another five for the showroom."

"I will attend to it this morning," Federica promised. "I will telephone later today with the particulars of when and how you may expect delivery of the cars. Congratulations, Arthur, that is most excellent."

"Thank you," he said. "I confess I had wondered how we might fare, but am now most heartened and look forward to more sales in the months to come."

"Do you have any advice for me on a manager for the showroom here in Slough?" she asked.

"I will think upon that and when you telephone later, hope to have some suggestions for you," he replied. "If you will excuse me, I have a customer who has just come in. I look forward to hearing from you later in the day, good day, Mrs Wheelwright."

Federica sat back and smiled. That was a good start to the week. Now it was time to see Ian Stuart and arrange delivery of cars to London.

Ian Stuart was in deep discussion with Winston Fox. Federica joined the discussion and learned that several of the castings from the foundry had been at fault. Winston Fox was there to review things and work out what had gone wrong and how he would fix the issue.

"Never fear," Fox said. "I will address this issue and right soon, I will get you new parts by the end of the week. Do you have enough for the interim?"

"I do, we have thirty blocks in stock at the moment, so enough for four or five weeks," Stuart confirmed. "Will you take back the discrepant parts?"

"I will," Fox said. "I want to look them over carefully to determine what went wrong with the cast, whether it was the mould or the melt."

"Have you had many problems?" Federica asked.

"No, Madame," Fox replied. "I have installed a new mixer for the mould sands and am wondering if we have not set that quite right. I need to check other castings made about the same time to see if we have more defective parts."

"I am sure that you will resolve things," Federica encouraged. "I do have news that I am sure you will both wish to hear. All the cars that were in London have been sold, and Mr Dent has orders for another twenty and would like a further five for the showroom. We also have enquiries for another twenty delivery vans."

"That is excellent," Stuart said. "We have ten cars finished and unsold, and I will instruct the line to start on the other cars right away. When will you be able to confirm the vans?"

"Perhaps later this week," she thought. "In the meantime, why don't you put five vans in the production line anyway, and we can add others as we confirm orders."

"I will do that," Stuart promised. "Winston, when do you think we can have more good engine blocks?"

"Let me investigate and I will call upon you as soon as I have resolved the issue," Fox said. "I will add your requirement to our order book and work out delivery with you as soon as I can."

"Fair enough," Stuart said. "I also need to look at our other parts and see what we need to order."

"I will confirm with Mr Dent that we can deliver ten cars this week, then with the rest to follow in the next two weeks," Federica said.

"That would be fine, Madame," Stuart said. "I will call Pickfords to have them delivered as soon as possible."

"I will leave you, gentlemen and see Mr Coates," Federica said. "He will need to be ready with the right number of car bodies. Perhaps on Monday morning next, we might meet and review the order book and decide on what we should build. Would you both be at the office at, say, eight in the morning?"

"Of course," the others chorused.

Federica went next to the body works and found Andrew Coates poring over some panels.

"Good morning, Mr Coates," she greeted him. "Is there a problem?"

"There is indeed, Ma'am," he replied. "The paint finish on these panels is quite unacceptable. I am trying to discover what was done while we were at the Show and what was changed to give this result."

"Have we lost many panels?" she asked.

"A little over one week's worth of these side panels," he said.

"Can the parts be refinished?" she asked.

"I believe so," he replied. "But, I need to determine what occurred so that we do not continue to produce inferior parts."

"I am sure you will solve the problem, I have every confidence in you," she said. "I came to tell you that all the cars we delivered to the London showroom have been sold, and that Mr Dent is asking for twenty-five more, and that we have enquiries for another twenty delivery vans. I have told Mr Stuart to put five vans in the production schedule and will confirm the rest as soon as I can."

"That is excellent news," he said. "Clearly, I need to resolve this paint issue forthwith."

"One other thing," she said. "I have decided that we, we being yourself, Mr Stuart, Mr Fox, and Mr Wilson, should regularly meet on Mondays at eight in the morning to review the order book. Would you be at the office this coming Monday for our first meeting?"

"I will indeed, Ma'am," he confirmed. "We might also review anything, such as my recent paint problems, that would affect our ability to make cars."

"That is a good idea," she agreed. "So, a general production meeting with problems to be reviewed, as well as orders and shipments. It is beginning to sound more like the Abbey biscuit works each week."

"They have such meetings?" he asked.

"They do indeed," she confirmed. "Mr Robertson has the heads of his various departments report on conditions each week, and they decide what they will make, and they discuss problems with the various pieces of equipment they have."

"What sorts of machines do they have?" he asked.

"They have mixers, shapers, machines for adding fillings, ovens and other specialised equipment for making biscuits, some of it seems to

261

break down just when we need it most," she explained. "But they have worked out good ways to fix the machines and not incur unnecessary delays or produce poor quality biscuits."

"Do they have much that is not suitable for sale?" he asked.

"There is always some," she said. "It used to be as much as one-tenth, but we have steadily improved things, and we have much less now."

"What happens to the biscuits that they cannot sell?" he asked.

"We bag them up in plain brown bags and sell them to our staff at much reduced rates," she explained.

"Sadly, we cannot do that," he lamented. "So, I must work out just what happened here and decide how best to fix the problem."

"I will leave you to your deliberations then," she said. "Good morning, Mr Coates."

Later in the day, Federica called Arthur Dent and promised ten cars later that week, as soon as Pickfords, their haulier, could arrange transport. She then asked him for his views on a sales manager for their Slough showroom. Dent had thought about this and even had a person in mind who lived in Windsor. He gave Federica the name and address of Charles Cox and suggested that she contact him directly. Federica asked for a little background and learned that Cox was currently a salesman for a bicycle firm and that he had a record of achievement with that company. Finally, Federica asked Arthur about his lessons with Mabel Lloyd.

"It went most excellently well," he said. "She grasped the concepts and the techniques very quickly and by the end of our first lesson, she was quite capable of driving the car, but she says she wants another lesson to cement in her mind what to do when things do not go well."

"I hope she does not have it in her mind that our cars are prone to breakdowns," Federica said.

"Not at all," he assured her. "I think she is just being cautious, as she told me she plans to take the car on a tour of England and Scotland."

"I suppose that makes sense," Federica admitted.

"We were hailed by a number of admirers," he said. "Several wanted to know what type of car we were driving, and she obliged us by pointing out the name of the front and suggesting that they call upon me at the showroom."

"That was nice of her," Federica said. "Thank you for the sales, Arthur, we are off to a splendid start for the year, let us hope that it continues as well."

"Indeed, Madam," he agreed.

"Tell me, Arthur, would you be able to join us at the office on Monday next at eight in the morning for a meeting to review our production and sales numbers?" she asked.

"Of course," he said. "I will be spending the weekend in the country, so that would be quite agreeable."

"What did you do today, George?" Federica asked when she arrived home that evening.

"I went to Abbey Biscuits and went through production pans with Mr Robertson, and we also discussed some expansion plans," he replied.

"Expansion plans?" she asked.

"Another sandwich biscuit line," he explained. "Our sales of sandwich biscuits have been brisk, and we could take orders for quantities greater than we can produce. The question is whether to simply replicate the line we have now, or consider a new approach."

"Have you any views?" she asked.

"I am leaning towards a new line that uses machines that Carrs built with Baker and that would produce as much as the old line, but with less investment," he replied.

"You are becoming quite the business tycoon," she laughed. "Next, you will be telling me all about rates of return and sinking funds and the like."

"I doubt that," he demurred. "But, I confess I have found it stimulating and have learned much."

"What of our other enterprises?" she asked.

"Well, our Mr Painter has a new line of women's coats that he is preparing for the autumn and some summer dresses that are ready now," he replied. "We have signed a supply contract with Carrier and Bulstrode and would like to add Harrods to the list. We will see what transpires. As to Handy Cross, spring will be upon us soon, and the ploughing season will start in earnest. Mr Edwards has already rented out all the ploughing engines. We took delivery last week of four Foden lorries for transport, and we already have three contracted out for long-term projects and are using the fourth for short-term engagements. The transport engines are all rented out for various jobs, and we have an active client list for future jobs."

"You have been busy," she remarked.

"I have the easier job of merely maintaining existing enterprises; you have the more challenging task of creating an enterprise," he said.

"Well, things certainly look as if they are off to a good start this year. We will have to see if it continues," she commented. "Arthur has already sold those cars we delivered from the Show and has orders for some twenty more already placed. We also have a number of enquiries for delivery vans, including the one we got at the show from Carrier and Bulstrode."

"What of our portfolio of shares?" he asked.

"I confess not to have followed it all too closely of late," she said. "But I think that Sophia has been watching things and would let us know if anything was amiss or if she felt it would be to our advantage to buy into something new."

"What oil companies do we have interests in?" he asked.

"As I recall, we have shares in Burmah Oil, Royal Dutch Petroleum, Shell Transport and Trading, Standard Oil, Gulf Oil and the Texas Company. That covers the Far East and America," she enumerated.

"Do you think we should increase our holdings?" he asked.

"I don't think so," she replied. "We have quite an investment in oil shares, and I believe it would be prudent to retain as much diversity as possible."

"Enough of business and the like, do you know what Jane has conjured up for dinner tonight?" he asked.

"I asked when I first arrived home," she replied. "Eleanor told me that we are having trout."

"What would you like to drink with that?" he asked.

"Do we have any of the *Côte de Beaune* left that we bought last month?" she asked.

"We do, I will fetch some and open it for dinner," he replied. "If you would let Eleanor know that we can eat at any time, I will fetch the wine.

Thursday of that week, Federica received a telephone call from Professor Walker asking if it would be possible to bring his students to the factory the following Monday. Federica agreed that it would be possible and further offered to provide transportation from a railway station. Walker said that he planned to bring the party, all forty-three of them, to Slough on an early train from Paddington, arriving in Slough at 8:30 in the morning. That agreed to, Federica then wondered just where she was going to get transportation from for that many people. She recalled a conversation she had had at the Crystal Palace show with some people from Thomas Tilling, the bus company, and they had told her that they were working on the development of a motor-powered bus. Perhaps they might be the perfect solution. She found the business card of one of the Tilling people and made a telephone call. The upshot of the call was a commitment to provide two experimental buses to transport the students from the station to the factory and back. In return, she agreed to pay a hire rate and to include all the Tilling people who came on the tour. As they did not compete, she saw no problems with that. Now all that remained was to inform Ian Stuart and Andrew Coates of the visit and prepare what they would be willing to disclose.

Federica drove out to the factories and found the two closeted together, poring over some parts.
"Is there a problem?" she asked.
"There may be," Stuart said. "The new axles we received today from Bradwells are not the same as previous batches. It seems Bradwells has made a change."
"Does it affect the way the axles work or how we fasten them to the car?" she asked.
"It does," Stuart said. "These lugs here, which we would use to secure the axle to the springs, are different. This is an old axle, and this is a new one. You can see the difference."

"Can we modify our design to allow for that change?" she asked.

"We can easily do so, Ma'am," Stuart replied. "But will we see further changes in the future?"

"We should contact Bradwells and get an explanation," she said.

"We have done so," Coates said. "They will be here tomorrow."

"Does this affect the body as well?" she asked.

"Not directly," Coates replied. "But the changes to the springs and the attachment points change where the springs attach to the chassis, and because of that, where we attach the body to the chassis."

"So everything has a consequence," she commented.

"It does indeed," Stuart agreed. "We now must look at how many of the old axles we have and when we should introduce the change. That means also changing the drawings, both of the chassis and of the body."

"Perhaps when Bradwells are here tomorrow, I should join you and ask for some explanation for the change and require in our purchase orders some notice period when they plan future changes," she said.

"We plan to meet at ten in the morning here," Stuart said. "I will have an old axle and a new one, plus the specifications that we sent with the order. Unfortunately, it seems that we did not specify exactly what lugs there should be and where they should be, so we were rather at fault."

"I'm so sorry," Federica said. "When we created the drawings, I must have omitted notes on that matter."

"It is not of major consequence," Stuart assured her. "Just a minor item that is an irritation at most, something that we can readily correct. But, I think it would behove us to look at all our purchased parts and how we specify them."

"Of a surety," she agreed. "And we should do so forthwith. Our two other issues, the engine block castings and the body panels, how do we fare with understanding what occurred?"

"Edward Fox tells me that their new sand mixer was not set up right and that he has made a change and is now happy with the moulds he creates. He has already given me two test pieces, and they seem to be just fine," Stuart explained. "I have given him authorisation to resume his production."

"I discovered the problem with the paint finish on our panels," Coates said. "We moved the work around a little to better flow through the factory. Unfortunately, some parts were then close to windows, and those were open during a rain shower, and the panels got wet. The water affected the finish. We have looked at putting awnings above the windows to keep any rain out in the future. I would prefer to keep the windows open in that area, moisture in the air is fine, but direct rain spatter is not."

"A lesson that we have learnt then," Federica said.

"It is indeed, Ma'am," Coates agreed. "We now have agreed that if we move things around, we will ask ourselves more questions and see if we cannot foresee problems such as these."

"Very good," Federica said. "I am pleased that you were both able to quickly identify our problems and find solutions. Thank you."

"It is our pleasure, Ma'am," Stuart said, speaking for both of them.

Federica related her adventures for the day to George later that evening. "I have failed," she said finally.

"Why, because we omitted a note on an order for parts?" he said. "If that is the only problem we have, it will surprise me."

"But, George, I should have thought of that," she moaned.

"I should have thought of a lot of things when I was riding in the veldt," he replied. "But, I did not, and I still survived, even with people shooting at me. To more important matters, what will you show and tell the students on Monday?"

"I thought to start with the first concepts we had and then show how we modified the chassis frame because of the cracking, and then the engine and finally a little about the design of the body," she replied.

"How much detail will you go into with the body?" he asked.

"I think we should say that the panels are pressed together pieces of different materials for weight and strength, but I am hesitant to reveal all about what materials we use," she said. "It is conceivable that some of these students are aligned with competitors."

"Will you do the explanations or will you have Nastia do it?" he asked.

"I think Nastia mostly," she said. "Much of it is her design, and it will help her with the professors. Then I think I will have Ian Stuart and Andrew Coates lead tours with some explanation along the way."

"To the more mundane, will we provide any kind of lunch?" he asked.

"I had not thought of that, but I think yes, no better way to endear oneself to students that feed them, so I will talk to Alice in the morning and let her work her magic, perhaps we should provide for the factories in general, that way none of the workers is offended that we treat these students better than we treat our own employees," she replied.

Alice had ideas when Federica posed the problem to her of feeding the five thousand, as she put it. Alice suggested they contact Lyons, who were well known as caterers and get them to manage things.
"Is there a budget for this?" she asked of Federica.
"I confess not to have thought upon that," Federica replied. "Please use your best judgment in contracting for a reasonable lunch of perhaps two courses plus a dessert, no wine or beer, I think, but I think coffee to follow the dessert."
"Yes, Mrs Wheelwright, I will also arrange for tables and chairs and will go and see Mr Stuart about the best place to set out the luncheon," Alice said. "I also have here forms of agreement for car dealers for your review, and we have received four more enquiries regarding delivery vans. It is almost as if they have generated more interest than our car."
"It certainly seems that way," Federica agreed. "But, perhaps that is because someone interested in a car walks into the showroom, whereas a potential customer for a van writes to us wanting to understand how they may get their name emblazoned upon the sides of the van."
"I will attend to the luncheons for next week, if you will excuse me," Alice said. After she had gone, Federica looked over the agreement for possible dealers, made two minor changes and then marked the papers for transmission to their solicitors for final review. She set a date by which she wanted to see a response from the solicitors; it had been her experience that they tended to drag their feet and not respond as quickly as she would like. She then called Sophia to see if she was going to come to Hedsor over the weekend. Sophia was going to come, but Anastasia would stay in London and journey down with the rest of her class on Monday morning. She wanted to be fully included in the outing and felt that joining them on Monday at the factory would not be the best thing to do.

William Forester, the farm manager, sought the attention of George and Federica on Saturday. He was planning spring sowings and wanted to know if they had any preferences as to crops. He also had a short list of new equipment that he wished to purchase for the farm. He was looking for a new sickle bar mower and a McCormick Harvester, plus some smaller items for potato planting and harvesting. He had numbers at hand for the costs and delivery dates. George and Federica quickly looked over the numbers and approved the purchases. As to the crops, they looked to Forester for guidance, and he had certain wheat and oats crops in mind as well as an expansion of the market garden he had been building up. That had turned out to be a very profitable venture, and he was now supplying several of the major hotels locally and four greengrocers. The business of the day done, Federica turned to other matters,

"How do your girls fare in school?" she asked.

"Very well," he replied. "I am delighted with their progress and am looking to the future. Catherine is enjoying the Halidon School, and I intend to also enrol Elizabeth for the new school year starting this September."

"That is quite a journey for the girls each day," Federica commented.

"It would seem so," he agreed. "But Catherine travels with another girl who also attends the school and whose father drives her with his trap on his way to the station in Slough. The girls' mother meets them after school and drives them home. My Elizabeth, from time to time, will help out by taking our trap into Slough and bringing the girls home."

"So later this year, Elizabeth will join the other two girls?" Federica asked.

"She will indeed, as will another girl from a large house situated close to us," Forester explained.

"That could be fun and noisy, or a long journey, depending on the mood of the girls," George laughed.

"You're right, Sir," Forester agreed. "But, as far as I can tell, the girls are quite amicable and I have seen no squabbles, certainly no tears. I was wondering if the farm might get one of the delivery vans like the Abbey Biscuit van, that we may use to deliver produce to the various hotels and grocers that we supply?"

"I think that could be arranged," Federica agreed. "What should we put on the outside as a name?"

"I had wondered if we could use the name, Beeches Farms?" Forester suggested.

"That sounds reasonable," George agreed. "The farm, after all, is amid large beech woods. Were you thinking of a painting of a beech tree on the sides of the van?"

"I was indeed, Sir," Forester said. "I fact, my wife has made a sketch of a possible sign."

"Very nice," George agreed, looking over the paper that Forester gave him. "What do you think, Fede?"

"Delightful," she agreed.

"If we may take the sketch, we will have the sign writer put it and the name on the sides of the van, and we should have one available for you shortly," George said. "One other thing, can you drive a car?"

"I regret not, Sir," Forester admitted.

"Never mind," Federica said. "I will have one of our factory people come with a car to the farm and teach you. You will have to get your own driving licence from the County, but that is simply a question of being there and paying the fee."

"Very good, Ma'am," Forester said. "I look forward to the lessons."

The first formal production meeting of the Sirius Car Company was held on Monday morning at eight in the morning. Ian Stuart and Andrew Coates quickly described their production plans for the week and assured Federica that there were no current problems. Winston Fox asked if he could get a view of what production requirements might be a month away, so that he could properly manage his foundry schedules. Unfortunately, that information was not available, so Federica made a guess and suggested that he start with that and that the following week they would look at the numbers again and see what may have changed. Douglas Wilson then asked a number of questions about parts they had or order or needed to purchase, and he added quantities to a chart he had, showing what was needed and when.

"Now, to the visit," Federica said, after the business of the production meeting was concluded. "Are we ready?"

"We are," Stuart assured her. "We have a couple a frames set on stands away from the production line and the various parts that will attach to them."

"I have also taken a completed body and several panels to the assemble area and have also set them on stands for the students to view," Coates added. "That way, we can avoid showing them the details of the panel assembly stages."

"And if they question how the panels are made?" Federica asked.

"I will describe the process without disclosing the exact nature of the materials we use," Coates explained.

"I have no idea what kind of questions these students may ask, but they may be prompted by the professors, so expect some quite technical discussions," Federica said. "I am relying on Anastasia to answer many of the questions, as she had such a hand in the design of the car. But, it is possible that we may all be asked about the assembly process. I trust we are all ready for that?"

"Speaking for Andrew and myself, we are indeed," Stuart assured her. "If these students are like many that I have known, the notion of a free lunch will be as attractive as any factory."

"You are probably quite right," she agreed. "Well, perhaps, gentlemen, we should repair to the factory and await the onslaught."

At a little after 9:30, two motor buses pulled into the factory of the Sirius Car Company. The buses attracted almost as much attention as the students, and the Tilling people were all smiles when they were introduced to Federica and her managers. Apparently, the buses had met expectations, and trials were to continue before deliveries were to be made to London as part of a new motor bus service. Federica introduced herself and the others to the assembled crowd and then led the way to the area where Ian Stuart had placed the frames on stands. Federica deferred to Anastasia, who pointed out the design features of the chassis and then moved on to the engine, gearbox, and other parts that made up the car. She finished her talk with a description of the body and then pointed out features on the body that had been brought to the display. Then she asked for questions. The questions came, first slowly, then in a flood, and she enlisted the help of Ian Stuart and

Andrew Coates in answering all the questions posed. While the questions and answers flowed back and forth, George motioned to Federica and indicated that he had a question of his own, "Which one is William McIntosh, do you think?"

"I have no idea," she admitted. "Perhaps that one, he seems to have more of a tan than the others."

"Ah, yes, look at the shoes," George pointed. "*Veldtschoene.*"

"What?" she asked.

"Shoes, typical of the Dutch in South Africa," he said. "But here is Professor Walker, we may ask him."

"Ask me what, pray?" Walker wanted to know.

"How is the visit, and who is that young man?" George asked.

"Splendid, most instructive and as an added treat to ride a new Tilling motor bus before it is even in service, how did you manage that?"

"I made a call," Federica said.

"Remind me to stay friends," Walker laughed. "If you can conjure up two new motor buses with just a call, I dare not think what you might call up if I were to antagonise."

"You will join us for lunch?" George asked.

"I would be delighted," Walker said. "If I might get the others of our faculty to sit with us?"

"By all means," Federica replied.

"Oh, and that young man is McIntosh from South Africa," Walker said. "I gather from Miss Wheelwright that you were there yourself, Sir, during the recent conflict?"

"I was," George admitted. "I did some service in the Field Intelligence unit."

"I imagine there is a lot more behind that simple statement," Walker said. "Excuse me, I will get my colleagues."

Lunch was served for everyone in the assembly bay. Lyons brought in tables and chairs and, in record time, had them set up and laid out and the crowd seated. Federica, George and Sophia had Professors Walker, Brand and Dallender and the Tilling representative with them which gave the students the chance to talk to Ian Stuart and Andrew Coates without their professors listening and potentially critiquing their every word. Anastasia sat with Andrew Coates and helped him dance around the exact nature of the body panels they had invented. Federica had asked Winston Fox to join them, and he sat at a table with another group of students and the drivers from Tilling. Fox was bombarded with questions about castings, not only for the cars but also for railway parts and other uses. He, in turn, asked the Tilling drivers about the new motor buses and who had made the various parts that went into the construction. The drivers were actually from the factory where they were built and were quite happy to talk about the development and about the management of the company. Something Fox declined to be drawn into. He had no quarrels with the way either Federica or George interacted with him and the foundry business. After lunch, Professor Walker made a short speech of thanks and wished the Sirius Car Company well, and then the students were whisked away by the Tilling buses and normalcy returned to the factory. Anastasia went with her class, and Federica saw that she was in deep discussion with two of the professors who were obviously full of questions. Federica hoped she had answers, but was confident that she would be able to hold her own.

"Well, how do you think this morning went?" Federica asked George that evening.

"I think very well," he said. "The questions and comments we got from the professors at lunchtime led me to believe that they were quite impressed."

"I got that as well," she agreed. "I did see the Tilling man paying very close attention to the discussion on the side panels of the car. Perhaps he sees an application for similar concepts in their buses."

"I had a brief chat with William McIntosh," George said. "I asked him where he was from, and after he had told me Kimberley, I told him that I had been there in the recent war. His family had been in the siege of Kimberley, but had sustained no particular hardship or losses, except to develop a deep mistrust and dislike for Rhodes, which does not surprise me, the man can be most manipulative."

"What is McIntosh like?" Federica asked.

"I liked him," George said. "He seems to be straight straightforward sort of chap, who I see as doing well at whatever he puts his hand to."

"Is he a fortune hunter?" Federica asked.

"I don't believe so," George replied. "His family has money enough; they apparently sold their holdings to De Beers before the war and had moved much of their money to Scotland. Perhaps they intend to return there one day, or perhaps they saw storm clouds brewing and took precautions against the loss of their investments."

"Speaking of South Africa, there was a letter from Koos today, he wished to know if we could provide him a delivery van, but with a flat platform instead of the box that we currently provide, rather like a small version of the lorries that Mr Edwards now has at Handy Cross," Federica said.

"I like the sound of that," George said. "I could see many uses for such a motor. Would it be difficult to provide one to Koos?"

"Not at all," Federica said. "We just need to omit the walls and doors of the current van and perhaps extend the floor a little towards the side. I need to ask Koos if he wants the back floor to be simply flat or does he want some sort of edge that may be folded down. He also sent a picture of a car near Beaufort West modified to run a pump and wanted to know if we could not do something similar."

"Did he say how this was done?" George asked.

"I should have brought the letter home, but as I recall, it was an Olds car that they had put up on a frame and then removed the chain drive from the differential and had it instead drive a sprocket which in turn drove a belt which they ran to the pump," Federica replied. "He goes on to say that Olds is selling quite a few cars through the Raleigh Cycle Company."

"Wasn't there an item in the Automotor Journal in the last issue with a picture of that car?" George asked.

"Now you mention it, yes, there was," she agreed. "I will look at it again in the office tomorrow."

"Can we do something similar with our car?" he asked.

"I am sure we could," she replied. "But, do we wish to complicate our assembly process by the introduction of too many different options?"

"Perhaps we could create a small factory that attends to special options," he suggested. "That way, they could take a standard car or van from the assembly line and then make modifications to suit special requests."

"That sounds reasonable," she agreed. "I will talk to Ian Stuart on the morrow and see what he thinks. Meanwhile, I think it would not be difficult to design a small gearbox that attaches to the main gearbox, from which we could run a shaft either to the front or the back of the car and provide a pulley with which to power some equipment."

"Perhaps a new market for cars?" he said. "A small traction engine if you like, suitable for small holdings."

"I will talk to Nastia and see if she has any ideas," she said.

A setback?

"Have you seen the paper?" Federica asked George.

"No, is there something of note?" he asked.

"A most dreadful car accident," she explained. "And, it was one of our cars."

"What happened?" he asked.

"The item in the newspaper is not clear, but it would appear that the car was somehow crushed by the overturning of a lorry laden with a large load of sacks and the two occupants of the car were killed," she said.

"How did that happen?" he asked.

"The newspaper item again is not clear; in fact, there are precious few details of any use to provide any clue as to what really occurred," she complained. "I am concerned that it was our car and the newspaper is making free with our name, almost as though we carry blame for the accident," she said.

"Surely we cannot be held liable for something that happens on the open road?" he asked.

"One never knows," she said. "I think we should try and learn as much as we can about this accident so that we may forestall any criticism of our design or our car."

"Where did this accident occur?" he asked.

"A little north of York, apparently just outside the city," she said.

"Should I contact the Yorkshire Constabulary and see what I can learn?" he asked.

"Do you think they would tell you anything?" she asked.

"Perhaps, perhaps not," he thought. "It may depend upon who I speak with. Are all the papers reporting upon the accident?"

"That I don't know," she admitted. "Perhaps we should take some of the other papers and see if the versions of events vary."

"I will drive into Maidenhead this morning and collect a variety of papers," he said.

"This is such a shame for the people involved, and for us it may be a setback. Things have been going so well of late, for March, April and May we had good sales of cars, we seem to have solved the production issues and have resolved things with our various suppliers, now this," she said. "It is quite disheartening."

"Don't be downcast," he told her. "We did not cause the accident, most likely it was a combination of a heavily laden lorry, perhaps bad roads and, who knows, perhaps poor driving. Does the article say whether or not the car was attempting to pass the lorry, or were they travelling in opposite directions?"

"The article does not say, but I am sure there will be a coroner's court and perhaps there we may learn more," she suggested.

"That is a good idea," he agreed. "I will find out when that is likely to be held and attend."

When the next issues of the motoring journals came out Federica was distressed to see that they also covered the accident and even hinted that the deaths may have been caused by the fact that the car was fully enclosed and that that may have constrained the ability of the people in the car to jump to safety when the load toppled upon them.

"I think that is arrant nonsense," George said when she read out the article to him. "If the load toppled upon an open car, the result would have been the same."

"But, could they not have been thrown clear?" she wondered.

"We still don't know the circumstances of this accident, and for the journals to speculate is unjust and irresponsible," he stated. "Perhaps it is time to call our solicitors."

"Let's wait until after the coroner's court," she suggested.

"I'll do that," he agreed. "The court is on Friday, so I'll leave tomorrow and drive to York, and then attend the court."

"Should I come with you?" she asked.

"I don't think that is necessary," he said. "I will find a telephone and call you after the hearing to let you know what the coroner rules."

"Will he be able to reach a decision quickly?" she wondered.

"It will depend on how thorough a job the police have done at the scene of the accident and if there were any witnesses," he said. "I rather think that the court may actually be in session for some days before a ruling is handed down."

"Drive safely tomorrow, will you reach York in one day?" she asked.

"I doubt it," he said. "The days are long because we are almost at the summer solstice, but it is well over two hundred miles to York and apart from the speed restrictions on the roads, I doubt that high speeds are possible anyway and I am sure every little town has its speed trap, so I expect it to take me a day and half at least."

"What time will you leave?" she asked.

"I thought no later than seven," he said. "I will get breakfast on the road somewhere and stop for the night, probably in Stamford, or if I can, north of there. I have booked a room at the Royal York Hotel for three nights. I can always leave early if the ruling is handed down quickly, and I am sure that I can extend my stay if the hearing continues."

"I will miss you," she said.

"And I you," he said. "But I will telephone each day."

"What will you do today?" she asked.

"I thought to check the car to be sure that it is in good condition for the drive north and perhaps visit Abbey Biscuits to see how our new lines are performing," he replied. "And you?"

"I have some orders to attend to," she said. "Although we had good sales in the past months, if it had not been for Papi and Koos, things would have been quite slow. I would have expected more after Crystal Palace."

"Well, at least we are getting good orders from outside the country," he said.

"Indeed," she agreed. "The sales of the vans with the flat bodies like that of a lorry have been most encouraging. The new line we set up that takes the basic car before the body is added, and then adds the new cab that Andrew designed, is working well. I wonder just who Koos is selling these cars to."

"Whoever is buying them, the results are good," he commented. "Has the new line upset things?"

"Not very much," she said. "We take the frame of the car and simply add a different body. Andrew has had to make the most changes with three lines in the factory for car bodies, one for cars, one for vans and now the new one for the small lorries. I wonder if we should invent a name for those?"

"Should the frame of the car be modified for the hard work that those cars that we ship to the Cape be put to?" he asked.

"I will ask Koos," she thought. "Perhaps a larger engine and more robust springs on a slight deeper frame. But, then we would need two lines for our car factory, I would need to look at the accounts and see how that might work."

"Would you need two lines, or just different pieces being taken to the same line?" he asked.

"It would require quite some planning and control, perhaps still just the one line," she thought. "But, all things are possible. I will ask Ian to look at the problem and see if we can be more flexible without sacrificing our cost advantage. If we did that, then we could also accommodate the cars with a steering wheel on the left that Papi is now asking for."

"Would you have time to luncheon with me?" he asked.

"Always," she replied. "Do you have somewhere in mind?"

"I was thinking of trying the new establishment in Windsor on Thames Street," he said. "Both Ian and Andrew have spoken well of it."

"Shall I see you there at noon then?" she asked.

"Perhaps a little later, shall we say one?" he countered.

"One it is," she agreed. "Look at the time, I must fly or I will never get done all that I had planned. I will see you later. *Ciao mia stella.*"

"*Ciao, non vedo l'ora,*" he said, literally telling her that he could not see the hour and thereby implying that he could not wait.

Federica and Alice quickly reviewed the correspondence for the day, then sat and talked over coffee about the accident near York and what that might imply for their business. Federica asked Alice to try and get some local papers from the York area to see how the accident was being reported locally. The Times, Telegraph, and the Manchester Guardian had all carried follow-up stories that were, for the most part, balanced, or at least withholding judgement until such time as the coroner released his report, unlike the initial reports that seemed to lay the blame on the car. There was even a small item in the Daily Mail, which was quite unusual because Alfred Harmsworth of the Mail was known to be a great supporter of cars, even to the extent of instructing his editors not to publish reports on car accidents. Federica then went to the factories to check on progress of current orders and to discuss a possible new model car with Ian Stuart and Andrew Coates. She was thinking of a slightly larger engine, with a pump for lubrication, a deeper frame and larger springs to carry the heavier weight. A new model also possibly meant a new gearbox and differential, so there would be much work to be done.

Ian Stuart was busy checking over a batch of the small lorries when Federica arrived.

"Good morning, Mrs Wheelwright," he greeted her.

"Good morning, Mr Stuart," she replied. "Are these the next batch to go to the Cape?"

"They are indeed," he confirmed. "We should have them to the docks for loading on Wednesday next."

"I wonder who Koos is selling them to?" she said. "There cannot be that many people in South Africa who wish to buy a car."

"Perhaps there are," he said. "I am given to understand that the distances between towns are great and there is little in the way of public transport beyond the limited reach of the railways, so perhaps it is business owners and farmers who see our cars as an alternative to ox wagons and horses."

"You may be right," she agreed. "Mr Wheelwright is going to York on the morrow to attend the coroner's court investigating the accident with our car."

"It was surely careless or irresponsible driving," he said. "I wager that the driver of the car was trying to pass the lorry and road conditions, an overloaded lorry and fate intervened."

"Well, we may know in the next few days," she said. "I hope that early reports and suggestions that our enclosed cab somehow contributed to the deaths do not discourage buyers."

"We may see some lessening of sales," he said. "I have heard talk in a few places that leads me to believe that there may be a period where people avoid us, but I do not expect that to last. The first good rain or snow, and people will again see the benefits of the enclosed cab."

"Let us then pray for rain," she laughed. "If we do have a period of fewer sales, will we have to reduce the number of employees we have?"

"Possibly," he said. "But I have some ideas for the factory that may help us through a slow period."

"Please include in your ideas some time for thoughts on a new car," she said. "We have been thinking of a new model that has a larger engine and all that that entails, so would require a larger, deeper frame and heavier springs. I would imagine that the gearbox and differential may also have to be changed."

"I see no major problems with any of that," he said. "I will look to it and also to how we run production so as not to lose our cost advantage in our production methods."

"Splendid," she said. "Perhaps you would include Mr Coates in your discussions. We should have a new body for a new car, perhaps one that has some more style to it, not the simple box we now have."

"We will bring ideas to the next production meeting, perhaps we could take an hour after the meeting to review what we need and how long it will take to create a plan," he suggested.

"That is a most excellent suggestion," she agreed. "We also need to find a better way to get petrol to the engine. The gravity feed tank we have now is fine, but we are limited in size and therefore limited in how far the car will go before the tank needs to be refilled."

"Perhaps we could put a small reservoir above the engine and recharge with fuel pumped from a larger tank located under the car?" he said. "We would need to find a pump that would work with petrol and then work out how to power the pump."

"That is what vexes me," she said. "I have not been able to imagine a system that will work."

"I am sure you will in time, Ma'am," he commented. "I will get Mr White to look into the matter and see if he has any ideas."

"Suggest to him that he start by investigating how the Frenchman Levavasseur manages the fuel supply in his new engines. I believe it is some form of injection, so that implies a pump," she said.

"I will indeed," he agreed.

"Well, if you will excuse me, I must dash," she said.

"I'm sorry I am a little late," Federica apologised to George. "There was much to be done, and I was delayed at the last minute by a telephone call from Arthur in London. He had exciting news. He has an order for twenty of our vans to be delivered to the docks in London for shipment to Australia."

"Who is buying them?" George asked.

"Apparently, a bakery in Sydney," she replied. "I understand that one of their owners was at the Crystal Palace show and as a result of his researches, the company decided to place an order with us."

"Do they wish for their name to be emblazoned on the sides?" he asked.

"Arthur said not," she explained. "They apparently have a sign writing company that has done all their delivery wagons and carts before and will simply get them to apply the same design on our vans."

Their conversation was interrupted by a waitress who was hovering near their table. George ordered his lunch while Federica quickly scanned the menu. She placed her order and then sat back to look around and appraise the restaurant. What she saw met with her approval, and she returned to the conversation with George.

"Do you have enough petrol for your trip?" she asked.

"I have several tins, all full," he replied. "And, I'm sure that on the road north from London to York, there will be petrol available."

"Are you sure that you would not rather take the train?" she asked.

"No, I rather like the notion of driving there, and then I will not have to rely upon cabs to get around York," he explained.

"Well, drive safely," she said. "Telephone me when you can."

"I will," he promised. "Now, we should eat or you will be late back to the office!"

Federica was up early the next morning and saw George off on his trip north. She watched him go down the driveway and turn off onto the road that would take him to the Oxford road into London. She was puzzled for a moment, wondering why he chose that route rather than the road through Slough, but surmised that he had decided upon that road because it made his journey out of London on the main road north a little easier. Later that morning, she received a telephone call from Anastasia.

"Hello Nastia," she said. "How are you faring?"

"Fede, all is well," Anastasia replied. "I have a question."

"Of course, *Cara*, what is it?" Federica asked.

"Well, one of the young men in my year here is from Queensland," she began. "His family have a large sheep station and he was asking me if we could supply them with some delivery vans, but with some changes. They would like the back to be flat so that they can carry fence posts and wire and, most importantly, they are asking for enough petrol to drive three hundred miles."

"As to the first," Federica said. "We have already done that and have sold some. As for petrol, I was discussing the very matter with Ian Stuart only yesterday, I think it was. We are looking at how the French inventor Levavasseur manages fuel injection. To us, that suggests some form of pump. If we can pump petrol to the carburettor from a tank under the car and not rely upon gravity feed, then we can make the tank as large as will fit under the car, and we should be able to have enough petrol to meet their needs."

"Really?' Anastasia said. "How exciting, when can it be ready?"

"Nastia," Federica protested. "We have only started to think about the problem, it will be some time before we have a solution. Will your friend make do with tins in the meanwhile?"

"I don't know," Anastasia admitted. "I think they would probably make do, but it would be so much better if we solved the petrol pump issue."

"I agree," Federica said. "How are your studies?"

"They're going well enough," Anastasia said.

"And how is Mr McIntosh?" Federica asked.

"We attended the theatre last night," Anastasia said. "Then he took me to dinner at a nice restaurant. It was delightful."

"Well, enjoy yourself," Federica said. "But not too much!"

"Fede," Anastasia protested. "You almost sound like Mama!"

"Just remember you can always rely on me," Federica said.

"I know *Cara*," Anastasia said. "*Ciao*."

Federica called Ian Stuart and asked him if he could meet her for lunch at the Reindeer Inn and to bring Mr White with him. Over lunch, she told them of the request from Anastasia and the need to find a solution to the petrol tank problem. What had been something to be looked at as time permitted, now seemed that it would become of much greater urgency. The first to solve the fuel management problems would surely have an advantage over the other car builders.

"We could pressurise the fuel tank and push the petrol up to a small reservoir above the carburettor," Harold White suggested.

"We could try that," Federica agreed. "But how do we pressurise the tank reliably and with what?"

"For that, we would need a small air pump," Harold said. "My concern is that it might not be reliable, and then the driver would need some form of manual pump to move the petrol."

"That doesn't sound very satisfactory," Federica commented. "Is there no way to use some kind of mechanical pump?"

"I think the problem is one of control," Harold said. "How do we start and stop the pump to move the right amount of petrol, not too much to flood the reservoir and lose petrol and not too little to starve the engine of the fuel it needs. With air pressure, we can at least include some kind of air line that goes back to the tank, and the pressure difference will cause the fuel to flow."

"Is there no such thing as an electrical pump?" Federica asked.

"Not yet," Harold said. "Or at least not small enough for our needs. If we had such a pump, we would need some way of turning it on and off, perhaps a float in the reservoir with a switch that would activate the pump and refill the reservoir to a preset level."

"I like the sound of that," Federica said. "We should explore the air system and how to make either an electrical or mechanical pump to refill the reservoir. If we use an air pump, do we power it from the engine, and would that then require something to prime the reservoir if it is empty when we come to start the car?"

"Why don't you let me examine all these questions and see if I cannot find some solutions?" Harold suggested.

"Good," Federica agreed. "Do you have all the equipment and tools you might need?"

"I really cannot say at this time," Harold said. "My laboratory has most things I can think of, but if I needed some specialist equipment, could I come to you to buy the same?"

"Of course," Federica agreed. "Providing we are not buying a power station!"

"Of course not, Madame," Harold said in horror. "I anticipate that if we need any new tools or measuring devices, or equipment, it will be small."

"I did but jest, Mr White," Federica assured him. "Be assured that if we need it, we will get it. Now, I suppose you all read the item in one of the January issues of the Automotor Journal that described the factory of Oldsmobile. Is there anything we can learn from it?"

"I don't think there was anything that would cause us to reexamine how we build our cars," Ian Stuart replied. "But I did like the test bridge they had to check out brakes, clutches and gears for hill climbing."

"Should we try something similar?" Federica asked.

"I don't know that we need to build something, we have hills enough near here, but I like the idea of testing the cars to see that they will hold on a hill and they will climb the hills," Ian said. "Perhaps we should conduct a trial one day of the mountain passes in the Lake District, that would be quite a test?"

"Let's do that," Federica agreed. "Send a car with a driver and observer, and let's see how it performs. Has anyone seen the American Ford Model A?"

"I have," Andrew Coates replied. "They are like us in that you can have any colour you want as long as it is red. The engine is a flat twin, and it has a reputation for transmission issues. I like the Model B touring car better, it looks nicer, but even that does not have a complete body, only a Cape Cart type of hood."

"Should we be worried about them?" Federica asked.

"They will certainly be competition," Coates replied. "The prices of the cars are about the same as ours, perhaps even slightly lower, but there is the body difference to consider. We should keep a close eye on them."

"Where are you?" Federica asked George when he telephoned her that evening.

"The George Hotel in Stamford," he replied.

"Is it a suitable hotel?" she asked.

"It's old," he said. "It has a history going back almost to pre-William days," George said.

"William, who is William?" she asked.

"William the Conqueror," he explained. "Although it certainly is old, the owners have done modifications, and there are modern amenities."

"So, the latest in plumbing?" she laughed.

"Indeed, the latest in plumbing and a telephone here in the foyer," he added.

"Will you arrive in York tomorrow?" she asked.

"I fully expect to," he confirmed. "It may depend upon the weather and the state of the roads, but certainly now I anticipate no problems."

"Nastia telephoned me today," she told him. "One of the young men in her class is from a sheep station in Australia and he says that they would be interested in a van with an open flat back, which we can easily do, but they also want it to be able to travel for three hundred miles without having to stop and fill the petrol reservoir from tins."

"Is that possible?" he asked.

"I am not sure," she admitted. "I met with Ian and Mr White today and we discussed the possibilities. If we are able to solve the problem, then we will have something that we may advertise as a feature of our cars that others do not have."

"Could Nastia and her university class help?" he asked.

"I will put it to her," she said. "It would be a suitable project for the students to undertake."

"I miss you," he said.

"And I you," she replied. "*Ci vediamo presto amore. Buona notte!*"

"*Buona notte, ti amo,*" he said, before ending the telephone call.

"I am not surprised that a car overturned when trying to overtake a large lorry," George said when he telephoned Federica the next day. "The road at that place is appalling with large ruts and holes."

"When is the inquest?" Federica asked.

"Tomorrow," he replied. "I will attend, and if all the evidence is set forth and the coroner reaches some kind of decision, I will return home the next day."

"Where are you staying?" she asked.

"The Royal York Hotel," he replied. "It is an imposing edifice, relatively new, having only been opened in 1878."

"How was your journey?" she asked.

"Well enough," he replied. "Twice I encountered rain along the way, and I had an interesting altercation with an irate moustachioed country gentleman in Pontefract who complained about the infernal machine I was driving and told me that I and my machine should be banned from the roads."

"How did you reply?" she asked.

"As it was raining, I offered to transport him to his destination," he said.

"But, he said that he would rather walk than use such a machine."

"How did you come to encounter this person?" she asked.

"I was having lunch, and when I left, he was outside the inn looking at our car," he explained. "He told me that instead of running around the countryside in the car, I should be in the army."

"Did you respond to that?" she asked.

"Actually, I did have some fun with him," he laughed. "I asked him what rank and regiment he was with and learned that he was a captain in one of the Yorkshire regiments, so I put on my best officer voice and informed him that that was no way to speak to a superior officer."

"What did he do?" she asked, laughing.

"Went purple and stamped off into the rain," he said. "It was a shame because it was raining quite hard just then and I would have been quite happy to take him to his destination."

"Have you had other interest in our car, other than hearing that it is an infernal machine?" she asked.

"Yes, I had quite a crowd gathered here," he replied. "There must have been some twenty people looking at the car late this afternoon, just after I arrived."

"Did anyone express a desire to purchase one?" she asked.

"Three did, and I obtained their cards and will have Arthur Dent contact them," he replied.

"Have you dined yet?" she asked.

"I will when we are finished," he said. "It is a pity you are not here, you would much enjoy the view from the terrace, it is most pleasant."

"Perhaps we will go there one day," she suggested.

"Perhaps," he agreed. *"Buona notte, mia stella."*

"Buona notte, ti amo," she replied.

George sat in the public gallery of the courtroom the next day and watched the proceedings of the coroner's court. He had never been to one before, so this was all a new experience. He listened as the police gave their reports, the doctor attending, his report and the other reports made by the engineers for the county who had responsibility for the roads. Of great interest to him was the testimony of the driver of the lorry, which had overturned. The driver complained about the general state of the roads and told of previous problems with soft patches in the road that caused his lorry to sink in on one side and lurch terribly to that side, to the point of overturning. That led to questioning by the coroner as to the condition of his load and whether or not it had been properly tied down. The driver insisted that it had, but other testimony by two of the policemen who had attended the scene disputed that. The police did, however, agree that the condition of the road left much to be desired. In the end, the coroner handed down a verdict of misadventure with comments directed to the road engineers and to the police. The road engineers to improve the state of the roads and the police to cite persons travelling at unsafe speeds along those same roads, particularly those overtaking other traffic, be it horse traffic, locomotives or cars. To George's relief, the coroner dismissed any notion of the deaths being in any way as a result of the design of their car. He rather expounded at length upon the habits of drivers and the desire for speed that led to reckless behaviour, commenting that the persons in horse-drawn carriages had been known to suffer similar accidents in the past, so that the mode of transportation was not an issue, just the behaviour of the drivers.

"*Ciao bella,*" George greeted Federica when he telephoned her that evening.
"*Ciao,*" she replied. "Was your day of interest?"
"It was," he confirmed. "I sat through hours of testimony given by inarticulate policemen, a lorry driver who spoke with such a broad accent that I had great difficulty understanding him and a doctor who was long-winded to the point of absurdity. But, after all the testimony was done, the coroner's verdict in no way reflected upon us or the design of the car."

"Oh, that is good news," she said. "I am quite relieved."

"It will be interesting to see how the matter is reported in the papers," he said. "I will start to come home tomorrow morning early. I hope to get at least as far as Stamford again, perhaps even as far as Huntington or St. Neots."

"I will be waiting for you," she said.

Following the coroner's court verdict in York, there was much written in the various newspapers about the state of the country's roads and of the implied instruction given to the police, at least of York, to impose sanctions upon those speeding. The controversy surrounding the design of the Sirius car died down, but sadly, there was no concomitant rise in orders, whether due to lingering doubts or other factors. Arthur Dent managed to sell cars to two of the people that George had obtained cards from, so George was happy with the trip and the result. Federica delved into the problem of pumping petrol and had to admit that it was going to take some time and experimentation before they found a solution that was acceptable. There were also other things to think about, apart from cars. One of the biscuit lines had broken down and was possibly going to affect their ability to deliver biscuits to their major customers. George and Federica spent three days with Mr Robertson until they finally understood the problem and worked out a solution. Then they looked at their other lines and discovered the same basic flaw and set about correcting those as well. It was a salutary lesson in the need for proper and timely maintenance. Other areas of their various enterprises were performing well, all the traction engines were out on rental and jobs for the next six weeks had been identified and, in most cases, terms agreed. Federica was concerned that the lines of clothing that they offered through Windsor Garments were becoming dated, and she and Mr Painter finally agreed that they should retain the services of an additional stylist to bring new ideas into the company and to follow the latest trends and styles.

"We should have another party for everyone," Federica announced at dinner one night. "I was thinking that we could hire a larger boat on the river and take a cruise from Boulter's Lock up river through the Cliveden Reach to Cookham and back."

"That sounds like fun," George agreed. "Now that Nastia is down from University, perhaps she and Sophia would also like to come?"

"I think that would be delightful," she agreed.

"The trip from Boulter's to Cookham is not that far," he commented. "Perhaps we should go farther upriver into the Bourne End reach?"

"*Certo,*" she agreed. "At least as far as Spade Oak, when do the locks stay open until?"

"I am not sure," he said. "I'm certain, though, that a boat hire company would know, perhaps even have arrangements with the various lock keepers to work the locks late into the evening. It does stay light after all until quite late at this time of the year."

"Good, it is settled then," she said. "I will have Alice organise a trip and we will make an excursion on the river."

Three weeks later, the various factory managers and their spouses met just below Boulter's Lock on the River Thames and embarked upon their evening cruise.

'This is a steam vessel," Anastasia commented as they pulled away from the bank and started upstream. "I wonder how long it will be before the engine is replaced with an internal combustion engine?"

"I'm sure that it is simply a question of economics," Federica replied. "Until such time as it will be necessary to make major engine repairs, why spend the money?"

"So old-fashioned," Anastasia said.

"Yes, but it is an older vessel," Federica pointed out.

"Hello, Mrs Wheelwright, Miss Wheelwright," Mabel Lloyd said as she came up to them. "What a delightful idea to take a river trip."

"I have come to like this reach of the river," Federica said. "I like the aspect of the trees along the banks and the view of the Cliveden house up on the hills."

"I have never been on the Thames before," Mabel said.

"Not even in London?" Federica asked.

"Oh, I suppose I have been on the Thames," Mabel said. "It just does not look like the same river. Here it is green trees and stately houses, in London, it is muddy banks if the tide is out and industrial buildings if the tide is in, and one can see over the banks."

"Have you another theatre performance coming?" Federica asked.

"Actually, I have just agreed to work with Hepworth Studios to make moving pictures," Mabel said. "They are very active and are pioneers in the art."

"Are they busy?" Federica asked.

"They make short films regularly and have ambitious plans for longer pictures," Mabel explained. "It is very different work from the theatre, and the salary structure is quite different, but I am hopeful that the art will be successful."

"How exciting," Anastasia said. "Did you hear George, Mabel is going to be in moving pictures?"

"Congratulations, Mabel," George said. "I imagine that moving pictures will soon be popular. We even had some made in South Africa during the recent war there. I have not seen them, but I have been told that they are quite clear and are interesting to watch."

"Are we going in there?" Mabel asked, pointing as the boat entered the lock.

"Yes," George told her. "The river here is made navigable by a series of weirs and locks; we have to go up to the next level."

"I've not seen any locks in London," Mabel said.

"The last lock downstream is at Teddington," George explained. "Below that, to the Pool of London and the North Sea, it is a tidal river, which is what you are used to seeing."

"How far up the river can this boat go?" Mabel asked.

"I'm not sure about the upper reaches," George admitted. "But, this boat, probably at least as far as Oxford."

"How interesting, I must find Andrew and ask him about taking a holiday on the river, excuse me," Mabel said and then withdrew.

"Sophia," Federica greeted her. "Tell me about London."

George watched as the two women wandered off to the aft of the boat and talked about whatever they talked about. Since Sophia had moved to London with Anastasia, they had not spent much time together, and this was a good time to share news, gossip and opinions. He then spent time talking with the factory managers and their spouses. Since the start-up of Sirius cars, Federica had spent most of her time there, and

George had assumed more of the duties of managing the other, more disparate enterprises. All in all, he was happy with them. The sale of the carriage business had been a good idea, and they had toyed with the sale of the tractor business a couple of times, but each time the expected value from a sale had not been sufficient, so they kept it. He followed closely the developments of the heavy oil tractors that had internal combustion engines and would at some point make obsolete the steam engines, but that change looked as if it were still some time in the future. His view of that was shared by John Edwards, who loved his tractors.

Ian Stuart and Arthur Dent both approached George and told him of their researches into the subject of car maintenance.

"We have the basis of a plan," Ian said. "We think we should set up a new business that sits alongside our car sales showrooms but that deals with spare parts and repairs."

"That has been our intention," George agreed. "Do you have some ideas on how to structure that business and cost the parts and the work?"

"We do," Arthur confirmed. "We have been working with Douglas Wilson and suggest that for parts we use the cost to us and add one hundred per cent to make the price that we would sell a part to a car owner. That sounds like a lot, but we have to have the parts on hand, and they may sit in the warehouse for weeks or months on end if not used."

"If we make a change to the car and use a different part, how do we deal with old parts and older cars?" George asked.

"I think that would depend," Ian said. "If the new part can be used in place of the old part, then we just sell that; if the new part cannot be used in place of the old part, then we need to know when the car was made and what part will work."

"That sounds like a lot of bookkeeping work," George thought.

"It does," Ian agreed. "That's part of the reason for adding on to the cost to us of the part, someone has to pay for the work it will take to follow changes."

"I suppose it is impractical to make no changes," George laughed.

"It is indeed," Ian agreed. "A supplier may go out of business, and we have to get new parts, or we may discover that our car works better if we make a change, so I think that change is inevitable."

"How do we manage repairs?" George asked. "How do most owners effect repairs now?"

"As to the last, most owners are part-time mechanics and address their own problems, or if wealthy and having a chauffeur, the chauffeur does it. For the first, we take a car and have some of our workers disassemble it and see how long it takes to take it apart and then put it back together, much in the same way that I understand Mrs Wheelwright took apart your early purchases of the Daimler and the other cars you have," Arthur suggested. "That will then give us some basis for estimating the costs to do repair work."

"Do we tell customers before we start work what it will cost to repair?" George asked.

"That may not always be possible," Arthur thought. "We may have to do some work just to find out what is wrong. We should, I think, give the customer news as we progress and let them know as soon as we can what it may cost."

"When do we start?" George asked.

"There are mews behind our London showroom," Arthur said. "They would probably be suitable for storing parts and for doing repair work."

"Are they for lease or sale?" George asked.

"They are owned by the same person from whom Mrs Wheelwright purchased the building in which we have our showroom," Arthur explained. "I understand that he is in need of funds to shore up his country estate, so would be willing to sell."

"Arthur, take Douglas with you and negotiate the best terms you can and let us buy the property," George instructed. "When we know the purchase price, then we will determine the best way to acquire it to avoid taxes and other unnecessary burdens. What about someone to run the business?"

"I have a friend from Scotland," Ian said. "He, at the moment, travels the world repairing machines for Mirrlees."

"Would he be able to change to smaller machines and manage people and parts?" Arthur asked.

"I think so," Ian said. "He and I often talked of the problems we faced at Mirrlees, not knowing what we faced until we got there and then having to organise things locally for people to do work and for parts to be made or acquired."

"Should our parts have numbers that make them easy to identify?" George asked. "In the army, we all had numbers so that people could be tracked easily. Why not do the same for parts? If I look at enlistment papers, there is a description of the man, we do the same for a part, then for each person there is money associated, for us we add the price of cost of the part and then what we would sell it for."

"That sounds like a good idea," Arthur said. "To do that would take some administrative effort."

"It would," George agreed. "But I think it would be worth it if only to be able to identify all the parts and bits and pieces that go into the car."

"I will look at that," Ian said. "We should do it for the factory and then provide the information to the maintenance people."

"Good," George said. "Now, if you will excuse me, I need to talk to Mr Robertson."

Federica joined George by the rail of the boat as they sailed up the cut towards Cookham lock. "This has been nice," she commented.

"It has," he agreed. "I think everyone is enjoying themselves."

"How far above this lock should we go?" she asked.

"I'll ask the boat captain where he can turn around," he said. "He may have to go a little upstream of Spade Oak until the river is wide enough to make a safe turnaround."

"Nastia seems to have enjoyed her first year at university," she said. "She is full of tales of students and professors."

"How has Sophia kept herself busy?" he asked.

"She told me that she has taken to studying the machines that Babbage built and proposed," Federica replied. "I think she believes that she can invent some machine that will do mathematical calculations easily. She has acquired a number of slide rules and other calculating devices."

"I had not realised she had such an interest in mathematics," he said.

"I knew she had an interest," Federica said. "But I think her current ideas go far beyond simple calculations. I know she has looked at

Jacquard looms and the concepts of Hollerith to see if machines cannot be made to control other things, including she told me machine tools to manufacture parts for us."

"Ian Stuart and Arthur Dent have a proposition for the maintenance business for our cars," he told her.

"That is good," she said. "When will we have something?"

"I'm not sure," he admitted. "But I will meet with them next week, they are going to look at some premises behind our London showroom as a place to set up business. They are right, I think, there are more of our cars in the London area than anywhere else."

"That's everyone off and on their way," George said to Federica when they waved goodbye to Henry and Esmerelda Robertson. The trip had been a success, and there had even been talk of making it an annual event. Federica was now ready to go home and have a bath. She could smell coal smoke on herself, probably from the smoke from the steamer. They had been through one short patch where gusty winds blew the exhaust smoke back onto the vessel and made everyone cough for about a minute.

"Shall we go?" she said to Sophia and Anastasia, who were standing by the riverbank.

"Are you driving?" Sophia asked.

"No, I think I'll let George drive us home," Federica said. "I think I had too many glasses of wine and do not trust myself to be fully aware."

"Well, that was fun," Anastasia said. "I had forgotten what a pretty reach of the river this is. I don't know that I care for the Bourne End reach, but I do like this one. Do you all smell like coal smoke, too?"

"We do," Sophia said.

"You see, that would not happen with an internal combustion engine," Anastasia said. "One could probably even take the exhaust below the water to avoid such happenings."

"Ah, but one day people will long for the days of steam power, you will see," George said.

"Perhaps," Anastasia admitted. "But by then we will have perfected batteries and electricity will have displaced petrol engines."

A new model

"Are we ready to introduce our new model?" Federica asked her managers.

"We are," Ian Stuart confirmed. "We have a slightly larger engine that we have tested and find it to run better than our first engine. We made the distance between the axles a little larger and made the necessary frame and spring changes, and have improved the gearbox and the differential. Andrew has made some nice changes to the body, and although it is still clearly one of our cars, one can tell the two apart."

"Excellent," Federica said. "What do we call it?"

"Do we follow the convention and call it by the horsepower of the engine?" Andrew Coates asked.

"I would rather we went a different way," Federica said. "We are the Sirius Car Company. Perhaps we should name our cars for the stars?"

"What about Regulus?" suggested Douglas Wilson.

"I like that," Federica said. "Should we give a name to our first car?"

"I think Procyon, the star that rises before Sirius," Wilson suggested.

"I did not know you were an astronomer," Federica said.

"It is a hobby of mine," Wilson said.

"What do you all think?" she asked. The vote was a unanimous yes, so the names were agreed. Then came the matter of whether or not to apply a badge or mark to show the name of the model of the car. Winston Fox suggested that he could easily cast small badges in the form of the name that could then be applied to the body of the car. He said that he would take the enamelled badge that they had for Sirius and use the same print to make up a simple script word, that he would then cast.

"What else is there?" Federica asked.

"I would like some additional tools, equipment and parts," William McDonald said. "We have been busy of late and have almost used up all the parts that we initially stocked our small warehouse with, and we are finding that the one hoist we have is not enough for the work."

"Does that suggest that our cars are not reliable and that they break down often?" Federica asked.

"No, Madame," McDonald replied. "We have had some repairs that are the result of things breaking or failing, but most of our work is from car crashes."

"Accidents are then common?" she asked.

"More common than one would think," McDonald said. "It seems that the greatest challenge we and the other car makers face is teaching people to drive and how not to drive into things, particularly each other."

"What are most of our repairs then?" she asked.

"Repairs to the body," he replied. "Because of the unique construction we use, one cannot simply take a hammer and bash things straight after an accident. Perhaps we could look to some kind of buffers like the trains have to absorb some of the shock when two cars collide?"

"Ian?" Federica asked.

"It is possible," he said. "A simple bar across the front and across the back, perhaps with some springs to take the shock."

"Would you investigate for us?" she asked. "Do you have a list of parts and equipment that you need, William?"

"I do, Madame," he replied. "Here is a list of parts, and this is a list of the equipment I think we would need to improve our repair shop."

"Thank you," she said. "Douglas, would you take care of this, consult with Ian and Andrew and get the appropriate parts to William. For the repair equipment, do you have suggestions of where we could acquire what you need?"

"I do, Madame," McDonald replied. "I have here a list of suppliers who have what we need."

"Good, again work with Douglas and get the things you need," she said. "One final thing, do we take out a patent on the petrol tank system?"

"It would provide us with some protection against others copying the idea," Wilson said.

"It would," Stuart agreed. "But the information in the patent would also tell people how it works and give them something to start with to invent something similar. We may be better off just using the idea."

"If someone submits a case for a patent on our idea?" Coates asked.

"We will have evidence of use and can deny their claim of invention," Stuart said.

"Is there a way to write a patent that leaves out one vital piece of information?" Federica asked.

"If the examiner of patents is good, then no," Stuart said.

"I don't like legal battles over patents," Federica said. "The only people who really benefit are the lawyers for either side. Having said that, I will consult with our solicitors, who have advised us on patent issues before and may have an opinion."

"If I may, Madame," Stuart said.

"Yes, Ian," she replied.

"Winston and I have been looking at the van with the flat body, and we believe that another slightly larger model would sell," he said.

"Not a car but a van?" she asked.

"Yes, Mrs Wheelwright," Stuart confirmed. "We believe that for the moment the two car models are fine, they are not too expensive as to be unobtainable for the average man, but the vans are often purchased by companies and enterprises and we have seen brisk sales of the van, even more so than our car, and we believe that extending the line of vans and small lorries may be worthwhile."

"How much larger?" she asked.

"Well, the original van can carry two and a half hundredweight," Ian said. "The new Regulus model will carry about four hundredweight, and I think a slightly larger model that would carry five hundredweight would be attractive to many enterprises. It is still small enough not to attract the attention of Foden, Straker or Thornycroft, who all make much larger lorries, but large enough to be of use to many people."

"I like the idea," Federica said. "What would it take?"

"For Andrew, very little," Stuart said. "We would do what we have done with the Regulus version of the van, the driver's cab is the same and common to both models, we would use the same cab for a new model and all the real changes would be in the frame and springs."

"Would it not require a larger engine, gearbox and differential?" she asked.

"It would," Stuart agreed. "I propose that we add another two cylinders to the original engine design, lengthen the crankshaft and use the same pistons. For the gearbox, we do need to do some work there as we will with the differential."

"With the increase in carrying capacity and the basic weight of the van, are the wheels adequate?" she asked.

"They are Madame," Stuart assured her. "For the smaller cars and vans, they are probably more than is needed, but at the time we selected the wheel supplier, we opted for an existing wheel, which was actually larger than we needed, but cheaper than designing a new wheel."

"How long will this take?" she asked.

"Less than six months," Stuart said. "We are busy with the start of the production of the Regulus, so cannot have all the designers we would need, but two or three for now should be able to get most of the work done."

"Douglas?" Federica asked.

"I concur with Ian, Madame," Wilson said. "I have examined the costs of such an addition to our models and believe it to be a good idea."

"Winston, can you make the engine blocks that this would require?" she asked.

"Yes, Madame," he replied. "I could have a casting in less than a month."

"So, Douglas, what would we call this model?" she asked.

"I think Arcturus, the bear," he said.

"Fine, let's do it," she said. "When can we have some Regulus models to ship to South Africa and Australia?"

"Next month," Stuart said. "We have been building cars in anticipation of a general increase of interest in cars generally following the soon-to-be-held shows at Crystal Palace and Olympia."

"Ah, yes," she said. "We need a plan for who will be going next month. I withdrew from exhibiting at Crystal Palace after the Society of Motor Manufacturers and Traders pulled out and went to Olympia instead. But, it may be valuable for some of us to go to the shows to see what is new. If you would let Alice know which show you would like to attend and when. There is still the issue of what do we call the model of our van that has a flat lorry-like back to it, does anyone have any ideas?"

"Why don't we just call it a wagon?" McDonald suggested.

"That makes sense," Federica said. "So, we'll have the Regulus car, van and wagon and the Procyon car, van and wagon. Good, I'm pleased that we finally agreed on something. Alice, would you make up appropriate advertising materials with the three body types?"

"Yes, Mrs Wheelwright," Alice replied.

"Did you see the Spyker car?" Federica asked George after they had toured the floor of the Crystal Palace Motor Show late in January and were driving home.

"I did, how novel to have all four wheels driven," he said. "I wonder how complex the various gearboxes and differentials are?"

"Would that not be an advantage to the army?" she asked. "With all wheels driven, the car could go in places that most cannot."

"They advertise that having all wheels driven forestalls sideslip," he said. "I do not think that they have thought in terms of ability to go away from the road."

"Well, as it is a hill-climbing racing car, is it intended to stay on roads up hills or run away from the roads?" she asked. "How big was the engine, 40hp?"

"Forty," he confirmed. "But, that is for a racing car, for one of our vans with the flat back, we would not need an engine so large."

"We should look at this," she said. "Perhaps we could build one for trials and send it to Koos to test. I think we should call the project our Antares project."

"I like that notion," he said. "I like the name, and if we send a test car to the Cape, we could put it through no end of trials without having competitor companies seeing. I should ask Koos to properly record the trials, preferably with photographs, so that we have something to take to the War Office."

"I suppose the greatest challenge is the third differential that sends power to the front and rear axles and the front axle complications of driving through wheels that are steered," she thought. "I will ask Nastia to come down and take a close look."

"I was interested in the Straker Squire commercial vehicles," he said. "I think we should keep an eye on them. As our vans grow larger, we may find ourselves competing with them."

"Yes, but our vans are much smaller," she said. "Straker is talking about lorries from one to five tons, and we are at five hundredweight."

"I wonder if they will sell more omnibuses or lorries?" he mused.

"I imagine omnibuses," she thought. "But why I could not tell you."

"Did you see that the Straker has another gearbox that gives them six forward speeds and two reverse speeds," he said. "Imagine if we could combine that with the Spyker four-wheel drive, we would have a car that could truly go anywhere."

"It would surely be more expensive than the average man could afford," she commented.

"That is true," he agreed. "But, I think possible buyers would not be the average man, but people with a special need for whom the notion of paying a higher price is not such an issue."

"Do you think the War Office would have an interest?" she asked.

"I think the secret will be to find the right person to talk to," he replied. "The War Office and the Army are very conservative and probably still think in terms of horses and foot soldiers. For scouting, such a car would be perfect, if we fitted a large petrol tank, even with a larger engine, the car could still go three hundred miles, even away from the roads, doing that on a horse is hard on both the man and the horse."

"Would such a car have gone everywhere you did when you were in South Africa?" she asked.

"Not everywhere," he replied. "But most of the places. We would need to point out that such a car would be good for places like the Cape and the Transvaal, but not for England, where the fences and hedgerows constrain one almost to the roads. This would be a help in a quickly moving conflict, like we had in the Cape, but of little use in the more static conflicts like they had at the Siege of Ladysmith."

"Even so, I like the idea," she said. "I think the idea of sending one to Koos is good, we should add the second gearbox and give Koos the instructions to test it as if it were an army scouting car. Should it have any kind of gun attached, like the Simms Motor Scout?"

"I think that would be an excellent plan," he agreed. "But, I'm not sure where Koos might find such a gun."

"He might surprise us," she laughed. "Didn't you tell me once that he had a room behind a stable that was well stocked with guns?"

"That is so," he said. "But I did not see any machine guns there."

"Who knows what he may have picked up in the aftermath of the war," she said.

"Well, here we are home," he said. "Will you pour us some wine while I put the car in the stable?"

For the next month, with time out for a visit to the new motor show at Olympia, Federica devoted her time and attention to the new Regulus car and van and was quite happy with the results. She had been concerned that the number of variations in body style they now had would cause problems, but Andrew Coates and Ian Stuart had worked out a clever system of control that kept the lines running with little or no problem. Sales of vans and wagons now exceeded that of cars, but the overall numbers were such that the company was turning a profit, quite a nice profit in fact. All in all, things were going rather well. The only regret that Federica had at the moment was that she had been unable to secure space at the Olympia motor show or an invitation to the Inaugural Lunch of the Society of Motor Manufacturers. If she had been to the lunch, she would have been the lone woman in a sea of male faces. She was concerned with the number of companies now making vans of one type or another, from the 'Argyll' van made by Hozier to the White Steam Car delivery van. It probably did vindicate her strategy to push products for commercial customers, but she was concerned that the field was getting crowded. In the next months, she saw ambulances built on motor vehicles, post office delivery vans, other vans built up on the chassis of omnibuses and even a special van owned by the British Vacuum Cleaner Company, which had a pump and all the hoses necessary to provide a mobile vacuuming service. That vehicle had been built by Thorneycroft on one of their lorries. She was interested but did not want to get distracted by such speciality items. While they might be novel and interesting, they would have to be constructed away from the basic manufacturing line. The main lines were going so well and costs were well under control that she did not wish to disrupt the flow. Even adding extra items now called for special scrutiny.

"Good morning, Gentlemen," Federica greeted her management team. "I would like to discuss the item that William raised a little while ago about buffers. What have we learned?"

"Apparently, we were not the only ones who saw a problem," McDonald said. "The Simms Company has designed a pneumatic buffer that does just what we want."

"Is it expensive to fit?" Ian Stuart asked.

"I'm not sure," McDonald said. "Perhaps we should acquire one and see how it would fit and then test it to see if it works."

"Good," Federica said. "Would you do that, Ian?"

"Yes, Madame," he replied. "I'll have Harold White take one of the cars we use for testing and try it."

"We have been approached by the Smith Company to use their speed indicators," Federica said. "Has anyone seen one on a car?"

"I have," Arthur Dent replied. "One of my friends has had speeding summonses dismissed because he has one installed."

"Has anyone seen anything about the Davis Speedometer?" Federica asked.

"I have," Andrew Coates said. "It is a peculiar device; it functions in an entirely different way from the Smith instrument. Whereas the Smith device uses a mechanical drive from a front wheel and has a governor that is attached to the needle on the dial, the Davis system uses a pump driven by a wheel and the pump creates a vacuum in a tube that then draws up coloured water and shows speed by the height of the water column."

"That is a little different," Federica agreed. "I'm not sure about that for a speed indicator, but could we not adapt the concepts and use the pump as a better pump than we have now to move petrol from the tank to the upper reservoir?"

"I think we could," Stuart agreed. "I think I even have a notion of how to turn the pump on and off based on relative air pressures. I will talk about it with Harold and see if we cannot improve our current system."

"Had Smiths asked for an appointment?" Arthur Dent asked.

"They have," Federica confirmed. "They proposed Wednesday next at nine in the morning. Would that be acceptable to all?"

"I will be in London," Dent replied. "But, this will be mainly technical, so I have no real need to be present. I would suggest including Harold as he has tinkered with lots of devices like this."

"An excellent suggestion," Federica agreed. "We will meet at the factory and include Harold in our discussions."

The meeting with S. Smith and Sons was cordial and productive. At the end of the morning, the Sirius team understood the workings of the speed indicator and agreed that they would install it as standard on all new production cars. The same device could be used on each model, the only adjustment being where the drive was taken from on the front wheel, so that the change in diameter between the Procyon and Regulus cars did not affect the indicated speed. They opted for the version that showed speed in miles per hour, the maximum speed attained on any trip, and the mileage travelled. The maximum speed feature was popular for defence against summonses for speeding. Prices were agreed and the Smiths people departed, happy to have signed up another car builder. Some of their sales had been to motorists directly, but that had led to problems with installation and calibration. Smiths would rather the car builder install the instrument in the factory, where those issues could be dealt with professionally.

Anastasia came down from her second year at university, happy with her results and eager to do something over the long summer break. Federica gave her the Antares project and a free hand to see what she might come up with. Anastasia asked for a space at the factory and two helpers. Ian Stuart cleared out some space they had been using to store parts that were not quite right in one way or another and took the opportunity to make dispositions of those parts, either as usable or to be reworked or to be scrapped. The parts had been left over from very early days before they had become more rigorous with their suppliers, so it was a good time to clear the books. Anastasia took the Regulus engine and mated it to the normal Regulus gearbox, then she designed and had built a second gearbox that fitted directly behind the first. The second gearbox incorporated features from the Straker Squire lorry and the Spyker car.

So, now she had two shafts coming out of the gearbox, one running forwards and the other to the rear. Now her problem was to design a front axle that included a differential but also included mechanisms to transmit power to the front wheels even when they were turned for steering. She found the designs for a front-wheel drive car that had been created by a J. Walter Christie of the United States and felt that she could adapt those concepts to her car. It used telescoping universal joints at the ends of the front axle, so the wheels would drive even when steered. Concerned about the effects such a system would have at speed, she limited the use of the four-wheel drive feature to low speeds that came as a result of the Straker gearbox design. She used a modified form of the Regulus frame that was quite a bit shorter and reinforced in some areas to take the extra loads from driving the front axle, and for bodywork, she simply took the Regulus cab and cut the top off and omitted the doors. She used the wagon body and included struts for a Cape Cart Hood that could be used to cover the driver and any passengers or goods. She reasoned that keeping the profile of the car low would be of benefit, something she had learned from conversations with George. Late in September, before she went back up to university, she proposed a trial and selected a course around the estate, then ran through the woods, up and down hills and was both on and off the roads and tracks that they had. Federica, George, Sophia, Ian Stuart, Andrew Coates, Douglas Wilson, Arthur Dent, Harold White and the two helpers that had been with her that summer, David and Gareth, all gathered at the house to watch the first run of the Antares wagon.

"Who wants to ride with me?" Anastasia asked. "Fede, will you come?"

"Of course," Federica replied. "Perhaps when we get back, someone else would like to go with you?"

"I would like to," Sophia said.

"Good," Anastasia said. "George, while we are gone on this first trip, perhaps you could make a quick roster of who will be next?"

"I'll do that," he promised. Anastasia and Federica drove off down the driveway, and just before the gate, they turned off onto a side track and then into the woods. The Anastasia turned off the track into a clear area and started up a slope. Quite quickly, the rear wheels started to spin, and they were going nowhere.

"Let's see if this works," she said. She stopped and used the second gear lever to select the lower gears and also to apply power to the front wheels. The car moved forward and climbed the slope with only minimal of slip from one or other of the wheels.

"It works," Federica said, delighted with the result. "You have done an excellent job, Nastia!"

"All I did was take other people's ideas and bring them all together in one place," Anastasia replied. "The inventions were largely already done by the Spyker brothers and by the American Christie."

"Let's go back to the house and give the others a chance to see how it works," Federica said.

The last to take the tour with Anastasia were her helpers, David and Gareth. They were delighted with the experience and proud to have been part of the project. At the house, Sophia had a surprise for them all; she had had small badges made with the number four behind the word Antares. She gave one to all those who were there and asked Federica to also give one to Winston Fox, who had produced the axle castings in record time. Later that evening, when the family was discussing the events of the day, George came up with another idea.

"Nastia," he began. "Now that we have shown that our Antares car works, would it be possible to add one more item?"

"What do you have in mind?" she asked.

"Well, it occurs to me that although the car is very capable, it is always possible that it could get stuck," he replied. "If that happens, it would be nice to have a way to pull yourself out of difficulties. Could you attach a winch somehow and power it from the engine?"

"Something like the winches on the ploughing engines?" she asked.

"Something like that," he agreed. "But, much smaller, perhaps like a capstan winch from a small boat."

"In the front or the back?" she asked.

"I don't know which would be best," he said. "Or, how you would get power to it."

"The power is simple enough," she said. "We supply some wagons now with facilities to take power from the engine when the wagon is not moving. We would use the same addition to the gearbox and run a shaft probably back to a capstan mounted on the rear, yes, that would probably work."

"What if you wanted to pull yourself forward?" he asked.

"Always difficult," she laughed. "I think a pulley and a channel through which to run the rope, and it could come out the front."

"Can you add that before we ship this one to Koos in the Cape?" he asked.

"We can," she agreed. "I think we should build two more, send two to Cape Town to Koos and keep one here on the estate."

"That sounds like a good idea," Federica agreed. "Will you have time before you go up to London?"

"I will," Anastasia confirmed. "David and Gareth have become good at the job, and they can build the cars easily, even without me. I know Winston has some extra castings for the axles, and we built a couple of extra gearboxes to see that we had the design right, so the job should be quite simple."

"I think Nastia did a wonderful job," Federica said later when she and George were in the bath together. "She really is clever, and I think when she finishes at university, I will step aside and let her run the company."

"Do you think the managers will accept her?" he asked.

"Yes," she stated quite categorically. "I was watching them today, they think she is probably the most clever person they have met and yet she manages to get them to do things for her without any ill feeling, or without them feeling in any way inferior, they recognise her abilities and are happy to do what she asks."

"That is a rare talent," he said. "I met one or two officers in the army who were like that, but there were not many; most of them ruled by dictate and often not for the best. If you step aside and let Nastia run the company, have you other plans?"

"Yes," she confirmed. "First, I wish to visit South Africa and look at wild animals, and where you did your service and after that, I would like a child."

"As to the first, that is easily arranged," he said. "As to the second, we should practise to be sure we know how to make that happen."

"Ah, I wondered if that would cross your mind," she laughed. "I don't think you need any practice, but I do need to see if you are still capable. It has been a week since we last made love. Why is that?"

"*Mia stella*, I don't know," he said. "I hope we are not becoming too set in our ways to take the time for each other."

"Well, you can make up for lost opportunities now," she invited. "I am desirous of your attentions and have a notion for experimentation!"

The first production Arcturus rolled off the line barely two months after the idea had been first mooted. Sirius now had two cars, two vans and three wagons in their line. Federica was certain that there would soon be a demand for an Arcturus-sized van, so she instructed Andrew Coates to create a body for it. She was right. Not long after, the first Arcturus wagons were seen in the field, and a query came for a van based on the same chassis. What made their vans and wagons attractive was that the driver had a cab and sat inside, protected from the elements. There were not many other vans and wagons appearing, but all left the driver exposed. Federica was surprised that car makers had not all gone to enclosed bodies, even new models of Brotherhood and Daimler cars coming out left at least the driver exposed, if not everyone. She supposed it was a question of the cost of the body and the time it took traditional coach builders to put together a body that was the real problem. Koos sent reports from Oudtshoorn regularly documenting his excursions with the Antares wagons, which he was putting through their paces. He had been into the open veldt and up the mountains and was thrilled with the new wagons. Federica was not sanguine about the possibilities that the War Office would buy any of the wagons, as George had said to her many times, they were wedded to the horse and could not see past it, except for rail transport, even then they classified goods wagons by the number of horses they could accommodate. Once they had enough field test data, she was going to ask George to test the waters with the army and with the War Office, but she was placing no value on any future orders that might result. For them, the exercise had been valuable; they understood more about transmissions and gearboxes than they did before and had proven to themselves that they could design and build a speciality vehicle in short order, plus they had a superb wagon for doing chores around the estate.

"Did you hear from your friend in the army?" Federica asked George.

"I did," he confirmed. "I see him on Wednesday, I have the reports Koos sent, and I have the photographs."

"What part of the army is he in?" she asked.

"The cavalry," he replied. "So, technically, he should be interested in mobility, but he may like his horse too much to give us a fair hearing."

"What is the cavalry supposed to do?" she asked.

"They are supposed to find out where the other side is; they should be able to move quickly and engage the other side," he replied.

"So, mobility?" she asked, looking for confirmation.

"Yes, mobility is their primary advantage and function," he said. "We were shown up in the Boer War because the Boer forces in the latter part of the war did what they should have been doing all along and conducted a fast-moving mobile campaign."

"So, if the army is intelligent, our Antares should be useful to them?" she asked.

"That's a big assumption," he said. "Assuming that the army command is intelligent. I just don't think they are ready to embrace any new ideas. Look at the Marconi fiasco. In the Boer War, Marconi demonstrated wireless communications, but the army saw no benefit; they only saw the problems and challenges and would have nothing of it, so the navy is now pursuing it."

Federica placed no great hope in the War Office or the Army actually buying one of their Antares wagons, let alone any substantial order. For her, the project had always been more of an engineering challenge. She placed her hopes on the more mundane and general sales of cars, vans and wagons to individuals and businesses. Total sales of all vehicles now topped a thousand a year, or about three a day, which was quite an increase since their first production. They had three lines running, two for the Procyon models and a new line for the Regulus models, on which they also built the Arcturus models. She fully expected to add a second line for the Regulus models as demand increased, but most of the increase in production had come from small but regular improvements to their system of production, and she was gratified that both Ian Stuart and Andrew Coates kept looking for ways to speed things up through the lines. As changes were made, there were occasional imbalances between the body shop and the main assembly lines, but those usually only lasted a week or so until the other had caught up and made their own improvements. Also gratifying was the fact that although the total number of people had increased over time, the number of cars per person had increased substantially, so Douglas Wilson was happy to report healthy finances and profits. There had been pressure on wages and salaries as the demand for trained and skilled assembly mechanics and for engineers had increased, but even those increases had been offset by the production improvements.

When George returned from his meeting in London, it was with the news that the army would like a demonstration of the Antares wagon. They suggested the training ground on Salisbury Plain, the relatively new facility that the army had begun to acquire in 1897 and was now spread over 43,000 acres, more than enough space to test any vehicle. Federica suggested that George take David and Gareth with him, as they had a better knowledge of the wagon and how it worked than anyone. She was not sure how the army wanted to conduct the demonstration, but assumed it would be over a variety of terrains. She wondered how many of the various army departments might be present, but placed little hope in any speedy positive response. There was relative peace in the world. The Russo-Japanese War had finally come to an end, and the only conflict that had arisen that looked as if it would go on for a while was the Maji Maji Rebellion in German East Africa. So, she thought, perhaps she should approach the Germans and see if they had interest in the Antares project. She dismissed that idea as a poor use of time for all concerned, sending George off around the world to sell one or two wagons was just not worth the trouble and cost.

"So, *amore*, what did they think?" Federica asked George when he returned from his trip to Salisbury Plain.

"They found fault," he replied. "I wouldn't go where a horse might go, it was too slow, it was too fast, it was too heavy, it was not large enough, it was too large, it seemed that each officer there looked at it in their own way and chose not to like it."

"Did you expect otherwise?" she asked.

"Not really," he admitted. "Though I did think that William, who is supposed to be my friend, would have given me a little fairer trial and not wanted me to follow him on his horse through a large pile of rocks that looked to me like driving up a kopje in the Cape. We made it through, but not as quickly as the horse."

"They did not want anything to disrupt their lives?" she suggested.

"Exactly," he agreed. "They are wedded to the horse, and I am not sure what it would take to get them to change."

"Ah, well," she said philosophically. "Change takes time. When they decide that they do need our wagon, then they can pay dearly for it; in the meantime, we can use it around the estate, and when we visit South Africa next year, we know that Koos will have transport for us."

"If we are to go next year, what do we need to do to ensure that you can turn over the company to Nastia?" he asked.

"Not much," she said. "Nastia already knows the car designs, she saw the factories being built, she understands the accounts, so I expect that after a short while getting to better know the people, I can safely leave it to her. I have a yen to look at aeroplanes. After the Wrights made their flight in America, there are more people trying out different machines, and now the Wrights, with their Flyer III, have flown for over twenty miles in just under forty minutes. I think it would be interesting to see what we could do. Just imagine flying to South Africa instead of taking the boat. I wonder how long it will be before that is possible?"

"Flying over water," he said with a shudder. "What happens if things go wrong?"

"I suppose the simple answer is that you go into the sea, but perhaps a better answer is that things will not go wrong, because we have made a good flying machine that is reliable," she said.

"*Mia stella*, I could not lose you to the sea," he said.

"I have no intention of going into the sea," she said. "When I design an aeroplane, it will fly and fly!"

"What are they made of?" he asked.

"I think it is a frame of some sort covered with a fabric that is coated with paint or varnish. The frame has to carry the wings and the engine and the driver," she said. "I must study the news reports and pictures and see what I may learn."

"What will we do for Christmas?" Federica asked Sophia one day late in November.

"I think we go to Florence again," Sophia suggested. "But, this time we drive in our own car."

"*Bene,*" Federica agreed. "We should ask Nastia if she wishes to invite William McIntosh."

"I think that would be wonderful," Sophia said. "I think that perhaps when they finish at university next July then he may ask her to marry him."

"They are that serious?" Federica asked.

"They are," Sophia confirmed.

"Do you have any idea of what they may do if they do marry, go to South Africa, stay in England or what?" Federica asked, concerned that her plans to hand over the car company to Anastasia might be in jeopardy.

"I cannot say for certain," Sophia hedged. "But, I think that she has the notion that she will run Sirius and he will help."

"Perhaps we should discuss that with them at Christmas time?" Federica suggested.

"It would be good to do so," Sophia agreed. "I would also like to move back to Hedsor. London is fine, but that trip we took on the river was such fun that I realised how much I have missed the quieter life."

"I will contact Papi and arrange for us to stay in Firenze," Federica said. "It will be good to see the family again and introduce William to my relatives."

"Do we take one or two cars?" Sophia asked.

"I think two for comfort," Federica replied. "We can follow the same route that Papi took when he drove back from here in the car we sold him. I will go with George and leave you to chaperone Nastia and William!"

"Thank you," Sophia said wryly. "I think we should drive together with Nastia and let George and William go together."

"A compromise," Federica suggested. "Each day we move one person to the next car, so that by the time we reach Firenze, we will have driven with everyone else."

"Agreed," Sophia said. "Will I leave the planning to you?"

"Of course," Federica said. "Don't worry, I, or perhaps Alice, will book passage on the ferry and hotels in various towns we will pass through."

"Good, *ci vediamo presto,* perhaps two weeks," Sophia said. "*Ciao.*"

The sixteenth of December found the family on the ferry Invicta on their way to Calais. The cars had been shipped ahead of time and were awaiting them in Calais. William McIntosh had been thrilled with the notion of going to Florence, and his enthusiasm was only mildly dampened by the news that it would be a family outing to stay with even more family. Anastasia and William had come down from university and spent the night in Dover together with the rest of the family before taking the first ferry of the day to Calais. For the first stage of the trip, as far as Amiens, William drove with George, and the ladies travelled together. Apart from the weather, which was not the best, and driving on the other side of the road, a result of Napoleon's rule, the trip was uneventful. From Amiens to Florence, each day brought new drivers and partners, even going through the rotation for the second time, until they arrived at Florence late in the evening of Christmas Eve.

"*Ciao bella,*" Signor Beretta greeted Federica. "*Como vai?*"

"*Bene Papi, bene,*" she assured him.

"*Ricordi Anastasia e Sophia?*" she asked.

"*Si, me ricordo,*" he replied. "*E chi è questo giovanotto?*"

"*Papi, le presento Signor William McIntosh, il ragazzo de Anastasia,*" she said, making the introduction.

"*Ciao William, benvenuti in Italia,*" Signor Beretta said. "*Entriamo in casa.*"

They all followed their host into the house, where other members of the family were waiting. For William, it was all a little overwhelming to be greeted effusively by so many people, doubly difficult for him as he spoke no Italian at all. For Federica, it was a homecoming and a chance to talk to her mother and her sisters. Her sisters left quite early, all to go to their own homes and families, but with the promise that the whole family would descend upon the family home for Christmas Day. Poor William had no idea what was in store for him when the nieces and nephews were all there. Federica recounted for him the story of the bell attached to the marital bed, which made him blush deeper than beetroot red, if that was possible. But he would be spared such high jinks as he had been housed in the room George had used before his and Federica's wedding, well away from the room that Sophia and Anastasia had been allotted.

Christmas Day was chaotic with some family members going early to mass, others cooking and still more arguing about the weather. Federica was fond of her family but had come to enjoy the more staid and sober life at Hedsor Grange. She and her father had some discussions about aeroplanes, and he was also caught up in her enthusiasm. He was still interested in the car business and was delighted with the results of the Sirius Car Company and the dividends he was receiving, but powered flight was the next frontier, and he wanted to be part of it. They agreed that if Federica pursued the idea and formed a company, then he would again take ten per cent of any issued shares. Signor Beretta promised her an introduction to a friend of his, Gaetano Crocco, who taught at the University of Rome and who was researching the principles of flight and aerodynamic stability. Federica already knew from the works of George Cayley that everything depended on four factors, thrust, lift, drag and weight. She felt that she could manage thrust by the design of the engine and propellor and the weight of the materials that the frame, skin and wings were made of. Lift was going to be a function of wing design, and she was still researching. Obviously, the Wright brothers had hit upon at least one combination of the four factors that worked, and they were now improving their design to be able to control the flight. She had spent time reading about the many failures in the search for powered flight and was determined not to repeat those failures. She was intrigued by the radial engine that Manly had designed and which had been used by the American Langley in his failed Aerodrome tests. She felt that she understood why things had come apart and was certain that she could design a frame that would accommodate the stresses of the engine. Although the American press and the government had been critical of Langley, she felt that his errors were of great value because they pointed the way to possible success. Her greatest challenge was going to be the wings. Her early studies of the works of da Vinci had given her clues about airfoil designs, but no one yet seemed to have been able to achieve a really good design that was also controllable.

George finally managed to entice her away from technical discussions with her father and got her to spend time with the rest of the family.

"You are miles away?' he said to her.

"I was dreaming of flying to see Koos in the Cape," she laughed. "I think I have some ideas of how we might build an aeroplane."

"What about Sirius?" he asked.

"Sirius can also fly," she said. "I will transfer running of the company to Nastia and Sophia, they and I have already discussed it. We spent some hours between Calais and Amiens deciding how to make the transfer. Then you and I will go to South Africa, and after that I will build an aeroplane."

"Just like that?" he asked.

"Just like that," she confirmed. "No, not just like that, it is a much greater challenge than designing and building a car, but it can be done, and one day people will fly from London to Cape Town without a stop."

"Can you design an aeroplane that will fly in the rain?" he asked.

"I think that with what we know today, weather will be an issue," she replied. "Perhaps if you go high enough, you can be above the clouds, but does that bring its own problems?"

"I've noticed that as you go higher, it gets colder,' he said.

"It does," she agreed. "One more problem to solve. But, we should take things in small steps, first build an aeroplane and learn to fly it, second improve the controls so that you can direct the flight, third add enough petrol so that you can fly from here to London without stopping and then see what is next."

"Most would say that you have lost your sanity," he said. "But, if I look at how quickly car designs are changing, as more aeroplanes are built, more will be learned, and who knows, perhaps one day what you dream of will be possible if not done every day. When you and Sophia, and Nastia discussed Sirius, did you discuss how William will be involved?"

"We did," she confirmed. "William's dream is to produce three times as much horsepower from our current twelve-horsepower engine, without making the cylinders larger."

"How will he do that?" George asked.

"He talks about piston design and shape, head design, fuel mixtures, valve timing and so on," she said. "I think give him a small machine shop, a test bench and a dynamometer and Nastia and he will be as happy as a man can be."

"Is the company sound enough that it can afford the costs of that development?" George asked.

"More than," she confirmed. "We are seeing splendid accounts and can readily afford the costs of the research."

"When do they plan to get married?" George asked.

"Nastia and Sophia are negotiating," Federica laughed. "But, I think it will be an August wedding. William wanted to know the date well in advance to give his family the time to arrange passage from Cape Town to either London or Southampton."

"Where will the wedding be held?" George asked.

"I think at the Hedsor church with a reception for guests at the house afterwards," she said. "I will leave it to you to arrange transport once we know how many people will be in attendance."

"I am sure that I will be able to manage that," he assured her. "What will you do?"

"I will be there supporting Nastia," she said. "At some time, I will even buy a new dress for the occasion!"

Changes in management

"I William Duncan McIntosh take thee Anastasia Katrina Wheelwright. to my wedded wife, to have and to hold from this day forward, for better for worse, for richer, for poorer, in sickness and in health, to love and to cherish, till death us do part, according to God's holy ordinance; and thereto I plight thee my troth."

"I Anastasia Katrina Wheelwright take thee William Duncan McIntosh to my wedded husband, to have and to hold from this day forward, for better for worse, for richer, for poorer, in sickness and in health, to love and to cherish, till death us do part, according to God's holy ordinance; and thereto I plight thee my troth."

"Well, that's done," Federica whispered to George as the priest finished the marriage rites and pronounced them man and wife. "Have you a handkerchief? I said I would not cry, but it is a happy day."

"We should follow the bride and groom outside," George said. "I have arranged cars to take everyone to the house."

As George had said, outside was a line of cars, all waiting to transport guests to Hedsor Grange. They watched as Anastasia and William left in the first car, then as Sophia left with Mr and Mrs McIntosh, then they got into a car with Robert and Elizabeth, brother and sister of William, whom they had met three days earlier when the party had arrived in London from Cape Town.

"She's just so beautiful," gushed Elizabeth. "I hope that one day I can look as pretty."

"You look beautiful," Federica assured her. "Brides are supposed to outshine everyone else on their wedding days."

"Where did you get married, Mrs Wheelwright?" Elizabeth asked.

"In Firenze," Federica asked.

"Florence in Italy," George explained after noticing some confusion pass over Elizabeth's face.

"You are originally from South Africa, Sir?" Robert asked.

"Yes, I was born in Beaufort West, but moved to England after my mother died," George explained.

"Were you there during the last war?" Robert asked.

"I was," George confirmed. "I was assigned to military intelligence and spent my time riding fruitlessly around the veldt."

"We were too young to be involved," Robert said. "I was only thirteen when the war started, and Lizzie was ten."

"I did go to Kimberley when I was there," George said. "I was part of the drive north to relieve the siege. What was it like in the town during the siege?"

"It was exciting enough for a young boy," Robert said. "I had a rifle and Lizzie was there to pass me more bullets if we needed them, but we never did, and when all the troops finally came, the people treated them like heroes."

"Be glad you never had to shoot at anyone," George said. "It is not an enterprise to be sought after."

"When do you return to Kimberley?" Federica asked.

"At the end of the month," Elizabeth replied. "We go to Scotland to see family members I have never met, then we journey back to London and take the boat back to Cape Town."

"And then what?" Federica asked.

"Robbie goes back to university," Elizabeth explained. "And I back to school. Robbie goes to the Transvaal Technical Institute, which used to be the South African School of Mines, right in Kimberley, but now it has moved to Johannesburg, and I am working to be accepted at the University of Cape Town, where I wish to study medicine."

"Well, I wish you every success," Federica said.

"Will said that you and Nastia designed these cars," Robert said.

"We did," Federica agreed. "Nastia did most of the work, I just prodded in the right direction occasionally."

"And now, we understand that you are putting Nastia in charge of the company," Elizabeth said. "How exciting, but won't she have problems with all the men in the factory?"

"When we first started, there were those who thought us incapable," Federica confirmed. "Some realised that knowledge and learning are not limited to the male sex, some never did learn, and if they worked for us, they did not for long, and if we had to do business with them, we tried to find others that were more rational and less afraid."

"You think it's fear that causes men to not think that women are their equals?" Robert asked.

"*Certo,*" Federica said with feeling. "They are afraid that they will lose control of us. They want an ignorant and compliant so-called weaker sex."

"Well, here we are," George said. "Please come in and enjoy yourselves."

"Where are Nastia and William going for their bridal tour?" George asked Federica as they watched the happy couple being driven off to the railway station.

"Scotland," she replied. "I understand from Nastia that there are some distant relatives who were unable to journey south for the wedding, and they will see them, and then they go to Skye for a romantic interlude."

"After they return, how long do you wish to spend with Nastia and Sophia before turning the company over to them?" he asked.

"I think a month will be quite adequate," she replied. "Sophia and I already have a plan for what we will do until Nastia returns, and that will help considerably. Sophia plans to use her mathematical studies to put in place some form of better system to manage the inventory of parts."

"So, I could book passage to Cape Town in early October?" he thought.

"That would be splendid," she agreed. "Is that not also the beginning of spring to summer?"

"It is," he confirmed. "The weather should be getting warmer, and the rain should be getting less. The coolest months are July and August, and they are also among the wettest months in the Cape."

"I am looking forward to the trip," she said. "It has been many years since I was on a long sea voyage, not since we came back from Hong Kong to Italy."

"I will attend to it on Monday," he said.

"Now, we should join the others and not leave Sophia on her own to entertain the relatives and guests," she said. "*Andiamo in casa!*"

George went to London to the Union Castle offices in Fenchurch Street and booked their passages to Cape Town out on the RMS Kildonan and back on the RMS Armadale. He secured two berths in an Outer Deck Cabin at £88 16s 6d each for the outbound and return trips, with a baggage allowance of thirty cubic feet each. He was also told that the portmanteaux that they had in the cabin should not exceed fourteen inches in height, two feet in width and three feet in length, so as to fit under the berth. He took note and that and procured two new portmanteaux that met the dimensions. While he was taking care of that, Federica and Sophia met with the managers of the Sirius Car Company and set out their plan for transferring the reins to Anastasia. They were all comfortable with the change. They knew that Anastasia understood the designs of the cars, and they all were quite content to have her in charge. Federica and Sophia then met with the managers of their other enterprises and let them know that for the next three to six months that Sophia would be conducting the monthly meetings and that she was the person to turn to for approvals of expenditures, *et cetera*. That done, Federica took some time for herself to find a suitable wardrobe of clothes to take to South Africa. She supposed that she had to have some formal gowns for dinners on the boat, but after that her clothes should be of a more basic nature, better suited to the veldt and for sunshine and heat. She took one of George's old khaki uniforms and visited her friend Madame Garnier, who had made her wedding dress and other special occasion dresses and put the problem to her.

"Mon dieu," Madame Garnier said. "You wish me to do what?"

"I would like a similar blouse and some riding breeches made of a twill that would be lightweight, easy to wash out and dry, without the use of an iron and which will wear well," Federica explained. "I am going on an African adventure with my husband and do not wish to be in any way constrained by dresses."

"I suppose it is possible," Madame Garnier grudgingly admitted. "But, why so dull?"

"My husband tells me that it is better to wear simple, dull colours when approaching animals," Federica said. "I do not wish to frighten them away before I have a chance to look upon them closely."

"I can get twill woven from cotton, and I can also get whipcord that I think I will try," Madame Garnier said. "How many blouses and how many pairs of trousers do you need?"

"I think ten of each," Federica said. "I would also like some jackets like this uniform jacket, with pockets and places to put personal items. I think four of those should suffice."

"When do you need these garments by?" Madame Garnier asked.

"I think the last week of September should be fine," Federica replied. "With perhaps a fitting earlier in September. We do not depart for Cape Town until the beginning of October. I also would like four dresses that are suitable for dinners on board the boat."

"Ah oui," Madame Garnier said, much cheered by this addition. "The latest fashion *oui?"*

"Of course, Madame," Federica agreed. "I thought one in cerise, another cobalt, another tyrian and one jade, what do you think? Oh, and I need another in burgundy for George's cousin's wife. She is my height but with more of a motherly figure. Could you manage that as well?"

"Certainement," Madame Garnier agreed. "That I will enjoy, the other I do for you because we are old friends, *mon Dieu,* dull brown, what do they call it, carker?"

"Khaki, they call it khaki," Federica said. "It is, I believe, a word from India, because it is there that the colour was first used by the British army."

"Bon," Madame Garnier said. "We will have two wardrobes then, one for the travel on the boat and one for the expedition into the wilds of uncharted Africa."

"I don't think my husband and his cousin will be taking me anywhere uncharted," Federica laughed. "But, I do need to equip myself with the right clothes, boots and hat."

"Will you not also require a bathing dress and daytime dresses for the boat trip?" Madame Garnier asked.

"I will," Federica agreed.

"For how many days should we be thinking?" Madame Garnier asked.

"I believe seventeen or eighteen," Federica replied. "So, if you would put together ideas for me, we may discuss them when next I call."

Federica's next stop was her milliner friend, Signora Schirano. She took in the bush hat that George had acquired from one of the Australian regiments and asked for a similar hat for herself. Signora Schirano was not as horrified by the idea of such a wardrobe item as Madame Garnier had been over the khaki clothes, but she did suggest two other hats that

Federica might like to take as well. She promised to have the hats all ready by the last week of September, then Federica excused herself from the usual coffee as she had to call on a boot maker. He was intrigued by the notion of making boots for Federica to take to Africa. He had been in the Sudan in one of the campaigns there and understood very well the type of boots that Federica was looking for that would withstand the rigours of trekking in the bush. He took the requisite measurements and asked about heels, to be raised or not. The only concession Federica made was to have one pair as riding boots in case she had occasion to be on a horse in the Cape rather than the car. Federica's last stop of the day was at the gunsmiths. She explained her needs, and he was delighted.

"I have here a new Mauser," he said. "It has been designed for settlers in German East Africa and German South West Africa, not surprisingly, they call it the Africa Model. It was introduced last year. It is a very fine gun."

"May I take one home to try?" she asked.

"Of course, Mrs Wheelwright, take it and try it and let me know how you like it," he said. "Will your husband also be requiring a new rifle?"

"I think I will make him a gift of one," she said. "So, if I like this one, I will take seven, one for each of us, one as a gift for George's cousin in South Africa and one for each of his boys. Should I also take a pistol?"

"The one you have is quite adequate," he said. "But perhaps something new for the trip?"

"What do you suggest?" she asked.

"I think simplicity," he said. "You do not want failures just when you might need things to work. I would suggest the Colt single-action gun that was designed for the American frontier."

"Do you have one?" she asked.

"Of course, Madame," he said. He reached back into a cabinet behind the counter and brought out the revolvers. "Please," he gestured.

"Thank you," she said. "It has greater heft than my current pistol. I like the feel of it, may I also take this to try?"

"Of course, Mrs Wheelwright," he said. "Let me know what you think and how well it shoots. If we need to make adjustments, then we can do all that before you depart."

"I have something for you to try," Federica told George when she arrived home. "I am thinking of buying a new rifle for our trip to the Cape and have this Mauser on approval."

"It is a nice-looking gun," he said. "When must you decide?"

"I don't think Mr Seagrave is in a hurry," she said. "He told me to take the rifle and make sure I like it. If I do, and you do, I was going to buy us one each and another to take for Koos and one each for his sons."

"That is thoughtful of you," he said. "When shall we try it out?"

"Perhaps this weekend, in the large dell at the western side of the woods," she suggested.

"I will have some targets ready," he promised. "What else did you buy today?"

"Clothes," she replied. "Clothes for Africa and for the boat trip, and boots and hats."

"You were busy," he laughed. "Am I now supposed to go and acquire new suitings?"

"I imagine you will wear the scruffy clothes you brought back from South Africa with you," she said. "But for the boat, we need some better clothes as we are expected to dress for dinner at least."

"Am I permitted to buy new shirts and trousers for South Africa as well?" he asked.

"Oh, you mean you will be giving up those frightful clothes you had when you first came back?" she asked.

"I was thinking of it," he admitted.

"I will arrange for you to have new trousers, shirts and jackets," she said. "Do you also need new boots and a new hat?"

"Boots, yes," he replied. "Hat, no."

"I will take care of those, and what did you do today?" she asked.

"I went with Sophia to Abbey and to Windsor," he replied. "I wanted her to see the changes we had made at Abbey and for her to meet the new designers that we retained for Windsor. Tomorrow we will visit with Fox at the foundry, and then we will go to Handy Cross."

"I do believe things will be in good hands with Sophia and Nastia," she said. "I am quite happy leaving them in charge."

"Even with Sirius?" he asked.

"Even with Sirius," she confirmed. "Our cars have proven to be quite successful, and our vans and wagons more so. I see a good future there."

Anastasia and William returned from their trip to Scotland, keen to start their new adventures. Federica had had a workshop created for William equipped with an engine test stand and dynamometer, and a small shop attached with machine tools and other equipment, and he was happy to closet himself away and tinker. Anastasia, Sophia and Federica spent time with Ian Stuart, Andrew Coates and Douglas Wilson, then, when she felt that things were going well enough, Federica started to withdraw from daily operations, leaving more and more to Anastasia. After three weeks, George asked her how things were progressing.

"We could leave now, if you desired," she replied. "I confess to having somewhat mixed feelings. On the one hand, I am delighted with the ease with which Nastia has taken to the rôle of manager, but on the other hand, I cannot help but feel a little distressed that I was so easily replaced!"

"That only speaks to the organisation that you created and the fact that you have so well guided Nastia that she can so easily take over," he said.

"I know you are right," she said. "But it would be nice if they needed me more."

"Yes, but if they needed you more, we could not go away, and you would then berate yourself as having failed to properly educate and train Nastia for the job you wanted her to do," he pointed out.

"As ever, you are right *amore*," she said. "What do we need to do before we take passage to Cape Town?"

"I think just pick up the clothes you had ordered," he said. "I purchased several steamer trunks for the voyage, and you may pack into them what you will. Remember to differentiate between those things you will need on the voyage south and those things that may be stowed in the hold."

"I think all the Africa clothing may be stowed," she said. "That and the gifts I purchased for Anna and their children."

"Should we take a camera?" he asked.

"I think yes," she said. "It would be nice to have photographs that we look upon later in life and remember our trip."

"What did your father buy?" he asked.

"A Kodak No. 3-A Folding Pocket Camera," she replied. "I remember precisely because he repeated the name to me many times. Would you buy one and some film to go with it?"

"I will take care of that," he promised. "Is there anything else?"

"Only how much money should we take with us?" she thought.

"I imagine that there will be expenses on the boat and we cannot expect Koos and Anna to fund our trip into the veldt, so I will draw some funds in sovereigns and take them with me," he said. "Now, should we join the rest of the family for dinner?"

Over dinner, Federica put to William a request for an engine, an engine not destined for cars but for an aeroplane. She outlined what she knew about the engine that the Wright brothers had used for their powered flights and asked him if he could do better.

"Now I know why you acquiesced so easily to my request for a place for William to do engine development," Anastasia said. "You had your own motives quite apart from our Sirius cars."

"I confess it had crossed my mind," Federica admitted. "But, I am sure that whatever William learns, either developing engines for cars or for aeroplanes, could be applied to the other."

"Did you have some idea of how many horsepower and how much weight?" William asked.

"Well, the Wright engine is about twelve horsepower, weighs about one hundred and eighty pounds, is a simple four-in-line water-cooled side valve engine with a gravity fuel feed," Federica said. "I was thinking of the same weight or less with a target fifty horsepower."

"Fifty!" William said. "That is quite a leap from twelve."

"It is, I agree," Federica said. "I was thinking of four cylinders, either in a Vee or horizontally opposed with air cooling and pumped fuel."

"What about more cylinders arranged radially around the crankshaft?" he asked. "The Manly Balzer engine produces over fifty horsepower and yet only weighs one hundred and thirty-six pounds."

"If you think that is the best solution, then yes," she said. "I would leave it with you. We have time enough, I do not see anyone stealing a march on us, but one day I would like a Sirius Aeroplane Company."

"What brought this about?" Anastasia asked.

"I think seventeen days on a boat to get to Cape Town," Federica said. "How long before one can fly there and how long before one can fly there without stopping?"

"That is a dream, I admit," Anastasia said. "To be able to fly to Africa, now there is something that would capture the imagination of almost anyone, it is the stuff of the writings of Jules Verne. So, my job is to produce as many cars as possible to fund this dream?"

"No, I have the funding," Federica said. "I need the mechanical parts and the aeroplane itself. I think once we have a workable design and some actual flights, then the project will fund itself."

"Well, Will, what do you think?" Anastasia asked.

"I have a design for the Sirius engine that increases horsepower by quite a lot, in fact in almost doubles it," he replied. "I need to build some test engines and run them to see if the design works. Once I have done that, I think I will try a Manly Balzer engine and see how many horsepower I can get out of it."

"When do you return, Fede?" Anastasia asked.

"Four months from now," she replied.

"Will, would it be possible to have something to show Fede by then?" Anastasia asked.

"I think so," he replied.

"That would be fine," Federica said. "I would like to see the car engines done first. If we can either increase the horsepower without increasing the weight, we would have a better car. If Will can get a Manly Balzer engine built and tested, I still have to work out how to build a frame for the aeroplane and the wings, the wings, I think, will be the greatest challenge. While I am away, could you see if you can get some tubing of various sizes made from aluminium and rivets as well, I want to see if it is possible to make a frame from aluminium."

We will," Anastasia stated. "I think we had better send you off to Africa before you dream up some other new notion!"

On Saturday, the 6th of October, Federica and George waved goodbye to Anastasia, William and Sophia, who had come to Southampton to see them off on their trip to the Cape Colony. Their vessel for the journey, the Kildonan Castle, was one of the newer vessels on the mail run, having been in service a mere four years. For the next seventeen days, they would be steaming south in the open Atlantic with only a short stop in Madeira. Federica examined the cabin to which they had been assigned and pronounced it to be quite adequate. Their luggage wanted on the voyage, had been stowed in the cabin, and she had watched as the balance had been hoisted up over and down into the hold to remain there until they docked in Cape Town. She had also had the pleasure of watching the crew load six of their vans into the hold, vans that were destined for Johannesburg. George had sent word ahead that they were coming, so she fully expected Koos to be there to greet them when they arrived. It was exciting to be going. As she had told George before, her last trip had been from Hong Kong to Italy, but that had been some years earlier.

"So, shall we visit the lounge and take an aperitif before dinner?" she asked.

"I think that would be a good idea," George agreed. "It will give us a chance to review our fellow passengers and decide whom to avoid."

"George," she said, trying to appear scandalised.

"Well, some of them may just be unpleasant people who have opinions of themselves quite undeserving."

"True," she agreed. "Let us go and categorise."

The roster of first-class passengers was mixed with some emigrants, some returning residents, and some like themselves off on an adventure. Federica found herself a comfortable seat, and a waiter appeared and took her and George's orders. When the drinks arrived, they were joined by a couple who asked if the other seats were occupied and then sat down.

"I should introduce us," the lady said. "This is my husband, Major John Robinson of the cavalry, and my name is Esme, and you are?"

"Federica and George Wheelwright," Federica replied, uncertain yet in which bucket to categorise the Robinsons. "Are you visiting or going out there to live?"

"John is going to show me the battlefields," Esme said. "We hope to visit Durban, Kimberley and Johannesburg as well as Cape Town. John was part of the relief of Kimberley and did sterling service chasing down the Boers in the latter part of the war. Are you visiting or going to stay?"

"We are but visiting," Federica replied. "This will be my first trip to the Cape, and I am looking forward to the adventure."

"John tells me that it can be hot and dusty," Esme said.

"It can also be cold and wet," John said. "I remember in September of 1901, I was in Beaufort West and the weather was awful."

"We have met before," George said.

"We have?" John said.

"It was in Beaufort West, I had been summoned by General French and arrived from the western Cape and en route we had an incident on the train. After my meetings with General French and Colonel Haig, I was assigned to Field Intelligence," George explained.

"Ah, yes, what did I say, something about a scruffy Dutchman," John said. "I'm sorry about that, I had no idea where you had come from or, for that matter, where you disappeared to after those days."

"I spent most of my time in the veldt looking for the Boer commandos, particularly that of Smuts," George said. "But, as it transpired, I was in the east and he was in the west."

"Too bad," John said. "But you must let me buy you a drink. Are you still on active service?"

"No, I resigned my commission, but they wanted to be able to call on me in the future, so they put me on the reserve list," George explained.

"Well, I hope we don't see anything else for a while," John said. "This last war was hard on the local people and led to distrust, hatred and much suffering."

Federica's verdict at the end of the evening was that John was a little pompous, but generally passable, but Esme was too gushing and too caught up in the glory that was her husband. George laughed and told her that it got worse with colonels and generals, and whereas they might be reasonable people, often their wives were unbearable. For the next few days, they sailed through the Bay of Biscay and beyond in the drear and mist until they reached Madeira. After that, sunshine prevailed, and it became hot, hot enough that Federica would have preferred to sleep out on the deck if that had been possible, but not being so, she had to content herself with wearing nothing at all in the cabin and only thin summer clothes on deck. Dinners were uncomfortable because it was hot, and it was expected that one dressed for dinner, so that meant long dresses, which were just too hot for the conditions.

Cape Town was a welcome relief; they had left the oppressive heat of the tropics and were in a more temperate zone. While they were clearing customs and immigration, Koos came up to them.

"Koos," George said. *"Hoe gaan dit man?"*

"Baie goed, dankie," Koos replied. "Good morning, Fede, so nice to see you again."

"Good morning, Koos, where is Anna?" she asked.

"She stayed at home with the boys," Koos said. "I have the car, and we will drive there when we leave here."

"How long will that take?" Federica asked.

"It is about two hundred and seventy miles," Koos replied. "So, two days should suffice. "We will stop on the way, possibly at Swellendam. Oh, and you will need this."

"What is it?" Federica asked.

"It is the required imposter's licence to bring your firearms into the Colony," Koos explained. "You must have one signed by a magistrate."

"But, you've signed it," George said.

"I did," Koos said. "I'm really respectable now, even a magistrate."

"We have lots of luggage," George apologised.

"No problem," Koos said. "I have Sol with me, he will be driving the van in which we will put the luggage. Did you see in Southampton if they loaded some of our vans?"

"They did," Federica confirmed.

"We will need to wait until they are unloaded and I have cleared them to be transported by train to Johannesburg," Koos said. "I have booked hotel rooms here in Cape Town for tonight. I will have Sol take you there now and will follow with the luggage and the van when I have taken care of the vans."

"Fine," Federica said.

When they finally left the boat, they saw a man standing next to one of their vans and beside that was the Antares wagon they had sent out to Koos for testing.

"Sol," Koos beckoned. "This is my cousin George and his wife Federica, please take them to the hotel and be sure they have what they need, I will bring the van and the luggage as soon as I can."

"Yes, Baas," Sol said.

"I see you have the Antares wagon here, but you painted it a different colour and you took the top of the cab off," Federica said.

"Muddy green better fits the purpose, and I thought that it would be more practical in the veldt without the top," Koos said. "But, we may talk more of that over dinner, I must see the port agents, excuse me."

Sol waited until they had got into the Antares, then he stowed the luggage they had with them on a rack that folded down at the rear. He then drove them through Cape Town, pointing out the sights until they came to the Queen's Hotel in Sea Point. The Queen's did not have the cachet of the Mount Nelson, nor did it have the cost, and to boot, Sol could stay there as well. That might change in the future, but for now, providing the room was paid for, any guest was welcome. Federica was anxious to bathe and change clothes. Bathing on the boat had been adequate, but she longed to luxuriate in a nice hot bath. She also was keen to try out her new blouses and trousers and felt that the Queen's would not look as askance as the Mount Nelson would at her wardrobe. They were taking tea with Sol when Koos finally arrived. He told them that he had supervised the loading of the vans onto the train and that they were now on their way to Johannesburg, destined for the explosives factory there at Modderfontein.

"So, tell me the news," he suggested when they all sat down later for dinner.

"George's sister Anastasia married a man from Kimberley," Federica replied. "She has just finished university and she is now in charge of the Sirius Car Company."

"I understood that from George's communication with me, telling me that you were coming," Koos said. "From what he told me when we were together in the veldt, she will succeed."

"I think she will," Federica agreed. "No, I do not think, I know. My interests now lie with aeroplanes, I would like to design and build one and learn how to fly."

"Her dream is an aeroplane that can fly from London to Cape Town," George explained.

"It is a dream, I grant you," she said. "But, it was not so long ago that the idea of a self-propelled carriage that did not rely on horses or steam was also only a dream."

"Aeroplanes would be good here," Koos said. "Our distances are great and roads are poor, if they exist at all, so travel is slow."

"You said it would take us two days to get to Oudtshoorn," George said. "Which way will we go?"

"I think from here to Swellendam, over Sir Lowry's Pass, then from Swellendam we may go inland through Barrydale and Ladismith over the Tradouw Pass. I have used that route before and the Antares wagon is most useful, because we often use it to tow our van up the passes, the drive on all four wheels and the large engine make it perfect for that."

"So, it is performing well?" Federica asked.

"There are the usual repairs and maintenance that one should expect," he said. "But, yes, it is performing well. How were your trials with the army?"

"They were lukewarm," George said. "They tried to get me to take it where a horse would go through rocks, which in time I managed, but they had no real intention of giving up their horses."

"I still use horses," Koos said. "But on the open veldt, the Antares is a marvel, and I would protest greatly if you asked me to return it. I have even towed out horse and ox wagons that have become mired. The winch addition was a brilliant idea, and I have used it many times. For trekking in the veldt, I added some tools, two jacks to lift the wagon, a shovel, a sledgehammer hammer and some long pins, an additional rope for towing and shackles to connect it, and some ladders with close-set rungs to put on the ground if I get mired myself. The ladders provide a path for the wheels and stop them sinking further into the mire. I also added a rack in front here for a rifle, which, when we go to Beaufort West, I will use to take a gun so that we can get dinner when we return."

"How are the roads from here to your farm?" Federica asked.

"None of them is finished like some roads we saw in England," Koos lamented. "They are all various grades of dirt, sand, mud and dust, so when we start out tomorrow, do not wear good clothing. Sol will be fine in the van, but as you know, the Antares does not have a cab, so we will be open to the elements."

"Will it rain?" she asked.

"That is very unlikely," he said. "We are past the rains, now it will be hot and dry, so please do wear a hat."

The drive the next day from Cape Town past Somerset West brought back memories for George, who had ridden in the opposite direction at the end of the Boer War. After Somerset West, they started uphill up the Sir Lowry's Pass, and soon they had to stop and attach the van to the Antares wagon. Koos did not use a rope but a solid bar, which had been stowed under the van and which he and Sol manhandled into place. At the top of the pass, they unhitched the van and drove up and down the rolling hill country to Swellendam. There was a good place to take a break and rest overnight at the Royal Hotel, a quite reasonable hotel with rooms for 7s 6d a night. Federica was enjoying the trip. Everything was new and different, from the baboons by the side of the road to proteas that grew in profusion on the hillsides. They even saw some antelope crossing the road three separate times.

"Are there elephants here?" she asked of Koos.

"No, we must go further east towards Knysna and Addo before we see elephants," he said.

"What is in the van that makes it so heavy?" she asked. "Surely that is not just our luggage?"

"No, if we go to Cape Town, we usually take the opportunity to bring back things that we cannot get in Oudtshoorn, so it is full," Koos said.

"We have not seen many other cars," Federica remarked.

"No," Koos agreed. "Most of the traffic is still horse or ox wagons, but you will see cars, especially where we have been able to talk to possible owners."

"I know that you are still selling quite a number," she said. "We ship cars and vans to you regularly."

"The wagons are becoming very popular," he said. "I think I may have even sold some of the latest Arcturus models."

"Natia will be delighted to hear that," she said. "What will the drive tomorrow be like?"

"We pass through the Langeberg Mountains into the little Karoo," he explained. "We will use the Tradouw Pass, which is quite spectacular. While we drive through, watch out for kudu, they are large antelope with spiral horns. We could also see a blesbok or a bontebok, but they are becoming rare as people hunt them out. I will point out what we see."

Federica was entranced by the drive through the Tradouw Pass. It was only really steep in a few places, where they had to tow the van; otherwise, it was a gentle winding climb up through the mountains. They did see kudu and klipspringer and more baboons, but no blesbok or bontebok, but to even the surprise of Koos, they saw a leopard. He was drinking from a pool in the river that the road followed, and they were able to watch it for a few minutes before it disappeared into the thick brush. Federica was thrilled to see eagles soaring above the hills, Koos identified them as variously, black eagles, booted eagles and even a Verreaux eagle. She pointed them out to George and noted the wing shape and the way that some of the feathers moved to direct flight as they soared above them. After they left the pass, they drove past the occasional farm until they came to the final pass of the trip, the Huisrivier Pass into Calitzdorp, and then it was a fairly flat run to Oudtshoorn. Anna was there to greet them when they arrived and introduced Federica to the four boys, Johannes, now eighteen, Nicolaas, sixteen, Koot, thirteen and Danie, ten. The boys all remember George and regaled Federica with stories of George's prowess with a rifle and the four guineas he took from a town guard near Swellendam four years earlier. That set her to thinking, it had only been four years since George came back from the war, and in that time they had started a successful company, had sold a lot of cars, vans and wagons, and now she was getting ready for the next enterprise. George interrupted this reverie by handing around the gifts they had brought. It seemed they had chosen wisely because all the family was delighted with their gifts.

The boys wanted to go out there and then to try out their new rifles, but Anna put her foot down and said that that could wait until the morrow.

"Can we go to Beaufort West?" Federica asked George. "I would like to see where you are from."

"We can," he assured her. "It is about a day's travel, but there is a good road there."

"What about seeing elephants?" she asked.

"As Koos said, we would have to go closer to Knysna or Addo, which are to the south and east," he said. "So, after we go to Beaufort West, we could go to George and then along the coast towards Knysna."

"I was watching some buzzards early this morning," she said. "It amazes me to watch them fly, they wheel around the heavens so effortlessly, I am even more determined now to build an aeroplane. I would like to see the world from their point of view."

"If some of the ostriches that Koos had could fly, I wonder how big the wings would have to be?" he mused.

"I would think vast," she said. "I don't know what buzzards weigh, but it cannot be much, what do you think about two pounds and the wingspan must be four and a half feet, the ostrich weighs, let's say three hundred pounds, that would mean a wingspan of over six thousand feet, no that can't be right, no six hundred feet, no wonder they don't fly?"

"No wonder," he agreed. "Have you given any thought to what you will build your aeroplane from?"

"I looked at all the available images of the Wright plane," she replied. "They use a wooden frame, and the wings are wooden ribs covered with fabric, and they also use a lot of wire to brace and stiffen the wings."

"What is the wingspan of their aeroplane?" he asked.

"A little over forty feet, it's odd because the right wing is longer than the left wing to account for the engine, which is not mounted in the centre," she replied.

"How much does it weigh?" he asked.

"With the pilot, seven hundred and fifty pounds," she said.

"That doesn't fit with the buzzard numbers," he commented.

"It doesn't," she agreed. "But the Wright plane was a biplane, it had two wings, one above the other, I believe the total wing area was about five hundred and ten square feet, I wonder what the wing area of a buzzard is? If I look at the wing span and we assume that it is four and a half feet and look at how far back the wings go, that must be about a foot, so, if we include the body and the tail, a wing area of four and a half square feet, or two and a quarter square feet per pound, whereas the Wright plane was much less than one square foot per pound. No wonder the buzzards soar so easily."

"What are you two talking about?" Koos asked, interrupting.

"We were discussing the technical aspects of flying," George said.

"Well, tell us on the way," he said. "Anna and I are coming with you to Beaufort West. It has been a little while since we were there. We go to George of Mossel Bay if we need anything that we cannot get at home, and we ship some of our produce from Mossel Bay."

The Antares performs

Koos drove east from Oudtshoorn towards De Rust, which they reached in just over an hour, then he turned north into the Groot Swartberge mountains. The road started to climb and crossed back and forth over a river many times. The going was slow as the road had been damaged by water when the river had run high and over its banks.

"Who built this road?" Federica asked when they were negotiating one particularly muddy and rutted patch.

"There was a roads engineer by the name of Thomas Bain who did much of the work on the current line," Koos explained. "There was an old bridle path through here, but a farmer by the name of Meiring wanted a better road through the mountains to get his produce to wider markets. The road was built in the mid eighteen hundreds and has been closed a few times since because of water damage. In fact, when they first brought Bain in, he decided to build another road that went over the mountains, so he built the Swartbert Pass, then came back to this one."

"Does the drive on all four wheels help?" she asked.

"It does," Koos assured her. "We could probably get through with one of the other cars, but we would probably be pushing it here!"

"It is spectacular," she said.

"It is," Koos agreed. "Not far ahead, there is a waterfall which should be flowing well because of the recent rains we have had."

"It looks like someone is stuck," Anna said, pointing ahead.

"Ag man," Koos said. "Well, we'll see if we can help."

"Môre meneer," Koos said. *"Kan ek u help?"*

"Sorry, don't speak Dutch," the wagon driver replied.

"Can I help you?" Koos asked again,

"That would be appreciated," the wagon driver said. "We've come up from Mossel Bay, and I did well until now."

"A long drive," Koos said. "I am Koos Englebrecht from Oudtshoorn."

"John Butler from Port Elizabeth," was the reply.

"You're a long way from home," Koos commented.

"I got a contract to haul china from Mossel Bay to Beaufort West, but it may cost me if I cannot get loose soon," Butler complained.

"What is the problem?" Koos asked.

"I hit a soft patch and the offside wheels sank almost to the axles. I have been digging, but it will take some time yet," Butler replied."

"Let me take a look," Koos suggested. He walked around the wagon, then up the road a little way, then back around the wagon, then again up the road, stabbing at the sides of the road with a stick, looking for soft patches.

"Let us try something," he suggested to Butler. "Unhitch your team and walk them up the road until it is good going again."

"What are you going to do?" Butler asked.

"Tow you out," Koos said.

"In that?" Butler asked incredulously.

"We'll try," Koos said. "Fede, will you guide me past the wagon on the left, I want to stay as close as I can without hitting it. George, will you help Mr Butler unhitch the team and walk them up the road, then I want you to hitch the d*isselboom* to the towing pintle at the back of our wagon."

George did as requested and helped Mr Butler move the team well up the road, then he watched as Federica guided Koos past the wagon, with the two wagons almost brushing. Twice, Koos got into soft soils, but the drive on all wheels of the Antares pulled him through. Once past the mired wagon, he reversed up until George told him the stop. Koos then looked at the *disselboom* and his own tow hitch and opened up a toolbox at the back of the Antares. He took out a short length of chain and proceeded to connect the two. Satisfied that it was as secure as he could make it, he asked the others to get back into the Antares to add weight over the wheels, engaged the lowest gear he could and started forward. To everyone's delight, they were able to slowly pull the mired wagon out of the soft patch and farther up the road to solid ground. Federica had been watching closely, and she observed some wheel spin a few times and wondered if there was a better way to manage the differentials on the axles and between the two axles, so as not to let the loss of traction on one wheel stop the forward momentum. It was something to discuss with Anastasia when they returned to England.

"What is that car?" Butler asked.

"A Sirius Antares," Koos replied. "Designed and built by my cousins here."

"Remarkable," Butler said. "You have a wonderful car there, Sir."

"It's not my design," George said. "My wife is the designer and the builder, I just help."

"Truly?" Butler asked.

"Truly," George confirmed.

"Well, thank you, Madame," Butler said. "Without your wonderful invention, I would have probably been stuck here another day or two. I was at the point of starting to unload the wagon so that it would be light enough for my team to pull it out."

"Well, good luck with the rest of your trip," Federica said.

"You've been a lifesaver, Madame," Butler said. "I'll be watching the road more closely now for soft patches."

Koos waved goodbye, and they drove on up the pass, past the oxen who were patiently waiting to be yoked up again and on until they came to the waterfall. Federica wanted pictures; she had, after all, purchased a camera especially for the trip and had only taken a few photographs so far. The waterfall was worth a picture, and she had the others pose in front of it. From there, they drove on up the pass to the summit and then down to Klaarstroom, after which the going was much better and they were able to pick up some speed. There were no speed limits on these roads in the Cape and no Constable Platt to look out for. Koos assured them that in time, the notion of speed limits would find its way to the interior, and they might even have constables issuing summonses. "But, as I am the magistrate for part of the district, I would have to hear my own case," Koos laughed. "So I think, for the moment at least, the constables will leave me alone."

"It occurs to me that there could be sales of a wagon built especially for towing," Federica said. "People do get stuck on occasion, and we have used teams of horses in the past to pull wagons out of trouble, or we use one of our steam engines."

"So a heavier version of the Antares built for towing?" George thought.

"I think so," Federica confirmed. "If we were to take the larger Arcturus frame, add the second gearbox and a driven front axle, and add the larger engine, it should tow most things."

"How many might we sell?" George asked.

"Ah, therein lies the problem," Federica agreed. "We would have to do quite some engineering work, and what might we sell, one hundred or so altogether, it may not be worth it."

"But if we have the parts, just give them to your special options team to put together," George suggested. "Then you can keep it from the main line, and the special team can work out the engineering needs as they go on a trial basis."

"Is this how your projects usually start?" Anna asked.

"It is," Federica confirmed. "Usually, something comes up or we see a need for a particular car or van, then we design one that we think might work. I have the wild ideas, and George usually drags me back to earth."

"What fun," Anna said. "When we return home, Danie wants to ask you about your cars and vans; he is fascinated with the idea of a transport company, moving goods around the country."

"He would like the new Arcturus then," Federica said. "It is larger than our other cars but not as large as the lorries made by Straker, Foden and the others. Perhaps Danie should be looking at them as well. Although they are now all steam, there are tests for internal combustion engines underway and before long, steam will be replaced."

"How is the petrol pump working?" George asked.

"It's fine, I added an additional tank underneath, so now have the range of about five hundred miles, which is sometimes necessary here because finding petrol can be a challenge," Koos replied. "I put some clear tubes on the outside of the tanks so I could see how much petrol was in them, but some sort of gauge like the speedometer would be useful, and to have it mounted here where I can see it."

"Is that possible, Fede?" George asked.

"I am not sure," she admitted. "I will add it to the list of projects to consider when we return home. There was a man in London, name of Davison, who has done what Koos has, except that his petrol tank is in front of the dash so the sight gauge is always visible, but it does not solve our problem as the tank size is limited to space by the engine, we cannot do that and have sight gauges from tanks under the floor."

"Here we are at Beaufort," Koos announced. "I don't think it has seen much change since you were here last, George. We have a choice of three hotels, The Royal, The Masonic or The Queen's. The Masonic is a little more than the other two at 10s a night, but the extra comfort is worth the little extra in cost."

"Do you see much change, George?" Federica asked.

"There are a lot fewer people," he replied. "When I was here in the war, there were camps of soldiers and horses everywhere. But, even so, the town has grown since I was a child."

"Do you remember where your house was?" she asked.

"I do," he said. "Perhaps after we get rooms at the hotel, we can take a short drive and I will show you."

"I thought that tomorrow we would visit the farm where they use the Oldsmobile car to drive a pump and various other farmyard machines," Koos added. "I think you will enjoy talking to the farmer; he is quite the inventor."

"I like that idea," Federica said. "Shall we go to the hotel? How far away is Renosterkop? Is that not where your family lived before Beaufort?"

"It is where my father and George's mother grew up," Koos said. "It is about twenty miles along the road to Bloemfontein."

"Why is it called Renosterkop?" Federica asked.

"Well," Koos said. "Literally, it means rhinoceros hill, whether that is because someone thought it looked like a rhinoceros or whether they found a rhinoceros there, I don't know."

Following the visit to the house of George's childhood and the trek to Renosterkop and the visit to the farm of the inventor, it was time to retrace their steps back to Oudtshoorn. Koos did not simply go back the way they had come, but instead took the road to Prince Albert Road, an unremarkable railway station that served Prince Albert, some twenty-eight miles distant at the foot of the Groot Swartberg. Prince Albert boasted an extensive irrigation system that was fed from the mountains. The route to Oudtshoorn went over the Swartberg Pass, which started out following a river and quickly went into a steep-sided canyon with high walls. They crossed the river twice, wading the car through the water, which was still high from snow melt. Soon, they started to climb out of the canyon and up and around hairpin bends in the road.

"Who built this road?" Federica asked.

"The route was scouted and planned by Thomas Bain, but it was built by convict labour," Koos explained. "There is a ruin ahead of a camp where the convicts stayed while they worked on the road."

"What is that antelope over there?" Federica asked, pointing off into the distance.

"That is a grysbuck," Koos identified it. "And the ones over there behind it are grey ribbok. As we go, watch out for baboons and vervet monkeys, they are common here."

"It feels as if it is getting cooler," Federica commented.

"It is," Anna confirmed. "At the top, it will be very cold and windy, but behind the seats here we have some of the motoring coats that you make that we use when it gets cold."

"We will stop up ahead for a coffee break," Koos said. "When we start out again, then we'll use the coats."

The view from the summit was spectacular. To the south was laid out the farms of the Little Karoo, and to the north a range of bluish hills. Koos had been right, at the summit it was windy, very windy, and that made it feel really cold.

"Now starts the most difficult part," Koos said.

"What, are there more of those hairpin bends?" George asked.

"No," Koos said. "It is a steep descent, and braking is always an issue. I usually go down in a low gear so that the *bakkie* does not run away."

"The brakes need improvement, then?" Federica asked.

"They are adequate for normal use," Koos said. "But, this is a fairly severe test; if you do make improvements in the future, then brakes on all four wheels would be good."

"Not far from the bottom of this pass are the Cango Caves," Ann said. "We'll stop there are explore a little. I have lanterns with us."

"Are they big caves?" Federica asked.

"They are quite extensive," Anna replied. "There was a survey just before the war, and twenty-six chambers were recorded. Johnnie van Wassenaar, who is a guide there, says that he travelled more than twenty-nine hours following the tunnels, and he guessed that he had gone over fifteen miles under the ground."

"I think we could agree that they are extensive," George said.

"The tales around here are that the Bushmen knew all about the caves and used them before they were pushed north into the Kalahari," Koos said.

"So your mother's ancestors may have lived here once?" George asked.

"I suppose it's possible," Koos agreed. "But I have no idea where they came from, only that Pa met up with them in Bechuanaland."

"Well, here we are," Anna said. "Are you ready for an adventure?"

When they were leaving the caves, they noticed a circle of admirers or critics surrounding their car. It seemed that there was an outing of school teachers who had been intrigued by the car, particularly when one man had noticed the differential on the front axle as well as the rear axle. That had led to debate and conjecture.

"Good afternoon," Federica said as she worked her way through the throng to the car.

"Good afternoon, Madame," one of the men said. "Is this your car?"

"It belongs to Koos here, but it is of my design," she replied.

"Your design?" he asked quite archly.

"Yes, I do assure you," Federica said. "My design."

"She tells you the truth," Koos said as he came up to the car. "I am Koos Englebrecht and I am the dealer in Oudtshoorn for the Sirius Car Company that built this car, the company that Mrs Wheelwright is the managing director of."

"Are we correct in thinking that it has drive to all wheels?" the man asked.

"It does," Federica replied. "We took the idea from a Dutch company, Spyker, and added a second gearbox to transfer power to the front axle as well as the rear and to provide for lower gears. We have two of the cars here in the Cape for testing. We have other cars, vans and wagons in South Africa, but they are all of a more conventional build."

"I have seen some," another man commented. "Yours are the cars and vans that have the fully enclosed cab that shelters the driver and the passengers or goods."

"That is right," Federica confirmed. "We have supplied vans to the Cape Argus, and some are at the moment on their way north to the explosives factory at Modderfontein."

"Are they expensive?" a third man asked.

"I am sure that Koos would be happy to discuss models and prices with you," Federica said. "We tried to design and build a car that would be within the reach of most professional people, including teachers."

"What about this one with the drive on all wheels?" the first questioner asked.

"We have not yet made the decision to enter into production," Federica replied. "We are still conducting tests and trials to assure ourselves of its reliability."

"Do you have a card?" the first questioner asked of Koos.

"I do," Koos assured him, and then handed out cards to all those who were interested.

"Did you come over the Swartberg?" another man asked.

"We did," Koos confirmed. "We drove north earlier in the week up the Meiringspoort, where we pulled a wagon out of the mire, and then this morning we came over the Swartberg."

"And your car dealt with the gradients and curves with no difficulty?" the man asked.

"None at all," Koos assured him.

"I think I will contact you soon," the man said. "And I," chimed in another.

"Will we see sales from that?" Federica asked Koos as they drove south towards the Schoemanspoort and the way back to Oudtshoorn.

"I think so," he replied. "Many were captivated by the car, and the fact that we had just driven over the Swartberg meant a lot to them. We may get enquiries both for the Antares and for the Procyon cars."

"I wonder if we should build the Antares in production?" she mused.

"What size of order from me would be adequate to help you make the decision?" Koos asked.

"I think I would need some idea of where we might sell at least twenty," she replied. "I should send you some cost estimates when we return home, and you tell me if there would still be an interest. The Antares is a more expensive car than the Procyon or the Regulus; it has more parts and a reinforced frame."

"True, but it has less bodywork," Koos pointed out.

"Do you think you would want them without a covered body, or even the driver's cab?" she asked.

"I think just a Cape Cart hood would be fine," he said. "As we go north, the weather gets hotter, and then only the rain is a problem. In the far north in Bechuanaland and Rhodesia, shade is important, but so is ventilation, as it gets really hot there."

"I will consider that," she promised.

Federica and George spent the next three days in Oudtshoorn, during which Johannes took Federica hunting, and she shot a very nice kudu that was then cut up and taken back to the farm to be eaten. George contented himself with being the observer on that trip. They were also rewarded by the sight of several Mountain zebra, a type of zebra confined to parts of South Africa and German South West Africa. It looked different to the common zebra found farther north in Central and East Africa. Johannes told them that the zebra had become nervous because they were being aggressively hunted for their skins. On the fourth day, the family set out for George and Knysna. They took both of the Antares cars as the boys were joining the older members of the family. Federica really wanted to see an elephant, and Koos had told her that the best chance, without going really far afield, was in the Knysna area or the Tsitsikamma forest, just beyond Knysna. He warned her that the elephants there had become skittish because of hunting and had learned to recognise the crack of a whip used by ox team drivers, which usually meant hunters. So, going in the cars, they were at an advantage because no one had yet started to use cars seriously for hunting. They used the Outeniqua Pass down to George, paying their toll to use the road. Koos joked that they could easily have avoided the toll house by the use of a side track that he knew, but as the local magistrate, that was hardly in keeping with his position. From George, they followed the coast to Knysna and put up at the Royal Hotel, reasonably priced at 8s 6d per night. But they did take four rooms and their meals, so the proprietor was happy to see them.

From Knysna, they took the road that leads up to Prince Alfred's Pass, the long drag up to Avontuur. Koos stopped them partway up and said that he was now going to take a side track and that they should be on the lookout for elephants. After an hour, he stopped and got out of the car to study some tracks. The others gathered for a quick lesson.

"Eight elephant," he said. "Moving west, six adults and two small ones, see here and here. They were here less than an hour ago."

"How do you know?" Federica asked.

"Look at the sand ridges made by the feet," he explained. "The wind in time knocks down the sharpness of the ridge. This is what I would expect after about an hour. Also, the piles of dung here are fresh, and the insect activity around them and the temperature confirm that, and look here, where some have urinated, the ground has absorbed some, but it is not yet completely dry."

"Oh," Federica said. "I had no idea there was so much involved. Do we follow them?"

"We shall," Koos said. "We will take the cars as far as we can, then we may have to walk."

They followed the tracks through the brush, and soon there was other evidence that the elephants had gone through there. They were now feeding as they went, and Koos pointed out broken branches on trees and other signs. He stopped suddenly and turned off the engine in the car he was driving, and Anna did the same in the second car. He pointed west and then pointed to his ears.

"I hear," whispered Federica. "What is that?"

"The rumbling noise you hear is a sound the elephants make," Koos explained. Then they heard a much different sound as an elephant tore a branch from a tree. Koos signalled that they would now walk. He picked up his rifle and indicated to the others to do likewise. Now they walked in single file following Koos. Federica noted how he watched carefully where he put his feet and how he stopped occasionally and picked up leaf debris and let it fall, testing the wind direction. Then he stopped completely and pointed forward. Federica looked to where he was pointing and saw nothing. But she reasoned Koos must have seen something, so she looked again. Then she saw it, an elephant behind a tree. Then she saw another and another. Koos motioned to them all to follow him, and he went north a little way up a kopje he had seen. Once at the top, they could look down on the elephants.

"That is wonderful," Federica said. "Don't you think so, George?"

"It is," he agreed. "I have not seen an African elephant since I was a child. I saw them in India, of course, but these are much larger. Do you have the camera?"

"I do," she confirmed. "Here, take my rifle while I try and get a picture of them all. Is the one with the big tusks the male?"

"No, that will be *ouma*, grandmother," he said. "There are no adult males in that group, one very small male, all the others are female."

"Is that usual?" she asked.

"It is," he confirmed. "All the breeding herds are led by females."

"What do the males do?" she asked.

"They go off on their own or in bachelor groups," he explained.

"So a lot of the stories about big bull elephants protecting the herd are wrong?" she asked.

"Most, yes," he agreed. "It is the grandmothers and aunts who manage things."

"Look, they're moving off into that thicker forest," she said. "Goodbye, elephants. You don't shoot them?"

"What for?" Koos asked. "We don't want the ivory, there's more meat on them than we could use in a long while."

"Didn't your father try his hand at ivory hunting?" she asked. "George told me that he went north to do that, but things went wrong."

"He started out thinking he would make a fortune hunting ivory," Koos agreed. "Then things began to go wrong, and it was only because of the bushmen and my grandfather that he survived. I had a sister once, but she died in a fight with slavers from Portuguese West Africa. My father and I walked back to Bechuanaland and then to Cape Town."

"That sounds like a very short version of a real adventure," she laughed.

"It was what it was," Koos said. "Shall we start to go home?"

Koos knew a fruit farmer in Avontuur who was happy to accommodate them for the night. It was not quite the Royal Hotel in Knysna, but he was generous and welcoming. Shortly after dinner, Federica excused herself. The farmer was trying hard to be hospitable, but he was struggling with English. Federica knew what it was to try and converse in a language that was not your first and how hard it was, so she did not want the poor man to labour through the evening. She heard as she left the room all the others switch to Dutch, and the farmer visibly relaxed. George did not stay long with the rest of the party, as he said the conversation had switched to crops, yields, water and all the things that farmers talk about. There was one item of news that they had all talked about, and that was the new railway line being built from Port Elizabeth to Avontuur. It had reached Krakeel, so only had about another thirty-eight miles to go and was expected to be open all the way to Avontuur by January. It was of interest because it was a narrow gauge line, even narrower than what was now called the Cape Gauge of 3' 6"; this new line had a gauge of only 2'. The farmer was excited because he would be able to ship his fruit to Port Elizabeth for export. George had a passing interest, but had to admit that Federica was a much greater attraction, even against a new railway line.

"Are you happy that you saw your elephant?" he asked.

"Oh yes," she confirmed. "I was amazed at how quiet they can be. When they moved away, I did not hear them at all. So, now I have seen lots of antelopes, zebras and now elephants. What else should we see?"

"We will have to go north to see lions and other animals," he said. "Many years ago, they might have been here, but they have been pushed out by people or killed by people."

"Where do we go?" she asked.

"Koos and I were talking," he said. "He recommends that we take the train to Johannesburg and then go east from there to the Sabi Game Reserve and the Shingwedzi Reserve. He says that we will see all manner of animals there."

"How much longer do we have in South Africa?" she asked.

"We have several weeks yet, so we have plenty of time," he assured her.

"Let us stay with Koos and Anna another few days and then go north," she suggested.

On the way back to Oudtshoorn, Danie plied Federica with questions about cars, vans and lorries. He told her that one day he would like to have a transport company to move goods and freight. She told him all she knew about the various manufacturers and what developments were afoot. Eventually, his brothers came to her rescue and directed the talk to things other than transport. They wanted to hear about Hong Kong and life in Asia. None had been beyond the borders of South Africa, so the world was a mysterious place. Johannes was clearly a farmer, and his heart was set on continuing the family farm. Nicolaas was interested in grapes and winemaking, Koot was undecided about anything, but as Federica told him, there was time enough to decide. Over dinner that evening, Koos told the boys that they were all going with Federica and George to the reserves that had been created in the eastern Transvaal. They would travel by train to Johannesburg and thence to Komatipoort on the railway to Lourenço Marques. He had been in touch with Major Stevenson-Hamilton, and arrangements had been made for them to visit the new reserves. Koos told Federica and George that the Sabie Game Reserve had been declared by President Kruger under the then Transvaal Republic, and it had been redeclared a reserve under the Milner government following the war. It was amazing to Koos that two such intractable foes could have the same vision when it came to one of the natural assets of the country. They knew from the Cape that pressure from people either drove animals away or they were killed, so if the country wanted to keep one of its real assets, they would have to protect it.

The journey to Johannesburg was interrupted by a stop in Kimberley to visit the parents of William, Hamish and Fiona McIntosh. Federica and George had met them at the wedding and had been invited to stop and see the family. Koos and family were welcomed as well, even though the Englebrechts were generally supporters of the Boer cause in the past war. As Koos and George pointed out to the boys, Hamish did not start the war; in fact, he was just caught up in it as they had been. The people to blame for the conflict were the politicians and ambitious businessmen who looked for a found an excuse to foment discord.

Hamish had done well with early diamond diggings and had sold out to the De Beers company at a healthy profit. He was now considering his next enterprise and had had several ideas, but had not yet fixed upon one. Federica and Koos both suggested that he might consider being a dealer for Sirius cars. Trade that he might do would not affect that of Koos, and there were quite a lot of people who could well afford one of their cars. Hamish was taken by the idea and suggested that he and Koos work out some form of dealer arrangement that left Koos as the agent for Africa and funnelled orders and such through him. That sounded fine to Federica, who would then only have to deal with one person in South Africa. That done, the family was treated to a tour of the mine workings around Kimberley. The next day, they continued their journey to Johannesburg and then on to Komatipoort.

The lower eastern Transvaal, the Lowveld, was hot and damp, and that meant that the grass was springing up, making finding and watching game a challenge. The party had been provided horses, mules and a guide and a wagon to carry the equipment and tents to be able to camp in the reserve. Federica and George were thrilled with sightings of lions, leopards, elephants, giraffe, zebra, hippopotamus, rhinoceros, wildebeest, buffalo, eland and any number of smaller antelope. Koot found his calling and decided that above all, he would like to join the organisation that Major Stevenson-Hamilton had and become a ranger. He could shoot, he could track, and he decided that he could learn the other skills he needed from the rangers who were there. He particularly liked Major Fraser, who looked after the Shingwedzi Reserve, a huge area between the Letaba River and the Limpopo. Koot decided that would be the life. Federica looked at the reserve as an opportunity to sell motor cars, but she knew that it would be some time before the reserve was developed enough to permit cars. Still, there was always the possibility of selling some of the Antares models. They were singularly well suited for the purpose of transporting people and goods in undeveloped areas.

All too soon, the trip came to an end, and the family made its way back to Oudtshoorn. There, Federica and George stayed for a few days. Koot challenged George to a shooting contest, so it was arranged, and then the whole family, plus farm workers, turned out to watch. Johannes took charge and paced out one hundred paces, then set up targets. It was decided that they would use the new Mauser rifles that Federica had brought, and Nicolaas handed out ammunition. Danie came with a coin, and they tossed it to see who would shoot first. George won the toss and asked that Koot shoot first. He suggested that they each be allowed two trial shots to test the wind before the competition start, so they each shot off the two rounds and studied where they had hit against where they thought they would hit. They gave them a sense of the wind and how the rifles behaved. Koot then shot his ten competition rounds and was thrilled that they were all in the centre of the target, clustered close together. George then shot, and his results were as impressive. Danie then suggested that they actually measure the spread of the impacts to see who had the better grouping. It was George; he was still the expert.

"Now, my young friend," he said to Koot. "Have Johannes step off two hundred paces and let us see how you fare."

"That is a long way, *Oom* George," Koot said.

"It is," George agreed. "But, I think you will do well."

Koot did do well, but his groups of shots now began to spread more, whereas those of George still stayed tight.

"He is still the master," Koos said. "Keep practising, son, and one day you will be able to do that."

"How is it done, *Oom* George?" Koot asked.

"As your Pa says, practice," George replied. "Know your rifle, study each part and see where the imperfections are, watch how it changes as the barrel heats up, check the air temperature and humidity and the wind speed and direction, is it little gusts or a steady blow, notice everything and you will be fine."

"Do you remember the day you won money from the captain of the town guard in Swellendam?" Nicolaas asked.

"I do," George said. "He thought he was so clever, but his trooper who did the shooting was quite good."

"*Ja,* but not good enough," Johannes laughed.

"It's dinner time, everyone," Anna said. "*Oom* George and Fede will be leaving soon, so we should entertain them while we can."

"Sadly, we leave tomorrow," Federica said. "Your Ma and Pa are going to drive us to Cape Town. I think I will leave some of my veldt clothes here, please find a good use for them. I will also leave the ammunition we brought; there is no need for us to take it back to England. Is there anything I may send you from England when we return?"

There were a few items that the boys suggested, none very large, and she thought that she could get them all and send them out by mail to the Cape.

"Will you come back?" Anna asked Federica as they examined the boat cabin that Federica and George had been assigned.

"I would like to," Federica replied. "Will you come to England again?"

"Perhaps," Anna said. "Perhaps the next time I go, it will be in the air!"

"I suspect that it will be some time before we can fly from Cape Town to England." Federica laughed. "But, it is a notion that intrigues me."

"Enjoy the trip home and think of us," Anna said.

"I will, thank you for your company and hospitality," Federica said. *"Tot siens."*

"Tot siens," Anna replied, then she hugged George, who had been talking to Koos, and then she and Koos left the boat as the ship's siren had just sounded a warning to all visitors to leave before sailing.

"I like her," Federica said to George as they watched Anna and Koos walk down the gangplank to the quayside.

"She and Koos are well matched," he said. "I have enjoyed the trip, and you?"

"It was wonderful," she said. "To see the town and the house where you grew up, and then to see all those animals, it was such a treat. I am glad we came, perhaps as Anna said, one day we might fly here and not have to take the boat for seventeen days."

"Perhaps," he agreed. "I wonder if it will be possible in our lifetimes?"

"When I was a child, I thought that it was not possible to have a cart that was not pulled by horses or powered by steam, now look. We have made so much progress so quickly. We know men can fly; the Wrights proved that. Now we need to improve their designs and extend the time of the flights, and increase the speed. The Wright flyer would be hopeless on a journey to South Africa, it is too slow, this boat goes faster, and that is without the effect of the wind that may be blowing against you, so there is much to do," she opined.

"Look, is that not John and Esme Robinson?" he said, pointing towards the couple who had just come up on deck.

"Do we flee or do we stay?" she asked.

"We should probably stay," he thought. "They are at least reasonable; there might be others who are unbearable, and we cannot stay in our cabin as hermits the entire trip."

"Ah, well met, fellow travellers," John Robison said. "Did you enjoy your visit to South Africa?"

"We did indeed," Federica replied. "We were able to visit relatives of George and take an excursion into the veldt and see all manner of wild animals, and you?"

"We looked at dry and dusty plains that John assures me were the sites of many famous skirmishes," Esme said. "We visited Ladysmith and saw the siege works, which were actually very interesting; it reminded me of history I learned as a child and sieges in the Middle Ages."

"Now for home and the cold," John said.

"I wonder if we will see snow this winter?" Federica pondered. "I hope not, I have become used to the heat again."

"You say again, were you here before?" Esme asked.

"No," Federica said. "But I spent most of my childhood in Hong Kong, where it was perennially warm, if not hot."

"Well, that's the siren blast for us leaving," John said. "I see they are casting off fore and aft. Well, goodbye South Africa again."

Federica and George looked for and found Koos and Anna standing on the quayside. They waved as the boat was pulled away from the quay by the tugs and continued waving until they could no longer see them.

"How did you travel around South Africa?" John asked.

"We were driven by car," Federica replied. "Except for our excursion to the Sabie Game Reserve, which is in the Transvaal, that we did by train and horse."

"I saw a few cars," John said. "They seem to be getting popular here. What type of car did you travel in?"

"A Sirius," Federica replied.

"I have seen those," John said. "Esme likes the fact that the body is all enclosed and provides the driver and passengers shelter from the rain and such."

"We own the Sirius Car Company," George said. "Federica did most of the design work on the different models we have."

"I say, really?" John asked.

"It's true," Federica confirmed. "The car we used here is a new model that we sent out here to be tested in extreme conditions."

"They would be that," John agreed. "Well, fancy, a car designer."

"You said that your new car is in South Africa for testing," Esme said. "What have the tests shown?"

"I think the one item that I would like to address quickly is brakes on all four wheels," Federica replied. "We went over a high and steep pass in the mountains, and coming down was quite an adventure."

"I had not thought of that," Esme admitted. "Do you have any ideas?"

"I have some," Federica replied. "But I need to talk to my co-designer, George's sister, to see what she thinks."

"Your sister also designs cars?" John asked.

"She does," George confirmed.

"Well, bless my soul," John said.

"We have been thinking of buying a car," Esme said. "Where might we see your Sirius cars?"

"If you are in London, we have a showroom where we offer cars for sale, we also provide driving lessons and have a facility there to effect repairs and maintenance," Federica said. "This is the address, and if you go, be sure and speak to Arthur Dent, who is our manager there."

"Right ho," John said. "I say, isn't that the gong for dressing for dinner?"

"You're right," George said. "We will see you in the dining room."

Design improvements

When the boat docked in Southampton on the 22nd of December, it was chilly, damp and not welcoming at all, except for the reception they received from Sophia, Anastasia and William.

"Welcome home," Anastasia said. "I was afraid that you might get eaten by wild animals."

"We had too many protectors for that to ever happen," Federica assured her.

"Did you enjoy the trip?" Sophia asked.

"Immensely," Federica replied. "I saw where George grew up, I saw where his cousin lives, and I saw wild animals. We even passed through Kimberley on our way to Johannesburg when we went to one of the new game reserves. We saw Will's father, in fact, he is to sign up with us as a dealer in Kimberley."

"He has signed with us," Anastasia said. "We have been receiving wires from Koos with agreements, orders and such."

"Already?" Federica asked.

"Already," Anastasia confirmed. "Mr McIntosh is not one to wait; he has already placed orders for ten cars, fifteen wagons and twelve vans. Apparently, he and Mrs McIntosh travelled down to Oudtshoorn to meet with Koos, and there they inspected and tried out our cars. Mr McIntosh particularly liked the Antares, so I decided to build a few more and have just shipped one out to him to use as a car to advertise the company."

"This is all very well," Sophia interrupted. "But, I would like to go home, and I am sure that Fede and George would also prefer to have this conversation in the drawing room and not on the quayside."

"Of course, Mama," Anastasia said. "What was I thinking of? We have a car and a van for the luggage. Who would like to ride with whom?"

"I will ride with William and the luggage," George offered. "That way, you can carry on your conversation as you drive home."

On the drive home, Sophia guided the conversation away from cars and more towards general matters, like fashions, food and trips into the veldt. Federica gave a detailed account of their trip from the boat ride out to the boat ride back. She promised to have her photographs all developed as quickly as possible so that they could see some of the places, people and sights. At the house, they were greeted by Eleanor and the rest of the staff, who were happy to see them a agog to hear of their adventures. After the luggage had been unpacked, Federica went to the kitchen and found the staff there. She passed out the gifts she had brought back with her for them and related stories behind each one. She had other gifts for Mr Forester and family and for the managers of their various enterprises. George, meanwhile, had been sharing his story with William, who wanted to know how his parents were faring and his brother and sister. George was sad to tell him that they had been unable to see either, as they were both away studying.

Dinner was a noisy event as it seemed that everyone was talking at once. Still, that was infinitely preferable to stony silence, which seemed to be often the case in English country houses.

"What did you enjoy most?" Sophia asked Federica after dinner.

"Following the elephants with Koos," she said. "It was fascinating how he looked at the footmarks and was able to tell me so much about the animals and when they had been there."

"What was the reserve you went to?" Anastasia asked.

"The Sabie Game Reserve," Federica replied. "It was first declared by the Boers in 1898, I believe, and it was declared again by the British only a few years ago, after the war. It is large, but there is an even larger one to the north, the Shingwedzi Reserve. The reserves are home to all manner of animals, lions, elephants, rhinoceroses and antelopes of all kinds."

"Did you drive anywhere?" Anastasia asked.

"We drove from Cape Town to Oudtshoorn," Federica replied. "And then we took a trip to Beaufort West, on the way back, we went over this spectacular mountain pass."

"And the car worked well?" Anastasia wanted to know.

"It worked really well," Federica said. "We towed a wagon that had got mired in soft ground and were able to save the driver the work of unloading the wagon to make it light enough for his oxen to pull it out, but we do need to talk about brakes, coming down the mountain pass was an adventure, to say the least. If Koos had not driven down in one of the low gears, it might have been less than pleasant."

"Were there any other issues with the cars?" William asked.

"Koos would like a petrol gauge on the dash, so that he does not have to get out of the car and check the sight gauges on the sides of the tanks," Federica replied. "Otherwise, no, the Antares ran well, and the van that we used to transport our luggage also ran well. Koos did tow the van up two of the passes we went over to get from Cape Town to Oudtshoorn, but those roads are steep, the surface is unfinished and rutted, and it was more of a precaution than anything."

"We should talk about all those things tomorrow at the office," Sophia said. "I am sure that Mr Stuart and Mr Coates would like to hear about your travels and about the car's performance."

"Good morning, Mrs Wheelwright," Alice greeted her as Federica came to the office. "Was your trip all you expected?"

"That and more, thank you, Alice," Federica replied. "I have something here for you that I think you may like."

"Oh, thank you so much," Alice said, delighted with her gift. "May I get you tea or coffee?"

"I think coffee, thank you, Alice," Federica said. "Have you been busy?"

"We have," Alice said. "Mrs McIntosh is really nice to work for, and we have been busy with new orders, including those that just came in from South Africa."

"Well, I do not intend to interfere in any way, Anastasia is now running the company, but I would like to discuss some possible improvements from things we learned in South Africa," Federica said.

"We have a normal meeting this morning," Alice said. "Ah, here is Mrs McIntosh."

"Fede, good morning," Anastasia said. "Did you sleep well?"

"The ground did not move like the boat, so it was a little strange at first," Federica said. "But, I soon fell asleep and slept well. You were up and gone early?"

"I went to see what is happening at the factories. I was hoping that I did not wake you when I left. This morning we have the regular business meeting," Anastasia said. "I think after that meeting we should discuss possible improvements to the cars."

After pleasantries had been exchanged and gifts distributed, Anastasia got down to the serious business of running the company. Federica sat back and watched, and was pleased with what she saw. Anastasia had a good grasp of what was happening and knew when the ask the next question and the next to unearth what her managers really thought and not what they thought she might like to hear. At the end of the regular business, Anastasia turned the meeting over to Federica.

"Thank you, Nastia," she said. "When we were in South Africa, we got to travel some distance in the Antares wagon. It truly is a useful vehicle in those conditions. We towed a wagon from the mire, we traversed a high mountain pass, and we took it away from the roads. Not everyone is looking for that ability, but the one item that really was obvious was brakes. I think we should look at brakes on all four wheels."

"I believe that the Spyker brothers brought out a system in 1903," Ian Stuart said.

"Do you have any details?" Federica asked.

"No," he said. "But we will look closely at what we can find and see how we may apply the system to our cars."

"I think one of the real questions is how to apply the brakes evenly around the four wheels so as to avoid skidding on one wheel," Andrew Coates commented.

"You are right, Andrew," Anastasia said. "At the moment, we use cables to pull on the lever system to apply the brakes; we should look at how we can equalise the force so that all the brakes are applied evenly."

"I am sure you will investigate this thoroughly," Federica said. "But, how do you accommodate the movement of the front wheels as the car steers and still apply the brakes?"

"We can do that," Ian said. "I was thinking that if we put a drum on each wheel and then have brake shoes inside the drum expand out and cause the braking. It is a new system to us, but I recall seeing something written about it in one of the journals."

"Excellent," Anastasia said. "Would you look into that, and I will look at a mechanism to apply the brakes. Fede, did you not also have a question about gauges?"

"Yes," Federica agreed. "Koos has fitted extra petrol tanks, so he can now run for over five hundred miles, which might sound far here, but in South Africa, petrol availability is not the same as here. He would like a gauge on the dashboard that shows him how much petrol is in the tank. I think he may be an extreme case, but I think most motorists would like to know how much petrol they have without getting out of the car and looking at sight gauges."

"That is a tricky problem," Ian said. "I agree with you, I would like a gauge on the dash, we have been thinking of ideas, but we have yet to find a solution. We will investigate electrical methods next and see if we can find a solution. How did the rest of the Antares run, the engine, gearbox and other elements? How far is it from Cape Town to where you went?"

"We had no problems while we were there," Federica said. "And Koos did not bring anything up. It is two hundred and seventy-five miles from Cape Town to Oudtshoorn, and we also drove to Beaufort West, which was another hundred and twelve miles there and a hundred and forty-five miles back, and the last long trip we made was to George, Knysna and back, which was another hundred and ninety-eight miles. The roads are all gravel or dirt and not always the best, and we went up and down seven major mountain passes. How are our investigations proceeding for a starting mechanism that does away with the handle?"

"We have looked at springs, explosives and a few other ideas," Ian replied. "We have not found one yet that would be satisfactory. The best idea would be an electric motor, but we would need to design one that would withstand the rigours of starting the engine. Then, we would need some mechanism to engage and disengage the electric motor from the flywheel, which is where I would propose fitting such a device."

"One thing that has come up is that there is now a glass available that uses the celluloid sandwich to protect the driver from breaking glass," Anastasia said. "It is being sold under the name of Triplex, so we no longer have to make our own."

"On the subject of windows," Ian added. "We have started using an adaptation of the windshield wiper that was invented by the American

Mary Anderson. At the moment, it is manually powered, but we are looking at ways to add an electric motor and a switch."

"Is there anything else?" Federica asked.

"There are always minor improvements that we can make," Ian said. "But these items, and perhaps an engine change when Mr McIntosh perfects his improvements, are all that I see for the moment. You said you went over high mountain passes, how high were they and did the engine performance change?"

"The Swartberg Pass was the highest one we went over, I think the summit is well over five thousand feet and yet the engine ran well," Federica explained.

"Is there anything else at the moment that we need to ask?" Anastasia said. "No, well, thank you, Fede, we should probably get back to work."

"Thank you, Nastia, for the time and thank you, gentlemen," Federica said. "Nastia, will I see you later?"

"You will indeed, we have much to talk about," Anastasia said. *"Ciao."*

"Well, how am I doing?" Anastasia asked Federica that evening.

"Very well," Federica replied. "I had no doubt that you would."

"Sometimes I worry that I have not made the right decisions, and if I should have tried something different," Anastasia said.

"That is something that we all face," Federica assured her. "We can only make the best decision we can at the time and with what we know at the time, sometimes we learn afterwards that things were different and that we were not right. But, we cannot let that stop us from making a decision, good or bad, or we do nothing. The secret is to learn from the mistakes we make."

"I have missed your counsel," Anastasia said. "I may be in charge of the company, but there are matters that I really need advice upon. Sophia helps where she can, but on design issues, she admits to lacking and points me elsewhere. Now that you are back, I have someone to turn to, unless, of course, you plan to completely closet yourself away to design aeroplanes."

"I will always have time for you, Nastia," Federica assured her.

"Good, then I see a prosperous future for Sirius Cars," Anastasia said.